Praise for

WOLF BY WOLF AND
BLOOD FOR BLOOD

"**Wild and gorgeous**, vivid and consuming. **I loved it!** I can't wait for the sequel."

—Laini Taylor, *New York Times* bestselling author
of the Daughter of Smoke & Bone trilogy

"**A haunting portrayal** of one girl's courage in the face of a vicious world. I was racing along with Yael until the book's heart-pounding conclusion. **A triumph.**"

—Megan Shepherd, author of *The Madman's Daughter*

"Ryan Graudin opens one of the darkest chapters in history and spins a what if into an **incredible tale** of survival, identity, and purpose. This is the kind of book you can't put down, and the kind that follows you long after you have. It is, quite simply, a **masterpiece.**"

—Victoria Schwab, author of The Archived series

"The rush of an action movie combined with a **flawlessly executed history,** this is the book I've been waiting for."

—Jackson Pearce, author of *Sisters Red* and *Tsarina*

"Filled to the brim with **tension** and **intrigue**, nonstop action, and a vivid cast of characters, you'll feel every bump in the road they ride. **I simply couldn't stop reading**—and wherever Ryan Graudin rides next, I'll follow."

—Amie Kaufman, *New York Times*
bestselling author of *These Broken Stars*

★ "Graudin...crafts another **fast-paced, enthralling tale of sacrifice** and dogged determination as she fuses alternate history and spy-thriller suspense. A provocative rumination on self-preservation, the greater good, and the boundaries that keep heroes from becoming as cruel as those they fight."

—*Publishers Weekly* (starred review)

★ "Graudin's writing is beautiful, her story **exciting and consuming** all at once." —*Booklist* (starred review)

★ "**Gripping and intricately plotted...**this haunting, historical what-if fantasy balances the atrocities of this alternate world with touches of innocent romance."

—*VOYA* (starred review)

BLOOD FOR BLOOD

BY RYAN GRAUDIN

LITTLE, BROWN AND COMPANY
NEW YORK BOSTON

Copyright © 2016 by Ryan Graudin
Iron to Iron copyright © 2016 by Ryan Graudin
Excerpt from *Invictus* copyright © 2017 by Ryan Graudin

Cover art copyright © by Laboca. Cover design by Marcie Lawrence. Cover copyright © 2016 by Hachette Book Group, Inc.

Little, Brown and Company
Hachette Book Group
1290 Avenue of the Americas, New York, NY 10104
Visit us at LBYR.com

Originally published in hardcover and ebook by Little, Brown and Company in November 2016
First Trade Paperback Edition: September 2017

Little, Brown and Company is a division of Hachette Book Group, Inc. The Little, Brown name and logo are trademarks of Hachette Book Group, Inc.

The publisher is not responsible for websites (or their content) that are not owned by the publisher.

The Library of Congress has cataloged the hardcover edition as follows:

Names: Graudin, Ryan.
Title: Blood for blood / by Ryan Graudin.
Description: First edition. | New York ; Boston : Little, Brown and Company, 2016. | Sequel to: Wolf by wolf. | Summary: In this alternate version of the 1950s, after the Axis powers win World War II, Yael, a Jewish skinshifter, fails in her mission to kill Hitler and finds herself being hunted while trying to finish what she started.
Identifiers: LCCN 2015043452| ISBN 9780316405157 (hardcover) | ISBN 9780316405140 (ebook) | ISBN 9780316405133 (library edition ebook)
Subjects: | CYAC: Government, Resistance to—Fiction. | Nazis—Fiction. | Hitler, Adolf, 1889-1945—Fiction. | Jews—Fiction. | Fantasy.
Classification: LCC PZ7.G7724 Bl 2016 | DDC [Fic]—dc23
LC record available at http://lccn.loc.gov/2015043452

ISBNs: 978-0-316-40516-4 (pbk), 978-0-316-40514-0 (ebook)

LSC-C

10 9 8 7 6 5 4 3 2 1

TO KATE—TALENTED WRITER, TRUE FRIEND

SON OF MAN, CAN THESE BONES LIVE?

—EZEKIEL 37:3

PRELUDE

THREE PORTRAITS OF CHRISTMAS EVE 1945

I

The family room was cramped. Too small for a mother and her three children and the crooked branch the older son had sawed down for a Christmas tree. Everywhere Felix Wolfe turned there were pine needles, tinsel, and the faces of his family. Each child stared eagerly at the trio of modest parcels under the spindly branch, waiting for their mother's blessing.

"Make sure you don't tear the paper," she instructed them. "We need to save it to use again."

Martin, as the oldest, went first. His gift was the smallest and held a secondhand pocket watch. Felix opened his own parcel with delicate fingers, carefully unfolding corners and smoothing out creases to find a toy car. It wasn't new—there was a dent in the far right door and some scratches on its bright red paint—but Felix didn't mind. New toys, his schoolteacher had said, were selfish and took away materials the Führer needed to win the war. Metal was needed for Mausers and bullets, not child's play.

Adele tore at the edges of her parcel. Inside lay a doll, with yellow yarn hair and eyes made from the blue buttons of one of their mother's old silk blouses. The doll's dress was made from scraps of its cobalt fabric, sewn with cramped stitches and care.

Felix knew, as soon as his twin stopped and stared at the gift, that she was unhappy. He always knew these things.

"I made other dresses," their mother said. "You can change her clothes every day. And I'll teach you how to braid her hair."

Adele's own plaited pigtails whipped her cheeks as she shook her head and shoved the box away. "I don't *want* a doll! Why can't I have a car like Felix?"

Their mother's mouth pinched. Her eyes went all shiny, the way they sometimes did when she read their father's letters from the front. The sight twisted Felix's stomach.

"Here." He pushed his own present toward his sister. "You can play with my car."

Adele's eyes lit bright as she grabbed the toy. She started making motor sounds and pushing it across the floor. Martin was busy winding his watch. Felix wasn't really sure what he should do without his car. At least his mother was smiling again, wiping her eyes as she watched her children playing.

"There's one more gift," she said.

All three Wolfe children froze. Felix looked under the tree, but there were no packages left. Perhaps they were getting oranges. Or *maybe* their mother had saved enough rations to bake gingerbread!

Their mother made her way through the room, dancing through bent paper and children's limbs and forgotten toys. She reached the door to her bedroom and placed her hand on the latch. Her smile was wider than Felix had seen it in a long time.

4

The door opened. Standing at the edge of the bedroom, arms outstretched, was their father, still wearing his army uniform. His field cap slouched over sun-pale hair as he knelt down to greet his children.

Adele was the first child to barrel into his arms, with the delighted shout of *Papa!* Martin—since he now owned a pocket watch and was practically a grown man himself—tried to contain his excitement to a firm handshake. Felix hung back, taking in the sight of his whole family together: Mama grinning by the doorway, Papa pulling both Adele and a not-really-reluctant Martin into a bear hug. Felix's heart warmed while he watched them, brighter than the cinders in the wood-burning stove.

He wanted to capture this moment, hold this feeling inside him forever.

"Felix! My little man!" His father smiled. Even with two children in his embrace, his arms were long enough to reach out for his son. "Did you look after this lot? Keep them out of trouble?"

Felix nodded as he joined the hug.

Their father explained that he was home for good. The war was winding down on the Eastern Front, and the army no longer needed him. He didn't have to say good-bye to them anymore.

No more good-byes. The warmth inside Felix stoked and flared. After years of letters from the front—and Felix always fearing that the next would spell out his father's death—the Wolfe family was together again.

II

Luka's father had been home for many months, compliments of the artillery shell that ripped his left arm off. The Kradschützen, elite motorcycle troops who'd been a key part of attacking the Russian front, had no use for limbless drivers, so Kurt Löwe and his remaining arm were shipped back to Germany with a Silver Wound Badge and a second-class Iron Cross. Scars and medals: the marks of a war hero. Luka was awed by both.

There were no hugs or smiles involved in the greeting, just a stern nod on his father's part. Luka's mother told him later it was because his father was tired. (After all, he'd been at war for six years.) He just needed time to rest.

Luka's father rested. He sat in a chair for hours and days at a time, staring blankly at the portrait of the Führer that hung over the mantel. When he spoke, it was never to ask Luka how his classes were going or to praise his wife's cooking, but about the war. He told them about the endless, snowy kilometers he drove on his motorcycle. The firefights he and his fellow soldiers endured. How many Soviets he shot and killed. All for the sake of *mein* Führer.

Kurt Löwe rested for months, but the smiles and hugs Luka's mother had promised never appeared. Not even for Christmas Eve.

The Löwe family sat around the small table, eating roasted carp in silence. It wasn't the contented, holy-night type of silence that filled the holiday's church services, but a strained one—full of chewing and scraping forks. It made Luka squirm in his chair.

"Stop fidgeting," his father growled from the other side of the table.

Luka's mother shot her son a meaningful look. He stopped moving. He felt as if he were sitting on eggshells. As if something was about to break . . .

His father was dividing the carp into neat little pieces with his fork. "When I went on night patrols on the front, we had to be quiet as ghosts. We moved without a sound. Had to, or else we would've been shot."

His mother cleared her throat. "Kurt, I'm not sure this is very good table talk—"

"Good table talk?" Luka's father set his fist on the table. He was still holding his fork, tines up, tattered fish meat hanging from the metal. "Losing my *verdammt* arm for the Fatherland earns me the right to talk about whatever I want at the table."

His wife didn't reply. Instead she set down her own fork and looked at Luka. "Would you like to open your gift now?"

Luka straightened in his chair, nodding. He'd been waiting for this moment for weeks. A bicycle (shiny and red) was the only thing Luka wanted. Sometimes Franz Gross let him play with his. Both boys took turns pretending to be Kradschützen motorcycle troops, revving imaginary engines as they stormed lines of invisible communists.

"Your gift is by the Advent calendar," his mother said. "Go and fetch it!"

There was no tree this year, but Luka's mother had set up the family's Advent calendar on the mantelpiece. Most of its twenty-four paper doors hung open, revealing a hand-painted Nativity: Mary and Joseph and the Christ Child all gathered in a barn, surrounded by curious animals and poking hay. Blue-eyed angels hovered over the Holy Family. Above them hung a single brilliant star. And above the star...

The Führer's immortalized face loomed, its painted eyes following Luka as he ran to the package by the hearth. The box was much too small for a bicycle and wrapped in old newsprint. Dated headlines told of the advance of the Wehrmacht through Russia, the Reich's impending, undeniable victory. Inked across the package was a picture of the Führer giving a speech about the future of the New Order. Luka ripped through it all to find a set of new shoes and a toy pistol. He stared at them, disappointment bitter in his throat.

"What do you say, Luka?" His father had followed him into the sitting room, watching the whole affair in silence.

"I know you wanted a bicycle"—his mother's voice was soft in the doorway—"but the ones at Herr Kahler's shop were too expensive. Maybe next year, when the war is over."

No bicycle. After weeks, months, years of waiting, still no bicycle. A crying feeling crept up Luka's throat.

"What do you need a bicycle for?" his father asked. His hand strayed up to the second-class Iron Cross that hung from the button on his tunic. "You walk to school."

"I—I want to play Kradschützen with Franz." As soon as the words left Luka's mouth, he wanted to swallow them back. But they were out, along with his tears, swimming through the sitting room.

"Play?" His father's face went hard. Something in his eyes reminded Luka of the painting above the fire. Blue and lifeless. "You want to *play* Kradschützen?"

"I want to be like you."

In a single blitzkrieg movement, Luka's father dropped his Iron Cross and grabbed the boy by his collar. Nina shrank against the doorway as her husband dragged their child past, into the kitchen, out of the house.

It was a snowy evening. Luka's father plowed through the spinning flakes, into the street. His knuckles stayed tight around Luka's collar as he stopped in the middle of a growing snowdrift. "You want to be like me? I spent more nights than you could count in weather far colder than this. Curled up in a *verdammt* foxhole while the commies tried to put a bullet through my skull. You think I spent that time sniveling?"

Luka shook his head. There were more tears now, blurring against his eyelashes.

"Don't show emotion." Kurt Löwe gave his son a rough shake. "Don't you ever show emotion. Tears are weakness. And I won't have any son of mine being *weak*. You're going to stand here until you stop crying."

Luka tried, but the squeeze in his throat only grew worse. The tears that had already fallen were starting to hurt his cheeks: burning cold.

His mother shivered barefoot in the doorway, on the verge of tears herself. "Kurt! He'll freeze!"

"You've let our son grow soft and ungrateful, Nina. Filling his head with art and fanciful *Scheisse*! If I could endure an entire winter in this snow, the least he can do is stand ten minutes in a drift."

"You had a uniform to keep you warm! Luka doesn't even have a coat."

Kurt Löwe took another look at his son: hunched over, teeth chattering, shin-deep in the snowdrift. He stepped back into the house and returned moments later with his prewar brown leather riding jacket and his dog tag. Both items were shoved into Luka's arms. "Put them on."

The jacket was far too big; its sleeves dragged far past Luka's fingers, into the piling snow. The dog tag hung all the way down to his belly button.

"A German youth must be strong. Tough as leather, hard as steel." His father pointed at the jacket and the dog tag in turn. "Stand your ground. Don't bother knocking on that door until the tears are off your face."

Kurt Löwe's arm cut like a scythe through the falling snow as he marched back to the house, hooking around his wife's waist to usher her inside. When the door shut, Luka tried to wipe his cheeks with the oversized sleeve. His father was right. The leather was hard, too tough to blot the tears.

So Luka stood staring at the glowing kitchen window—minute after frigid minute, while his legs grew numb and his heart grew hard—waiting for his sadness to dry on its own.

III

A fresh pan of gingerbread sat on the ledge of the farmhouse window. The glass was cracked a few centimeters, just enough to let the cold in. The confection's heat clouded into steam, carrying scents of clove and ginger and molasses all the way across the snow-covered yard, into the barn.

Yael tried her hardest to ignore the smell. She'd already settled down for the evening, taking shelter in the scratchy piles of hay. The barn was warm enough, and the handful of oats she'd scooped out of the horses' feed bin kept the gnaw of her hunger away.

But the gingerbread…

Never in her seven years of life could Yael remember eating anything as good as that dessert smelled. Food in the ghetto had been scarce. Food in the camp had been scarce *and* rotten. (Bits of gruel, spoiled vegetables, moldy bread.) Ever since Yael escaped those barbed-wire fences by using her skinshifting abilities to look like the camp kommandant's daughter, her diet was substantially better. During summer the woods burst with blackberry thickets and mushroom caps. Orchards were so fruitful by autumn that the farmers' wives never seemed to note how the trees on the borders of their property lacked apples. Now that the weather was harsher, Yael took shelter in barn lofts, sustaining herself with horse feed, hoping the owners wouldn't notice that their horses seemed to eat twice as much without getting fat.

She'd lurked in this particular barn for a week. It was an unusually generous length of time, but the family who lived in the house had been too distracted by holiday festivities to pay much attention to clues of her presence. Yael had watched the whole process from the safety of the loft. The decorating of the Christmas tree, the singing of carols, the baking...

She'd watched the mother stir the gingerbread together into a deep brown dough. One of her blond daughters (the same one who trudged across the yard every morning through blank-slate snow; whose breath frosted the air as she sang "Silent Night" to herself and milked the cow; who had no idea that Yael was listening in the loft above) popped the pan into the oven. The other daughter peeled potatoes. Their two brothers played Stern-Halma at the kitchen table—a game full of laughter and elbows.

The family was off in the dining room now, eating dinner and waiting for the gingerbread to cool. The oats in Yael's stomach did not feel like enough as she watched them. She wanted to be in that house. Chuckling, full, and not alone.

That, of course, was impossible.

She was not one of them. She could never be one of them.

But she *could* snag a piece of that gingerbread.

The milking cow gave Yael a lazy, low greeting as she crept down the loft's ladder. She made certain before she stepped out of the barn that her sweater sleeve was rolled down to hide the tattooed numbers on her arm. Her hair, tangled though it was, was as golden as the straw. Her eyes were bold and blue. No one would recognize her for what she truly was.

Snow was falling thick enough to cover her footprints for a short trip to the kitchen window and back. After a few minutes there would be no sign she was even there. Just a cracked window and an empty pan.

Yael slipped across the yard, ignoring the sting of the snow through her thin shoes. The smell of gingerbread was stronger now, the family's laughter louder. She could hear one of the boys telling a joke—something about talking cows riding bicycles. The youngest sister giggled so hard she snorted.

Yael hunched under the window, reaching for the pan with hungry fingers.

"And then the first cow turned to the second cow and said—"

"OUCH!"

Yael, who was always so quiet, so careful, had not taken into account that a steaming pan meant the metal was still hot. She clamped her mouth shut, but it was too late. The youngest sister stopped laughing. Five different chairs scraped across the farmhouse floor as the family leapt to their feet.

"What was that?"

"Eric," the mother said to one of the boys, "go get the rifle."

Yael was off, sprinting across the field, leaving a whirl of footprints behind her. The farmhouse door opened to a yell. Yael did not stop. She did not look back. And it was a good thing, too, because—

KA-BOOM.

Silent night. Holy night.

All is buckshot. All is bright.

She was not one of them. She could never be one of them.

Yael could not go back to the barn (trigger-happy, cow-joking Eric would only follow the footprints, find her there), so she did what she always did.

She kept running.

PART I

EXODUS

CHAPTER 1

APRIL 2, 1956

Luka Löwe's evening had started out on a promising note. The most powerful men in the world were throwing him a party at the Imperial Palace in Tokyo. Champagne toasts prickled the air, Luka's name braided with praise from the lips of the Third Reich's highest officials. The Führer himself had offered Luka a job and called him a "fine specimen of the Aryan ideal."

The compliment was not undeserved. He'd conquered the Axis Tour—a cross-continental motorcycle race from Germania to Tokyo—not once but twice. A 20,780-kilometer journey of sandstorms, sabotage, and secrets. Two first-class Iron Crosses draped around Luka's neck, signifying that he was a double victor. The best of the best twice over.

So why was he standing outside his own party, staring through the towering windows, feeling like *Scheisse* on a shingle?

It had to do with a pang in his chest, near that cardiac muscle most people called a heart. It had to do with the fräulein in the scarlet-branch-patterned kimono, the one who'd been dancing in his arms moments before. The one who'd stared straight into his eyes and said, "I do not love you. And I never will."

Adele Wolfe. A fräulein like no other. There weren't many of the female persuasion who'd use her twin brother's identity to sneak her way into an all-male race. There were fewer fräuleins still who'd slid their way into Luka's heart so *effectively*. Not once, but twice.

He'd been such a *verdammt* fool. He should have learned his lesson after Osaka. After she'd chewed up his heart, bloodied his head, and won his race. To Luka's (very small) credit, he hadn't meant to fall in love with Adele again. He'd plunged into the 1956 Axis Tour bent on a single thing—revenge.

His plan was this: Watch Adele Wolfe like a hawk. Pretend he still loved her. Gain her trust, her alliance, her heart, and cement it with a kiss (which happened to be laced with a soporific that would knock her out for hours and give him a solid lead, another victory).

The plan played out well at first. He watched her through the curtain of rain at Germania's Olympiastadion. He watched her sitting in front of the fire at the Prague checkpoint. He watched her eating spaghetti at the Rome checkpoint. He watched all these things and came to a single conclusion.

Adele Wolfe had changed.

On the outside Adele was exactly the same: hair as light as snowdrifts, eyes a lonely, winter-sky blue. But there seemed to be a new depth to the fräulein. She cared about things she hadn't before. Asking about Hiraku's wreck. Going all bleeding heart over Katsuo's accidental death. She'd even saved his own *gottverdammt* life.

It was all very, very confusing.

The more Luka watched, the more he realized there was

a problem with his plan....He couldn't pretend he still loved Adele Wolfe, because he did. (The truth did not make a very good lie. Did it?)

He wasn't even sure when it'd happened. On the road outside Germania, when he'd flirted with burning rubber and death, and she'd stared unflinchingly ahead? In the middle of the desert, when she'd called his cigarettes *"Scheisse"* but smoked them anyway? In the guerrillas' camp, when she'd saved him from becoming Soviet target practice? On the train, when the kiss Luka had meant only as bait became all too real?

As sappy as it sounded, Luka decided it was the kiss that clenched it. When their lips met, he knew for certain that he was in love with this fräulein again. He loved her. *Scheisse,* he loved her. It was a painful, razor feeling. An emotion that rose up in him like a phoenix—made of ashes and burning, so much stronger than it had ever been before.

He'd even considered, for a moment, letting the race be a fair one: just him and Adele and the gnash of their Zündapps. But Luka's pride was just an ounce too inflated, a degree too wounded, to leave a second victory to chance. Yes, Adele had stolen his heart, but she'd stolen his victory, too. Only when they were even—a heart for a heart, a victory for a victory—could they be together. So Luka placed a soporific on his lips and kissed her a second time. He meant every moment of it. (Turns out, truths make the best lies.)

Luka Löwe won the race, but Adele had still managed to beat him.

Adele Wolfe. Who did not love Luka. Who never would.

So now he was here, standing outside his own *verdammt* party. The leather of his jacket was battered. Gone soft. The steel of his father's dog tag felt tinny and light, almost unnoticeable against everything else going on inside his chest.

Luka could still see Adele through the ballroom window. It was a special form of torture, watching her dance with the Führer. A strange, hungry look shimmered in Adele's eyes as she let the most powerful man in the world waltz her closer to the glass. A pure, concentrated feeling. Like love…

Or hate.

Luka wasn't sure he could tell the difference between these emotions anymore.

He tore his eyes away from the window, digging through his jacket pockets for a spare smoke and an almost-empty matchbook. Luka jammed the cigarette between his lips, plucked out the final match. The first strike came to nothing. So did the second. His third attempt sent the matchstick flying into the gravel of the Imperial Palace's garden path.

He was just leaning down when he heard pieces of Adele's voice through the glass. "I am [something]. I am [something, something, something]. I am [something] death."

Death? What was she going on about? Probably confessing to the Führer that she loved him to death. Like every other lemming soul in this—

BOOM.

Luka looked up and saw the Führer falling. His chest looked as if it had been turned inside out. Standing over the body—left hand outstretched, still holding the gun—was Adele.

She gathered up the hem of her kimono and turned, aiming her Walther P38 at the window. The pistol's muzzle flared; glass exploded in a hundred different angles. Luka flattened himself against the ground.

20

Adele flew past. A flash of teal-and-crimson fabric, pale hair, glinting pistol. Leaving gunshots, screams, broken glass, a shattered body in her wake.

Adele Wolfe had just shot the Führer.

It was all happening *again*. Just like the rally at the Grosser Platz, in front of the old Reichstag. Screams and blood and Adolf Hitler on his back...But this time, Luka realized, it was his fault. The only reason Adele Wolfe had been at the Victor's Ball in the first place was because Luka had been dummkopf enough to invite her. When the SS started putting the pieces of the evening together, his name would be at the top of their interrogation list. They would accuse him of collaborating, treason...charges not even Luka's Double Cross could shield him from.

Although there'd be no tears shed for the Führer on Luka's part, drowning in his own blood after days of torture was a fate he preferred to avoid. Only one person could clear Luka's name, and she was currently sprinting away from him. Running as if the very hounds of hell were at her heels.

They weren't, just yet. A glance back into the ballroom showed Luka that the SS and Imperial Guards were still floundering in broken glass and bloody floor tiles. All of them were another few seconds from reaching the window.

The hunt was all his.

Luka lunged to his feet. His medals clashed as he burst across gravel, rounding the clump of cypress trees in time to see the fräulein drop her kimono at the base of a lamppost and double back. Milky limbs, undergarments, and electric movement. She took four determined strides down the path before leaping over a hedge.

The kimono lay rumpled under the lamplight. Luka left it

for the SS. Let them get distracted, waste valuable seconds fussing over a false trail. He needed to catch Adele before they did.

The lampless part of the garden was a wasteland of shadow figures: bell-curve boulders, frenzied foliage, a silken nymph of a girl. When Luka spotted her, he slowed, crouching until the hedges were eye level. Adele's pistol still had six bullets left by his count. No need to go blazing in and get himself shot.

The fräulein was bent over a stretch of bushes, tugging a knapsack out of the leaves. She was breathing hard, pulling dark clothes from the bag and twisting them on. Luka held his own breath, edged closer. As his eyesight sharpened, he began to notice things he hadn't before.

There was a bandage on the lower half of her left arm. Its gauze must have caught on the window's jagged edge, for it had begun unraveling at the elbow, falling away faster and faster in Adele's haste to get dressed. The flesh beneath was wreathed in black. At first, Luka thought it was dried blood, but the longer he stared at the darkness, the more he realized it had form. Its lines ebbed and flowed in distinct shapes. Tails, paws, fangs...

They were wolves. Tattooed on her arm. Ink Adele most definitely did not have last year. These disappeared as Adele shouldered on a jacket and bent over to lace up her boots.

The SS should be finding the kimono now, fanning men and guns into all parts of the garden. Luka had to make his move soon. He was certainly close enough. It would take him only a second to leap out and blitzkrieg Adele.

Luka was just tensing his muscles, getting ready to launch, when the unbelievable happened.

Adele Wolfe became... not-Adele.

Her corn-silk hair changed color from the roots out, until it was all black. The blue in her eyes vanished, irises growing so dark they blended with the pupil. Even the shape of her face shifted—from Adele's long, oval features into those of a Japanese girl.

If Luka hadn't witnessed the change with his own eyes, he would've said it was impossible. Even now that he *had* seen it, he wasn't quite sure he believed it. Maybe he fell and hit his head when he went looking for the lost matchstick. This was all some strange revenge fantasy, playing out while Luka sprawled unconscious on the garden path and Adele danced happily in the Führer's arms.

That would make much more sense.

But no. It was all too real. Loud German commands rose just meters away. The fräulein who was not-Adele shouldered her pack and took off in the opposite direction.

Operation Save His Skin and Clear His Name had taken a drastic turn.

What exactly was he supposed to do now? Run down this Japanese fräulein and tell the SS guards she'd swapped out her body? Stay here and hope they believed his delusional story without trying to torture a more plausible truth out of him? Luka might as well just pull out his Luger now. Save them a bullet. Save himself a world of pain.

The cries of the Führer's bodyguards grated on his ears as they drew closer. The double victor—poster boy of the Aryan race, hero of the Third Reich—stood, his stare honing in on the fading form of not-Adele. He kept his eyes fixed on the vanishing darkness and started running.

CHAPTER 2

For the second time in a month, Felix Wolfe woke up with a headache. Not the dull kind sometimes acquired by sleeping too long, but the splitting type that afflicted people after their twin sister pistol-whipped them upside the head. One Felix was becoming far too well acquainted with.

He found himself staring at box springs—the underside of a bed. Rolling over was a difficult task, since Adele had bound his wrists behind his back with twisted bedsheets. She'd done the same with his legs, clearly trying to prevent him from wriggling free and ruining her evening.

Felix's feet thrashed the bed frame as he turned onto his side. Something silver dropped to the floor—Martin's pocket watch—lying open, cracked face showing. Beyond it, the Imperial Palace guest quarters were bathed in the light of the flickering television screen, empty. His sister was gone. Off to the Victor's Ball to complete her mission for the resistance: assassinate the most powerful man in the world.

Adele had always been a rule-pusher: pinching sugar from the Wolfe family's rations, reading issues of *Motor Schau* with a flashlight hours after lights-out, entering male-only motorcycle races under Felix's name. Growing up, Felix had kept a multitude of his sister's secrets, both big and small. They were—after all—a team. It didn't matter that they weren't identical: male versus female, homebody versus wanderer. They were Wolfes. There was iron in their blood, and it bound them together.

But this time his sister had wandered too far. This time the secret was too vast. One could not murder the Führer of the Third Reich and walk away from it. If Adele went through with her plan, she and the entire Wolfe family would pay the price.

It was ten past six, according to the spindly hands of Martin's pocket watch. The Victor's Ball had only just started. There was still time for Felix to stop this madness.

Guttural half curses pressed against Felix's gag as he rolled his body another ninety degrees, flailing his bound hands at the metal mattress springs above. There were nearly a dozen sharp points. Something had to catch....

It didn't. The mattress springs' hooked ends were small, demanding precision, which Felix—nose-first on the floor, with skull-splitting pain—did not possess. He kept trying, thrashing his numb wrists at the bed's underside again and again.

His dead brother's watch kept ticking. It was five past eight when Felix managed to slip the cotton over the pointed loop of the mattress spring. It was ten past eight when the first bit of bedsheet began fraying. At twelve past, the tie broke. Felix's arms flopped to his side, wrists braceleted in deep purple.

First order of business? Getting rid of this stupid gag. Felix's tongue was a vast, cracked wasteland. It felt too big for his mouth as he dragged himself out from under the bed.

Black, white, gray images of the Victor's Ball cast their spell through the darkened room. There on the screen was his sister, her teeth bared in a smile as she accepted the Führer's invitation to dance.

Their bodies started to whirl to some tempo Felix couldn't hear (the television's volume knob had been twisted into silence). He kept an eye on the screen as he sat up and started unknotting the three separate bindings on his legs.

Felix used to think he could read his twin's thoughts—her emotions hummed in his, and he often knew the words she'd say before they were spoken. But if their bond was so strong, then why hadn't he known until just over a week ago that Adele felt the world was wrong? That—at the risk of everything they held dear—she'd joined the resistance to right it?

Don't do it, Ad. Don't. Please don't. Felix hoped there was still some semblance of a connection between them. That these pleas weren't just beating useless against the glass screen.

Adele went rigid in Hitler's arms. Her mouth was moving, her features wrenched with an expression Felix had never seen before: a loathing so vast and deep it poisoned all facets of her face.

He'd witnessed his sister's anger—felt it buzz through his own veins—many times over. In the third year of primary school, when the Schuler boy tried to kiss her, Adele punched him in the stomach so hard he decorated the school yard with his lunch. After Martin's motorcycle accident, when their parents forbade the twins to race, Adele's face flushed redder than a Reich flag.

But this...this emotion was something else. A fury Felix could not understand, much less feel. It wasn't just in Adele's face. It raged through her whole being: Her arm, as it ducked into her obi. Her hand, as it drew out a pistol and pointed it at the Führer's chest. Her finger, as it squeezed the trigger.

Martin's pocket watch kept counting the seconds, its gears grinding through the room's stillness. *Tick, tick, tick* as the Führer collapsed to the floor. *Tick, tick, tick* as blood spread across Hitler's chest, oozing through the fabric and onto the television's pixels.

The screen cut to static.

Felix's fingers fell away from the knotted sheet on his knees. He retrieved Martin's pocket watch and snapped its warped casing shut without checking the hour. It didn't matter what time it was because he was too late.

There was nothing to stop.

The ballroom was a whole copper-roofed building away from Adele's quarters, but Felix could still hear gunshots as he slipped the watch into the breast pocket of his Hitler Youth uniform. Screams followed, punctuated by more bullets.

Felix tried not to think what each of them meant. He tried not to imagine his twin sister's body crumpled next to Hitler's, blood blending purple into her kimono. He tried not to imagine her gravestone next to Martin's.

What was he thinking? Adele wouldn't be given a gravestone. Not after what she'd just done. None of the Wolfes would. From this moment forward, the Wolfe family's fate was this: to be wiped off the face of the earth. All records that they ever existed would be burned by the SS. Forgotten forever and ever. Amen.

And there was nothing, *nothing*, Felix could do to save them.

He couldn't stay here. This room would be the first place the SS searched. If they found him . . .

Felix scratched at his leg bindings, but the harder he tried to undo the knot, the more it seemed to grow—double, triple, tenfold. He edged his way back to the mattress springs, looped the first twisted sheet over the metal, and began to saw.

One strip down.

The gunshots were gone. The screen was still a mess of electronic noise.

Two strips down.

Were those footsteps he heard or the thud of his own heart?

The third strip had just fallen from Felix's legs when the door slid open.

Footsteps, then. A trio of men stood in the doorway. All three wore the sharp black dress uniforms of the SS. All three had their Luger barrels pointed at Felix's face.

Felix lifted his hands above his head. He felt his own emotions well enough: Fear, piss-warm against his crotch. Shock, shaking under his fingernails.

The leader of the group frowned. His gray eyes raked through the room, trying to make sense of the shredded bedsheets, the fuzzing television, the boy in the middle of it all.

"Secure him!" he barked to the soldier on his left, then turned to the other. "Search the room."

The first man hauled Felix to his feet, binding his arms once more behind his back. The second—a beefy, yellow-haired soldier with a bulbous nose—kept his Luger out as he checked the quarters' more obvious hidey-holes: beneath the bed, behind the curtain.

They're still looking for Adele. Relief…Felix should not have felt it rushing down his throat, cutting new paths through his heart. But the emotion was there, reassuring him that somehow—in the midst of all those gunshots and screams—his sister had escaped.

"She's not here, Standartenführer Baasch," the second soldier announced from the washroom once he finished scouring it.

Baasch didn't look particularly surprised or displeased at the news. He pulled a spotless white kerchief from his pocket and coughed into it. A single, dry wheeze.

"No," he said once his throat was clear. "She wouldn't be. You saw how she moved through that window. She's had training."

Bulbous Nose stepped back into the bedroom, itemizing everything he saw. "Clothes, a phone, makeup brushes…It doesn't look like she left anything of use behind."

"Oh." Baasch turned. The screen's light caught the silver *Totenkopf* on the officer's hat: cracked skull, crossed bones, leering grin. The eyes beneath the cap were the same mixture of dead and shining as they settled on Felix. "I wouldn't be too certain about that."

CHAPTER 3

If the conditions are just right—on a clear, cold day, in a flat, treeless terrain—the sound of an average gunshot can travel several kilometers. The sound wave from Yael's cartridge went much farther. Ripping through cables and airwaves, from Tokyo to Germania/London/Rome/Cairo/anywhere with a working television set, in the span of seconds.

The world heard it. People of all stations, colors, creeds… Aryan mothers and fathers with broods of blond children, a balding shisha merchant in Cairo, an oily-faced adolescent in Rome. Many stared at the screen—mouths slack, stunned eyes—trying to process what had happened. Others who watched understood. This was the signal they'd been waiting for.

One—a frizzy-haired Polish woman by the name of Henryka—even smiled at her television, whispering, "That's my girl," before she stood and got to work.

For years Henryka's beer hall basement had been the nerve center of the resistance—relaying messages between the cells, gauging the readiness of every territory, housing operatives, providing a safe place for General Erwin Reiniger and other mutinous National Socialist officers to brainstorm military operations.

A pair of radios sat between stacks of cracked-spine encyclopedias, waiting to receive messages from all corners of the crumbling Reich. Each set was accompanied by an Enigma machine, meant to protect the resistance's airwave conversations from prying ears by encrypting outgoing messages and decrypting replies. For years these machines had been silent, gathering dust. Now they were brushed off, switched on. Four resistance operatives sat close by, their eagerness palpable. Brigitte, the only other woman in the room, had laid out not one but *two* sharpened pencils by her notebook, ready to encode messages. There was a third tucked through her honey-blond bun. Johann was already wearing his radio headset. Reinhard and Kasper stared at the map of the Axis-controlled world on the far wall, making bets on which territory would be first to secede.

There were plenty to choose from. The continents were littered with coded pins of operatives and Wehrmacht regiments, detailing the borders of the Third Reich's reach in wretched red. The color swallowed Europe, crept into Asia, stained the sands of northern Africa.

The resistance had twenty-four hours to change it.

The putsch—a full-fledged militarized occupation of Germania, including arrests of the Reich's highest officials and new leadership put into place—had to be quick. The old National Socialist government felled and Reiniger's new government raised within a single day. Otherwise, the leading minds of the National Socialist Party—Göring, Himmler, Bormann, Goebbels—would get over the shock of Hitler's assassination, declare a new Führer, and crush Reiniger's attempt to establish martial law.

Such an event would not mean defeat. But it would mean war. War in a way the world had rarely seen before—battles without borders, soldiers without uniforms. War that would ravage the bones of the Reich from within, with chaos like cancer.

Henryka stared at the red map, wrapped in a maelstrom thought pattern of what might/could/would happen when—

"What's going on?" The girl's voice would've been imperious had it not been muffled by several centimeters of steel. "Did I hear a gunshot?"

Henryka looked over at the doorway. Once, it had led to a supply closet full of filing cabinets, a broom, a lightbulb operated by a pull chain, and a spider or two. Now—with the help of a newly installed, reinforced door—it contained one very real Adele Wolfe (and, perhaps, still a spider or two).

At the beginning of the girl's captivity, Henryka's maternal side fought against the idea of keeping her locked up in a windowless room. These sympathies vanished after Adele's first three escape attempts. Her initial "cell" had been Yael's old sleeping quarters, but that door was made of mere wood, which took Adele only twenty-four hours to kick down. Henryka caught the girl before she reached the beer hall and relocated her to the closet. The girl's second break for freedom happened when Henryka tried to slip her some crullers for breakfast and Adele shoved the reinforced steel wide open. The third involved an unscrewed lightbulb smashed into Henryka's face and a dropped plate of schnitzel. Both attacks had come to nothing. Henryka still had cuts on her cheeks. Adele Wolfe now sat in the dark. Mealtimes were tenuous.

"I demand to know what's happening!" The next yell was followed by a blunt *THUD*. And another. And another.

Kasper, who'd been involved in the operation to bring Adele Wolfe in, eyed the shuddering door. "Want me to slip her a sedative?"

Henryka shook her head. "Let her kick. She'll break her toes before she gets through that door."

And it sounded like she might. *THUD* after *THUD*, Adele was giving the steel a noble fight. "What's going on out there?"

Henryka's gaze shifted to the static-filled screen and then back to the map. She wished she knew the answer to that question, but it would be some time before any real news started pouring in through Johann's headset and Brigitte's pencils. Right now all Henryka could do was record the facts she knew. (One day this would all be history. Someone had to keep documents for the books.)

So she walked over to her Olympia Robust typewriter, placed her fingers on its well-worn keys, and started to write.

Valkyrie the Second Operation Notes
April 2, 1956
1315 hours--The Führer Adolf Hitler is
dead.

33

CHAPTER 4

The Führer Adolf Hitler is not dead. Yael was no longer running, but this single, stunned thought still chased her. *Not dead. Not dead.*

Her getaway from the Imperial Palace grounds had been clean, though she was still dripping with moat water as she walked down Tokyo's streets. Despite her damp hair, the people passing Yael on the sidewalk hardly gave her a second glance. Why would they? Her face bore the same bone structure, pale skin, and dark eyes as theirs. She looked nothing like the girl who'd shot Adolf Hitler on live television.

Neither of the dancers on that screen had been what they seemed. Victor Adele Wolfe, blond darling of the National Socialists, had actually been Yael. Jewish daughter. Skinshifter. Adolf Hitler, the ruler of the Third Reich, was not the man she'd danced with and shot in the chest. The disguise had been as convincing as her own. He wore the Führer's clothes, spoke the Führer's words, perfected every wrinkle on the Führer's face, every silvering hair in the Führer's bristle of a mustache.

Yael did not know *who* he was. She'd only had enough time before her flight to see the truth—spilling white through his hair, flashing gold, green, blue, gray, black through his eyes. She'd killed a skinshifter. Someone like her.

For so long (so, so long) Yael had thought she was alone in this—changing, never truly owning her own skin. Now she realized she couldn't be. Experiment 85 was Dr. Geyer's triumph. Hadn't she been in the room when she heard Reichsführer Heinrich Himmler himself say it showed much promise? The doctor would not have stopped administering the injections simply because Yael escaped. Her impersonation of Bernice Vogt had shown the Angel of Death what was possible. He must have gathered new subjects, given them life-threatening fevers, and taken their skin, erasing their old identities needle by needle.

Her whole life Yael had struggled to find what was lost—the *her* before Dr. Geyer's syringes. For a moment, between the shout and the shot, she'd claimed it. She'd been fully herself: Yael. Inmate 121358ΔX. The Führer's death.

I am. I am. I am.

And now?

Now she was a murderer, her hands stained with the wrong man's blood. Now the real Führer—the one who'd ravaged continents with war and death camps, who'd murdered millions and millions (including Yael's whole family and people)—was still alive. Yael had no doubt that the world would soon know it.

She crossed the street, to the corner of an intersection. Something caught her eye as she walked. Movement—jerky and quick—about a block back: a hunchbacked silhouette darting through shop shadows.

All of Yael's instincts screamed one thing.

35

—YOU'RE BEING FOLLOWED—

Not such a clean getaway after all.

Who could have possibly spotted her disguise, trailed her all the way from the Imperial Palace? And why hadn't this person called for reinforcements?

Yael scanned the shop fronts' dead neon signs and locked entrances. She needed a nook, some sort of sheltered corner—

There! Between a shuttered tea shop and a modern, glass-walled department store sat an alley, lined with trash bags waiting to be hauled away in the next violet dawn. Several lamp-eyed felines looked disdainfully at Yael as she ducked into the side street and waited.

For a long moment there was no sound but cats clawing through bags and the distant clatter of an electric streetcar. Yael was beginning to wonder if she'd been mistaken when she heard the clip of boots against pavement, too heavy to be female, closing in fast. Whoever this was had obviously seen Yael change, which meant he'd seen her clothes, and possibly her wolves. If she allowed him to get away, he could return to the SS, give them a head start on where to search for her.

She'd left enough loose ends tonight.

As soon as her tracker's arm came into view, Yael sprang. Adrenaline surged as she wrenched the man into the alley, flinging him face-first into the pile of trash bags and pinning him there with her knee.

Garbage flew everywhere: gummy rice, limp seaweed, rotting fish, wads of kanji-covered newspaper. Cats howled and scattered. Another (more muffled) howling rose from beneath the man's jacket, which was draped over his head, as if he himself

36

had been hiding. "*Scheisse!* All right, all right! I surrender! You don't have to break my arm."

Something about the voice made Yael do a double take at the jacket. Old brown leather, soft as butter. There was only one German speaker in Tokyo with outerwear like that....

Oh no.

Yael let go of his arm and stood. The jacket fell away.

The last time she'd seen Luka Löwe, he'd almost looked like a gentleman: shaggy golden hair pulled back, jacket oiled, uniform starched and pressed. Now his hair stuck out at all angles. Bits of seaweed and rice clung to his face. The whole of him was soaked.

Any other person might have found cause to look self-conscious about these things. Luka Löwe, however, smiled in that half-cocked way of his as he sat up, gave her a once-over.

"Fancy seeing you here, Fräulein. You look good. But something's changed....Wait. Don't tell me." His eyes cut up and back. "New haircut."

Unbelievable. This boy was the very definition of the word. Cracking jokes and grinning (grinning!) with seaweed-strung hair in the face of a skinshifting assassin. If his intention was to disarm Yael, it worked. She was without words....

"Don't get me wrong. I like it. It's a *verdammt* good party trick. But we both know I didn't just traipse halfway across Tokyo to compliment you on your restyling choices." The boy rose from the trash bags and shook out his jacket. Some stray droplets dashed into Yael's face. She blinked them away.

"How did you—"

"Know?" Luka's dark eyebrows quirked, the way they always did before he launched into a sarcasm-riddled monologue.

"I had a front-row seat for the whole shebang. Fräulein shoots Führer. Fräulein runs like the wind, leaving me behind to get questioned and blamed. I wasn't about to let that happen."

"So you followed me."

"Yep." Luka shouldered his jacket back on. Yael realized that the swastika armband he'd worn on the sleeve throughout the entire Axis Tour was missing, torn off. "Excellent job, by the way. I guarantee you no one in the Third Reich saw this coming. First-class showmanship."

Excellent? No sympathetic National Socialist would use *that* word to describe what they'd witnessed in the ballroom.... Luka's loyalties had never been easy to pin, but there was something about the way the boy stood in front of Yael, soaked to the bone, notably *not* screaming for any nearby SS, that made her doubt his allegiances lay with the Third Reich.

"It wasn't a show," she managed.

"It *was* a live television broadcast," Luka pointed out, then relented. "Fine. First-class assassination, if you prefer. Hitler's been dodging a violent demise for years—"

Yael's hearing—still flying high on adrenaline—bristled at a new sound. More footsteps. She held up her palm in front of Luka's face. It was a signal from her shorthand language with her old trainer, Vlad, but the victor understood.

—SILENCE SOMEONE IS COMING DON'T LET THEM SEE—

Yael pushed Luka's back against the alley wall, shielding him with her own body. Whoever walked by would glimpse her dark hair. Nothing more.

They stood, chest-to-chest, face-to-face, as the footsteps drew closer. Yael couldn't help but notice how Luka's jaw clenched, how his skin went a shade paler. It reminded her that his mask of confidence was just that—a mask. The mechanics of defense at its finest.

Was it only this evening she'd last seen it slip? When they were dancing in Emperor Hirohito's ballroom. When Luka had practically proposed to her. When Yael's heart had felt something other than anger, pain, hurt. When she knew there could be nothing between them (because of who he was, because of who she was not). When she'd been forced to cut him off with *ending* words: *I do not love you. And I never will.... Good-bye.*

But here they were—covered in trash, soaked in moat water, hiding for their lives—and what did Yael find herself staring at?

Luka's lips.

They weren't chapped, the way they had been on the train to New Delhi, when he'd leaned in and kissed Yael like the world was ending. They weren't smooth with soporifics, the way they had been on the *Kaiten*, when Japan's mountainous shores had loomed on the horizon and Luka had kissed her a second time, knocking her out and winning the race.

In this moment they were tight, pulled back with something like fear.

The footsteps came—from the sound of their tread and the quiet conversation tickling her ears, Yael suspected they belonged to a middle-aged couple, harmless—and went. But Yael kept staring at Luka.

Luka stared back.

"What now?" he whispered.

It was a simple enough question. Two short words that led to a vast, answerless chasm. All of Yael's life had been leading up to this mission. She'd given everything to it: her years, her grief, her soul.

What now?

Now the wrong man was dead. Now she was standing in an alley with the boy she'd wanted so terribly to hate but didn't. Now she had no mission or orders. Now she was supposed to be free, but instead she felt…lost.

"I—I have to go." Yael backed toward the alley's entrance.

Luka stepped forward. The distance between them hadn't changed at all.

"Not so fast." He hopped around so that his squared shoulders blocked the way to the street. "Don't you know it's rude to run out on your date? This would make twice in one night."

"You were Adele's date. Not mine," Yael told him. "If you don't get out of my way, I will break your arm."

Luka's lips pulled tighter (from frightened to terrified), but he didn't move. "You can't just abandon me, Fräulein. My Japanese begins at *konnichiwa* and ends about there, too. My hair stands out like a one-thousand-watt lightbulb. And my face is… well…my face!"

—*GET OUT LEAVE HIM*—

Yael didn't owe this boy anything. It would be simple, easy even, to snap Luka's radial bone and slip off into Tokyo's ripening night.

"You leave me here, and it's only a matter of time before the SS snag me for questioning. We both know that when that happens, I'm as good as dead. And if you're the girl I think you are, that wouldn't sit too well with you."

"You know *nothing* about me," Yael snarled.

"Do I not?" The victor held his hands up. "Don't get me

wrong. You were a *verdammt* good Adele, Fräulein, but you lived by a code she never did. You went back for Yamato and me when the commies caught us. And don't even get me started on Katsuo—"

Katsuo. The Japanese racer who'd died in a wreck Yael had caused trying to get ahead. Technically speaking, the death had been an accident, but this had done nothing to salve Yael's guilt. Tsuda Katsuo was dead because of her. The first name on a growing list: Tsuda Katsuo, unknown skinshifter...

Yael had started off her mission with a nameless list, bloodless hands. She had grown up in the shadow of death—death, so much death, and all for what? She'd watched so many fall into its jaws—Babushka, her mother, Aaron-Klaus—and she'd wanted, so desperately, so helplessly, to stop it.

For a while, she thought she could.

Yael wanted to be like the Valkyrie maidens in the old Norse lore. Winged women who rode to war on the backs of wolves, choosing which soldiers lived and died. She'd thought she could make death mean something, if she wielded it right. (A death to end this death.) So she'd aimed her gun at that man in the ballroom and made her choice.

"Point is," Luka kept talking, "you've got a heart. And right now, I'm wagering my life on that."

Life or death?

Yael was getting sick of choices.

"How do I know you won't contact the authorities as soon as my back is turned?" she asked.

"I considered it," Luka said with a shamelessness only he could pull off. "But your face is...well...not your face. If I dragged you back there looking like that, who'd believe me?"

Life? Or death?

Death? Or life?

There were enough names on the list without Luka Löwe's at the end.

"Take off your clothes," she told him.

Luka burst into a grin as he threw off his jacket and started unbuttoning his uniform to reveal his damp white undershirt.

"Not all of them," Yael said before he could peel that off, too. "Just the big tells. Swastikas, Iron Crosses, anything that will make you stand out."

Luka balled up his uniform (pins, brown shirt, black tie, and all) and tossed it among the trash bags. The two Iron Crosses—a culmination of over forty thousand kilometers, five years of Luka's life—were next to go, landing beside food bits and torn paper. The victor retrieved his jacket, slung it over his shoulder.

"How's this?" he asked.

Yael gave the boy a quick study. No party eagles, no swastikas... He'd worn his motorcycle boots to the Victor's Ball instead of the standard Hitler Youth footwear. *Not*, Yael reminded herself, *that Luka Löwe has ever been a boy prone to convention*. His trademark jacket (stitched out of vintage brown leather, where every other Axis Tour racer's jacket was standard-issue black) was evidence of that. He'd worn it for the past three races. There were years' worth of Reichssender footage with Luka Löwe sporting this very article of clothing.

"The jacket?" She nodded at it.

"Stays."

Funny. She'd expected more of a fight over the Iron Crosses. Not this worn piece of leather. But Luka's grip on the jacket tightened, as if daring her to rip it from his grasp. Yael could have. She might have, if the victor's face weren't so Nordic and his hair weren't as blazing as a high-noon sun.

"Fine. Use it to cover your head again."

Luka obeyed, positioning the leather so it hung over his hair, shadowing his face. Not the most subtle of disguises, but (Yael tried to reassure herself) it had gotten him this far.

—LEAVE HIM—

She had to.

She couldn't.

"If you get yourself caught," Yael told him, "if I think you're going to betray me in any way, I will leave you. Understood?"

"Aye, aye, Fräulein." Luka nodded under his jacket. "Lead the way."

—LEAVE HIM LEAVE HIM NOT SAFE—

Yael's instincts kept screaming, but she pretended not to hear. She pretended not to remember that they were usually, almost always, right.

43

CHAPTER 5

When Felix was younger, his favorite place in the world was his father's auto shop. Every day after school, when Martin was off at Hitler Youth meetings and Adele was playing football with the Schulers, the younger Wolfe boy sat cross-legged on the auto shop's floor, listening to his father narrate the ailments of Volkswagen engines while he picked through their grease-smeared guts.

"The spark plug's been fouled in this one. See all the oil corroding the tip?" His father held up the part, wiping his spare hand on his navy coveralls. "Keeps the engine from starting properly. All we have to do is replace it, and the car should run like new."

Things in the auto shop made sense, the way his father explained them. There was always a solution. Through the eyes of a nine-year-old child, there seemed to be nothing his father couldn't fix. It was only three years later, standing on the edge of the Nürburgring racetracks that Felix learned the terrible, terrible truth: This was a lie. Some things were too broken to be fixed. Martin's crushed neck vertebrae couldn't just be swapped out with replacement parts.

The auto shop was gone now, too. Its towers of tires, its cinder-block walls papered with engine diagrams, its rows of wrenches arranged by size and type…Felix had sold all of it to Herr Bleier for enough Reichsmarks to bribe his way into the Axis Tour, to keep his sister from getting too entangled in the resistance plot Hans Schuler had warned him about.

But Adele wasn't just at risk of being in the plot's path. She *was* the plot. Felix had tried his best to stop her, to fix just one more irreparable thing. He'd tried his best, and the garage was gone and so was his sister, leaving him to deal with the consequences of her mess.

Very, very painful consequences.

SS jackboots—with their hobnailed soles and iron heel plates—were tailor-made torture instruments. It took Bulbous Nose only three kicks at Felix's side before he felt something crack.

There was no fixing this.

Felix knew he was a dead man. He knew the moment he looked into Baasch's eyes, saw his lack of future there. All he could do now was bear this agony, buy his sister the time she needed to make a clean getaway.

Another kick. Another crack. The fire in his side was spreading, coal hot and ember deep. A thickness in Felix's breath made him choke. There was something sticky on his lips….

"Herr Wolfe." SS-Standartenführer Baasch's own jackboot tapped against the floor. "Time is not a luxury we can entertain this evening. Where did the girl go?"

"I d-don't know."

Baasch leaned over and muttered something to Bulbous Nose, who uncuffed Felix's wrists and splayed his right hand flat on the floor.

"You're a mechanic, are you not? Engines are made up of so many small pieces. The coordination you must need in your fingers to get it all right…" The SS-Standartenführer's pause filled the room. "Tell me who the girl is working with."

The resistance. Start with the Schuler boy from Wolfsgang Street. He knows—no. Felix caught himself. *Don't say it. Don't even think it.*

At least one Wolfe had to survive. Adele's life depended on his silence.

Baasch's jackboot lifted over Felix's ring and pinky fingers. Its heel plate landed with a sickening crush. The pain inside Felix became a living thing—rising, roaring. The heat in his side met the shatter of his fingers and took animal form, tearing from his mouth in a scream.

Baasch did not lift his foot. He sounded almost bored when he spoke. "Tell me. Why do you feel the need to protect this girl? After she tied you up, left you for us to find?"

"I will not"—even Felix's teeth felt broken as he cobbled these words together, blood rusty inside his mouth—"betray my sister."

"Your sister?" Baasch's laugh shimmered off the floor's bare wood. His heel lifted. "You were watching the television. Didn't you hear what the girl screamed before she pulled the trigger?"

"Volume's on zero, Standartenführer." Bulbous Nose jerked his head at the screen. "No sound."

"Ah." The commander walked over to the volume knob, twisting it until the speakers emitted a long, low buzz. "It's noble of you, Herr Wolfe, to bear so much pain for the sake of your family. You're a fine example of 'blood and honor.' But I'm afraid your suffering has been in vain. The girl who fired the gun in that ballroom was not your sister."

The pain in Felix's fingers mixed poorly with the officer's declaration. *Not* (splintered fingernails) *your* (blood, sticky, on the floor) *sister* (Was that a piece of bone sticking out?).

He couldn't believe any of it.

"You shouldn't feel so bad," the SS commander went on. "Inmate 121358ΔX fooled quite a lot of people. Racing officials, Reichssender press, even the Führer. She must have studied Fräulein Wolfe for quite a long time to impersonate her so well. The girl was one of the initial test subjects in the Doppelgänger Project. She can manipulate her appearance at will. Look like your sister one minute and a complete stranger the next."

These words did not make sense.

But . . . they did.

They made perfect sense, Felix realized, because he'd *seen* this change. Back in Cairo, he'd followed the girl he thought was his sister through the night market, down dark and winding streets, all the way to a shisha café. When he'd walked in to confront her, he'd found an Egyptian girl—dressed in the same clothes. Later, Adele had explained to him she'd known he was coming and traded garments with a girl in the café.

She'd lied. It wasn't clothes she'd traded, but faces.

The girl he'd ridden over twenty thousand kilometers with, the girl who'd twice bashed his face with a pistol, the girl he'd tried and tried to reconnect with, the girl he'd given up everything to save ... was not his sister.

"There must be blood to pay for what happened on television, Herr Wolfe. I'm sure you can appreciate what a delicate situation this puts us in. The world watched your sister shoot the Führer. If we fail to retaliate in kind, then people will begin to question our resolve—" Baasch broke off in a cough. He brought his handkerchief—still pure, spotless white—to his lips.

Retaliate in kind. Words to match the SS-Standartenführer's handkerchief. First-class fancy, covering a much more sinister meaning: shooting Adele. No, Felix corrected himself, if they executed his sister publicly, it would be in the traditional manner: guillotine blade. Rolling heads made much more of a statement than bullet holes.

"You can't!" Felix rasped. "What about the girl?"

"What about her?"

There was so much Felix wanted to ask. He found the idea of this girl shifting from face to face fascinating. How did she make her eyes match the exact blue of Adele's? How did her skin replicate the finest pattern of his sister's, all the way down to freckles and scars? How was it even possible for a human body to piece and re-piece itself together like that?

But pain flared through these curiosities, bubbling with the blood in Felix's mouth, seeping into the roots of his teeth, burning up all but the basest emotion: anger. Funny how only minutes ago he'd struggled to comprehend such a fury. One that consumed every centimeter of a person's being.

Now it was Felix and Felix was it.

"She's the one who d-did this. She's the one who sh-should—"

48

He stuttered on his own blood. There was too much to swallow back, so he spit it out. Flecks smeared the edge of the SS commander's boot. "P-pay."

"I agree." If Baasch was bothered by the spit, he didn't show it. He nodded at Felix's ruined hand. "Which brings us back to my first question. Where did the girl go?"

His thoughts swirled—in fire, on pain. Adele's head rolling, rolling, blond hair tagged in blood. More blood—his own—still streaming out, anchoring his fingers to the floor. *Where did the girl go?* How would Felix know? She hadn't told him any of her plans. All she'd done was lash her pistol across his head—

Stop. Think. Go back.

There was one thing.

The last time Felix saw his sister (No! Not his sister…the inmate) she'd pinned him to the ground with the curtains and reached for her gun. The motion pulled back the sleeve of her kimono, revealing a column of running canines.

Not one thing, but five. Not said, but seen.

"I'll tell you what I know." Felix had to stop himself from spilling all—hot anger tongue. He still needed to defend his sister— his *real* sister—to the end. "But I want a pardon for Adele."

"A pardon?" A clinical smile (turned lips, eyes still dead) slashed along the SS-Standartenführer's face. "Quite the bargainer, aren't you, Herr Wolfe?

"Unfortunately, the authority to pardon your sister is above my rank. So let's start with this." Baasch lifted his heel again. Its iron plate hovered just over Felix's middle and index fingers. "Tell me what you know, and perhaps I'll choose not to pulp what's left of your hand."

Felix looked back down at his fingers (eight whole, two crushed, more maroon now than red). He could keep his silence, watch the rest of his fingers crumble under the SS-Standartenführer's iron heel. Or he could offer up what he knew, hope for mercy.

Felix was not going to play the martyr. Not for this…this… girl. Not for blood that was not his.

"Dogs," he said.

The smile slipped from the SS officer's face. His heel hovered. "What?"

"There were dogs on her arm. A t-tattoo. Five of them."

"Which arm?"

"L-left. The ink went up to her elbow. Like a sleeve."

The SS-Standartenführer's jackboot hung, kept hanging. Globules of Felix's own saliva salted the sole, close enough to count. One, two, three…no crushing…four, five, six… Baasch brought his shoe down. It hit the floor, just shy of Felix's fingertips.

"Thank you, Herr Wolfe. That information is most useful."

The room's door twitched open. Another SS soldier poked his head through the gap, his face mortared with a grim expression. "Standartenführer?"

"What?" Baasch snapped.

"We finally made contact with Germania, Standartenführer. But there's a situation—Reichsführer Himmler wishes to speak with you."

"The Reichsführer? Very well." Baasch turned to Bulbous Nose. "Have Obersturmführer Thiessen send out a notice about the doppelgänger's marking. Tattoos don't change for their kind.

The dogs will be on any form the girl takes. With any luck we can use them to make a positive ID."

Baasch started walking to the door. The heel of his right boot marked his path in Felix's blood: *C C C* stamping the wood at odd red intervals. "Oh, and get Herr Wolfe some water. I have a few more questions for him when I return."

CHAPTER 6

Wet leather smelled like *Scheisse*.

The stench clawed at Luka's nostrils as he watched Fräulein cross the street. Not-Adele looked at home in the darkness, on the move. Velvet hair swung against her cheeks as she walked, blending so perfectly with the shadows that for a moment Luka found himself choked with the fear that the girl herself would melt away. But the fräulein's form was still corporeal when she halted on the other side of the street, surveying their surroundings before calling Luka over with an old Wehrmacht hand signal.

Where had not-Adele learned the Wehrmacht hand signals? For that matter, where had Fräulein learned any of what she knew? Planting tracking diversions, scaling walls, swimming moats, tackling and besting someone with considerably more muscle mass... As far as Luka was aware, the League of German Girls did not school young women in any of these subjects.

Who the hell was this girl?

"You got a name?" Luka asked as he scuttled toward not-Adele.

"Why should I tell you? You'd never bother using it."

She had a point.

Luka shrugged. "I suppose 'not-Adele' has a certain ring to it."

"If you don't stop speaking German, I will leave you in the gutter," she hissed and kept moving forward.

Luka—half-blinded by his own sleeves, choking on the smell of damp, dead animal—trailed the nameless girl and reviewed his options:

Option 1: Overpower Fräulein. (Amendment: *Try* to overpower Fräulein. She had kicked his *Arsch* in the alley.) Call the authorities. Hope they didn't laugh their heads off at his crazy tale of her changing skin.

Option 2: See where this goes.

Right now, this was going south at a painstaking crawl of 0.0002 kilometers an hour. Every few steps, not-Adele signaled for him to halt. Luka was forced to hang back in the shadows as she scouted ahead. Whenever people passed, the girl pulled the same stunt she had in the alley—leaning in for the almost-kiss, her nose crinkling at the wet-leather-*Scheisse* smell. Luka didn't quite know what to make of her closeness. It seared him, just as it had on the train, on the *Kaiten*, in the ballroom. His was a body plagued with hangover feelings: love, mixed with hate, stirred with shock.

Who the hell was this girl? Why did he still want to kiss her?

Not-Adele is not Adele, he told himself, over and over again as he stood motionless, showing no emotion, waiting for the danger to pass.

They worked their way through the city. Down blocks, through alleys, past parks, over bridges, slowly, slowly. The stars were high and the night was deep by the time they arrived at the edge of Tokyo's harbor, halting just across the street from a collection of docks. Luka was no architect, but he could tell they were a postwar addition to the capital's waterways, with shiny light fixtures and unsplintered boards. Dozens of boats— passenger ferries, fishermen's dinghies, sleek motorboats—sat in the slips.

"So." Luka nodded at the docks. "We're stealing a boat?"

The girl turned on him. Delicate nostrils flared. "I thought I told you not to speak German," she hissed in that very language.

"I can't speak anything else!"

"Then do us both a favor and shut it."

Luka's usual response to an order was to smirk and do the opposite. But he'd already pushed his luck in the alley, and he knew it wouldn't take much for this girl to ditch him. Without her, he'd be a poster-boy fugitive stranded in downtown Tokyo. (Translation in Luka-speak: dead meat.)

He kept his mouth shut.

"*I'm* stealing a boat." The girl continued in Luka's mother tongue, low and sure, so he'd understand. "You're staying put."

"Here? Alone?" Luka sucked in a breath, immediately regretting it as he gagged on the damp leather stench. "I don't think so!"

"It's been several hours since everything happened. The SS has likely asked the Japanese to amp up security around the city's departure points. There could be patrols. If I'm discovered poking around the boats, I can lie my way out of it. That would be considerably more difficult if you were with me.

"I'll come back for you when we're ready to leave." The fräulein stepped across the street before he could argue. This time

54

she truly did melt away, hair, jacket, face becoming one with the shadows of the harbor.

Luka found himself alone, craving a cigarette, squinting at the docks for signs of not-Adele's return. Harbor water glimmered, mercurial against the lamplights. Once or twice the darkness streaked with pint-sized movements that could belong only to rats.

No patrols. No Fräulein either.

Minutes passed. His urge for a cigarette gnawed and grew. The dead meat/*Scheisse* smell cloaking his head had become nauseating. Luka's tally of things-not-Fräulein was up to three passing cars and five rats when the certainty hit him, as slamming as Felix Wolfe's right fist.

Not-Adele was gone. And she wasn't coming back.

Luka couldn't blame her. Not-Adele's escape was a certain thing without his face in tow. If he'd been in the fräulein's position, juggling odds of 100 percent against *no chance in hell,* he would've done the same. He was more flustered at how he'd allowed himself to be hooked by the girl's *I'll come back* words, leaving him dangling like bait, waiting for the SS sharks to descend.

He'd wagered she'd had a heart. He'd begun to fear he'd had one of his own....

A voice—not so unlike his father's—circled his thoughts. *Tricked by a girl. Again? Serves you right for being such a softhearted dummkopf.*

Luka was done being chum. He tore his jacket off his head and shouldered it on, crossing over to the harbor. The docks were more extensive than they had appeared from the other side of the street, a labyrinth of industrial lamps and kanji-covered helms, branching out into dark waters. Luka walked down the main stretch—jaw clenched, heart fuming—passing dock after empty dock.

The fourth dock was not empty. A human-sized shadow skirted around islands of lamplight, pausing every few steps to study boats in their slips.

Luka's pulse steamed into his throat as he called out, "Can't shake me that easily, Fräulein!"

The person turned, stepping into one of the pools of light. Where Luka expected to see a black biker jacket and nostrils wide with rage, he instead found an olive-green field cap, a canvas jacket, the slender barrel of a rifle....

Not not-Adele, but a member of the Imperial Japanese Army.

Scheisse.

The two regarded each other, a stunned moment slipping between them. Then the soldier yelled words Luka's ears could not decipher. At least in the literal sense. He gathered the gist of them well enough. (Translation in Luka-speak: The hunter had become the hunted.)

Luka Löwe swore again (this time out loud) and started to run.

CHAPTER 7

There had been a few candidates for getaway boats along the docks, but Yael didn't waste time weighing their various merits. The boat she chose was as good as any: small enough to be subtle on the coastline, with enough engine power to handle the chop of deeper waters, enough to get her and Luka across the East China Sea, back to the mainland.

When Yael pried out the motorboat's starter panel, she found its wiring wasn't so different from the setup Vlad had used to teach her hot-wiring: tangled and colorful, ultimately simple. It would take only a few seconds to get the engine started.

"He's over here! I need backup!"

"*SCHEISSE* on a *verdammt* stick!"

Two yells in two different languages, both just a few docks over. Yael dropped the panel when she heard them, cursing Luka in every one of her six languages. She should've known the victor would refuse to stay put. But Yael hadn't counted on the boy being brainless enough to blunder into a patrol.

More yells—all Japanese—rose from various locations around the docks. One a few meters northeast. Another from the west. A cry from the south. At least four soldiers, by Yael's count. Not a manageable number of opponents to take on alone.

Not impossible either.

—LEAVE HIM GO GO GO—

The starter panel dangled from its wires—red, yellow, black. Ten seconds was all it would take to cross them and crank the engine.

Ten seconds and a life.

—DON'T BE A HERO NOTHING CAN FIX WHAT YOU'VE DONE YOU'VE CHOSEN DEATH ONCE WHY NOT AGAIN?—

Why not again?

The shouts were drawing closer. Even if Luka somehow made it off the docks by himself, he wouldn't make it out of this city. He was too blond, too loud, too *there*.

She cursed Luka again. She cursed the soldiers for patrolling this exact dock at this exact hour. She cursed herself for jumping out of the motorboat and pulling the P38 from her pocket.

Yael did not run straight into the fray, gun blazing. Vlad had taught her better than that. She clung to the darkness instead, skipping from boat to boat, clambering along their bows until she reached the highest one. From there she was able to assess the situation.

It was not good.

Luka was trapped on the main dock by a trifecta of Arisaka Type 99 rifles. Their muzzles were leveled at his chest, aimed by patrolmen who looked just as shaken as Victor Löwe did. The three soldiers chatted excitedly among themselves.

Soldier one: "It's one of the victors!"

Soldier two: "What is he doing here?"

Soldier three: "He's the one who invited the inmate to the Victor's Ball. He must have fled when she did—"

Luka (in frantic German): "Are you going to put a bullet in me or not? If so, I'd rather you get it over with."

Soldier one: "Is that *rice* on his face?"

Soldier three: "He smells like a dog's ass."

The men's dialogue spiraled into a contest of insults. None of them seemed too concerned about *what* to do with the German victor now that they'd caught him. There was no sign of the fourth soldier. He must've gone to radio in their discovery.

If Yael was going to save Luka, she had to do it now.

She rose from her surveillance pose on the bow and crept her way to the dock, stalking closer to where the soldiers bantered. Two of them stood with their backs to her, and the third was too distracted by his comrades' jokes to notice the shifting shadows on the far dock. Luka's arms were propped above his head, all his attention focused on the three rifles. His jaw was set on edge.

During the course of the Axis Tour, Yael had seen Luka break noses and disarm Soviet guards with brutal, decisive elegance. The victor was a good fighter when he wasn't hemmed in by Arisakas. He needed a distraction and she was the one to provide it.

Yael disengaged the P38's safety, drew its hammer, and aimed at the water. Her finger cradled the trigger, waiting for just the right moment to pull.

It never came.

An O of metal jabbed into her back, followed by an order just as sharp: "Don't move."

The fourth soldier hadn't gone to radio. He'd been waiting for her.

"Over here!" he called to the others in Japanese.

Yael's heart trilled its old chorus: FLASH, *THUD, VER-DAMMT!* Her brain scrambled through Vlad's training, against her own dread. Most people would've found an Arisaka Type 99 rifle pressed against their flesh paralyzing. Not Yael. She turned and lunged. The fourth soldier pulled the trigger a fraction too late. His bullet missed Yael (though she felt the graze of its breath, death almost death, passing her over once more), plowing straight into the patrol. Yael grabbed the soldier and wheeled him off the edge of the dock. Then she turned to face the rest.

The round had missed every one of them, for when Yael looked at Luka and the other Imperial Army soldiers, she saw not blood but confusion. Rifles swung, arms flailed. Luka sprang at the nearest soldier; the pair became a green-and-leather blur. The other two patrolmen lined their Arisakas' sights on Yael's end of the dock and fired. Their aim was sloppy, frantic. One shot splintered the wood by Yael's toes. The other hissed over her shoulder.

Both men fumbled with the bolts of their guns—giving Yael valuable seconds to stow her P38 and jump. One abandoned his reloading efforts, drawing his bayonet instead. Yael didn't have time to go for the knife stowed in her boot. They met: hand-to-blade combat. He was a gifted fighter: anticipating her first punch, dodging it, throwing a swipe of his own. Yael's sidestep wasn't swift enough; the tip of the bayonet dragged across her jacket, slicing all leather, no skin. Her second hit was more successful. Yael felt her bones connect with flesh, crack into cartilage.

The soldier spun away from her, free hand clasping his face, red leaking through his fingers. Yael was just about to put the man in a headlock when she heard a series of heart-dropping sounds.

Bad: a spent casing tumbling to the dock. Worse: a slick twist and click of a rifle bolt pushed into place. Worst: a command issued first in Japanese, then again in German so precise it was surgical: "Arms up. Or I'll shoot."

The second soldier's reloaded Arisaka was aimed straight at Yael. He was too close, too ready—there was no dodging this bullet. She held her hands up. A side glance showed her that Luka's fight had fared no better. The victor was on his back, lips snarled, the third soldier's Nambu semiautomatic pistol shoved against his throat.

"I'm afraid there's been a mistake," she began, trying to keep her Japanese fluid. Unrushed. "I was only out here cleaning my father's boat—"

"Check her!" the fourth soldier barked from the edge of the dock, where he was pulling himself out of the water.

Blood kept rushing down the first soldier's face as he grabbed Yael's left sleeve. Pulled. The fabric gave away to wads of unraveling gauze, which the soldier tore off. Beneath, a scene of ink-and-whirlwind wolves: Babushka, Mama, Miriam, Aaron-Klaus, Vlad. Her pieces, her pain, herself. Stripped back, exposed for all to see.

The wounded soldier jabbed a finger at Yael's skin. His nail landed on the bared fangs of Vlad's wolf. "These are the markings the SS told us about. It's her. The inmate."

"Excellent. Let's get them back to the palace."

But . . . how could the SS know about the wolves?

Felix. The other boy she tried to leave behind. (And did.) Yael had hoped that when the SS found Adele's brother tied up and gagged in her room, they'd assume his innocence. After all—she'd shouted her own true identity to anyone who cared to listen.

Yael's stomach swan-dived to her toes. She should've known better. Innocence and guilt were irrelevant in the courts of the SS. They judged with far harsher laws.

What had they done to Felix to get him to talk?

What were they going to do to her and Luka?

Yael already knew the answer to these questions. It was the reason many of the resistance operatives hid cyanide pills in the soles of their shoes. It was why after shooting the Führer three times in the chest on May 16, 1952, Aaron-Klaus swung his own pistol to his head and did the unthinkable. It was why her stomach kept falling, past her toes, into despair.

Life or death.

Yael had made her choice in the middle of that boat.

This time, the death would be hers.

CHAPTER 8

Luka's life was marked by a trail of bread-crumb rebellions. In the early days, these were small, insubstantial side effects of an overbearing National Socialist father. A tongue stuck out at the Führer's portrait. A cigarette inhaled (but mostly coughed out) behind Herr Kahler's shop. Things Kurt Löwe hated. Things that made Luka feel like Luka and not a loyalist lemming.

But there was always a part of him that yearned for that shiny red bicycle. The same part of Luka that wanted his father to clap him on the shoulder and say, "Well done, my son." The same part that made Luka dust off Kurt Löwe's old BMW R12 and enroll in the Hitler Youth's Axis Tour training program. The same part that made him get back on his motorcycle again and again, through heat and snow, after countless crashes.

This part of Luka wanted to be as strong as his father, stronger even: leather tough, steel hard. This part pushed him, pushed him, pushed—all the way to his 1953 Axis Tour victory.

Everything changed after he won. Luka met the real

Führer without sticking out his tongue (though he couldn't stop his neck hairs from prickling; that response was purely instinctual). The victor became not simply a part of the system that stifled him, but the very image of it. His face was immortalized on *Sieg heil* posters all over the empire's streets. *We are strong*, the Aryan people thought whenever they saw it. *We are so invincible a fourteen-year-old boy can race across continents and win.*

But whenever Luka looked at these posters, he did not feel strong. He did not feel right. He felt...swallowed. People saw him—a boy wearing a black jacket, hair clipped military tight, arm planked in a high salute—but they did not see *him*.

So the bread crumbs of Luka's discontent grew bigger, bolder. A carton of cigarettes a week. A brown jacket donned instead of the standard black racing uniform. An angry word— or two, or three—about the state of things, always and only in the right company. Luka's rule-breaking was very calculated. Just enough to set him apart, never enough for a one-way ticket to the labor camps.

But after Fräulein had come back for Luka, after she fought the Japanese soldiers and lost, after their weapons were seized and their hands bound, after they were stuffed into the patrol wagon with about as much dignity as a *verdammt* hay bale, Luka knew he'd made a mistake.

Actually, he mused as the transport rolled through Tokyo's streets, *I've made quite a few mistakes*. Wandering down to the docks. Chasing not-Adele out of the garden. Inviting her to the Victor's Ball. Falling in love in the first place (and the second, for that matter).

The fräulein sat next to him, eyes out the window, as they rolled through the main gate of the Imperial Palace.

"Back so soon," Luka muttered.

He watched her and waited. For an eye roll. A retort. Anything. But not-Adele kept staring out the truck, face eggshell white. Luka would much rather have her yelling. Angry words and accusations he could brace himself against. But silence . . .

He never did well with silence.

The sound of it was everywhere. Just yesterday Luka had crossed the Imperial Palace's main gate to a storm of cheers and flashing cameras. There was none of that now. The palace grounds were strangely quiet for a place that had just seen the Führer shot. No more frantic SS men rooting through the garden. Very few lamps were lit; most windows had gone dark.

Luka and not-Adele were handed over to the SS guards, dragged back to the ballroom. The place had been stripped of music, cleared of guests. Its Reichssender cameras were unmanned—six views gone blind—ringing a dance floor covered in glass. Adolf Hitler's body lay in the midst of this shattered scene. Someone had draped a sheet over the corpse before the blood fully dried. Stains had seeped through. Red now fading . . .

The Führer, a man who'd always been so much larger than life—whose face was everywhere, always (above Luka's parents' mantel, on their television screen, inside every textbook)—was now just worm food waiting to happen. Luka—apart from the possibility of being implicated, tortured, executed—wasn't terribly torn up about the death. Oddly enough, the SS bodyguards didn't look too miffed about it either. The highest-ranking among them was actually smiling: a stiff expression not framed by dimples or laugh lines. It had no business on the man's face.

"Victor Löwe," the SS officer growled as the pair was shoved in front of him. "I expected so much *more* from you."

There was no time like the present for Luka to tell his tale of woe. He'd always had a knack for talking his way out of things. (Exhibit A: Convincing the Axis Tour officials that, yes, he *was* wearing the brown jacket in honor of his veteran father. Wasn't the whole point of the race to honor bloodlines and war victories?) But, Luka realized, the story of how he valiantly pursued this girl across Tokyo to make a citizen's arrest would not work for one simple reason: The fräulein had come back for his sorry *Arsch*. She'd *fought* for him the way she would fight for an ally. A friend.

The evidence was stacked against Luka in a way no swaggering grins or loophole reasoning could erase. His fate was bound to not-Adele's. For better or worse.

At the moment, it was looking very much worse.

He searched the SS officer's uniform for rank. The man's middle finger shone with a gold signet ring—engraved with double *Sieg* runes. Two silver-threaded oak leaves haltered his neck via a collar. The surefire symbol of a "Standartenführer—"

"Baasch."

"Thank you, Standartenführer Baasch." Luka nodded. "I believe you just came up with the title of my autobiography."

Luka Löwe: We Expected So Much More. It would probably be better reading than that *Mein Kampf* headache....

The SS-Standartenführer cleared his throat, his gaze sliding to where not-Adele was being held in place by an SS-Sturmmann. Her left sleeve was shoved up: wolf pack loping from wrist to elbow, beneath the chandeliers' glow. "As for you, Inmate 121358ΔX. I would never have expected one of Dr. Geyer's lab rats to accomplish so much. You truly had me and my men convinced you were Fräulein Wolfe."

Inmate? Lab rat? What was the SS-Standartenführer talking about?

"Even after all this time you *Saukerl*s can't stand to use my name," not-Adele said.

All thoughts of Luka's own story fell away as he watched Fräulein's features change. The process looked different out of the garden's dream-filled dark, under the ballroom's light—much more brash and factual. The angles of her face shifted; all traces of Asian heritage vanished. Hair pulled—long silk, pure white—out of her skull. Her skin was just as pale, pigmentless. And her eyes…they burned. An impossible fluorescent, shop-light blue. One that put Adele's bright irises to shame.

"I am Yael," she said.

Yaaaaaaaaah-ell. The name had a sort of poetry to it—one that didn't jibe with any of the German names Luka knew. It didn't sound Japanese or Russian either.

"It's hardly my concern what your mother called you. What does concern me is who you're working with. I need names. Addresses." Glass from broken champagne flutes crunched under the SS-Standartenführer's feet as he walked toward Yael. It was the same restless stride Luka's father used to perform. The one that created threadbare circles on the Löwes' sitting room rug. The one that set Luka's teeth on edge because he knew what often followed it.

The officer's fist flashed out. There was a dull, wet noise that reminded Luka of the evenings his mother made schnitzel, when she stood over the butcher block, hammering pieces of veal until they were paper-thin.

Yael's head twisted back, white hair streaming. A flag of no-surrender.

That signet ring had to hurt like hell, but the girl didn't make a sound. Color spread through her pale hair, and at first Luka thought maybe she was doing her trick again. But as Yael spit the strands out of her face, he realized it was blood. The *Sieg* rune ring had left a split along her cheekbone. The cut flowed freely, as bright and red as any.

Her mouth stayed closed. Her eyes blazed.

"Names!" SS-Standartenführer Baasch tossed his fist again. There was another thud, just as wet and deep and sickening as the first.

Silence.

Another hit (more silence), another (more), another (more). Blows so hard the SS-Sturmmann who held Yael struggled to stay in place. If her flesh *had* been schnitzel, it would've been long finished, ready for the skillet. Luka kept expecting her to break— to yell, scream, anything—but *Scheisse* if this strange-named fräulein wasn't tough. Pain seemed like nothing to her. Maybe it was. But from where Luka was standing, it was too much.

The color, the silence, the blow after blow . . .

It was all too much to watch.

"Hey!" he heard himself yelling.

The thuds stopped, replaced by the heavy, bloodful sound of Yael trying to breathe. Luka couldn't see the extent of the damage, with her hair plastered to her cheek the way it was. But that was enough of a thrashing for any man to take, much less a fräulein her size. Even the SS-Standartenführer looked tired as he retrieved a kerchief from his pocket, toweling pink spray off his knuckles. He spent an extra few seconds polishing his signet ring before letting the soiled fabric fall to the floor.

SS-Standartenführer Baasch's eyes met Luka's. They were the color of sharkskin. Too calm.

"You don't happen to have a cigarette, do you?" Luka asked. "I could really use one right now. Helps my nerves. They're a bit jangly—"

A fist. A flash of gold. The signet ring *did* hurt like hell.

Luka shook the sparks from his eyes, working the *Sieg* rune pain out of his jaw. "Could you avoid the face next time? I need to keep it pretty for my press release."

"It's a bit too late for that," the SS-Standartenführer said. His face stayed smileless. "Victor Löwe has asked for a cigarette. Should we oblige him?"

Seconds later, a cigarette and silver lighter appeared. *Click, whoosh!* Smoke crept in tendrils out of Baasch's thin lips; fire flared circle-bright off his fingertips. "We used these a good deal in the early days. Easy torture tools that fit in your pocket. Ever since the Aryan Health Laws were instated, they've become much less convenient. Illegal, expensive. Though I hear you're quite partial to them."

"Like I said. Helps my nerves." Right now Luka's nerves were the furthest from calm they could be. Prickling, jabbing, SCREAMING as the SS officer brought the cigarette's smolder closer to the victor's skin.

"You know what happens when you play with fire," the SS-Standartenführer said.

You get burned. On the collarbone.

The fire ate into his first epidermal layer, fizzling along Luka's nerve endings. He would be steel hard, leather tough. He would push, push, push through this....

Luka managed not to scream. He bit through his lip instead.

"Stop!" Even Yael's voice sounded weeping-meat wet. She spoke in short chops of sentences. "Luka had no part in this. Neither did Felix. They know nothing."

Scheisse. It was a nice gesture. Luka was genuinely touched. But the SS-Standartenführer was right. It was too late for that. The victor braced his boots against the ballroom floor—the very one they'd danced on—and got ready for the next burn. But the cigarette hung limp in the SS officer's fingers. His face looked... thoughtful. "These two...they were found at the docks?"

The SS-Sturmmann holding Yael nodded.

"In what order?" the SS-Standartenführer asked.

"Victor Löwe was restrained first," the SS-Sturmmann recounted the Japanese patrolmen's report. "They caught the girl trying to rescue him."

"An assassin with attachments. How unique." There was that *smile* again. The expression would've looked more natural on an actual shark than it did on the SS-Standartenführer's face. The sight of it dragged tooth tips along Luka's spine.

"Luka and Felix are innocent." Yael's protest smudged through her battered face. "Let them go."

Again, nice gesture. But the end of an era lay too close by, death rusting through the white sheet, as tangy as the taste edging Luka's own lips. Blood...mixing with the charred stink of his own flesh. Just the beginning, he knew. He could see it in the edge of Baasch's smile. Shark-hard, drifting closer, expecting so much *more*.

The SS-Standartenführer lifted the cigarette again, but this time he flipped it. Wedged it butt-first between Luka's lips. Ash and surprise—the victor almost choked on it.

"Keep these two here," Baasch instructed his underlings. "I have a few calls to make."

CHAPTER 9

Felix couldn't keep down any of the water that Bulbous Nose had brought him, so he poured it over his fingers instead. It was a shoddy cleaning. His left hand, still cuffed to the bed, slopped the liquid over his injuries in uneven jolts. Felix had nothing but the hem of his Hitler Youth uniform to pad the mess dry. He wasn't even sure why he bothered.

The SS-Standartenführer was gone much longer than the average phone call. When the officer finally did return, Felix braced himself against the bed frame, crippled hand clutched close to his uniform. But Baasch didn't seem set on breaking any more fingers. Nor did he order Bulbous Nose's jackboots back into position. Instead he started pacing, treading through the bloody water on the floor.

"I've been encouraged by your recent cooperation, Herr Wolfe. Your information regarding the girl's markings has already proved useful."

"You—you caught her." Felix's stomach turned. He couldn't

tell if it was from this realization or the constant pain relaying through his tendons or the smoke stink rolling off the SS-Standartenführer's uniform. (All three of these things made him want to retch.) "How?"

"The girl possesses more sentimentality than the average assassin. It does not work to her advantage."

But…if they had the girl, they had no need for Felix's answers anymore. What was Baasch doing here?

Felix's spine felt crooked against the bedpost, as if Bulbous Nose had kicked that out of alignment, too. He watched Baasch's jackboots closer than he would a fanned-out cobra as they splashed back and forth across the room. Wafting that awful ill-wind, burning smell…

"The girl isn't the only one we caught." Baasch halted at the bedside table. His hand went for the rotary phone—picking up the receiver, sliding through a series of numbers.

What was the SS-Standartenführer talking about? Felix's gut wrenched tighter as the officer murmured into the phone, "You've connected with Frankfurt? Good. Put them on the line."

Frankfurt. Home. Oh God…

Baasch carried the phone as far as its cable would allow, pressing the receiver—hard—against Felix's ear. There was a crackling quiet, and then: "Felix? Is that you?"

"Papa?" It *was* his father's voice. A raspy baritone lined with age and arthritic pain, made faint by tens of thousands of kilometers of distance. "Papa, where are you? Where's Mama?"

The sound of tears, high and frail, answered Felix's last question.

"Some men came to the house. Gestapo. They took us.…I

don't know where we are. Are you hurt? Where's your sister? What's happening over—"

Baasch's finger punched into the switch hook. Silence sliced through his father's voice.

Gestapo. Felix's parents were being held by the Gestapo. It was among his worst fears. One he'd voiced in this very room just hours earlier, to the girl who was not his sister: *If you succeed, what do you think the Gestapo will do to Mama and Papa? You'll destroy them.*

But the girl didn't give a *Scheisse* about the Wolfes, did she?

"You're quite a remarkable person, Herr Wolfe. Not many brothers would travel the lengths you've gone to for your sister's sake. Twenty thousand kilometers, ruined fingers..." The SS-Standartenführer's eyes flickered over Felix's stained uniform. "Family is clearly important to you. Tell me, how much further would you go to keep your parents from harm?"

Felix's heart jump-started, rattling electric against Martin's pocket watch.

"I'll do anything," he said, and meant it.

"I thought as much," Baasch said. "The situation has changed. The girl posing as your sister was only a single piece in a much larger plan. The Fatherland is in peril. As we speak, there is a putsch taking place back in Germania."

A revolution? In Germania? It didn't seem possible, not with the hold the National Socialist government had on the population. Every few years, there were small rebellions in the outer territories—uprisings in the mining camps and oil fields—but news of them hardly reached the Reichssender screens before they were squashed. Cleaned out with the ruthlessness of a root canal: quick, brutal, painful.

To have a movement deep enough to launch an assault against the very heart of the Reich? That wasn't just a cavity. That was *years* of hidden rot.

"Some generals have used the Führer's apparent demise to trick their Wehrmacht units into seizing the capital. They've started arresting key National Socialist officials. This attempt to overthrow the government appears to be highly organized. They might have gotten away with it if not for a crucial flaw in their plan." Baasch paused, letting his eyes pick Felix to pieces: toned arms, hair paler than pale, crooked bridge of a nose. "How old are you, Herr Wolfe?"

"Seventeen."

"So young." The SS officer tutted. "Too young to remember...There was a situation like this years ago, during the war. The Führer was betrayed by those in his closest confidence, men who planned to assassinate him and take over the government. They smuggled a bomb into Hitler's Wolfsschanze headquarters. When it went off, these traitors attempted to use the Führer's death as an excuse to overtake Berlin. But Hitler survived the explosion. The resistance was quickly squelched, its conspirators arrested and tortured. They spilled the names of more conspirators, which led to more arrests, more torture sessions....Can you guess, Herr Wolfe, how many were executed in the wake of that incident?"

Felix had no idea. "Three hundred?"

"Five thousand. Five *thousand* traitors were eliminated. And yet here we are, nearly twelve years later, facing another putsch. Clearly the roots we tried to pull up survived. Regrew..." Baasch drifted off. Shook his head. "We must take a different approach this time. The resistance should be crushed beyond regrowth, *all* who are involved exterminated. You—Herr Wolfe—are going to help us."

"But I know nothing. Even when I thought she was Adele... the girl gave me no information. I didn't even know Ade—I mean, the girl—was involved in the resistance until halfway through the race." It hurt to think of those conversations, now that Felix knew the truth behind them: lies, lies, all lies. The girl's manipulation—flesh and feelings, right and wrong—was nothing short of masterful.

"Oh, I'm not going to torture the information out of you." The SS commander glanced back down at the marbled pink puddle. "We've both had quite enough of that, I think."

"Then... how..."

"If you let a rat out of the trap, where does it go?" Baasch didn't wait for an answer. "It scurries straight back to its nest. It's true that we've managed to capture the girl with the help of your tattoo information. We could continue torturing her in the hope that she'll give us a name or two, but she seems to be even more adept than yourself at resisting pain. It's far easier to let her lead us straight to their headquarters. Of course, I can't have any of my men tail her. She's too well trained. She'd get scared off."

"You want me to do it," Felix finished.

The SS-Standartenführer nodded. "We'll give you the tools you need to escape. You're to gain this girl's trust and follow her back to the resistance's headquarters. When you discover where they're hiding, you'll contact me through the channels I'll provide you. No one will lay a finger on your parents as long as you keep to the plans of your mission."

It was amazing, how many ways the SS-Standartenführer

could make a threat without actually verbalizing it. Felix preferred the nuts-and-bolts version: *Fail and we'll kill your parents.*

"What about Adele?" he asked.

"I've already spoken with Reichsführer Himmler about the pardon," Baasch said. "Should you succeed, Adele's name will be cleared."

What the SS-Standartenführer was asking him to do was not a simple fix. No mere swapping out parts. This was more like the few times Felix watched his father rebuild an engine from scratch. Exhaust manifold bolts, valve covers, cylinder heads, rod caps... every piece of the machine had to be taken apart, sifted through, and refitted with unforgiving precision. The job took weeks to complete and could be ruined by a single misplaced part.

Faking an escape, tracking a trained killer back to Germania, infiltrating the resistance, and leading the SS to its stronghold. This was no simple fix, but it *was* a solution. If Felix pulled this off, his family—Mama and Papa and Adele—would be safe.

And the girl...if Felix's veins hadn't been so thinned out from blood loss, they would have kept boiling. But he was exhausted, and his anger was sinking into something deeper. The girl had lied to him, used him, made him *care*, left him for dead. The girl had tried to hurt his family.

The girl would pay for what she'd done.

Speaking of compensation... Felix jerked his chin at the television. "What about the 'blood to pay'?"

The question had hardly left his mouth when the screen's static vanished, giving way to a familiar scene: a National Socialist flag hanging above a chair. It was the same piece of furniture

77

from Adolf Hitler's weekly *Chancellery Chat*s: high-backed, upholstered in velvet.

It was not empty.

The Führer sat as he usually did—meter-stick back, shoulders slightly turned like a portrait of some long-dead king. A pallid face and raging eyes bored into the camera.

It was a recording. It had to be. Even if the Führer had somehow managed to survive a point-blank shot to the chest, he wouldn't be *sitting up in a chair* just hours afterward.

Yet when the Führer spoke, all resemblances to a ghost vanished. His words were as strong as ever, made of Krupp steel syllables. "My fellow countrymen. Our great empire of peace and purity is under attack. Earlier this evening, many of you witnessed a desperate attempt on my life—"

Felix stared at the screen, trying his best to believe.

Not a recording. Not a ghost.

Not even a scratch.

"The hand of Providence has, once again, protected me—"

"Mark my words, Herr Wolfe." Baasch's voice swelled over the Führer's speech. He watched the television, a half smile breaking his face. "There will be blood. There will be more than enough. The world is about to drown in it."

CHAPTER 10

Henryka's map was beginning to change.

Cairo had been the first news to come through, at 1430 hours. The message Brigitte decrypted—letter by penciled letter—was simple:

> **Reichskommissar Strohm arrested. National Socialist forces surrendered. Republic of Egypt declared. More to follow.**

The other operatives whooped and roared when Brigitte read them the news. Kasper smiled so hard his left cheek dimpled. Johann raised an imaginary glass. *Cheers!* Reinhard used another imaginary glass to clink it. Henryka took a marker to her operations map—its deep indigo ink blotting out Egypt's borders.

One Reichskommissariat down. One and two half-continents' worth to go.

More reports trickled in, creating a web of battle lines all across Henryka's map in the form of thin yarn, held in place by thumbtacks. Riots were springing up across London and Dublin.

Rome was burning. Violence had not yet broken out in Germania because the revolution there wore a uniform. Many of the mutinous generals had guided their regiments to key points throughout the city without trouble. Reiniger and his portion of the army had marched down the Avenue of Splendors all the way to the Volkshalle, where they were making quick, quiet arrests. Göring had already been apprehended, control of the Luftwaffe air force seized along with him. (According to the report, he'd been sitting in his office, smoking a celebratory cigar at the news of his "promotion.") Goebbels was still in Tokyo, which left just Bormann and Himmler unaccounted for.

The crimson tide was turning. Bit by bit, the red was ebbing away.

Adele was kicking the door again. The sound of her foot against steel provided a metronome for the map room's work. *THUD, THUD.* Receive a transmission. *THUD.* Key the letters into the Enigma machine. *THUD.* Write down the decoded message. *THUD.* Type out notes. *THUD, THUD.* Relay the news to General Reiniger about the victory in Egypt. *THUD.*

Occasionally, Adele added words to her solo: "All of you are going to pay for this!" Henryka drowned out her cries with the clatter of typewriter keys, wondering if the girl ever got tired. She was mulishly stubborn. Almost as much as Yael.

This thought reminded Henryka that they still hadn't heard from the girl. There'd been nothing in Yael's mission protocol stating she had to report, and getting a message through on the run was almost impossible. Henryka looked up at Japan's dark gray smattering of islands on the map.

Was she still in Tokyo? Surely by now she'd gotten out....

"Henryka." There was a strangeness in Kasper's voice that made her look at him. His dimple was gone. The radio's handset hung limp in his hands.

Brigitte's pencil had dropped to the floor, but she made no move to pick it up. Reinhard and Johann wore shattered-glass stares. All four operatives were looking over Henryka's shoulders, in the direction of the television.

When Henryka turned around, she saw why.

The Reichssender was back on the air. Adolf Hitler sat in front of the camera. Alive and, by all appearances, very well.

This was what he had to say: "My fellow countrymen. Our great empire of peace and purity is under attack. Earlier this evening, many of you witnessed a desperate attempt on my life. Victor Wolfe, in her feeble, feminine state of mind, was brainwashed into believing the world would be a better place without me in it. The hand of Providence has, once again, protected me against those who would seek to destroy our way of life. Despite their best efforts, I am not dead.

"But the danger has not passed. I call now upon the people of the Reich to remember the oath you swore to your Führer. Remember this great world we have built and do not let the pure blood of your fathers be shed in vain."

"*Scheisse*," Kasper whispered.

Henryka's swear was far louder, far worse.

The *THUD*s inside the closet faltered, died. Henryka would've bet ten thousand Reichsmarks that Adele's ear was pressed to the door, listening to the Führer's impossibly alive voice as he raged on.

"Our retaliation will be swift and without mercy. We must

take blood for the blood that was taken. For the bullet that was shot in Tokyo, thousands more will hail down on traitors to the Fatherland. Resistance will be crushed without hesitation...."

Henryka's arms seemed to move of their own accord as they shot out, fingers joining with the Olympia Robust's keys, shoving past them. The typewriter went crashing off her desk, clattering to the concrete floor in a pile of broken metal and inky ribbon. The document Henryka had been working on was spattered with stray keys. The greatest victory—The Führer Adolf Hitler is dead—and the smallest—Cairo declared a republic—undone with FJKÖÄ ZUIO QWER, the most random of letters.

Valkyrie the Second's history in the making stopped here.

CHAPTER 11

Yael held her gun fencing style: left hand up and out and straight. Adolf Hitler stood in her sights, alive again (still). His mustache fringed his lips; stodgy veins wreathed his temple. His eyes crackled, manic blue.

—*KILL THE BASTARD*—

Yael obeyed: finger to the trigger. Her bullet whistled through the ballroom's golden air, into the Führer's chest. At first, there was only nothingness—a gap of not-flesh where flesh had just been.

Then came the blood. Pouring out and everywhere.

Adolf Hitler did not scream or fall. Instead he changed. His hair frothed white, then sleeked black. His eyes flashed dark, darker, darkest, until they were the same shade as Tsuda Katsuo's. They *were* Tsuda Katsuo's. The Japanese victor stood in the Führer's place, his gaze all the more sharper in death. The red circle on his chest kept blooming.

I'm sorry I'm sorry I'm so, so sorry is what Yael wanted to say.

Instead her finger fell, unstoppable, on the trigger. A second hole appeared in Tsuda Katsuo's chest.

He changed again, taking the shape of Aaron-Klaus's face— the way Yael had last seen it. His zealous features were lit with *belief* that he could change things.

She shot him, too.

Again and again. Shot, change, shot, change. The skin-shifter wore face after face after face. Miriam's dark curls. Mama's evening-shadow eyes. The Babushka's piano-key smile. Yael fired more bullets than the chamber of her P38 could possibly hold. Holes riddled their chests, more than any living person could stand. The faces kept changing, revolving through an endless litany of ghosts.

They would not die. They would not stay dead.

There were buckets of blood now, pouring from the wounds Yael had made. Pooling on the floor, lipping up the edges of her zori sandals.

"Isn't this what you wanted?" Aaron-Klaus asked her. "Isn't this what we trained so hard for?"

BANG.

"You left me," whispered Miriam. "You left me to die."

BANG.

"Monster!" wailed her mother. "It's a monster!"

BANG.

The blood rose to her shins, rose, rose, kept rising, warm around her knees. There was a crowd behind Yael, but they did not seem to notice the red staining their kimonos, soaking their dress uniforms. They held glasses of champagne, the nothingness of their conversation hummed loud, louder, loudest....

It was a strange waking. Not like the ones that followed most of Yael's nightmares. No rapidly pounding heart, no flailing limbs, no sweat-soaked undershirts. There was just darkness, noise, pain, and the stab of Yael's blood-matted hair against her cheeks as she lifted her head, took in the dim surroundings.

Walls: metal and . . . bending? Unforgiving floors. Seats upholstered in scratchy ochre fabric. Luka Löwe was sprawled in the seat across from her; the cigarette burn on his collarbone rose high, dipped low as he snored. The buzz of the nightmare crowd droned on, unbearably loud.

Airplane engines.

She remembered now.

After the SS-Standartenführer's punches and the silence Yael forced herself to keep, the officer disappeared. Yael and Luka and the guards stayed in the ballroom with the ~~unknown skin-shifter's~~ sheet-covered corpse. The hours passed and kept passing. Dawn light peeked through the windows, stretched through the morning and into noon. Their guards changed. The bloodied shroud and the Führer's dead body double were removed. The day crawled on. When the SS officer finally returned, it was with Felix Wolfe in tow. From a distance, it looked as if the boy wore a glove of patent oxblood leather. But when SS-Standartenführer Baasch dragged him closer, Yael caught sight of the right hand's final fingers: crushed.

He didn't deserve this.

Yael knew the moment Felix saw the wolves, saw *her*. The Wolfe boy flinched. Up, up his blue eyes scathed: through the Babushka, Mama, Miriam, Aaron-Klaus, Vlad . . . over the blood and bright of her default face, until their gazes finally locked.

Both stares were clouded with pain, inside and out. Yael wanted to say something, but the SS-Standartenführer was speaking, telling the trio they were being flown back to Germania for "a more thorough interrogation" and a trial at the People's Court.

They were driven to an airstrip with the rest of the SS bodyguards and loaded onto the Führer's personal plane: *Immelmann IV*. Yael, Felix, and Luka had been stuffed into the tail section, locked behind a steel-plated door, denied the luxury of cotton ball earplugs and orange juice. SS-Standartenführer Baasch and the rest of the guards left them alone, retreating to the Focke-Wulf Condor's front end.

The gesture struck Yael as odd, but then again, what was the point of stationing a guard? Their hands were cuffed, secured to the cabin's various unmoving elements. (Yael's wrists were locked around a table leg, Luka's bolted to the frame of his own seat.) Even if they managed to free themselves, where would they go? They were trapped in a steel tube, thousands of feet over the middle of nowhere.

None of this stopped Felix Wolfe from trying. The boy sat in the chair next to Yael's, his hands clasped to the other table leg. There was very little light in the cabin—their plane was flying west, too slowly to keep the night at bay—but Yael could still see the mess of torn skin and garnet clots that was his right hand.

(No wonder she'd dreamed of blood.)

Felix's right thumb and forefinger, at least, seemed functional. He was using them to try to twist the cuffs' lock apart. His lock-picking tool was crudely clever—he'd managed to loosen a badge from his Hitler Youth uniform, bending its pin into shape against the table's edge.

But—as Vlad had told Yael when she first started learning—tricking locks open required delicacy. Precision Felix's mangled fingers did not allow. The raw wounds kept scraping against metal cuff, until they bled freely again. Every few seconds, he slipped, swore, barely keeping his grip on the pin. His fair, freckled face mirrored agony.

"Stop!" It was hardly the first (or only) thing Yael wanted to say to him, but she blurted it out anyway. "You're just hurting yourself!"

Felix kept twisting the pin. He did everything he could not to look at her. And Yael did everything she could not to watch the blood—seeping down Felix's skin, along his cuffs, gathering into the sleeve of his Hitler Youth uniform.

After a few more grimacing, twisting minutes, the lock clicked. His left wrist snapped free. It took him considerably less time to jimmy the right lock open. The cuffs fell to the floor with a resounding *CLUNK*.

"Give us a hand, Herr Wolfe?" Luka was awake now, staring at the other boy. "I don't mind if it's half of one."

Felix turned. There were so many wounds on his face, visible even in the cabin's scarce light. His nose was still taped from Luka's roadside punch, temple bruised from Yael's last pistol-whipping, lips scabbed red from SS torture. He looked nothing like the black-and-white pictures from Adele's files. Nothing like the boy who'd given up everything to help Yael on the road.

Felix knelt down, twisted Luka's cuffs free. He made no move to undo Yael's restraints.

"Where is my sister?" This second gaze between them was not painful so much as...dangerous. There was a wild edge in Felix's eyes, but Yael was not surprised.

She'd taken someone he loved. It was enough to make anyone dangerous.

Four times over (four wolves inked) was enough to turn someone into a *monster*.

"Safe." Yael hoped this was the truth, and not just for Felix's sake. After knocking out Adele in her Germania flat, an operative named Kasper had smuggled the girl to Henryka's beer hall basement. That office was the heart and soul of the resistance. If it wasn't safe now...

"That's not what I asked." Felix's edge grew sharper. His good knuckles clenched.

Yael eyed them. Half wishing he'd throw the punch they held. Fully knowing the SS would crush the rest of those unsplintered bones to reap whatever information they could out of the maimed boy. She didn't blame him for telling the SS about her tattoos, but if there was even a chance that Reiniger's Operation Valkyrie the Second was still a go, Yael would risk it for nothing.

"That's all you need to know," she said. "Adele is safe."

"I wouldn't fret too much, Herr Wolfe." Luka slid between them. "Your sister is more than capable of fending for herself."

"Adele—" Whatever Felix was about to say, he decided against it. He shook his head. "You don't know her."

Luka snorted and leaned back on his heels. "That makes two of us. Change-o-Face here had us both convinced she was your flesh and blood for over three *verdammt* weeks."

Felix's mouth dropped open, scabbed lips first. Wanting to speak, but not quite managing it.

"If she says your sister is safe, she's safe. End of discussion,"

Luka said. "I'd be more worried about our future disfigurement and probable beheading."

"There are worse ways to die." Felix's voice dropped low.

"Maybe. I'm more of a heart-croaking-out-in-your-sleep kind of guy myself," Luka retorted. "Fräulein here is our best chance of obtaining that, but she won't do us *Scheisse* if she's cuffed up. So if you don't mind handing over that pin?"

The *Immelmann IV*'s engines rattled and burned, the whole plane shaking through a patch of turbulence. Adele's brother dropped the Hitler Youth badge to the floor and walked away. Luka retrieved the pin, rolling his eyes as he turned back to Yael's bonds. She watched him work in silence, not knowing what to feel.

There were certainly plenty of choices. Anger—the righteous kind—for the dock incident. (Yael was still cursing it, six languages over, in her head.) Admiration—the earned kind—for the way he'd handled the SS-Standartenführer in the ballroom. And through it all, that nebulous, lost feeling.

What now? What now? What now?

Luka glanced up. Their eyes clashed—his stunning and stormy, hers all bright, eerie bright—and Yael realized she'd been staring too long.

"About the docks," the boy said. "Well, you've been around me these past few weeks. You know trust isn't exactly my strong suit. I was a dummkopf. A *Schweinehund*."

"Yes. You were."

"I should have waited."

"Yes," Yael said. "You should have."

He jabbed the pin—hard, too hard—into the lock. (Delicacy,

89

like trust, was not Luka Löwe's specialty.) Yael started to worry that he would bend the pin too far, beyond repair. She was just about to ask him if he really knew what he was doing when—

Twist, click, free!

One lock, two. Yael's cuffs fell to the floor. She wasted little time setting her broken nose back into place.

What now? What now? What now?

They were still trapped inside this plane. Wounded, outnumbered, weaponless. Even if they could get through the reinforced steel door between them and the SS guards and by some sheer miracle overwhelmed their captors, there was the very not-small matter of landing the plane. A skill Yael's years of training had not equipped her with.

Again, Felix seemed undeterred by these things. Adele's brother was rooting around the cabin, looking for anything of use. Pillows, blankets, crystal glasses, old copies of *Das Reich* (RACERS EQUIPPED WITH RIKUO 98s IN HANOI was the headline). He even pulled Martin's pocket watch out of his uniform, clipping the timepiece open and shut again before deciding it held no answers.

Luka picked up one of the glasses, tossed it in the air, and caught it. Heavy crystal smacked against his palm. "We could blitz them when they come to fetch us."

Barware against a mob of SS? Yael shook her head.

The *Immelmann IV* shuddered again. Yael felt the floor tilt beneath her, gravity shifting toward the nose of the plane. Were they beginning their descent? Already?

"What's that?" Felix nodded at an object on the far wall.

They all leaned in to look.

It was a red lever.

And then she remembered.

(How had she *not* remembered?)

The *Immelmann IV* was Adolf Hitler's personal plane. The only one he ever traveled in.

Yael started laughing. The sound left her more easily than it should have. Luka and Felix turned to look at her, variations of *Has she snapped?* shading both their faces.

In the early days of mission planning, Yael had spent hours with Reiniger, poring over the schematics of the Führer's security detail. After forty-nine assassination attempts, Hitler's defense was airtight, but that hadn't stopped the resistance from double-, triple-, quadruple-checking for holes. Roster lists, blueprints, transportation plans, anything and everything that might possibly hide a weakness. Reiniger barely glanced over the diagram of the *Immelmann IV* before tossing it aside. Yael retrieved the waxy paper from the floor, eyeing its swooping, avian lines, delicate tracings that reminded her of the Valkyrie etching she was so fond of.

"Why can't we do anything on the plane?" she'd asked.

"Apart from the lack of Reichssender cameras? The *Immelmann IV* is impenetrable." Reiniger had nodded at the plans in Yael's hand. "You never know when the Führer will depart, so you can't put a time bomb on it. The windows are made of fifty-millimeter-thick bulletproof glass. The Führer's cabin is fortified with steel and fitted with its own escape hatch. All the seat backs double as parachute packs. If anything on the flight goes wrong, Hitler just pulls a red lever, and out he goes."

Yael—the girl outside the memory, the one still laughing

because not everything was death (not today)—slipped her fingers inside the nearest seat back and pulled. Its cushion fell away to reveal a harness and, below that, a cord. She checked the next chair, and the next. Each was the same: detachable back cushions doubling as parachutes.

Yael slid her shoulders into the straps of the one she was holding and shoved a second parachute cushion into Luka's chest. "What are you waiting for? Put them on."

The victor clutched the tangle of straps, examining it much like he would a spiderweb—disgusted, about to drop it to the floor. "You want us to jump out of an airplane wearing just this?"

"I want you to die in your sleep. Old and gray," Yael told him. "Now, put it on. Make sure you're wearing your jacket. It's going to be cold."

Luka's expression balanced between sheer terror and the desperation to look unfazed as he salvaged some of the cabin's blankets, wrapping them around his torso before he buckled his parachute into place.

Not a bad idea. Yael grabbed more blankets, threading half of them through her own harness before collecting a third parachute-cushion and turning to Felix. The boy's face was filled with a terror far stronger than Luka's. Fear beyond fear, backed up by medical files. **Acrophobia: an intense fear of heights.**

She'd seen this in Felix before, on the road, when he'd had to guide his motorcycle along a cliff ledge. But that drop had only been twenty meters.... This one numbered in the thousands.

"Nononono." The whisper left Felix in a single stream. He shook his head, all of him shaking. "This wasn't...isn't..."

"Felix." Yael's voice was low, blunt. "Look at me."

He did this time. She could see how the terror was eating him alive, swallowing his pupils until there was no blue left. Yael held this dark, dark gaze as she draped the blankets around Felix's chest, slipped the harness over his arms, and cinched its buckles tight.

Once she was sure the boy was fastened in, she found his cord, placed it in his good hand. "I want you to count out fifteen seconds, then pull the cord," she said to both boys. "When you land, stay where you are. I'll find you both."

They stared at her. Luka nodded. Felix's face was blank with terror.

Yael pulled the scarlet lever. One moment the floor was a solid, certain thing. The next a piece of it yawned open, jaws wide to chaos. Darkness, cold, and roar poured inside the plane.

Yael had no idea what lay beyond, no way of guessing their distance from the ground. Who was to say there was ground beneath them at all? How many seas littered the landscape between Tokyo and Germania? Rough math (Focke-Wulf Condor engines averaged 335 knots an hour times about ten hours) told her they were somewhere on the Reich side of the Seventieth Meridian. If the pilot had chosen a more northern flight path, they'd be well away from any large bodies of water.

The only way to know for sure was to jump.

Luka edged his way over to the chute. Golden hair whipped back. Lips peeled into an unfeeling snarl. His eyes sliced over to Yael; his fingers twitched off his forehead in a non-*heil* salute.

Then he jumped.

Even expecting it, the sight was shocking. Luka there, then

not. Devoured by dark. Yael tugged Felix forward by his harness. They had to move quickly if they were to land close together. But Adele's brother fought her, every molecule of his body struggling to get away from the nothingness in the floor.

"You can do this!" Yael screamed; her muscles did, too. It was taking all her might to wrest him to the escape-door opening. "For Adele!"

They were at the edge now. Felix Wolfe's eyes met hers a fourth, final time: stark white, wide black, muddy fear, rage in all its shades.

Yael pushed.

The chaos swallowed Felix, too.

She stood alone on the brink of a hungry night. Dizzying darkness and heights unknown howled beneath her. The parachute straps around her chest felt as flimsy as parcel twine. For a moment, for more than a moment, Yael found herself understanding Felix's fear.

But the unbearably cold air tore at her fingertips, lashed at her blood-bound hair. Calling…

—*JUMP JUMP JUMP LIVE AGAIN*—

She threw herself into the night.

CHAPTER 12

Felix was falling. His throat clenched so terror-tight he could not even scream. Shutting his eyes made no difference in his level of fear. There was still darkness and falling, darkness and the cold claws of night against his face. His stomach felt closer to the cabin of the *Immelmann IV* than to his own body. His heart refused to obey even the most basic laws of survival, starting and stopping and starting again as he fell...

as he fell...

as he fell...

Count out fifteen seconds, then pull the cord.

"One...two..." Felix was moving his mouth, but he couldn't hear himself. There was the wind roaring past his eardrums, but there were also Baasch's many instructions. Intricate plan pieces rattling through his head.

Use the Hitler Youth membership badge on your uniform to pick the lock on your cuffs. Then you will free Inmate 121358ΔX. On the wall of the cabin is a red lever. Point it out to the girl, but not too quickly. You'll want to jump as close to the fourteen-hour mark as possible. Do you have a watch?

So much of what had happened in the past few hours had been staged. From the *Immelmann IV*'s flight path to their placement in the Führer's personal cabin to the manageable altitude. It was all part of the SS-Standartenführer's plan—releasing the rat from the trap.

But Felix's fear was far from fake. He'd thought he'd do anything for his family. But he knew now—shamefully, without a doubt—that he couldn't have jumped on his own. If the girl hadn't pushed him, he'd still be up in the Condor, on his way to Germania and more crushed fingers and the Wolfe family's gravestoneless fate.

But the girl had pulled Felix to the edge, looked straight into his eyes, and pushed.

For Adele! That was what she'd told him, without even knowing how terribly true it was. How much salvation and damnation there was in her single shove. The Wolfes were safe, but there would be blood. Blood for blood. Blood to pay. An entire world of it.

Salvation, damnation, salvation, damnation.

As he fell …

as he fell …

as he fell …

Count out fifteen seconds. Surely it had been that long! Felix pulled the cord. The parachute released, thin fabric pluming in the night. Its harness cut against Felix's arms. His world snapped into place.

The moon hung high above, gleaming as bright as Baasch's

Totenkopf. All was silver and dark. Far below he could see the peaked crowns of lush pines. Odd…should there be *this* many trees?

No. No, no, no…NO!

On the plane, when Felix went to check his watch, he'd found the hands stuck in place. Time stood still, and he'd had no idea when it had stopped. Five hours ago? Eight? Three? They'd already been flying for so long.

That was the moment the *Immelmann IV* started to tilt back to earth. That was the moment when Felix feared that Germania was only minutes away. Their fourteen hours was up, and it was *Now or never!*

But Germania—its sparkling collection of monuments, the thunderous curve of the Volkshalle's dome—was nowhere to be seen. The ground was lightless; velvet dark wilderness rolled out for kilometers. Not a farm or a town in sight. Just trees upon trees upon trees.

They'd jumped too soon.

To the distant right and far left, Felix spied the other escapees' parachutes. The lives of Luka and the girl hung by threads, just a few centimeters of fiber between them and *drop, fall, death.*

All of this reminded Felix that he was still falling. Still suspended in a place no man should be.

What would happen when he reached the ground?

INTERLUDE

THREE PORTRAITS OF
MAY 16, 1952

BEFORE

Emptiness dwarfed the Wolfes as they gathered around their television. This feeling was crammed into all corners of the family room—withering the wildflowers in the coffee-table vase, livering the silver picture frames with black tarnish spots. Everywhere Felix looked, he was reminded of *the absence*, but it was the chair that haunted him the most. Its sagging mustard-colored upholstery had been Martin's favorite place to read. How many evenings had his older brother sat there, leafing through an abridged version of *Mein Kampf*, trying to pretend he understood it?

Now it was a shrine. Empty for a reason none of the Wolfes talked about. The wool throw Martin had left crumpled there on the morning of the twins' twelfth birthday was unmoved. Two years' worth of dust fuzzed its sterling yarn.

There was a lot of dust in the Wolfe house these days. Drifts of it built up on shelves, settled on the pages of unopened books. Felix's mother seemed not to see it. Then again, she wasn't really looking. Most of her time was spent inside her bedroom, shades drawn. It was a rare morning that she got out of bed.

This was one of those rare mornings. Felix and Adele had both been excused from school to watch the New Germania rally. (A chance to watch the Führer speak, their headmaster explained, was far more important than class. It promoted national unity and raised morale.) Adele had wanted to use the free time to sneak off to the racetrack, but Felix decided that the Wolfe family could use a dose of unity and raised morale, so he persuaded his sister to watch the speech. He'd also urged his parents to join so they could watch as a family.

But even when they were all together, it wasn't the same. His parents sat on the sofa, one cushion between them. His mother's stare was on the television: glass meeting glass. His father's skin was scarred with days' worth of engine grease—over his knuckles, under his fingernails. Adele sat on the rug, her expression screwed tight in a way that meant she wanted to be somewhere else. *Anywhere else.*

Felix couldn't blame her.

He didn't quite know where to sit. Martin's chair was off-limits, and the cushion between his parents held the same untouchable aura. In the end, he settled on the rug behind his twin sister, in front of the couch.

None of them spoke as they watched the screen. The Führer had not yet appeared. A band was playing; the cameras switched back and forth between the musicians and the crowd. Frankfurt's morning was drizzly outside the Wolfes' windows, but Germania's skies spread cloudless against the Reichssender lenses. Rows and rows of rally attendees were singing party anthems, faces lit with sunlight and fervor.

His mother's foot started to move in time with the music,

tapping Felix's back. She began to hum, giving the song a skeleton frame. Papa started singing. He knew all the lyrics. His husky voice shifted through the dust, fleshing out his wife's tune. Even Adele joined in after a few stanzas.

It wasn't enough just to listen to his family's chorus. Felix opened his mouth and did his part. The song took shape.

For the last time, the call to arms is sounded!
For the fight, we all stand prepared!
Already Hitler's banners fly over all streets.
The time of bondage will last but a little while now!

There was still a space. But for a moment, Felix could make himself forget the silence of Martin's full baritone, never again to join theirs. For a moment, he could stare at the screen's light—at Germania's new stones and smiling faces, at the brass band and banners—and feel no distance at all.

DURING

Luka Löwe was lost in the forest of salutes and uniforms planted in the Grosser Platz. His boots were just one pair of the hundreds standing on the plaza's stones. There was other footwear as well—saddle shoes and wing tips, heels and flat-strapped Mary Janes—belonging to the myriad of press and civilians. Many of them were Germanians (though some, unused to the capital's new name, still slipped and called themselves Berliners), but others had traveled from all corners of the Reich to attend this assembly. The rally—meant to celebrate the Führer's immense architectural overhaul of Germania—was being held in front of the old, torched Reichstag building. The amount of humanity in the Grosser Platz felt impossible: thousands upon packed thousands. All of them eager for a chance to see Adolf Hitler speak.

Luka hated being there, though he'd had little choice in the matter. Every one of the Führer's public speeches was attended by a handful of carefully selected Hitler Youth. They always stood in a line—pressed uniforms, painfully identical—providing a gold mine of shots for Goebbels's propaganda films.

One of the rally organizers had arranged the boys' formation three hours earlier. Lining them up just so, angling their faces in view of the third Reichssender camera, instructing them to "look to the Führer and nowhere else."

But the Führer wasn't at the podium yet. A brass band had played "Horst-Wessel-Lied" beneath fluttering swastika banners, and some man named Albert Speer spoke at length about the grandeur and symbolism of the newly completed Volkshalle. (The dome of the monstrous building beside them was so high that the statue at the top—a Roman eagle clutching a globe in its talons—nearly touched the noon sun.)

Luka's neck was starting to ache. His legs tingled with a hot-pin sensation. The boys next to him must have been just as uncomfortable, yet no one dared to break formation.

When Adolf Hitler finally stepped onto the stage, it was to an almighty roar of *heils*. *Heil* to Hitler. *Heil* to victory. *Heils* rang throughout the Grosser Platz; the power of them buzzed through Luka's eardrums, made him cringe.

Eventually, the welcoming cries faded. Adolf Hitler started talking about communists and Aryans, building empires and destroying them. He'd gotten no more than a few words into what promised to be a long, spittle-flying, fist-pounding speech when Luka stopped listening. It wasn't just Hitler's yelling that bothered him, but the way the crowd yelled back during the speech's planned pauses—so eager to be heard by this man, so willing to take Hitler's words and make them their own.

Luka wanted no part in it, though he knew if he was caught withholding a salute, the consequences would be crushing. He realized at the next break in the monologue that he could swing his arm and move his lips without saying a word. No one would notice the difference.... The boys next to him were too busy shouting their own *heil*s, and the cameras couldn't pick apart Luka's voicelessness from all the other moving mouths.

No one could hear his silence.

The pause ended. Hitler's speech flowed on and a thirsty crowd listened. Luka's thoughts began steering back to all the Axis Tour training he was missing when something—no, *someone*—caught his attention. The man was in uniform. Brown shirt and boots the same as Luka's and those of hundreds of other rally-goers. His hair was an off sort of yellow, covered mostly by his cap. He would've been impossible to pick out from the rest of the crowd, except for one very simple fact: He was moving.

Every other brownshirt stood straight, eyes rapt on the Führer, as they'd been instructed. Luka couldn't help but watch this man inching forward, shifting from line to line in a slow, subtle way.

No one else seemed to notice.

The Führer's speech had reached the point of frenzy: red face, quivering mustache. "We've left the ruins of old Berlin behind, embraced the monumental splendor of Germania by building structures grander than any other in history! The Volkshalle shall be the shrine to which the world's eyes turn! The great witness for the progress of the Aryan race!"

The uniformed man was making progress of his own, slipping closer to the rally stage. He was only two rows away, and a few more Hitler Youth boys had started to notice. Like Luka, they all watched as he removed his cap. They all had mere seconds to register the dark roots along his hairline before something much more shocking claimed their attention: the pistol hidden in his hat.

Luka expected the man to shout, but he didn't say a word. He raised his gun, let his bullets scream for him.

One.

Two.

Three.

A trio of shots. Far more powerful, far more deafening than any of the crowd's *heils* had been. Every shot hit its mark: Adolf Hitler's chest.

The Führer choked on his own blood and words, collapsing down to some place that Luka—as close as he was to the stage— could not see. His eyes fell back to the marksman. There was a fire behind the man's face. He wasn't trying to run. It was almost as if, in his stillness, the marksman had forced everyone else to move. No other soul in the shadow of the Volkshalle was still. Brownshirts twisted and turned. Black streaks of SS uniforms tore to the base of the stage, Lugers drawn.

The flames behind the marksman's face roared. Strength like burning. He raised his gun again, all the way to his head.

There was a fourth shot.

The Grosser Platz writhed with the screams of the living. Panic, fear, agony, emotion, *too much emotion.* The boys who'd stood so calmly beside Luka for hours on end were now running with nowhere to go, threatening to trample one another with their own hobnailed boots in their herdlike panic. Luka stood his ground, soles planted in the Grosser Platz's stones. His mouth had fallen open, but no scream came.

For him, there was only silence.

AFTER

Yael saw things differently.

Pop. Pop. Pop.

She sat in front of Henryka's television screen, pencil in her mouth, homework forgotten, as she watched Aaron-Klaus—friend, survivor, the boy who ruffled Yael's hair and teased her about being too smart and helped her pretend she was somehow normal—do the unimaginable.

Pop.

Yael's pencil shattered at the sound of the fourth shot. Moongray graphite powdered across her tongue. A taste as acrid as ash.

No. Not him. Not him, too.

She'd known it was coming. Death always did. And Aaron-Klaus had been hungry to meet it—to stand face-to-face with the Führer, gun in hand. Wasn't it just yesterday that they'd talked about stepping up, killing the bastard, changing the world?

The rally's order was as smashed as Yael's pencil: Screams and SS men and civilians and brownshirts all blended together. The Reichssender channel fell into chaos, fuzzed into static.

Henryka walked into the office, squinted at the screen. She'd missed it all. "What's wrong? Did it break?"

Blond frizz tumbled over the older woman's forehead as she leaned toward the television, twisted its power knob off. Static to silence.

"Aaron-Klaus." His name felt different this time, when Yael said it. As if all of its letters were edged with lead. It was the way every one of their names felt, whenever Yael let herself think of them: Babushka, Mama, Miriam. Heavy, heavier, heaviest. All an equal weight of gone.

"Klaus," Henryka corrected her. "You mustn't let anyone hear you say his real name. He could get arrested and questioned."

Yael stared at the blank screen's glass. It was her own reflection inside the television now: twiggy teenage girl, blond pigtails, lichen eyes, the face she'd chosen for herself, so many years ago, when Aaron-Klaus found Yael by the river. She had not changed it since.

But it looked like someone else's. It *was* someone else's (she'd stolen most of the features from a League of German Girls recruiting poster). Yael watched as the strange girl inside the television started moving her mouth. "Aaron-Klaus just shot the Führer. Aaron-Klaus just shot himself."

Unreal words. True in the worst of ways.

———

Yael knelt in the middle of the cinder-block office. The television screen was still dark, dead, dark. There was a candle by her knees, a match in her hand, and a memory in her heart.

You must never forget the dead.

This had been Miriam's commandment to her after Yael's mother passed. The older girl had taken pieces of straw from the mattress and woven them together into a memorial candle. It had been waxless and wickless, but it hadn't mattered. They'd had nothing to light it with anyway.

There was a flame this time. Yael dragged the match across the floor—red chemicals at its end shivered to life. Life, life, something was *alive* and burning. It danced hot against her fingertips as she guided it to the wick, where it caught. Kept.

Religion was one of the many things she'd left behind in the camp. Mama's healing prayer, Miriam's candle, faint memories of a Passover feast...these were the only pieces of her people's faith Yael could remember. She did not even know the mourning Kaddish prayers. Aaron-Klaus might have: He was the only person Yael knew who shared her numbers, her blood. Who might have known how to say good-bye to himself...

But lighting a memorial candle was something Yael knew how to do. She sat with crossed legs, watching the flame dance through the dark. It was a small and humble burning, but it made a difference.

He made a difference.

It was this thought alone that kept Yael feeling real. Through the sounds of Henryka's tears and Reiniger's curses. Through the unforgiving silence of the television. Aaron-Klaus was gone, but his death had meant something. He'd done exactly what he'd promised Yael he would do: Step up, change things, kill the bastard.

And that was something...something to hold on to.

Wasn't it?

Yael gathered her knees to her chest, and as she stared into the flame, as the tears blurred its light all across her eyes, she decided that it was.

It had to be.

———

Question: How long can one candle burn?

Answer: Until it has nothing left to give.

Aaron-Klaus's candle burned for twenty-six hours. The flame was already dying—shrinking into a sickly fringe of blue—when Reiniger stormed into the headquarters. The leader of the resistance slammed the door shut with such force it created a gust. The wind rolled through the beer hall basement, licking the edges of Henryka's stacked files.

The candle's light vanished. Smoke rose, wraith tendrils reaching up to the paper airplanes she and Aaron-Klaus had made together. Yael was the only one in the room to see it. Everyone else—Henryka and the other Germania-based operatives—watched the National Socialist general, breath held, waiting for a verdict.

"He's alive," Reiniger said. "The *Saukerl* survived."

No one said a word. Yael kept her eyes on the smoke, watching it rise. Fading until not even a haze was left. She knew he wasn't talking about Aaron-Klaus.

As soon as the news that the Führer was not dead reached the public, the television sprang back to life. Its pixels blaring, brighter than ever. Adolf Hitler—in what the Reichssender was calling a miracle—had survived the three bullets Aaron-Klaus lodged in his chest. Assassination attempt number forty-nine.

Question: How many times can one Führer live?

Question: How many times can one not-assassin die?

Answer: As many times as the Reichssender chooses to air it.

They showed the clip again and again and again and again.

All four shots.

Survival immortalized.

Another useless death.

PART II

THE WILDERNESS

PART II

THE WILDERNESS

CHAPTER 13

Walking was not Luka Löwe's ideal mode of transportation. It was slow, with a poor energy-expended-to-distance-actually-covered ratio. His biking boots were starting to eat into his heels with every step. He was fairly certain that if he took them off, he'd find blisters with the size and relative explosiveness of Mount Vesuvius.

But he hadn't had a chance to remove his boots. His initial landing had been not so graceful, into tangled pine limbs. It had taken Luka the better part of a half hour to get out of the harness and navigate his way to the ground without breaking both legs. By that time, Yael was calling for him. It was like a game of *Blinde Kuh*: dark, yell, dark, yell, until the fräulein came bursting out of the forest with a very queasy-looking Felix in tow.

"Let's move," she'd said, her arm tightened over a refolded parachute. "We shouldn't linger, in case anyone saw us land."

Being seen was a possibility Luka was very much beginning

to doubt. There was no sign of other human eyes, much less civilization. They'd been walking for hours, through winter-snow leftovers, past pine trunks, fir trunks, ash trunks, endless rows and rows of trunks.

Yael, at least, seemed to know where she was going. Her appearance hadn't changed since the ballroom—hair still white, eyes electric bright—which only added to the quicksilver feel of her movement. Equal parts flowing and lethal. She took them south and east, into a heavy-cloud sunrise. They halted a few times by ice-riddled streams, taking long, stinging gulps of water. Yael snapped a few branches off a nearby pine, plucking their needles like chicken feathers and handing them to each boy.

"Chew on these," she told them. "It'll help stave off the hunger until we find a place to camp."

Luka popped the needles into his mouth. "Tastes like Christmas."

They kept hiking as the morning gave way to noon. Down hills, up hills, until Luka was just as sick of inclines as he was of trees. His blisters ballooned inside his boots until he felt one of them pop, oozing through his socks. His collarbone kept charring with heat—as if an invisible SS-Standartenführer walked alongside, perpetually jamming a cigarette against skin.

What Luka wouldn't give for a nice long drag of smoke. He'd been too shocked to take advantage of the one Baasch jammed between his lips. It tumbled out in seconds—dashing ash and burning a shallow hole in the dance floor before the SS-Sturmmann stamped it out. What a waste...

While Luka was wishing, he'd take a Zündapp, too. Not

that a motorcycle would've done much good out here. Wherever *here* happened to be...

"Does anyone know where we are?" he asked.

Felix shrugged. He hadn't uttered a word since the plane. His pace had been stalwart, but in the past hour or so, Luka had noticed the boy's steps slowing.

Yael looked over her shoulder at the pair. Her nose was definitely the worse for wear; the thick red line over its broken bridge matched the signet-ring cut on her cheekbone. The rest of her face was a puffy, bruised mess.

"Somewhere in the Muscovy territories," she said.

The Muscovy territories. Former Soviet stomping grounds. No wonder it was so *verdammt* cold. Luka's father had spent many postwar years ranting about the place—tales of frigid foxhole nights and frozen motorcycle fuel.

"We're somewhere in the taiga," Yael went on, walking and talking, "and with this kind of forest and wildlife, I'd wager we're not far from the Urals."

"The Urals?" Felix's face went sharp. "But—that's *days* away from Germania."

"Longer by foot," Yael said.

"Is being days away from the people who want to lop off our heads not a good thing?" Luka asked.

But the mechanic was back to his sullen silence. His airplane blanket flapped behind him, going capelike when Felix stumbled on a root. He threw up his good hand to steady himself. The right one stayed tucked out of sight, under his stained shirt.

"We're much better off here," Luka told him. "Muscovy

territories. Land of endless edible pines and...what kind of wildlife did you see again, Fräulein?"

"I saw a sable earlier. And those"—she nodded at a nearby patch of snow, its flakes gray with dirt, crushed in an odd assortment of places—"are wolf tracks."

"WOLVES?"

"We are in the wild," Yael reminded him.

"And we probably smell like a *gottverdammt* butcher shop." Luka glanced at the fräulein's bloody face, Herr Wolfe's bloodier shirt. Maybe they *weren't* better off here.... "We're a feast on six legs."

Yael stepped directly into the snow patch, her own slender footprint stamping out the wolf paw. "They should be too scared of people to come forward."

"And if they're not?" Luka asked.

"We should keep going. Find a good place to camp before dark," she said.

So they kept going. Their afternoon view didn't change much. Trees, trees, snow, more wolf prints (now that Yael had pointed the first set out, Luka saw them everywhere), trees, trees, a frozen brook, trees. And finally, a road! When Luka first caught sight of it, he thought he might be hallucinating. The track looked feral, covered in frozen mud puddles and the carcasses of long-dead weeds. But Yael saw it, too. She knelt down by the mud, examining it.

"It has to lead somewhere." Luka moved up behind her. (But not too close. He'd seen her reflexes in action and wanted his solar plexus/nose/testicles to remain intact.) "Right?"

"That's what I'm afraid of." Yael frowned. "We're back

in Reich territory now. It's not just wolves we have to worry about."

Right. Luka wondered if the WANTED posters had gone to press yet. They'd likely use Felix's Axis Tour entry photo. For Luka, they could use one of the old propaganda posters from his 1953 victory with the *Sieg heil* text at the bottom blotted out. He imagined Yael's picture as a big question mark.

They were a feast on six legs, heads topped with a price.

"Look, as much as I enjoy pine needles, we need actual food," Luka said. "Food and medicine and beds and not getting eaten by wolves. Following this path is our best chance of obtaining those things."

Yael nodded, but her frown stayed. The expression looked downright vicious on her blood-blushed face. "We'll walk along the road. Not on it. If we come across somebody, we're in no shape to run, much less fight."

They walked for more hours in stumbling silence, too tired, too aching to talk. Felix's steps grew slower and slower, winding down to a collapsing stop. Knees into the earth, face and chest flat against the crusted, wolf-pawed snow. Even though the air was freezing, there was sweat on his forehead, plastering his fair hair to his face.

He fell with such a solid stillness that Luka wondered if the boy had just up and died. But when Yael rushed over to the mechanic, he started spluttering, pushing feebly against the ground with his good hand. "No. K-keep going. Have to s-save…"

His voice wilted off into a cough.

"He has a fever." Yael turned Felix onto his back, tugged

the boy's injured hand out from under his shirt. "The fingers are becoming infected."

So they were. Even the boy's uncrushed fingers were puffy and red, flesh inflated to the size of small bratwurst. Now that Luka was closer, he could identify a *smell*. It made his empty stomach churn.

Adele's brother would not be taking any more steps, which meant they wouldn't either.

"So this is camp." Luka glanced around. Somber pines surrounded by a thick carpet of fallen needles. A bad place to hole up if you wanted shelter from the arctic winds ripping between the trees. An even worse place if you wanted to avoid getting eaten by wolves.

Yael dropped the parachute she'd been carrying and began fraying one of its cords against the edge of a nearby rock. "I'm going to set some snares. See what other food I can find. Stay here and keep an eye on Felix. Try to get a fire started. When I get back, we'll rig the parachute into a tent."

It took Luka a grand total of ten minutes to collect wood and stack it for a fire, following vague instructions from his Hitler Youth days: kindling first, small sticks next, larger logs on top, leave plenty of room for air. His jacket was still damp from his dip in the moat (well over a day later, but such was the stubbornness of leather). This hadn't bothered Luka much while they were walking, but as evening temperatures began to plummet, he realized he needed to get the fire started. Fast.

He grabbed two sticks, started rubbing them together.

Felix's skin was marbling—flushed and paling. The mechanic shivered beneath the parachute and extra blankets Yael had draped over him. His lips moved in a frantic mutter: "Jumped too soon. Keep going. We have to keep going. Führer's gonna kill…s'all. N-not, not safe."

They were ranting, feverish words.

"Hitler's dead." Luka rubbed the sticks as fast as he could. Faster, faster, until one of them cracked. Somewhere, far behind the tree line, a branch snapped back. The sound made Luka jump.

Maybe the wolves were coming out early.

Forget cigarettes and motorcycles. He wanted his gun.

"He's not dead!" Felix's voice rose from lilting rave to madman. "He doesn't die! Can't die! Won't die!"

It was all a little too loud and crazy for Luka's taste. Felix might as well have been screaming *Tasty meat here! All you can eat!* to the region's apex predators. The victor was considering the easiest ways to shut him up when Felix's voice dropped back to a whisper all on its own.

"S'her fault. All this…the project."

"What are you talking about?"

"The Führer never dies." Felix struggled to push himself up. To Luka's surprise, the boy managed a few dozen centimeters. "You! You're an *Arschloch*!"

"I know," Luka told him. "And you're delirious. Now, sit down and shut up."

Miraculously, he did. Luka wasn't sure if it was because he'd suddenly decided to be agreeable, or if the effort of his insult had caused him to faint. Whatever the case, he was thankful for the cease in *Come and eat us, wolves* volume.

But the cracks and snaps in the woods were growing louder.

Closer. Luka abandoned his attempts at friction and grabbed one of the larger sticks from his fire-to-be. If the forest creatures *did* decide to make a meal out of him, there was no way on this frostbitten earth he'd go down without a fight. Luka gripped the base of the pine branch and watched the trees. Something did emerge—bright eyes first, running toward the boys with fearsome speed.

It was Yael.

It wasn't until Luka saw her bursting from the trees that he realized he hadn't been afraid she *wouldn't*. It had not even occurred to him that she might've decided to ditch them in this snow-laden taiga.

Huh.

She strode straight over to Felix and lifted the parachute from his body. She laid the fabric flat on the ground and started rolling the mechanic on top of it.

"Help me move him," Yael said as she gripped one end of the parachute and pulled. She was turning it into a stretcher! Smart. Though, when Luka grabbed the other end and Felix disappeared into the white fabric, it reminded him more of a body bag.

"Move him where, exactly?"

The fräulein's hair was a mess of blood-matted knots, and her face was even messier as she turned to Luka. He did not expect the smile he saw—wild, white-toothed, lighting her whole expression into something triumphant.

"I found a house."

CHAPTER 14

Yael hadn't found just a house, but a whole village of huts. A gray ramshackle collection of cabins set along a stream too large to be frozen. Her initial approach had been tactical. She hid for several minutes in the woods on the settlement's perimeter, scanning for life. But there was no orange glow behind the windows. No smoke whispering from chimneys. No men splitting piles of wood with their axes. No wives calling them inside to dinner. There was just the river sliding by: a low and steady murmur.

The whole place was deserted. From the looks of things, it had been for years. Some of the cabins' roofs had collapsed, bowed down by one too many snowfalls. The few cellars Yael peered into yielded jars of preserves (still intact) and potato sacks (empty, their contents long ago liquefied and evaporated). Cabin after cabin told the same story: plates on the tables, pools of wax sitting where candles once burned, chairs overturned, doors kicked in. Life interrupted.

When Yael reached the opposite end of the settlement, she

saw the truth splayed out in the path between the cabins. This village wasn't simply deserted.

It was dead.

Their bones were a tangle, worn down by wilderness and time, scattered by animals. Counting the bodies was impossible; the skeletons were too far gone. All Yael could tell was that there were many of them. All sizes, all ages, all shot dead to make room for future Aryan settlers. The carbon-writ signature of an SS blitzkrieg. Henryka had conveyed similar stories of horror from her own home country—raping, looting, mass executions. Entire cities disappeared as the SS advanced, claiming the land as Lebensraum. Land they didn't even use. This village had been slaughtered and forgotten. Flesh left to rot with the potatoes.

Yael's approach with Luka, and Felix in the parachute-turned-stretcher, was different. She chose a house on the end of the row, farthest from the bones. It wasn't the largest cabin, nor the best stocked, but the roof was intact, and it was a few lunges away from the shelter of the woods.

Just in case.

She felt as if she was about to collapse when they dragged Felix into the sitting room, setting him (parachute and all) in the corner. But there could be no rest yet. The temperature was dropping, and they needed sustenance. Badly.

Fire first. Food second. Then she had to tend to Felix's wound.

The first two tasks were relatively easy. Whoever massacred the villagers hadn't even gone to the trouble to raid their houses properly. Dishes were stacked in cupboards, the drawers full of long stick matches and tallow-fat candles. Any woodpiles had long rotted away, so Yael sent Luka out with an ax to piece apart one of the neighboring cabins. The wood was dry, and it burned well.

For food, she scavenged some canned vegetables from the cellars. These were still edible, though Yael wasn't really sure *what* vegetable it was. Both she and Luka were hungry enough to scarf down their individual jars without comment. Yael grabbed a third jar for Felix, along with a sealed bottle of vodka she'd found in the seventh house, and returned to Adele's brother.

He was unconscious in his corner, shivering. Pinned down by fever-fire.

Yael's years with Vlad had trained her to survive in the harshest conditions. And though her medical knowledge was basic (cleaning wounds, setting bones, sewing sutures), it told her in no uncertain terms that Felix's hand was not well.

Looking at the broken fingers in the candlelight, Yael was beyond amazed that the boy had been able to pick cuff locks, that he'd been able to function through the pain at all. The fingers were broken, and not cleanly. White bits of bone tore out of his joints, clumped with dry blood. And through it all an awful scent: the beginnings of rot.

Yael twisted the vodka bottle open and poured it over Felix's wound. There was a second of stillness before the cold burn of the alcohol overcame the rage of Felix's fever. His eyes snapped open, his arms flailed high as he screamed.

There were words in his agony: "YOU'RE THE DEVIL!"

"I'm sorry, Felix!" *I'm so, so sorry.* Yael tried to soothe him, but the boy seemed deaf in his pain. Felix's wounded hand caught the vodka bottle, sent it flying across the floor. Luka appeared in the doorway, retrieving the unshattered container before too much alcohol spilled.

"He's like this with everyone. Called me an *Arschloch*." He nodded at the crumpled parachute, where Adele's brother was still screeching in pain, spitting curses in her face. "I wouldn't take it personally."

Yet Yael did. Luka *was* an *Arschloch*. (Most of the time.) And she was…maybe not a devil…but definitely something dark. There was blood on her hands, on the parachute, in her dreams to prove it.

"Hold him down." A mess of tears and frantic saliva mixed with the sweat on the boy's face. There was no way Yael could treat those fingers by herself.

Luka cocked his head. "It wouldn't kill you to ask nicely."

Yael felt too exhausted, too close to tears, to argue with him. "Luka. Please."

The victor took a swig of vodka, handed the bottle to Yael, and did as he'd been told. In prime form, the boys were an equal match in strength, but after Felix's beatings in Tokyo, there was no contest. Luka pinned Adele's brother down through the screams, "devildevilmonsterdevil," steady enough for Yael to clean the hand, set the fingers, and wrap them in a makeshift splint. At some point in the process, Felix fainted.

When she was finished, she stared at Adele's brother— looking so much *smaller* than himself in the stuttering candlelight— and couldn't help but think it wasn't enough. The vodka trick was something Vlad had used solely on smaller cuts.

Not only that, but the boy had lost a lot of blood—it was everywhere but inside his blanched body. Yael wished she could give him some of her own, but her makeshift medical resources had been tapped to their fullest extent. All she could do now was wait, hope that the night was merciful and that the vodka did its work.

"Don't die," she whispered, prayerlike, into Felix's ear.

Luka let out a hard, exhausted breath as he flopped onto a pile of blankets. The victor spread his jacket out to dry by the wood-burning stove and stretched himself out as well, his lounge lionlike. The smooth of his Victor's Ball shave was gone, a shadow of stubble in its place. Felix's blood slashed across his undershirt; Baasch's burn wound marked the end of the scarlet line—a raw exclamation. Despite all this, the boy seemed…unfazed. As if all the past hours and days had not happened. As if they were right back in the middle of the desert, sharing a cigarette and a canteen and all the tensions of Adele and Luka. All their history and secrets…

The tension was different now. Different, yet not. Luka was still looking at her with the same flinting gaze. As if she were a riddle to be solved. As if they were still engaged in a dance Yael did not know the steps to. As if something between them could spark and detonate at any moment.

"You owe me some honest talk, Fräu—" Luka caught himself midword, switched to a term that was so much less familiar coming from his lips. "Yael."

Yael. That's who she was now. Yael. With her own history, her own secrets…

"I—I don't even know where to start," she told him.

"Beginning's always a good place," he said.

The beginning. Grainy ghetto, clattering train, barbed-wire fences, smokestacks black and billowing. First, second, third wolf…

Yael's hand wandered into her jacket pocket, found the tiny lump of wood there. The smallest doll. The Babushka of Barrack 7 had carved an entire matryoshka set for her, but this was the only piece that remained. The others—the ones Yael left behind with Miriam (savvy, smart, sincere Miriam) the night of her escape—were just as gone as her real family.

So long ago, so close. Gaping, splintered loneliness. It wasn't something Yael could bring herself to share, so she squeezed the smallest doll tight and shook her head. "Not there."

The victor gave a one-shouldered shrug. "Fine, then. The middle. Or the end. Start anywhere you want, just give me something."

The middle. Chocolate crullers. Calculus problems. Fourth wolf sorrows. Fifth wolf sweat. Making herself ready, ready, ready for…*the end*. It should have been at the Victor's Ball. It should have been the fall of everything—the death of a Führer and his empire of bones.

What now? Where to start?

The starting line—inside Germania's Olympiastadion, beneath the rain and the eyes of thousands—made most sense to Yael. It hadn't been *her* beginning, but it was a beginning. Several beginnings, actually. The beginning of the tenth Axis Tour. The beginning of her life as Adele. The beginning of her and Luka.

"I've been using my...skill to impersonate Adele Wolfe since the start of this race," she began.

"Your skill," Luka repeated with a tilt of his eyebrow. "You mean switching out your faces?"

"I call it skinshifting." She'd come up with the word not long after her escape from the death camp. Dr. Geyer probably had a different term for it.

"Was it something you were born with?"

"No. I was...made." It wasn't the right word. *Made* implied there was some sort of caring creator behind the process, instead of a madman with an endless supply of syringes. "I don't want to talk about that."

Luka gave a gruff nod. The light of the woodstove scattered across his face.

"Anyway it is—*was*—my assignment. Race as Adele Wolfe, win the Axis Tour, attend the Victor's Ball, get Adolf Hitler in front of the cameras, and kill him. There are resistance cells all across the Reich. They've been recruiting and stockpiling and planning for years. The Führer's death was supposed to be a signal for the partisans to revolt."

Luka Löwe took all this information in stride, his expression decidedly unchanged. Yael marveled at the composure of it. Grim jaw, lax lips, equally keen and flippant, as mixed up and hard to read as his kisses.

"You said 'supposed to be.'" The victor tilted his head. His free hand moved up to his neck, catching the dog tag there, running his thumb over its engraving: 3/KRADSCH I. 411. "What went wrong?"

Yael took a long breath and said, "Hitler isn't dead."

This information at least seemed to rattle the boy. He straightened. Dog tag dropping back to his breastbone. "What? But you shot him. I saw him fall. There—there was a body. We were in the same *verdammt* room with it!"

"I killed the wrong person," she whispered. "He was someone like me. Impersonating the Führer."

"*Scheisse*," Luka swore at the fire. "No wonder the man has nine lives."

"Forty-nine—" Yael caught herself. Forty-nine belonged to Aaron-Klaus. Her assassination attempt sported a different number: "Fifty, now."

The victor's jaw went tight. "Felix knew. Back in the woods he was babbling about how Hitler wasn't dead. I thought he was just spouting off fever crazies. Never crossed my mind it was actually true."

It was true. Too true. Impossibly true. Fifty times true.

"I was there, you know, the last time. In fifty-two. At the New Germania rally. I was standing right there in the Grosser Platz when it happened." Luka reached out for the vodka bottle and took another swallow. "Everyone was screaming and scared and sad, and I just...wasn't. The Führer got shot in front of my eyes, and I felt nothing. Maybe it was shock.... I don't know. All I could do was stand there while everyone else lost their minds to panic. I almost got trampled to death."

A piece of me was there. A piece of me died that day. Yael tasted graphite dust in her mouth all over again. Fourth wolf and Luka Löwe—two fragments of her life that never should have touched—were now crammed together in a strangely intimate way. Yael almost rolled up her sleeve then and there, almost pointed to the loping lines of Aaron-Klaus's wolf, almost told Luka everything she was.

But Luka was playing with his father's dog tag again, and Yael found herself wondering if Kradschützen troops had rolled through this very village, letting their motorcycles idle as the SS made it a pile of bones. She wondered if Luka had any idea how their pasts tangled and tore at each other's throats.

"So if Hitler isn't dead, then what's happening out there?" Luka asked. "Are your resistance friends fighting?"

"I have no idea. The fact that Baasch felt comfortable enough to transport us back to Germania means he either had no idea about the putsch or..." *It's already over* was what she meant to say, but couldn't.

"Hitler never dances" is what Yael said instead. This fact had seemed like such a small thing when Vlad stated it, the day she first received her assignment. Reiniger had certainly thought so. But now Reiniger might be dead. Reiniger, Henryka, Kasper, the thumbtack operatives scattered across the map... they could all be dead. "I should have known it wasn't him. I should've—"

"We've been down this road before. Back on the *Kaiten*. You did what you did, Yael." The metal disk glimmered between the boy's fingers. Luka kept twisting it; the chain tightened around his throat. "You did what you had to."

Did she?

"I killed the wrong person." Did she have to?

"You made a mistake," Luka said. "A few drops of blood doesn't make you a devil."

How much blood *did* it take?

131

"Have you ever killed anyone?" Yael asked.

"Not that I know of . . . Might've shot one of those commies a few weeks ago." The victor fell silent for a moment, twisting the dog tag until he couldn't anymore. The letters of his father's fight and pedigree spun when he let it go. "I've known quite a few devils, though. You're nothing like them."

He said this as if he knew her. Yael wanted to believe it. Wanted to believe *him*. But there was blood all over this room, far more than just a few drops: on Luka's shirt, on Felix's parachute, on Yael's face. Aryan and Jewish. All red. All her fault.

Yael glanced to where Adele's brother moaned restlessly against the parachute. She grabbed the vodka bottle. "We need to save it for Felix's wounds."

"Might want to use some on your own." Luka's expression went a notch darker as he nodded at her face. "Baasch bashed you up pretty good."

This was true. Yael had been able to block out her pain with the adrenaline of sheer survival, but all that was thawing now. The hurt had settled deep, lacing her every word and movement.

"I was expecting worse," she said. (This was also true.) "It would have been. If you hadn't distracted Baasch."

"What can I say?" Luka shrugged. "I really wanted that cigarette."

Yael's eyes went to the boy's own twilight-purple knot of a bruise, trailed down to the glistening burn on his collarbone: marks of loyalty, far more meaningful than any swastika armband. "You could have told the Standartenführer you had nothing to do with it. You could have let him keep hitting me. But you didn't."

"You should have left me at the docks. But you didn't," the victor said. They stared at each other for long seconds. Bruise to bruise. Blue to blue. "I wanted to keep things even between us."

Even. But there were so many things swirling through the gap their bodies made—the woodstove's heat, motes of dust kicked up by Felix's struggle, hurts and victories, distrust and kisses. Memories, so many memories, Yael + Luka mixing with the past of Luka + Adele. Gossamer feelings strung between them, as sticky, fragile, complex, and beautiful as a spider's web silvered in morning dew.

So many things belonging to so many people…it was impossible to keep track. What was Luka seeing when he looked at her—girl in the fire's glow? Who was he reaching for when he leaned through the amber light, brought his fingertips to the barest edge of her face?

A prickle ran through Yael, one that did not belong to pain or loneliness.

She wasn't completely sure it belonged to her either.

"I'm not Adele," she said, soft but firm. "You know that, right?"

Just like that, some of the threads between them snapped. Luka's touch dropped—away, down to the vodka bottle.

"It's a good thing, too," he said while he dashed some alcohol onto one of the blanket's corners. "Or else we'd be a wolf buffet right about now. Adele's a good racer, but I don't think her wilderness survival skills are quite up to par for this type of situation. Which is why"—he held the soaked cloth up, waiting for Yael's nod before padding the disinfectant against her wounds—"we don't need you getting infected and going all fever crazy, too. You're the best chance Felix and I have at staying alive."

Alcohol hissed into her cuts and scrapes. Healing hurt. Yael clenched her teeth and cast one eye at Felix. Still breathing. *Keep breathing*. "We're not out of the woods yet."

In the other half of her vision, Luka Löwe cracked a smile. "Here I was thinking I was the only one who could make terrible puns."

Yael, despite her aching, on-fire cheeks, smiled back.

—————

The nightmare had returned, pressing down on Yael—bloody, thick, suffocating. It was worse this time. Yael knew she was dreaming, but this did not stop the death. Felix stood next to her—face sour, hand dripping blood as he watched her shoot those she hated, those she loved.

Adolf Hitler (*BANG*), Mama (*BANG*), Aaron-Klaus (*BANG*), Tsuda Katsuo (*BANG*), the Babushka (*BANG*), Miriam (*BANG*), Adolf Hitler again (*BANG*).

The crowd was still there, but this time it was silent. The only noises apart from the endless *BANG BANG* of her P38 was Felix's haunting hiss: "devildevilmonsterdevil*monstremoнcmp*."

Yael woke with her heart thrashing, wild-animal frantic against her rib cage. The woodstove's fire was still simmering, casting a low glow throughout the room. Luka was curled in the blankets, deep in sleep of his own. Felix lay on his parachute, the rise and fall of his chest slow but steady.

Yael listened to the cadence of their breaths as she rolled up her left sleeve and looked at her five wolves. Stark black, fleeing from the woodstove's dying light. Babushka, Mama, Miriam, Aaron-Klaus. Her constant, her cost. All the pain Vlad had ordered her to capture and keep. For the longest time, Yael had pressed the ghosts close and let them become a part of her. The part of her that never changed.

Or so she thought.

Her ghosts—both the living and the dead—were becoming more vengeful. And with every one of their nightmare whispers (*You left me to die! Monster! Isn't this what you wanted? Isn't it? Isn't it?*), Yael felt something inside her shifting. Not just skin, but soul.

Who was she then?

Who was she now?

How much blood does it take to create a devil?

How much red would it take to change things?

Would the world ever be even?

These questions spun—answerless—through the dark as Yael tugged her sleeve back down, feeling even more undone than before. She curled herself back into the blankets, heart crying through her pulse. The same light that had resurrected her wolves was shining on Luka. The boy slept facing her. Ember orange melted over his maskless features. Yael lay still, watching it pour across his eyelids, his Roman nose, his lips.

You're nothing like them.

Luka had said these words the way he said so many things—with cocky confidence. Yael wanted Luka to be right. But he didn't know her.

Not the way the wolves did.

CHAPTER 15

For nearly six years, Felix had carried Martin's timepiece. Where Felix went, the pocket watch followed. The *tick, tick* tempo of its gears beat through varied fabrics: his Hitler Youth uniform, his grease-streaked coveralls, his racing gear.... It was his second heartbeat.

But now the beat was gone. Its absence was gaping over Felix's chest as he fought for consciousness. Fluttering in, out, into fever-haze nightmares. The dreams were strange. A lifetime of pieces—shifted, rearranged in a way that didn't work. Driving a motorcycle backward through the Axis Tour, kicking up desert sands in reverse. Adele's rag doll (the one that sat on a shelf, gathering dust) rode beside him. Yellow yarn hair snagged his wheel, threw him out, out.... He landed on a familiar patch of earth. The one he visited every year on May 2. Grass—bright with spring—peeked out under his knees. The gravestone loomed, its gaping, granite-wound letters: M followed by A followed by R followed by A ... No wait, that wasn't right....

The letters of his brother's name were disappearing, re-arranging. A new name appeared on the stone: A followed by D followed by E followed by L...

NO! Felix's whole body jolted awake. He found his skin burning against cool air. The sight above him did not belong to bedsprings or blue sky, but wooden rafters: old to the point of splinters and gray.

Felix's heart fluttered, questioning itself. *Is this real? I'm still alive, aren't I?* The pain—the one that was creeping through his tendons, into his arm, all the way to his mind—told him *yes*.

Somewhere outside, wood was being chopped. The sound was irregular, *thud, thudding* at the wrong tempo. But there was no *right* tempo. Not anymore. Felix reached up to his breast pocket, felt the lump of metal there. All at once, he remembered:

His mission had already failed.

According to Baasch's timetable, the trio was supposed to land somewhere in the web of small towns outside Germania, close enough to reach the capital in a few hours. Instead, they'd jumped out of the plane thousands of kilometers away. Dumped into the snow-laden, wolf-infested Muscovy territories, not just days but possibly *weeks* away from the resistance's headquarters.

Is this real? The watch sat under Felix's palm: pulseless. *My family's still alive, aren't they?*

That question wasn't so easy to answer.

Thud, pause, *thud* went the distant ax. Felix's heart pumped so hard he felt as if his insides were sweating. Maybe he could find a radio, a telephone, some way to contact SS-Standartenführer Baasch and tell him he was still coming.

Felix's brain fired clumsy synapse signals to his body. *Get up.*

Out of bed. Call Baasch. But he had only enough energy to roll onto his side. The cabin floor spread out before him: empty jars, rumpled blankets, rat feces, rotting wood. It wasn't hard to tell that the place was abandoned.

There was no radio or telephone here, and even if there were, Felix couldn't reach it. He didn't even think he could say a word properly, much less string enough coherent sentences together to plead for his family. Already his fever was starting to flare again, burning away at his mind's lucid borders....

"Felix!"

A flash of white filled his eyes. Not pain, but hair. *Her* hair. The girl knelt by his parachute. Out came her hand, fingers cold as snow crust against his temple.

"How are you feeling?" she asked. Her touch lifted.

How...was he...feeling? The absurdity of the question almost made Felix laugh. Not so much the query itself, but because *she* asked it. Did she care? Did it matter to her that he felt utterly ruined, that *she* was his ruination? His family was probably being tortured to death, hanging from piano wire in a Gestapo dungeon, getting carved to pieces, fingers, ears, nose, and toes whittled slowly away, because this girl had stolen his sister's face.

The girl's new face was just a few bruises short of terrifying. Broken in, framed by features too perfect, too bright to be real. Felix tried his best to focus on the eyes, expecting to see evil there, some sort of darkness to balance out that brilliant tracer blue. But all he saw was a girl and her sadness. A great and intricate sorrow, long past emotion, made of hundreds of parts...

Did she care?

139

Did *he* care if *she* cared?

No, Felix decided. He'd cared too much already. Look where *that* had landed him.

"I'm going to check your wound, okay? Try not to move. You lost a lot of blood last night, and I don't need you spilling more." The girl began unwrapping his bandages. Whatever she saw beneath them made her breath sharp, scratched harder edges around her lips. "I tried to set the fingers... but..."

Some things are too broken to be fixed. This was what Felix told the girl back in Tokyo, when he thought he was trying to save Adele from herself. This was what he felt now, all the way to the dust of his shattered bones. His injuries had gone too long without proper medical attention—the SS-Standartenführer had refused to dress his injuries beyond a splash of antiseptic, telling Felix the resistance would patch him up once they landed outside Germania.

The wound can't look too clean, the SS-Standartenführer had said. *We don't want Inmate 121358ΔX getting suspicious.*

The wound was not too clean. It was infected.

And the girl was not suspicious. She was *sorry*.

She muttered this word—over and over—as she splashed more vodka-fire onto his wounds, as she rewrapped them, as she tried to spoon-feed him some of that awful jar-muck, as she pressed dirty snow to the heat of Felix's forehead. "Sorry, sorry. I'm so, so sorry," she kept saying. As if one word could erase everything she'd done. Make everything right again.

It would take so much more than a single word for that.

Felix screwed his molars tight. The rest of his head was starting to feel swimmy. Nightmares skittered along the borders of his conscious thought, darkening everything—the cabin's shadowed corners, the bruises on the girl's face, the rot inside him.

The faraway ax kept thudding. The pocket watch felt ten ounces heavier over Felix's heart, jealous of every breath he took. The girl's eyes stayed on him as she packed more ice against his face. How did they still look so much like Adele's? Wrong shade, right stare. Sister-to-brother strength.

Felix couldn't stand it. He shut his eyes, let the darkness take him.

CHAPTER 16

This village was giving Luka the creeps. It wasn't so much
the collection of bones as the stillness. The emptiness where
life should be. It was the same feeling he had when they drove
through North Africa's skeleton villages and Baghdad's gutted
streets. The same unsettling sensation he got as a child when he
caught the Führer's fireplace portrait staring at him: seeing nothing, seeing all. They'd spent two nights in the haunted town,
waiting for Felix's fever to flag. No such luck. The boy was no
longer spitting delirious insults, but his skin was still furnace hot.
Faucets' worth of sweat soaked through his Hitler Youth uniform, and as far as Luka could tell, there was no shutoff valve.
Yael barely left the boy's side. Luka kept himself busy splitting
wood, scrubbing the bloodstains out of their clothes in the river,
scouting the rest of the cabins for anything of use. The spoils? A
dozen more jars of vegetables turned into tasteless mush, three
more bottles of liquor so strong it had the potential to blind you,
and a lone hunting knife. He didn't find a single cigarette.

The nights were just as still as the day. They should have been more disturbing, with the darkness everywhere, but Luka found himself enjoying the evenings around the fire. It was warm, there was food, and there was *her.*

Conversations with Adele had never been easy. Luka likened them to sparring matches—filled with witty words, cutting remarks, insults disguised as fondness. He was always, always on the offensive. Always looking for the best worst way to say something.

But as Yael had so effectively reminded him, she was not Adele. Luka found himself telling Yael things. Things that mattered. Things he didn't even *know* mattered until they'd spilled out of his mouth.

The Führer got shot in front of my eyes, and I felt nothing.

He'd never told anyone that.

Adele would've punched Luka's arm (a little too hard), called him a traitor in a way that was teasing (but not really). His father would have gone empty-eyed, throwing a punch that hurt twenty times worse than Fräulein Wolfe's. But Yael had listened to him. She'd more than listened. She'd understood.

He had…feelings…when he was with her. The same ones he'd experienced on the streets of Tokyo. Carbon-copy emotions spilling over from his days with Adele. He'd loved Adele as Adele. He'd hated Adele as Adele. He'd hated Yael as Adele. He'd loved Yael as Adele. But now Yael was Yael, and his whiplash emotions were still a step behind. Giving him a *verdammt* headache.

It was tempting to blame everything on the vodka. But Luka hadn't drunk that much, and he was sober now as he walked through the frigid noonday forest, checking the parachute rope snares Yael had set. The first two were empty. Wolves had already reached the third trap—the bloody remains of a feast on four legs was all that was left. The fourth trap's rope held a sable. The creature twisted at the sound of his footsteps, its sleek coat glinting under a bare-bulb sun.

Luka reached into his jacket pocket and pulled out the hunting knife. All it took was one quick flick and the animal stopped twitching. The sable's fur blended perfectly with the pine needles on the forest floor. The longer Luka stared at the body, the more his skin prickled, until all his arm hairs stood on end.

The stillness had followed him.

The woods were leaden with silence. The birds had gone songless, Luka realized, as he picked up the animal's body. He could hear every snap of vegetation under his boots as he walked toward the fifth trap.

When Luka heard the engine, he froze, trying to reconcile the vastness of the wilderness around him with the sound. A truck...people...

The dead sable beat against Luka's shoulder as he ran for a closer look, careful to keep a screen of trees between himself and the road. He recognized the truck instantly: a ZIS-5 transport. The same vehicle they'd stolen from the Soviet guerrillas after their Axis Tour ambush.

It was the first of many. A whole line of transports rumbled down the road.

When he was younger, Luka had spent many afternoons imagining the Soviet army. He'd killed hordes of commies with an invisible gun, screaming a series of *BANG*s and *POW*s as he kicked the pedals of Franz's rusty bike. The odds were always against Luka and Franz—hundreds to one—but the boys never failed to emerge victorious. They fought and shot a bloodless war and were never afraid.

Fear was getting the better of Luka now, as he crouched behind the vegetation watching truck after truck after truck roll past. Their beds were lined with Soviet soldiers, men and women alike, twenty to a transport. All were dressed in uniform. All carried rifles. All were headed in the direction of the village, where a thin stream of smoke rose into the sky.

How many of them, Luka wondered, had spent their childhood afternoons shooting imaginary National Socialists? How many would shoot the double victor and Felix Wolfe on sight once they discovered the two German boys?

Luka didn't even take the time to swear. He burst into a run, sprinting all the way back to the village.

"Put it out!" he gasped as he crashed through the cabin door. "Put the fire out!"

Yael knelt at Felix's side, a palmful of snow dripped through her fingers, onto his face. She frowned at Luka. "What's going on?"

Luka dropped the sable, grabbed the snow from her hand, opened the woodstove, and tossed the melting heap in. It did nothing but fizzle against the heat. "Soviets. Coming. Up. The. Road."

If Yael was surprised or afraid, she did not show it. "How close?"

"Half a kilometer." Less now, with the way those transports were rolling.

"They'll have seen the smoke," Yael said. "They'll know someone's here. You're certain they're Soviets? Not Wehrmacht?"

145

Luka nodded. "No swastikas in sight, and they're driving ZIS-5s. They're Soviets. At least a hundred of them, all armed."

Felix groaned in the corner. Mumbling and kicking and very much *not* ready to make a run for it. They were as trapped as that sable.

"You're a better fighter." Luka pulled out his hunting knife and offered it to Yael. The blade hovered between them: sharp, small, still wet with the sable's blood. Everything about it was a bad joke.

Yael shook her head. "I won't need a weapon."

Her face began to change. It was the third time Luka had seen her skinshift, but that made it no less jolting. Yael's hair shrank to a wiry shortness, a touch grayer. Fifty years' worth of life folded into her skin. Her eyes went dark, as did a few of her teeth. The only thing that remained the same was the signet-ring split and bruises wreathing her healing nose. In the end, she stood before him an old, hunched, disarming woman. Even her movement was elderly and unoiled as she picked up one of the blankets from the floor and wrapped it over her shoulders, covering her more obvious warrior-wear.

"Stay with Felix," she instructed him. "Do not make a sound. Do not leave this house."

146

CHAPTER 17

It was only when Yael stepped outside into the clean air that she realized how much the inside of the cabin reeked of rot. Despite the vodka cleanings, Felix's fingers (and accompanying fever) had taken a turn for the worse. The SS had crushed the life out of those bones. If Yael didn't do something about it soon, the death would spread.

But there was a more immediate threat to worry about. Yael could hear the engines as she shuffled to the side of their cabin and grabbed the ax Luka had been using to split firewood. She started swinging, bringing its rusted edge down onto a piece of wood. Yael swung and split, trying not to think of Felix's hand. Trying not to think of what would happen next, when the first truck rolled into the village.

Luka was right—they were Soviets. Not Wehrmacht. Whether this was a good thing or not remained to be seen. Yael's experience with Comrade Commander Vetrov—the Soviet offi- cer who'd kidnapped the Axis Tour racers between Baghdad and New Delhi—had been questionable at best, and the guerrillas who often raided the Urals were notoriously merciless when it came to National Socialists. If they discovered Luka and Felix in the cabin . . .

Yael brought the ax blade down a final time, resting it on the ground and double-checking to make sure her blanket covering was secure. The transport drew to a stop. And another after that, and another after that, and another after that . . .

These aren't dart-and-run guerrilla fighters, Yael thought as the fifth transport rolled up. *This is an army.*

A man wearing the markings of commander leapt out of the first truck. He was younger than Vetrov, with a fuller head of hair and eyes that had seen fewer years of bloodshed. This did not stop him from staring warily at Yael and her ax.

"Good afternoon," she greeted him in Russian. (Another gift from the Babushka, passed to her word by word during Barrack 7's frigid nights. Honed into perfect accent and syntax, years later, by Vlad. In this moment, Yael thanked both wolves for it.)

The sound of his mother tongue from an old woman's lips put the officer at ease. His hand slid off his holster. His eyes ranged down the pitiful row of houses, taking in their caved roofs and sagging window frames. "Are you alone, Grandmother?"

"Da." Yael nodded. "For many years. The National Socialists killed my family and my neighbors while I hid in the cellar. Then they left this place and forgot it."

The Soviet commander kept staring down the main path. Was he noticing Luka's faint, too-large footprints along the borders of the cabins? Was he questioning the depth of her wrinkles against the harshness of the surrounding wilderness?

Yael's hands tightened around the ax handle.

The officer's stare turned back to her. Yael became all too aware of the military-grade boots and leather jacket under her blanket. One flutter of breeze is all it would take for her story to unravel.

"What happened to your face?" he asked.

My face? Oh, right, her face. In all the fretting over Felix's wounds, Yael had almost forgotten her own. The days had been mirrorless, and she had no idea how badly the SS-Standartenführer's fist had messed up her features. "My steps aren't so steady anymore," she told him. "I fell."

The officer's mouth wilted into a frown. Behind him the soldiers were starting to climb out of the trucks, stretching their limbs and walking about.

"I have a medic in my company," the commander said. "Let him examine your face."

—DO NOT LET THEM GET CLOSE—

But they already were close. The fact that the soldiers' footprints covered Luka's was a useless comfort as they drew nearer to her smoking cabin and its dingy windows and the two very recognizable German boys.

"*Nyet, nyet.*" Yael shook her head, drew the blanket more tightly around her shoulders. "Thank you, comrade. But I don't need your help. I'm used to being alone. I prefer it."

After a pause, the officer nodded. "Forgive me, Grandmother. I know this must be a shock. My comrades and I have been pushing hard for days, and we need a short respite. We'll

149

camp for the night and be out by dawn. I assure you my soldiers will be of no bother to you."

"Thank you, comrade." Yael—amazed at the boldness of her own lies and the ease with which the young officer chose to accept them—rested her hatchet against the cabin.

It was at that very moment Felix Wolfe chose to scream.

The sound was stripped of words—torturous, undeniable. Yael's heart stuttered. She wished, very much, that she hadn't let go of the ax handle, but retrieving the weapon would've done little good. A whole unit of soldiers faced her, armed to the teeth. A handful rushed toward the cabin, breaking down its door with a single kick. In seconds they returned with a foulmouthed Luka. Felix was carried out, too, still howling in his bloodstained parachute.

One of the men nodded at Felix's Hitler Youth uniform. "They're National Socialists, Comrade Commander Pashkov!"

"Not simply National Socialists," the commander said as he stared at the boys. "They're Axis Tour racers. The very same ones who slipped out of Vetrov's grasp." He turned back to Yael. "What strange company you keep, Grandmother."

Another pair of soldiers grabbed Yael. Her blanket twisted off, landing in a heap by her boots.

—FIGHT RUN RUN RUN GET OUT AS FAST AS YOU CAN—

She didn't try to fight or run. Her thoughts grasped for an excuse that might get her and Luka and Felix out of this alive.

"And what strange clothes you wear." Pashkov stared at Yael as if she were some fairy-tale creature, set to vanish if he blinked. "Vetrov said the racers had a face-changer among them. A girl who called herself Volchitsa. He also said she spoke flawless Russian."

A dozen watered-down lies flowed through Yael's head—*I don't know them; they're not who you think they are; we're seeking asylum in Novosibirsk*—none of them good enough.

She dropped the old woman's appearance, features smoothing back to default. Not Yael's birth face, but her barest one: blank-slate hair and skin, eyes made of the most brilliant blue. One hundred soldiers watched this shift—ancient crone de-aging into young, supple thing. Every one of them reacted the exact same way: not at all. It was the same response she'd received from Comrade Commander Vetrov when she changed in front of him. Aweless, fearless, nothing.

Luka was the only one who spoke, muttering something about a "tough crowd" before a soldier shoved him to the ground, barking "SILENCE!" in a language the victor could not understand.

"Quiet, Luka," Yael instructed him.

His eyes met hers. He gave a slight nod.

There was nothing to be done about Felix. His wail was now a whimper. His injured hand hung off the parachute. The surrounding soldiers frowned at the blood-soaked splint, noses scrunched at the smell.

Yael turned back to the commander. "We're not your enemy."

"That's not for you to decide," Pashkov said, then shifted his attention to his men. "Take Löwe and the sick boy back into the warmth. Watch the face-changer until I return. I must radio Novosibirsk. They'll want to know what we've found."

CHAPTER 18

A night passed. Dawn had come and gone, but Pashkov's fraction of army showed no signs of moving. Through the window of her cabin-turned-prison, Yael watched as men bathed in the river and cleaned out their rifles. The door to her old cabin (the one that still held Felix and Luka) had been set back on its hinges, but even that hadn't been able to keep Felix's screams from tearing through the village. That morning alone the unit's medic had crossed the threshold over a dozen times. Every trip he held something different: rolls of gauze, bottles of pills, a canteen of water, a bloodstained Hitler Youth uniform that went straight into one of the soldiers' fires (along with the parachute). Yael tried to gauge the boy's well-being through these clues, but the task was impossible.

She gathered more questions than not, watching Pashkov's soldiers. War was what these men and women were armed for. Some of their equipment was over a decade old. Relics from the first invasion of the Reich. Yet a good deal of their weaponry was newer, fresh from the factory crate. Yael spied a few men walking past with Arisaka rifles slung over their shoulders. Type 30s and Type 38s: dated in name, but shiny in appearance.

What were the Soviets doing with so many new-old Japanese guns?

What were the Soviets doing here at all?

Comrade Commander Pashkov had refused to talk to Yael after he returned from his radio session. His only words had been for his men: "Keep Volchitsa under observation at all times. We mustn't have her swapping faces on us."

A trio of armed guards had whisked her away into one of the more intact cabins. They sat and watched Yael. They did not let their fingers slide from their triggers. They did not speak.

What were they waiting for?

There was little question they *were* waiting. The guards had the telltale signs of restless men: twitching feet, eyes flickering to the doorway. Outside, Pashkov paced the path between the cabins, from the caravan of parked ZIS-5s to the bones and back again. Every few steps, he craned his neck up to the cloudy sky. It looked almost as if he was praying.

At noon, the heavens brought their answer. Airplane engines droned through the sterling clouds, passing over the village once, twice, thrice before circling a final time and disappearing over the horizon. Comrade Commander Pashkov stopped pacing, his stare fixed on the woods.

It wasn't a *what* the men had been waiting for, but a *who*. A woman emerged from the trees, dressed in the full garb of a Soviet commander: coat, cap, a colorful collection of badges. She was far from old, but there was nothing young about her. She moved in a way that conveyed *authority*—clipped steps, set shoulders. Her greeting to Pashkov was perfunctory—an exchange of nods and a few words—before he pointed her toward Yael's cabin.

Yael couldn't help but notice how the guards shrank when the woman entered the room. All three took a subconscious step back.

"Out," the woman ordered them.

The middle soldier swallowed. "But Comrade Commander Pashkov said—"

"Leave us," she cut him off. "I will not ask again."

The guards shuffled through the door, leaving the unarmed newcomer with an unbound Yael. This situation should have read to Yael's advantage: tackle, knock out, change her face, change her clothes, make a break for it. But the evenness between them only made Yael uneasy. There had to be a reason this woman was fearless.

"You are Volchitsa?"

"I am." There was no use in Yael denying it. Not with one hundred eyewitnesses and their lives on the line.

"A very interesting name." The more this woman spoke, the more Yael could tell Russian wasn't her first language. Her words rose and fell in a cadence that did not quite fit. "How did you acquire it?"

It was a strange question to open an interrogation with. Yael had expected something along the lines of *What are you doing here?* or *Who are you working for?*

Those might have been easier to answer.

Volchitsa. Russian for "she-wolf." It was Yael's code name within Reiniger's resistance, but its origins went deeper than that. It was another one of the Babushka's gifts, handed to Yael along with extra crusts of bread. *Volchitsa*, the old woman used to call her. The girl who was *special*. The girl who would change things. The girl who was as fierce as a wolf.

Yael had never been able to put these memories into words. She tried, but found only eleven: "A friend gave it to me. A very long time ago."

"Your friend spoke Russian?"

Yael nodded. "We were in a camp together."

"You had different names on the television. Inmate 121358ΔX. Yael."

"I have a lot of names."

"That must explain why you're so hard to find. I've been looking for you, Volchitsa." The woman's accent suddenly fit her words; she'd switched languages to German. "For many, many years."

Yael's heart beat—faster, faster, faster—until the rest of her could not keep up. The woman drew so close that Yael could see the tiny ridges of her incisor teeth, the peach fuzz hairs on her earlobe, the premature strands of silver threading through her dark braid. HAZEL was the box the Soviet commander might check on an eye-color questionnaire, but even that wasn't broad enough to cover the gold—dusted and glittering—inside the woman's irises. Her skin lacked the scars most soldiers bore. It smelled like powdered lilies.

When the Soviet commander held out her left arm and lifted her uniform sleeve, these finer details faded. Yael's vision tunneled, erasing everything except the numbers on the woman's skin.

121048ΔX.

Numbers as crooked and dark as Yael's had once been.

Numbers she knew.

Numbers that belonged to Miriam.

CHAPTER 19

THE THIRD WOLF: MIRIAM

PART 2
SPRING 1945

Yael's disappearance was discovered at roll call. The women of Barrack 7 stood straight while the guards counted their frail and failing bodies. One, two, three, four...as the stars above drowned in morning light. Again and again the guards counted. Again and again they came up with the same result: They were one short.

Miriam and the rest of the women had been standing for three full hours when the doctor swept in. His physician's coat was aching white in the dawn light. His face lit with fury as he spoke with the guards in a low, hurried voice. Miriam watched his lips moving, trying to pick out words. When the doctor caught her staring, he stiffened, eyes going sharp behind his glasses. Miriam's own eyes snapped down to her clogs, but it was too late. Dr. Geyer was walking over.

He stopped an arm's length away. She could almost *smell* the anger on him, mixing with vicious cologne and morning coffee. The laces of his dress shoes were twine-fine, knotted in a tight hurry.

"How old are you?"

"F-fourteen." Miriam hated the tremble in her answer, but it couldn't be helped.

Dr. Geyer swallowed this number, considered it.

Miriam's heart fluttered—far and away—from her chest.

"Go stand over there." He pointed to the guards, who stood by the fence, holding their roll sheets and rifles.

Miriam's feet felt heavy in her clogs, every step throbbing. She clenched her palms (still crusted with fresh dirt) and kept on.

Escape from the camp was practically impossible, but it had happened. Whenever the guards discovered someone was missing, they forced the inmates to stand for hours upon hours until the prisoner in question was found. If the person wasn't, the executions began. Inmates were selected at random, made examples of.

Those left behind always paid the price.

Miriam had known this when she smuggled the ruffled yellow dress, sweater, and shoes from the sorting house. She'd known this when she instructed Yael to change her face and lie her way out of the gates. She'd known this when she rose from the straw mattress that morning and hid the matryoshka dolls in a safer place.

I am going to die. Miriam had known this and accepted this.

But that didn't mean she was ready.

Dr. Geyer kept walking through the rows, plucking girls

like daisies, tossing them out of the line with a point and a wave. *Go, go.* All were young. Bodies breastless and malleable. Eyes wide with fear. By the time the doctor was done, ten girls stood in front of the rest of Barrack 7.

We are going to die. Miriam looked at the guards' guns, slung so casually over their shoulders, and wondered which one would shoot her.

But when Dr. Geyer came back to the guards, all he said was, "Take these girls to the medical block and place them in the first observation cell. The rest of the barrack must be sent to the showers. They have lice."

"Yes, Dr. Geyer." The foremost guard nodded. "What of the missing inmate?"

"No need to worry any further about it. I'll make the report to Kommandant Vogt myself."

───

Every day Dr. Geyer stabbed Miriam and the other girls with his needles. He kept all ten of them confined to the medical block. He took notes on their progress; his scribbled paragraphs grew longer as their skin began to flake and their hair paled. Each and every session ended with the same question: "Can you change?"

Sometimes it was worded in the form of an order: "Change, *Miststück*!" Other times a plea: "Please change. It would make an old man like me very happy." A few times it was a threat: "If you don't change, I'll send you to the ovens!" Very rarely it was a bargain: "Change, and I'll give you extra rations."

Every day he stabbed them. Every day he asked this without fail.

None of the girls changed in the way Dr. Geyer wanted. Not in the way Miriam had seen Yael do. They sat in the observation cell day after day after endless day, picking at patches of loose skin, exchanging stories of *before* to pass the time.

Then the fevers came.

Six fell ill within the first month. All but two were dragged out of the observation cell, lifeless heels sliding over the tile floor. The doctor did not look particularly distraught when he found their bodies. Instead he took notes on the discoloration that seized the girls' features postmortem. Albinic skin and hair, eyes stripped of their natural color—the very same paleness that had washed out Yael after her sickness.

The pair who survived the fever carried these same shades. Snow white, egg white, cream white. There was an offness in the way they carried themselves. One girl ranted only in rhymes. Another started pulling out her hairs one by one. "I don't want them, don't want them," she said. Dr. Geyer took notes on them as well.

The first girl died two days later. The lone survivor went madder and madder. Plucking hairs, picking skin, staring at the same mildewed spot on the ceiling for hours. Ignoring all of Dr. Geyer's threats, orders, pleas, cajolery to "Change, just change!" Her scalp was half raw, cleared of stubble, when she was taken to the operating room, where the corners shimmered with surgical knives.

She did not return.

Miriam's own fever came like a wave. One moment she was

standing steady. The next, dizziness was pushing her down, cheek-first on the grimy floor. Her last whole thought before the sickness? *I am going to die.*

She didn't. When Miriam woke up, her skin was like the others. Scrubbed of all shading. She was not ranting, nor did she itch to pull out all her curls. (She did pluck one, just to see the color: vertebrae white.) She felt unchanged.

But she *could* change. It was a voluntary process, she discovered. Much like deciding to walk or speak. Learned, but controllable.

When Dr. Geyer realized she'd survived the fever with a healthy mind, he moved Miriam into her own room (no scalpels), bribed her with extra food and warmer clothes. He watched her change features again and again, making endless notes: *Tattoo ink remains unaltered in host's dermis layer. Possibly because it's a foreign substance? Other scars, moles, freckles are removed at will. Bone structure and muscle mass also subject to change.* Along with facts he gathered blood—harvesting life in ruby tubes, setting it aside for further study.

There were only so many notes and vials the doctor could take. Miriam knew it was simply a matter of time before he wanted more than just blood. A lung, a brain, a heart... Although Miriam could change, she was ultimately disposable. Another girl from Barrack 7 had survived the fever with a solid mind, and Dr. Geyer was bringing in new test subjects: children fresh from the train, with full heads of hair and clothes meant for the outside world. Every few days a group of them was herded past Miriam's window, lined up against the hallway's white walls, and told to stare at the camera.

161

Their young faces were then immortalized, captured as a reference point before Dr. Geyer began testing improved versions of the compound.

It wouldn't be long before the syringes' change set in. When that happened, Miriam knew, her time was up.

I am not going to die. This was Miriam's promise to herself. Death had had enough chances where she was concerned. While the doctor had been examining Miriam, she'd been making studies of her own, watching the nurse as she set about cleaning scalpels and filling syringes. She made small notes on the woman's presentation: Green eyes, pretty but vacant. A reedy voice so at odds with her full figure. Her habit of pinching her lips and nodding at everything Dr. Geyer said. Miriam filed these things away for later.

It was this nurse who checked her vitals and prepped her for injections. It was this nurse who brought Miriam breakfast in the mornings. It was this nurse who discovered Miriam lifeless on her bed——hair spilled milk white over the sheets, glassy eyes to the ceiling.

"Scheisse!" She unlocked the door. "Not another one."

When the nurse came to the bed, Miriam sprang back to life. She was not a fighter, but neither was the nurse. One lunge from Miriam smacked the woman's skull against the floor, leaving limp limbs and a short window of minutes.

Miriam stole the nurse's clothing and features, retrieved the key ring, and locked the door. She started walking. Down the hall. Out of the medical block. Through the gates. Past some soldiers who smiled and waved. Along the road.

No one stopped her. She did not stop.

Though Miriam had the perfect face (any face), she had no official papers and damnable numbers in her dermis layer. She worked her way east, as far from the center of the Reich as possible. There weren't so many paper-checking patrols in the newly established Lebensraum territories. But there *were* plenty of struggling farmers looking for extra hands. They paid her nothing, but Miriam was glad for hot meals and a bed. She never stayed in any one place for long. Every few weeks she packed her bag, changed her face, and moved another town eastward. Farther and farther into the wilderness she went, where the farms grew smaller and the fear of Soviet guerrilla raids was as strong as the cold.

Miriam was fifteen and a half when she joined up with the Soviets. They almost killed her at first—bursting into the farmhouse with Mosin-Nagant rifles and a hatred for all things German. The farmer's wife sobbed protests as they ordered her husband on his knees. Took their aim.

I am not going to die.

Miriam did not know much Russian, but she'd gathered enough from the old woman who once slept across the way in Barrack 7 to manage these words: *"Prekratite! Pozhaluysta!"*

Stop! Please!

All eyes were on her: the looters', the farmer's, his wife's. Miriam's mind was wiped blank. She did not know what to say, so she changed her face instead. The Soviets swore and cried out in shock, but in the end they spared her. The farmer and his wife weren't so fortunate. And so Miriam left the Reich filled with a holy fear. The men she was with were not heroes, and she knew that if they hadn't been so shocked, they would have shot her, too. Some of them looked as if they still might, but the group's leader was fascinated by the girl, and he took her under his wing.

Miriam traveled with the guerrilla band for months. By the time she arrived in the hectic newborn capital of Novosibirsk, she knew quite a lot more Russian. She could shoot a Mosin-Nagant without getting a bruise from the rifle's recoil. She could even swallow vodka without wincing.

Word of her abilities spread. Mnogolikiy, the guerrillas called her. One with many faces. Girl turned into rumor into legend into myth. It wasn't long before the Soviets' skeleton government caught wind of what Miriam could do. They did not lock her up or poke her like a lab rat. They offered her a job in the army instead. Miriam was young, yes, but her face-changing talents and fluent German made her a perfect scout for border raids in the Muscovy territories. She rose fast in the Soviet army's ranks.

Life went on. She fell in love, twice. She rented a one-room flat in the heart of Novosibirsk. She did not sleep much, for whenever she did, she dreamt of the small girl in the yellow dress, stumbling through darkened woods, a dozen hungry wolves on her tail. Yael always ran, always disappeared into the trees, and whenever Miriam tried to find her, she discovered a stack of bones instead, picked clean by predators' teeth. Many of Miriam's night hours were spent walking the city's quiet, snow-dusted streets. Every year, in the springtime, she lit a *Yahrzeit* candle and remembered her dead.

She thought of Yael often—willing her nightmares to be untrue. Novosibirsk was brimming with refugees, its corners crammed with languages from all over Europe and North Africa. During the city's small bursts of summer, when girls wore short-sleeved blouses, Miriam found herself staring at their arms, searching for her lost friend's numbers. Nothing ever came of it, but Miriam never stopped looking.

After Comrade Commander Vetrov and his men botched the kidnapping of the Axis Tour racers, it didn't take long for the details of the field report to make their way to Miriam. The mission, Vetrov claimed, had been foiled by someone like Mnogolikiy. The face-changer was posing as Victor Adele Wolfe and on her way to assassinate Adolf Hitler. The girl called herself Volchitsa.

Volchitsa, one of the first Russian words Miriam had learned. That was what the elderly woman in Barrack 7 once called Yael. Yael, the face-changer.

Miriam was not the type of person who believed in coincidences. She wasn't surprised when the girl dancing with Adolf Hitler shouted her name and lifted her gun. *I am Yael!* The girl Miriam saved, the girl she lost (again and again and again in dreams), the girl she found for two and a half seconds before the television feed cut off.

Miriam tried to uncover Yael's fate. But the Soviets' contacts in Tokyo came up empty, and all of Novosibirsk's energy had been thrown into the invasion of the Muscovy territories. No one had time to look for a lost girl.

When Comrade Commander Pashkov's call came in a few days later—saying he'd found Volchitsa in the middle of the taiga, squatting in a rotting village with two National Socialist boys—Miriam did everything she could to ensure she was the sole questioner Novosibirsk sent out. (It wasn't hard. The army had very few people to spare. And it made sense that a face-changer be interrogated by Mnogolikiy.)

So she handed off her assignments to a fellow comrade, boarded a plane, and flew into the war zone. It was a short flight, made that much longer by doubt. *How can Yael be this far west? How did she escape an entire ballroom of armed guards? Why would she be with Luka Löwe and Felix Wolfe, of all people? What if this is some sort of trap?* Miriam wasn't a nervous gnawer—and it was a good thing, too—because her fingernails would've been chewed to the quick by the time she landed outside the village. She hid all these misgivings from Pashkov, presenting a stern face and striking features the way she always did. (For as high as Miriam had risen in the army's ranks, she never could forget the farmer and his wife. Cries for mercy cut short, brain matter flecking the farmhouse floor. These soldiers weren't heroes, and so Miriam kept fascinating them: hair streaked with holy-fear silver, eyes made of a color only found on autumn trees.)

Pashkov was a hard man to intimidate by looks alone, but Miriam had collected enough badges on her uniform to command his respect. The three guards in the cabin had heard enough mythic tales involving Mnogolikiy to recognize Miriam's war face and be sufficiently quelled.

Intimidation tactics, doubt, eleven years of searching through nightmares and summer crowds—all these things fell away when Miriam stepped into the cabin. The girl stared at her, and Miriam felt something inside her connect—ending hitting beginning, a circle finally closing.

She knew then. She knew with unshakable certainty.

She'd found Yael.

CHAPTER 20

Yael felt outside of herself as she stared at the other woman's numbers. Dragged back to another body, an earlier time, a harsher place. She felt the stab of Barrack 7's straw mattress beneath her knees. She heard Miriam's breathy encouragements: *People don't walk out of those gates. But you can. You are special, Yael. You can live.* The thrilling fear of escape crawled through her changeable skin all over again.

Yael was special. She walked out of those gates, and she lived. All because Miriam told her to. The older girl had been dead for years—living on only as a wolf on Yael's arm, a reason to fight. There was even a file in Henryka's office to prove it: the execution orders of Barrack 7, stamped and signed by the Angel of Death himself.

But the proof in front of Yael now was etched in more permanent ink.

121048ΔX.

Her third wolf was alive.

"I'm here, Yael." Miriam's numbers disappeared as she wrapped her arms around Yael—the embrace felt just as firm and protective as it had eleven years ago. Yael burst into sobs at the familiarity of it. For once, her tears were not made of pain.

They stayed in the cabin for hours. Exchanging lifetimes. Miriam spoke of her own injections, her escape from the camp, her life among the Soviets. Yael told her friend everything: fourth wolf, fifth wolf, the Axis Tour... all that happened after. The afternoon was long and pale by the time their stories converged.

"Experiment Eighty-Five... Dr. Geyer must have perfected the compound," Miriam whispered when Yael's tale came to a close. "The SS is using face-changers."

"And the real Führer is still alive," Yael added.

The young woman nodded. "He reappeared on the Reichssender only a few hours after you shot his double at the Victor's Ball.... He gave a call-to-arms *Chancellery Chat*. It's been playing on repeat ever since. There's hardly a soul in the world who hasn't seen it."

"General Reiniger's putsch... Hitler had to be dead for the plan to work...."

And now the whole Reich knew otherwise. Valkyrie the Second's wings had been clipped, its flight for freedom failed. Years of preparation and secrets and countless deaths were now falling into ruin, all because Yael killed the wrong person.

Before she could ask after Germania (*Any news? Any at all?*), Comrade Commander Pashkov appeared in the cabin doorway. "Comrade Mnogolikiy."

Miriam leapt to her feet and faced the officer.

"We've lingered as long as we can," he continued. "We've just received orders to meet up with units in Molotov. From there, we're to make the push to Moscow while Germania is distracted." Pashkov stopped, as if only then remembering that Yael was there and could speak Russian. "I trust your interrogation has been fruitful?"

"Very." Miriam's demeanor hardened in Pashkov's presence. Yael watched her old friend—standing straight, wielding a stare that made men shrink—and could not help but think, *I'm not the only one who's changed.*

Her third wolf was alive, and she was a fierce, fierce creature.

"I'll need more time with the prisoners. Volchitsa is to come with us. The boys as well," Miriam continued. "Have them ride in my transport."

Comrade Commander Pashkov remained rigid in the doorway, his eyes clashing with Miriam's another few seconds before he relented. "If that's what you think is needed."

"It is," Miriam said.

There was a tension in the sharp, spring air that made Yael wonder what the alternative was. She didn't think she'd like the answer.

"We move out in ten." Pashkov left the cabin.

Miriam stared out the door, watching the soldiers pack up their tents. Her fingers found the end of her braid, started tugging its silver-dark strands.

"We're going to have to be careful," she said, voice low. "If it had been just you and not the boys..."

"Felix and Luka are with me," Yael said and stood to join her. "They're not to be harmed."

Miriam frowned. "Why should you care what happens to them?"

Because of blood dreams and broken things. Because Adele's brother didn't deserve to be here, in the middle of the wilderness with a dying hand. Because Yael had crossed so many lines. (*Tsuda Katsuo. Unknown skinshifter.*) Because both Felix and Luka had unlocked things inside her. Terrifying feelings, making her more monstrous, more human in turn.

But how to say any of this? How to untangle the knot inside her chest? Smooth it out into words?

"I owe myself something," Yael said. "I've lost so many people, Miriam. I lost you. I *left* you to die."

Her friend's hand dropped away from her braid, came to rest on Yael's arm. "Is that what you think?"

"It's what I feel," she whispered. "It's what I've felt for years."

The face her friend wore now was much different from the one Yael remembered, but the sadness beneath it was unmistakably Miriam's. "You were just a girl. We were both just children. Children faced with impossible choices."

Life or death. It stretched so far back.

Had she ever known life without it?

"I'm not a girl anymore," Yael said. The knot over her heart only seemed to grow—thick with blood not hers. "I'm an assassin. I spent so many years learning how to kill, and it's just made things bloodier." A few drops plus more plus more … "I thought I could make all this death stop, but—"

"Yael." Miriam's fingers tightened. Her sadness turned into something stronger. "Don't put this on yourself. Facing

171

an evil so large, much less stopping it, it's too much to ask of a single person. If you hadn't escaped the camp, Dr. Geyer never would've used the girls of Barrack Seven for Experiment Eighty-Five. I never would have gotten out alive. If you hadn't shot the face-changer in Tokyo, the resistance never would have acted, and Hitler's reign would be going on uninterrupted."

That was a new way of looking at it. Yael had little trouble swallowing her friend's words and taking them to heart because her third wolf knew her.

"You gave me a chance to live," Miriam said. "You've given the world a chance to free itself. That's nothing to feel ashamed about."

It wasn't, was it?

"Now I have to give Felix and Luka a chance," Yael told her friend. "They're under my protection."

"And you're under mine," Miriam assured her. "But for now, it's safer if you act the role of prisoner. Comrade Commander Pashkov has no lost love for National Socialists. Nor do his soldiers. Many of them are refugees from villages like this one, or the old countries. Poland, Austria, Latvia… They've lost everything to the Reich. If Herr Wolfe and Germania's poster boy walked freely among them, it would not end well."

Yael took a closer look at the fighters filing past, listened a little more carefully to their conversations. Many had accents like Miriam's—betraying mother tongues from all over the map. *They're also*, she noted, *too well equipped*. None of this matched up with her previous intelligence about the white space on

172

Henryka's map—Siberian wastelands that housed mere remnants of the Soviet army. A place without infrastructure, reduced to feudal living.

"Comrade Commander Vetrov told me Novosibirsk was planning to reclaim the Muscovy territories...but I wasn't expecting any of this." Yael waved out the door. "How can Novosibirsk have enough momentum to reclaim Moscow? I thought it was a ghost state."

"We were. Even before the Axis's Great Victory, Stalin's regime was crumbling. His government was just as bloody as Hitler's, and there were many uprisings that led to its collapse. After Moscow fell, there was anarchy....Refugees from all over Europe and Africa as well as the Middle East kept pouring across the Seventieth Meridian, trying to escape the Reich. Many brilliant minds found their way to Novosibirsk—scientists, musicians, politicians, artists, rabbis. The city became a melting pot. Once things began settling, these men and women had a hand in building a new government. As for the armament...we've had some help."

"The Japanese," Yael guessed, thinking of the soldiers' Arisakas.

Miriam nodded. "Not officially. Never officially. The Greater East Asia Co-Prosperity Sphere has grown increasingly uneasy with the Third Reich at its doorstep. The Japanese knew Hitler was preparing for future conquests, so they decided it would be in their best interest to have a buffer state. They offered us rifles, ammunition, tanks, artillery, raw materials....Many of the original Soviets in Novosibirsk's government didn't want to accept, especially after the part the Co-Prosperity Sphere played in the war, but the lure of building an army was greater. We've been keeping an ear to the ground in Germania and distracting the Reich with border raids along the Seventieth Meridian while we rearmed in Siberia. We were already mobilizing by the time you warned Vetrov of the events that would take place at the Victor's Ball."

"But Vetrov…he told me we were being kidnapped for political leverage. To use as bargaining chips to reclaim the Muscovy territories. Why bother doing that if you had an army ready all along?" Yael thought aloud. "And why kidnap Japanese racers?"

"Novosibirsk thought that the public's love of the Axis Tour racers would put Germania under enough pressure to bow to our demands and let us regain territory without casualties. The Japanese actually encouraged it, so they could plausibly deny involvement," Miriam explained.

Plausible deniability. This also explained why the Arisaka models were older, yet new. Type 30 and Type 38 rifles had been floating around Asia and Europe ever since the Russo-Japanese War half a century earlier. If pressed, the Japanese could dust off their hands and claim that the Soviets salvaged the rifles from previous conflicts.

An entire army of refugees, with Soviet uniforms and Japanese guns, marching through the Muscovy territories. Had Reiniger known about this? He'd been in contact with Novosibirsk, but the intelligence they'd shared had been limited. Comrade Commander Vetrov hadn't even known the details of Yael's mission. All they'd known was that a putsch was on the horizon.

Adding a full-blown, unaccounted-for army to the mix changed the equation almost as much as the undead Führer had.

"Is the army strong enough to hold Moscow once they take it?" Yael asked.

"So far it's been simple." Miriam smiled, but the expression was guarded. "This portion of Lebensraum is a wasteland.... Most of the frontier farmers have been scared off by years of border raids, and the Reichskommissariat's military outposts aren't equipped to resist this kind of blitzkrieg. The farther west we push, the more that will change, especially as we close in on Moscow. We may have relied too heavily on the promise of the putsch to weaken the National Socialist forces. Until we have a better idea of what's going on in the central Reich, we're all shooting in the dark."

"No news from Germania, then?" Yael asked, trying to hold off the heavy-cloud feeling in her stomach.

Reiniger and Henryka were still alive. Still fighting. They had to be. But there was no way of knowing. Attempting to contact her friends with one of Pashkov's field radios would be futile. She needed an Enigma machine and the preassigned rotor combinations if she wanted to make any sense of the transmissions coming in and out of the beer hall's basement.

"Nothing, apart from the *Chancellery Chat*. There's little doubt that Hitler's survival changes things." Gone was Miriam's smile, stark determination in its place. "But there's no turning back now. We do the only thing we can."

"What's that?" Thousands of kilometers away, with no way of knowing if her friends were alive or dead, Yael was at a loss.

She'd already done so much. She hadn't done enough. Things were changing, changing, changing, out of her control.

But when Miriam's eyes met hers, burning gold and purposeful, Yael began to believe anything was possible. Her third wolf was alive! An army was on the move!

"We hope," Miriam told her. "We hope and we fight."

CHAPTER 21

The fever nightmares kept sprouting—mold-dark and webbing. Felix dreamed he was standing by the hatch of the *Immelmann IV*, gripping his parachute cord, only to realize it was just a mustard-colored thread from Martin's old chair, unraveling longer and longer the more he pulled it. A pack of dogs tore out of the dark, hurtling with Felix through the hatch and into the sky. They howled, Felix screamed.

He fell! He fell! *For Adele!*

Suddenly, the parachute opened, lifting around him, drifting down. It landed at the feet of an old woman, who stared at Felix the way his mother used to—eyes flashing love and fear in the same instant. The expression of a person prepared for loss, terrified of it. Felix wanted to tell her everything was going to be okay. He was going back to Germania. He was fixing things.

But then the crone's wrinkles began peeling—her face curled back like poorly pasted wallpaper, shredding into *the girl's* features. The parachute swallowed Felix again, lifted, drifted, whiteness and blood. This time, it fell at the foot of a half beast. Fur sprouted from the man's head and ears; his words were bear-growly, making no sense. There was a red cross around his arm; his hands were sharp with silver claws. The air was thick with an awful smell: spoiled apple, all its juices leaking out. No—not apple rot. Meat…

Felix knew—suddenly, frantically—that he had to get away. HE HAD TO GET AWAY! But there were hands, hands everywhere, holding him down as the silver claws drew closer to Felix's fingers.

The nightmare faded just as the creature started to feast.

————

Felix knew he was awake because of the throb in his fingers. It felt as if Baasch's boot were landing, again and again. Heel, crush, twist. He supposed the hurt was a good thing, signs of a mending body. *Healing pains,* Papa had always called Felix's racetrack scrapes. *You'll be back on the motorcycle in no time!*

Time…what was the time? Felix remembered too late that Martin's watch was broken. His left hand was already on his chest, seeking out his mechanical heart, only to find it *gone*! Someone had stripped off his Hitler Youth uniform, replaced it with a clean undershirt.

"Ah. Herr Wolfe!" Luka's face appeared. His hair flopped over his brow, smirk lost to thickening facial hair. Felix knew it was there, regardless. The expression was as essential to the victor's appearance as his smelly jacket. "Welcome back to this side of sanity."

Felix's vision focused on the ceiling above him. Knotted wood rafters. The very same rafters he'd been staring at before... They hadn't moved, and according to Luka's budding beard, too much time had passed. Baasch was still waiting back in Germania, his iron heel hovering... poised to take away everyone Felix loved.

"W-where's the girl?" he asked.

"You know, Herr Wolfe, you really should work on your name retention."

Name retention? That was rich, coming from the boy who considered it his personal calling to rename everyone in the most ridiculous way possible: *Change-o-Face? Grease monkey?*

It was hard to believe that once Felix had actually admired Luka Löwe. When fresh-off-the-press 1953 propaganda posters filled store windows and street corners, Felix had studied them with more than a twinge of envy. Who wouldn't be jealous of the youngest victor in the race's history? What red-blooded Reich boy wouldn't want to be posing by the newest Zündapp model in a flashy black jacket?

The twinge was different now. Had been for some time. Adele's stories from the 1955 tour were less than flattering (fist-worthy, even), and there wasn't much the victor had done to prove her words wrong. In the flesh, Luka Löwe was by far the most insufferable, smug *Arschloch* Felix had ever crossed paths with.

As irritated as Felix was, he knew yelling would only exacerbate the situation. "Fine. Where's..."

Luka raised his eyebrows. "Do you even *know* her name?"

Felix knew many things about the girl. She was a criminal.

(Baasch called her an inmate, and there wasn't much evidence to argue with the SS officer. Good people didn't kidnap, lie, murder....) She was the start of the Doppelgänger Project. She was strong, strong enough to knock Felix out cold in the Imperial Palace, strong enough to shove him out of a Focke-Wulf Condor in flight. She seemed sad, so sad that her soul couldn't hold it all, but she was also very, very gifted at acting, so good that in the end Felix had no idea *what* he really knew about her.

The girl's name, however, had managed to escape him.

"Do you know mine?" Felix countered.

"Of course, Fritz. As for Yael..." Luka's stare shifted toward the door. "I'm not sure where she is. How much do you remember?"

"I don't...I don't know." Remembering wasn't the problem. It was the extraction of reality from the nightmare that was giving Felix trouble. His fever had blended the two realms together. All those gravestone letters—changing, rearranging, becoming the wrong death. The old woman's face melting away. The red-crossed man-bear digging into his flesh with silver claws.

These parts were nightmares. They had to be.

"We jumped out of a plane," Luka began.

"I remember that," Felix said.

The other boy shrugged. "Figured as much. But it sounds more impressive if I start off that way. Anyway, we jumped out of a plane, hiked until you went all fever crazy on us—"

"I remember that, too."

"Are you going to let me tell the *verdammt* story or not?"

Again Felix wanted to yell. Again hurt like knives

spread up his broken fingers. Everything—inside and out—ached too much to argue, so he fixed his stare on the ceiling as Luka kept narrating his version of events. "We played house, I got a splinter chopping firewood, the Soviet army rolled in, and Yael used her nifty face-changing trick to divert them...."

Face-changing trick. That's right. The girl could change faces. The old woman melting *had* been real. And if she was real... With a good deal of effort, Felix raised his right, bandaged hand and held it in front of his face. What he saw made no sense at all.

The last two fingers were gone, severed at the base. Both were flaring: crushed bones, tendons on fire. Felix stared and stared. He passed his left hand over the space. It collided with nothing.

Luka was still talking, but his voice sounded as if it were underwater.

Felix's fingers were gone. And they hurt.

And they hurt.

And they hurt.

This was a nightmare. It had to be.

Felix screamed loud enough to hear himself through his shock. The sound was all pain, filled with the agony of his not-there wounds. The door to the cabin swung open, and the man with the red cross appeared. Only now, in the full light of feverless waking, Felix could see he wasn't a bear-man at all, just a medic wearing a fur cap, with flaps that went over his ears. The medic pushed Luka aside, twisting the top off a tiny, kanji-inscribed syrette. The air around Felix went cold as his shirt was shoved up. There was a pinch and a warmth.

Felix had never taken morphine before, but he knew its effects instantly. Heat tugged at his belly, lifting his insides up. His sob settled into a shudder. The medic checked his bandages and gave him a pill, plus a swallow from a canteen to wash the bitterness down.

"Where's our friend?" he heard Luka asking the medic when the man moved to leave. "What have you done with Yael?"

These questions made Felix want to scream again. The girl was no friend of his, no matter *how* much sorrow or sorry her stare held. Felix's fingers were gone—scrap yard bound, beyond fixing. The Wolfes would suffer the same fate, if they hadn't already. All of this—pain, loss, nothingness—was her fault. HERS!

The medic had no answers. The cabin door opened and shut.

Was the *Arschloch* frowning? His forehead held a crease Felix had never seen before—concern in the shape of a V. "Sorry about the fingers, Herr Wolfe. I saw that wound. If Yael hadn't cleaned it out, if the Soviets hadn't rolled in when they did, you wouldn't have been long for this world. Stone-cold crow food. Consider yourself lucky."

Lucky? Felix wanted to hit this *Schweinehund*, but when he tried to make a fist, the pain struck anew. Too strong, too fresh for the new dose of morphine to reach. He gagged on it.

"Easy there." Luka's brow wrinkles deepened. "You don't need to go throwing any punches."

No, Felix wouldn't be tossing any more right hooks. Nor would he be able to twist a Zündapp throttle or grip the many, many tools he used to fix things.

"I can still feel them," he whispered.

It wasn't a question, and Felix really didn't expect an answer, but Luka offered one anyway. "Phantom pains. Your body thinks that whatever is gone is still there. Will for a while. My father used to get them. He lost his arm in the war, made him a hard *Saukerl*...."

Phantom pains. There was no healing in this hurt.

The door opened again, flooding their cabin with the grumble of truck engines. A soldier motioned Luka to his feet, prodded the victor outside at riflepoint. Two other men came to either end of Felix's stretcher (a real one, he realized now, no more bleeding parachute) and hoisted him high. All this as the morphine opened up a sky inside his body, lifting Felix up, up with every next second into a painless atmosphere. Heights he did not have to fear.

CHAPTER 22

It was the third time in a fortnight Luka had been captured by the enemy and held at gunpoint while being yelled at in a foreign language. *This is a disturbing trend*, he mused as a soldier goaded him forward, past the ashes of the Soviets' campfires. Was it possible to be a magnet for mortal peril? He craned his neck as he marched through the village, looking for Yael. Her bright hair should've been easy to spot (assuming she hadn't swapped faces on him), but there was no sign of the fräulein. Just soldiers everywhere, all aiming stares that were nothing short of murderous in his direction.

He needed Yael. Not just for translating (it was *much* harder to smart-mouth your way out of trouble when no one around you spoke German) but also for staving off a sense of impending doom. After witnessing the bloody screamfest that was Felix's amputation, Luka had stayed up the whole night, watching the mechanic twist in his drugged sleep and listening to the guards outside the door laugh in raucous Russian, hoping that Yael would come bursting in at any moment with some far-fetched escape plan.

She hadn't. And now Luka was being herded like a horse to a glue factory, left to wonder if his traveling companion was even alive. The mystery didn't sit too well with him.

He halted midstep, wincing as the bayonet gouged his back.

"WHERE. IS. MY. FRIEND?" he asked in his loudest, slowest German.

"*Davay, idi!*" the soldier yelled at him.

This time Luka added hand gestures. "FRIEND. WHERE. GO?"

"*Durak!*" The prod was harder this time. Luka was fairly certain it drew blood.

The victor was about to use a different hand gesture—one so universally rude it needed no translation—when Felix's stretcher passed. The mechanic was asleep again, tucked under a blanket and looking so pitifully pale that Luka didn't really need the third prod to follow the stretcher-bearers into the empty transport. (*Someone* had to keep an eye on the boy and make sure the Soviets didn't eat him. Or whatever it was commies did to their National Socialist foes.)

Yael's arrival caught him by the throat. She was alive, moving with an assuredness that made Luka wonder why he had ever worried she might *not* be. He couldn't tear his stare away from her—ice-castle eyes, tangled-web hair, black leather everywhere—as she climbed into the truck. The sight of her was more than relief.

"Did they hurt you?" he asked. It was hard to tell, with all the bruises Yael had already acquired. (Though these were starting to make their purple departure.)

"No. You?"

The small of Luka's back stung, but it wasn't worth mentioning. All he did was shoot a dirty look at the two infantry guards perched on the back of their transport. "Didn't touch me. They even patched up Wonderboy Wolfe here."

"Did they save the fingers?"

Luka shook his head. Yael leaned over the stretcher, staring at the mechanic with an intensity that made Luka's chest twinge.

Was he ... jealous?

It wasn't until she pressed her hand to Felix's forehead— when Luka saw the skin to skin, wished it was his—that he realized he was. It was the same nasty feeling that clawed the cockles of his heart outside the ballroom window, while he watched the fräulein dance with the Führer. Back when he thought she was Adele. Back when he thought he was in love with her ...

Pang, pang, dummkopf heart.

"His fever's down." Yael pulled her hand away. Her eyes caught Luka's, narrowed. "What?"

"Nothing." Luka shook his head. *Get a verdammt grip, Löwe.* "It's nothing."

It's nothing, it's nothing.

The transport's suspension shuddered with the weight of a sixth body. A young woman (too young, Luka thought, for her salt-and-pepper braid) pushed past the guards' half-alert Arisakas. Her German was as impeccable as her Soviet uniform. "I just spoke with the medic. We're to keep him dosed with these every twelve hours. It'll keep the pain bearable." She held up a handful of morphine syrettes and placed them by the side of the stretcher. "Also, he found this in Herr Wolfe's old uniform."

186

She handed Yael a scuffed silver watch. "I thought it would be better if you gave it to him."

From the stricken look on the fräulein's face, Luka figured she felt the opposite. She pocketed it anyway. Her hand did not come out empty—a lump of wood lay in the center of Yael's palm. It was about the size of a Stern-Halma piece, weathered, old, nothing special. But when Yael offered it to the strange woman, Luka sensed a shift between them. Gravitas gravity.

"You kept it." The woman's sleeves were rolled up, and when she reached out, Luka couldn't help but notice the number inked along her inner left arm. Her fingers hovered over the token without touching. Someone had carved up the wood, a crude job. There were two shallow stabs of holes in the top half. Eyes maybe? "All this time." Yael nodded. "I didn't keep the others," the woman continued. "I couldn't. After you escaped…"

The woman's voice trailed off. Luka was beginning to realize he did not belong in this scene. This woman knew Yael. *Knew* knew her. Their history felt so strong that it filled the entire transport, squeezing him to the fringes.

When he cleared his throat, both women snapped out of their spell. Yael's fist closed over the wooden piece. The Soviet woman looked at Luka—eyes calculating.

"New friend?" he asked.

"An old one, actually," the stranger replied. Her tone lacked any overwhelming friendliness. "I'm Comrade Mnogolikiy."

"Come again?"

"Mnogolikiy."

"Mgiol—" Luka gave up half a butchered syllable in. "Sorry. That word is not going to fit in my mouth. I'm going to have to call you something else. Tell you what, since you're an old friend of Yael's, I'll let you have a nickname of your choosing."

The Soviet woman turned to Yael, speaking in rapid, rattling Russian. Yael nodded, responding in Russian just as fluid. Luka thought he heard his name tossed around somewhere in the mix.

Yael wasn't a *Soviet*, was she? Luka didn't think so, but then again, how did she know Soviet-speak? And how was she old friends with an officer? There was so much about the fräulein Luka did not understand. So much he wanted to . . .

The women's untranslatable words eventually came to an end. The stranger turned to him and said, "Call me Miriam."

Miriam. The name was as rare as Yael's, for one simple reason. (And, Luka suddenly realized, the *same* reason.) It was Jewish.

This woman and Yael were Jewish.

In his seventeen years, Luka had heard many things about the Jews. *Untermensch*, his racial sciences teacher had called them, citing facts about skull sizes and bloodlines. *Enemy of the Aryan race* had been his own father's terminology of choice, words parroted from one of the Führer's many *Chancellery Chat*s. *Thieves* and *devils* were also thrown out during some of Kurt Löwe's more rage-filled evenings. He would wave his good arm in the air, cursing them for the loss of the other while Adolf Hitler's painted blue eyes watched above the mantel.

Yael's eyes were a sharper blue: seeing Luka and being seen. He caught her gaze, watching her in this new light. She was Jewish! The first Jewish person he'd ever met face-to-face, exchanged words with, knew . . .

Was it really so surprising that Yael was nothing like the slurs Luka's father/teacher/Führer spewed? That out of all the souls Luka had ever come across, hers was one of the brightest? It held the bravery of one hundred Iron Crosses, melted down and forged into something purer—a courage not corroded by cruelty.

No, Luka decided. It took more than a few drops of blood—shed *or* inherited—to make someone a devil. He had to believe that, because if it wasn't true, then what did that make him?

His father's son.

Luka wanted to be better/stronger/more than that.

"Miriam." He turned back to the Soviet fräulein and offered his hand. "Call me Luka."

Miriam didn't take it. Her stare flashed full of gold flecks, piercing. The sticky sense of history was still flooding the truck, leaving Luka no room to *be*.

He dropped his arm.

"Luka Löwe. Double victor. Face of the Third Reich." His titles might as well have been crimes the way Miriam recited them. "I wasn't aware you were a part of the resistance."

"Makes two of us," Luka told her, then immediately wished he hadn't. He could almost see Miriam's verdict on his character plummeting: *Arschloch. Guilty. No chance of parole.*

"Why are you here?" she asked.

"I'm . . ."

Why *was* he here? His days had been so survival-oriented that Luka hadn't really stopped to consider something as basic as this. He should've been back in Germania, giving a series of prewritten speeches in front of the Volkshalle about the virtues of the Aryan race: strength, endurance, honor, purity. Afterward he would have sat on the ghastly green love seat in his flat, watching reruns of his speech on the Reichssender, smoking an entire pack of cigarettes. Made of restless limbs and an antsy heart. His phone would've rung every few minutes with press and admirers and well-wishers, but Kurt Löwe would never have been on the other end, saying *Well done, my son.* Luka would've hated how those four unsaid words made him feel. He would have kept listening to himself on the television, realizing that no matter how many cigarettes he smoked, he was just as much of a lemming as his father and everyone else. Worse— Luka was the jester lemming, dancing to Goebbels's propaganda tune.

And after that?

Luka saw his scripted life stretching out: Getting a job at the Chancellery, pushing papers, marrying a fräulein whose aim was to earn the Gold Cross of Honor of the German Mother in the form of eight screaming babies. Mouthing *heil* day after day, the double Iron Crosses growing heavier around his neck with each passing year. Kurt Löwe taking those four words to his *verdammt* grave because no amount of medals or scars his son collected would ever be enough, Luka's strength fading inside an expanding waistline, not feeling right, never feeling *right*...

Being here—sitting by Yael's side in a truck in the thawing taiga—was technically a mistake. A wrong turn and then some. But it felt *right* in a way Luka couldn't begin to describe. *I'm here because it's not boring* wouldn't cut it for the angry Soviet Jewish fräulein. *I'm here because I'm here* was too cheeky. *I'm here because of Yael* felt too...raw...to say out loud.

He shrugged instead.

"Along for the ride, then?" Not a real question. A scoff, made all the more cutting by Miriam's gaze.

"Miriam..." Yael's words melted into Russian, and the two women began conversing in a level beyond Luka.

Transport engines were being cranked to life all around them, rumbling through the forest. The truck bed shuddered under Luka's boots as their driver shifted into first, began the long crawl forward. Collapsing cabins gave way to the sea of skeletons. The sight—all white and tangled and still—settled into Luka's own bones as their truck shuddered past, pushed ahead through mud and trees. Miriam and Yael kept speaking low in Russian. Felix kept sleeping, his bandaged hand hanging along the side of the stretcher. Luka put his own hand against the dog tag under his shirt. Palm pressing to cloth, pressing to steel, pressing to proof of blood type A. The blood of Kurt Löwe. The blood of himself.

Though Yael and Miriam's words remained a mystery, Luka followed their tone well enough. Their conversation lasted several minutes—going from strained to sharp and angry to sullen—before Miriam finally sat down on the opposite side of the transport. The edge of her boots only a kick away from Luka's own.

"Get comfortable, Herr Löwe," she told him. "We have a long drive ahead."

Herr Löwe was his father's name, and there was no getting comfortable in this ZIS-5. (Bumpy road + shot suspension = good-bye, nicely aligned vertebrae!) But Luka kept both of these opinions to himself as he settled in.

The drive *was* long. Trees passed into trees, the lines of their trunks going from brown to dim to invisible altogether once the sun set. The transports flicked on their headlamps (dimmed to prevent enemy detection) and kept driving. Felix slept like the dead, and Miriam eventually nodded off, too. Yael sat next to Luka. Something about the way she was holding her knees to her chest, staring out at the growing night, reminded him of the train to New Delhi—the first time they kissed. When all their truths and lies came to a standstill and Luka's heart was clenched. His ventricles were clenching now, remembering it. The moonlight on the fräulein's face. The warmth from her lips seeping all the way inside his heart, making it *feel*.

Yael must have sensed him watching. She glanced over her shoulder in her fiercely beautiful, arctic wolf way. Eyebrow arched.

Luka cleared his throat. "I don't think your new-old friend likes me much."

"I didn't either when we first met," she said.

When we first met. It took Luka a moment to remember this moment—back in the Olympiastadion. Yael had been wearing Adele's face, speaking Adele's words. Her hair had been translucent, skin glossy with rain. Luka's own skin had burned with anger at the sight of Adele Wolfe in the flesh—his first since their bloody encounter in Osaka. "That's different. I thought you were Adele. If I'd known you were you..."

"It would have made things worse," Yael said quietly into the passing night.

"I'd like to think not," Luka told her.

Yael turned, facing him in full. The truck's shadows

wreathed her face, her silhouette edged by the sparse light of the trailing transport. Luka couldn't quite decide if her brightness reminded him of an angel or a ghost. All he knew was that he wanted to close the gap between them, wanted to press his lips against hers again—an honest kiss, sans poison and sabotage. But honesty required knowledge, and Luka knew he was sitting on the wrong side of a wall made up of so many unknowns: tattoos and wooden tokens and a Soviet officer with golden eyes.

He kept still instead. Counting breaths and secrets.

"Luka?" Yael asked on her fourth exhale.

"Yes?" he said on his fifth.

"Why didn't you join the resistance?"

Ah. There it was. The question he knew was coming. Eventually. "It's not like they walk around town knocking on doors and handing out pamphlets."

"You have plenty of black-market connections. You'd have to, to get your cigarettes," she pointed out. "You could have found us if you'd tried hard enough."

Try harder, be stronger, be more. Story of my verdammt life.

"You've seen what the SS does to traitors. Why choose to get crushed when you can survive?" As far as Luka could tell, it was a legitimate alibi. Backed up by the laws of nature itself.

"Some of us don't have that choice." Yael's words held a tightness: a new-old anger to match the new-old friend. "Some of us have never had that choice."

He swam in the heat of her voice, stared at her taut arms. The cuff of Yael's jacket ended a few centimeters short, so Luka could see tattoo ink: the tip of a wolf's tail, tickling her delicate wrist. He stared at these markings, carved dark into her skin.

They reminded him of the sketches his mother used to make on the corners of the telephone message pad (then crumpled up before her husband could see). They bore all the portents of *art*. So much detail in such a small space: hatching lines both wild and straight shaded out the animal's fur. It made Luka wonder what the rest of the wolves looked like up close. Just as detailed? Just as dark?

Was there a string of numbers beneath them, too?

He wondered so many things about Yael. The answers of her were only fractions: *Inmate. Lab rat. Jew.* Numbers he did not understand but meant something. Luka wondered at the long gaps between. He wondered and he wanted to know. "What happened to you?"

There was a moment, stretching into another moment, and another. When Yael finally shook her head, every one of her pale, pale hairs cut against the shining headlamps. *Why?* her eyes seemed to ask him. *Why don't you already know? Why are you here?* Everything about her—stillness, silence, feeling—pared Luka down, cutting to his core.

Why?

Why?

Why can't you be more?

"I was afraid." The links of Luka's dog tag chain bit into his neck. His words felt too honest for his voice. "Still am."

"Fear is not an excuse," Yael told him. "Fear is being human."

What else could Luka say? He had no *more* in him. His lips twitched, stretched, wanted to sneer, just so she'd stop looking at him the way she was: with ice (or fire?), hate (or love?), extremes of emotions pulsing through those irises.

She felt *right*. She felt so far away. Too far for someone like Luka to reach.

"You might want to get some sleep. Miriam tells me we'll reach Molotov by sunrise," Yael said. Her arms fell to her sides, and the wolf tail disappeared, swallowed by the sleeve's leather. She lay down on the truck bed, curling her body in the shape of a C. Luka could see the ridge of her spine against her jacket.

Luka had no idea where Molotov was, but he supposed it didn't matter. The angry Soviet with eyes of gold was right: He was just along for the *verdammt* ride.

CHAPTER 23

THINGS UNHEARD: A TRANSLATION

Bout I

Miriam: He knows your name?

Yael: Luka's not like the other National Socialists.

Miriam: No. He's their poster boy! The one they look up to and adore.

Yael: It's not like that. *He's* not like that.

Miriam: Do you really think so, Volchitsa?

Yael, nodding: There's something more to him. I've seen it.

Bout II

Miriam: He's all talk, no spine.

Yael: Luka is brash, yes, but that's not all he is. Give him a chance.

Miriam: A chance? Is that what they gave us, Yael, when they stuffed us into those cattle cars? When they put the numbers on our arms and burned our families to ash?

Yael: I remember it as well as you do, Miriam.

Miriam: If Luka Löwe was more than a National Socialist, he would have found a way to join the resistance. He wouldn't have hidden behind his blood and name while our people were slaughtered.

Yael: . . .

Miriam: You know I'm right.

Yael: I trust him.

Miriam: Trust. Are you sure that's all it is?

Yael: . . .

Miriam: Don't let your heart get in the way of your head, Yael. Luka Löwe might be on your side now, but when it matters, he'll be gone. Men like him only look after their own interests. That's how our world fell into this sorry state in the first place.

CHAPTER 24

Sleep was beyond Yael. It was not for fear of the nightmare, or for lack of exhaustion, but for the heart inside her chest. The one still fluttering from Luka's cobweb closeness. The one still high on the impossibility of Miriam *here*, alive. The one drenched in the blood of men and dreams. The one that did not know what to feel.

The pieces of Yael—life and soul—were clashing.

In many ways, she felt better with Miriam here. Solid, safe. Yael's third wolf *knew* her, grounded Yael in an older version of herself. But the little girl from the death camp did not fit with the boy in the brown jacket. The two were worlds and years apart. Deaths and deaths and deaths apart.

She couldn't blame Miriam for hating Luka. She'd hated the victor, too, at first sight. (And second. And third.) His swastika armband and swagger trained by goose steps had grated on her nerve endings. She'd looked at him and seen the enemy.

When Yael looked at Luka now—burn blistering his

collarbone, his indigo stare more question than claim—it wasn't the enemy she saw, but the boy behind the mask. An ally. A friend. *Something,* the prickling heat within her chest whispered, *more.*

What now?

Now Luka was afraid.

And so was she.

Yael lay awake, staring out of the truck into a forest she could not see. Hours passed. The road grew smoother—ribboning into asphalt. She smelled Molotov long before she saw it. *War* lay heavy in the air: peppery gunpowder, acrid ash. The sun was rising, but when Yael looked up, all she could see was a starless, blueless haze. Smoke spread across the sky, choking everything.

The city appeared street by street, in muted streaks of color. Yael imagined that the place filled with daylight and scrubbed of battle would be picturesque. Broad Baroque buildings painted in shades of daffodil and powder blue stood side by side with wooden merchant houses. Many of their windows were shattered, glass sparkling against the street. Some of the grander houses—the ones with the tatters of swastika banners still fluttering from their balconies—had been torched, doorframes edged in soot. Dark lumps littered the streets, lying with a stillness that screamed BODIES.

Other than the corpses, the Soviets' convoy met no resistance as they entered the city. When the transports pulled into Molotov's central square, Yael saw why. The area was circled with the units Pashkov had been ordered to meet—transports, fighters, even tanks. Inside this ring were the National Socialist soldiers of Molotov. Dozens of black-suited SS stood in the center—closest to the square's iron statue of the Führer—chins sharp, stance unyielding. Several hundred weaponless brownshirts gathered in nervous huddles. There was a sharp divide among them; a good number had torn their National Socialist emblems from their uniforms, substituting ripped cloth for swastikas and eagles. Others wore no uniform at all. Silver-haired grandfathers stood next to schoolboys who stood next to laborers with callused hands and wind-burned faces—men whose bones showed too readily through their skin.

All these prisoners were staring at the north end of the square. It was there Yael saw the bodies, piled in a heap, not so long dead. SS officers with sightless eyes were stacked on top of Wehrmacht men. The stones by their limp fingers and feet glistened with blood.

A future mound of bones.

Molotov's central square tore apart with a series of gunshots. Sounds that shook earth and sky and heart. The prisoners gave a collective shudder. Luka jerked awake. Miriam's eyes snapped open. Even Felix shifted against his stretcher.

Yael watched more bodies being dragged to the pile and felt sick.

These men were being executed.

This isn't right. Yael looked back at the men without markings. Why would Wehrmacht fighters tear their National Socialist badges from their uniforms? Why would a starving laborer fight alongside the SS against an enemy he hadn't even known was coming? And, for that matter, how had the Soviets managed to capture Molotov so quickly? The city was not small, and even in the event of a blitzkrieg, a resistance of this number would have battled for at least a few days.

Resistance...

Molotov hadn't been overthrown by the Soviets. It had been taken by its own people: partisan fighters. Yael's allies. Her only way to reach Henryka. Men the Soviets were mowing down—

Another round of death shredded through the square, ringing against Yael's ears.

—THIS ISN'T RIGHT DON'T LET THEM DIE—

She dropped out of the truck, boots to asphalt, dimly aware of the shouts behind her (Miriam's "What are you doing?" alongside Luka's colorful curses and the guards' yells) and the cries of Soviet soldiers surprised at the sight of the albino girl parting their ranks. Yael shoved past shoulders and card games and hot meals and fighters singing the patriotic hymns of their long-gone countries, all the way to the firing squad. Ten men were reloading their rifles as another round of National Socialist prisoners were dragged into the line of fire. Most were Wehrmacht, some stripped of their insignia. All of them scared.

There were only two men without brown shirts or fear on their faces, bookending the line. On the far left: a lone SS officer. To the right stood a tall man with silvering hair. Everything about him was gaunt: sunken eyes, frayed trousers, his interruption of an Adam's apple. Dried blood spackled his bandaged forehead. Yael would've wagered her life that he was fighting for Reiniger's cause.

In a way she was—running up to the execution squad, arms up, coughing between breaths, "Stop shooting! You can't just kill these men! The Geneva Convention—"

The squad's leader, the only man without a rifle, turned toward Yael. His eyebrows were the color of a fox's tail, quivering with rage. "Geneva? You think these bastards quoted the articles of Geneva when they invaded our lands? When they led our parents, our brothers and sisters, our spouses, our *children,* into the woods and shot them in the back?"

No. The anger in the squad leader's voice was in all the executioners' eyes, glinting off the brass of the spent shell casings at their feet. Yael knew it only too well. For so many years it had been her marrow, her core. A burn in her bones, a thirst for an answer.

"There are no rules in this war." The squad leader spit and yelled back at his men. "Ready!"

They pressed the buttstocks to their shoulders as a single unit.

"These soldiers were already fighting when you arrived in Molotov, weren't they?" Yael persisted. "That's because some of these men are part of the resistance. They hate the National Socialists as much as you do—"

"AIM!" The squad leader shouted even louder, determined to drown out Yael's voice. Ten gun barrels stared straight into ten sets of eyes, a single word separating life from death. One of the swastika-wearing soldiers in the very center of the line began crying, nose running like a schoolboy.

—NOT LIKE THIS NEVER LIKE THIS—

"Please!" The anger in Yael's bones stretched and grew, and she did not know where to put it. But this—bullets flying, blood at her feet—would not help. "Let me talk to them!"

The squad leader's rage was growing, too: flushing up his neck, until his face matched his eyebrows. Red. Quivering.

"Someone get this girl out of my way!" he shouted at the soldiers who'd gathered to watch.

Two of them lurched forward. A third uniform tore out of the crowd: Miriam. She moved faster than the others, grabbing Yael's biceps and yanking her close. Instead of shrinking back into the crowd, Miriam turned to the squad leader.

"What is going on here? Who ordered this?"

The squad leader seemed to recognize Miriam on sight. The knowledge paled him. "C-Comrade Mnogolikiy. It's an honor."

Miriam did not return the pleasantries. "I asked you a question, comrade. Who ordered this?"

"It"—the squad leader's eyes began darting around the square, as if his answer were hidden behind one of the bystanders—"was a mutual decision. These men are combatants, Comrade Mnogolikiy. Not civilians. We don't have the infrastructure for due process."

"That man"—Yael pointed to the tall, older man at the line's far right—"is a member of the resistance. More than half of these fighters are. Do any of you know what's waiting for you in Moscow? You're going in blind. You'll need to keep eyes on Germania. If you let me talk to these men, I can get you the information you need to continue your advance through Muscovy."

I hope. Every significant resistance cell had an Enigma machine with its radio equipment, plus a list of daily rotor combinations. If Yael could talk to the resistance leaders, she could contact Henryka.

If Henryka was still alive…How many days had it been since the putsch was thrown into action? Five? Six? For all Yael knew, her friends were as crushed and gone as Felix's fingers.

203

These thoughts did nothing to ease the frantic feeling in Yael's esophagus. This and the blood at her feet (so real, too real, nothing nightmarish about it) were starting to break her. All of Vlad's breathing exercises and compartmentalization techniques couldn't blunt the hysteria that crept into her voice. "You *can't* just shoot these men in cold blood!"

Miriam's grip around Yael's arm tightened. *Silence*, the pinch of her fingers said.

The squad leader did not look convinced. "There's no cold blood here. These men deserve to die. Have you not seen the villages? Do you not remember—"

"I remember," Miriam cut the squad leader off. "Believe me, comrade. But Volchitsa is right. We need information on Moscow's defenses as well as the state of Germania's retaliatory capabilities. These men should have access to communication channels that can help us acquire that information. Killing them would be foolish."

"Volchitsa?" The squad leader's eyebrows swept away under his lone-star cap. "I'm to listen to a prisoner of war on how to treat prisoners of war?"

"No," Miriam said firmly. "You're to listen to me."

The squad leader did not challenge her. "How do we have any way of knowing which of these men are absolved?" he asked instead. "Any one of them could tear off their badges."

"The resistance has security protocols. Pass codes and such," Yael explained, her voice a smidge steadier. "Let me talk to this man. If I can confirm his membership with the resistance, then he can point me to the group's leader. They'll be able to vouch for their own members."

"What do you suggest we do with the others?"

Yael looked back to the line. All ten men were watching her. Resistance, Wehrmacht, SS... their eyes scaled the range from basic hope to acid hate.

"You don't need to add any infrastructure," she told the squad leader. "The resistance has been planning the uprising for over a decade. They'll have a contingency plan for prisoners. Let me find the resistance leaders and talk to them. We'll get things sorted."

The rifles stayed high, still ready for that one word (*FIRE!*). The men's arms began wavering from the wait and the weight. Their aims drifted. The squad leader's face drifted as well. His eyebrows were back down to a reasonable level, and his skin was back to a normal shade. Neither flushed nor pale.

"Do what you must," he told Yael, before ordering his men, "At ease!"

They lowered their Arisakas. Miriam let go of Yael's arm. The middle, weeping Wehrmacht soldier hiccupped with relief. The gaunt man nodded.

Yael walked to him, leaned in to his ear, and whispered the first half of the resistance's pass code in German: "The wolves of war are gathering."

"They sing the song of rotten bones." The man's answer was as frail as his frame.

"I need to find the leaders of your cell," Yael told him. "Will you help me?"

He did. Many minutes of searching and many whispered pass codes later, Yael found herself standing in front of a man named Ernst Förstner. He looked close to Reiniger's age, with similar lines around his eyes and dips in his hairline.

His altered Wehrmacht uniform was a few sizes too tight, a few years too faded—last war's relic. When he greeted Yael, it was not with joy, but wariness. She couldn't blame him, with the pile of bodies less than ten meters away and the spit of Soviet soldiers flecking stones and faces alike. It also didn't help that Yael had acquired a train of officers: Miriam followed by Comrade Commander Pashkov, followed by Comrade Fox Brows, followed by five other top brass uniforms. Ernst Förstner and his band of wounded men regarded the entourage nervously.

"What happened here?" Yael asked the leader of Molotov's resistance.

"This cell has been growing for years," he explained. "When the signal was sent over the Reichssender, we seized control of the camps to the north and freed the laborers. Many joined us. It took two days of fighting to win the city. We surrounded the SS headquarters, arrested the leaders, and brought them here to the square. That's when the Soviet trucks started rolling in; they had us outnumbered and outgunned. When they demanded our surrender, we saw no reason to fight, so we laid down our arms. They made us stand here with the others."

"And then they started shooting?" Yael asked.

Herr Förstner nodded. "We tried to explain, but it made no difference."

Behind her, Miriam was translating the discussion from German to Russian. The execution-squad leader gave another grunt: far more uncomfortable than the first.

When Yael asked about a radio, Ernst Förstner's expression did not flinch. "I do have equipment for contacting the headquarters in Germania. I can take you to it, but first I want a guarantee of amnesty for myself and my men. I want the executions stopped."

Yael looked to the seven judges as Miriam translated this request. "Can you promise this?"

Their stares were as varied as those in the execution line. Traces of mercy jarring against *no cold blood here*. One of the nameless officers motioned to Ernst Förstner's faded Wehrmacht uniform. "Ask him how many of our comrades he killed in the war."

Yael didn't. "How many Germans did you kill?" she shot back. "How many of your comrades will die if we don't contact Germania and your army goes plunging toward Moscow without intelligence?"

None of the Soviet heads had an answer for her. They muttered among themselves instead.

"There's hundreds of prisoners, and we can't afford to leave whole units behind to guard them," Pashkov reasoned, loud enough for Yael to hear. "What will we do with the men?"

"Herr Förstner tells me there's a labor camp north of here. They'll have enough fences to contain your prisoners of war until Novosibirsk can arrange a tribunal." Yael shuddered at the thought but kept talking. "Amnesty for the members of the resistance and no more death. You can agree to this?"

More mumbling. More *war without rules* stares, old wounds rising to the surface of their whispers. It took some minutes, but finally they fell silent. Miriam looked to the resistance leader.

"The comrade commanders agree to your terms," she told him in German.

Ernst accepted the news with a nod. "Then it would be my pleasure to take you to the radio."

———

They made a strange parade through Molotov's scorched streets: eight high-ranking Soviet officers, an albino girl, a stretcher, and an Axis Tour double victor (Yael refused to leave Felix and Luka behind in the square), plus several Soviet guards (despite everything, they were still prisoners). Adele's brother stayed asleep, a blanket pulled over his recognizable features. Luka was once again using his jacket as a hood, which drew just as much attention as his regular face. He bumped into Soviets and bodies alike, mumbling apologies neither the soldiers nor the dead could appreciate.

At the head of all this: Ernst Förstner. The resistance-cell leader led them to a wooden house that looked as if it had been ripped from its foundations and rattled about. Its wood was unpainted, the borders carved with elaborate details of diamonds and flowers. A swastika flag hung in the front window.

"Please forgive the details," Herr Förstner said as he unlocked the door. "It's important to blend in, as you well know."

The dwelling's inside was just as jumbled as its facade. The front room was stacked with a decade's worth of *Das Reich* newspapers—ragged, yellowing editions disintegrating against a bearskin rug. The sofa could have doubled as a museum piece, if its velvet hadn't been worn bald by so many sittings. An upright piano blocked the side window: keys stripped of ivory, its lid spattered with candle wax. Adolf Hitler's portrait was propped halfheartedly above an ash-clogged fireplace.

The Führer's voice was there, too. It was the first thing Yael heard when she stepped inside. Red, red as ever, crackling through the Reichssender's airwaves. The screen showed Adolf Hitler sitting in his high-backed chair, looking just as he had in the Imperial Palace ballroom. Just as he did in Yael's dreams.

The sight of him—so frenetic and unbearably alive—sent a new rush of hatred through Yael. If she'd had a gun, she would've pointed it at the television, taken the shot all over again.

"Irmgard?" the resistance leader called down the hallway. "It's me!"

"Ernst? Oh, thank heavens! The others were telling me what was going on in the square. . . ." A woman peered out from one of the rooms, a pistol as aged as Ernst's uniform in her hand. When she caught sight of the newcomers, she froze.

"It's okay, love," Herr Förstner explained. "They promised us amnesty."

At this she rushed down the hall, into her husband's arms. "I thought you were dead!"

"It was . . . a misunderstanding," Ernst said into his wife's shoulder. "They killed Lutz and Günter. They might have shot all of us if one of Reiniger's operatives hadn't stepped in. She arrived with some of the Soviets. Convinced them we could help."

"Ernst tells me you have a radio with an Enigma machine." Yael tried not to sound too frantic, but television Hitler's promises of crushed traitors (embroidered in his needle-tip precise elocution) weren't helping. "May I see it?"

"Of course, of course." Irmgard was aflutter—proof of her husband's survival made her movements whole stones lighter as she pulled away from Ernst, hitched up the hem of her dress, and picked through the newspapers, stepping over ADELE WOLFE PULLS AHEAD AT CAIRO CHECKPOINT and GERMANIA PREPARES TO OBSERVE FÜHRER'S 67TH BIRTHDAY, all the way to the piano. Here the woman bent down, pressing the instrument's pedals in a quick pattern. The wood panel of the base swung away, revealing not strings but knobs and speakers. Irmgard flicked these to life, then turned to the Enigma machine.

"Today is... April eighth." Irmgard arranged the rotors into the day's correct combination. "There. Now we'll be able to understand what comes through."

Yael bent down into the gutted piano and took stock of the machinery. This radio was more complicated than Vlad's shortwave setup, but nothing she wasn't equipped to handle. She turned the dials to the correct frequency, trying to ignore the scarlet stab of Hitler's voice over her shoulder, trying to pretend there wasn't a lump of worry pearling inside her throat.

April 8. It had been six days since the failed assassination. Six days since the real Hitler first appeared on screens all across the Reich to declare himself *immortal*. History, Yael realized, was on a loop, as awful and repeating as the *Chancellery Chat* behind her. Just as Hitler had thwarted the first Valkyrie's bomb at the Wolfsschanze, so had he survived Yael's bullet. Both times Hitler had announced his providential resilience for all to hear. Both times he'd called for a settling of accounts, vengeance in the form of bullets and blood.

It had taken less than twenty-four hours for the original Operation Valkyrie to plummet into a series of brutal executions. Why should the second attempt prove any different?

Irmgard punched a greeting into the Enigma machine, jotting down the resulting code in pen and handing it to Yael. "Here. Use this to hail them."

Yael cleared her throat as best she could, then read the letters aloud in bursts of five: "*BRTJX. UGZJZ. EALST. QGJRW. G.*"

...Nothing...

Of course, Yael hadn't expected an immediate response. If her message had gotten through, it still had to be unscrambled into its true form:

VALKYRIE NEST, DO YOU COPY?

After that, an answer needed to be composed and encrypted. These actions took time.

But should they take *this* long?

The whole room listened, wordless. Luka had made a small throne out of the newspaper piles, biting his lip as he leaned into the crumbling pages. Irmgard's pen was still pressed to paper, blotting her notepad. The Soviet officers were a tableau of stretched patience. Ernst eyed the guards as they settled Felix's stretcher onto the bearskin rug, weapons at the ready. Miriam picked her way toward the piano and leaned above Yael, forehead pressed into its keys.

...Still nothing...

There was only so long Yael could wait. Only so many times her heart could leap inside her chest just to be met with silence. A vision of Henryka's ransacked office kept shoving into her thoughts: Map ripped from the wall. Radios smashed against the concrete floor. Gestapo picking through years' worth of the resistance's files...

....

The radio crackled and then—Kasper's voice! Yael recognized it in an instant. The sound—made tinny by thousands of kilometers and electronic speakers—crumpled her chest. She listened, breathless, as her fellow operative rattled off his own letter series. Irmgard typed these into the Enigma machine. Out the new letters came, which the woman respaced, and punctuated with her neat penmanship:

COPY. WHO IS THIS?

Write down, encode, recite an answer:

MOLOTOV CELL. VOLCHITSA.

CHAPTER 25

Chaos did not even begin to describe it.

Henryka needed more ears, more radios, more, more, more. News kept spilling in faster than she and the four operatives could listen, much less record or pass along. Over it all, the Führer's post-assassination *Chancellery Chat* was airing on repeat on the *przeklęty* Reichssender: "I am not dead....Despite their best efforts...Despite their best efforts...I am not dead."

Over and over, on and on. Thirty times an hour. Twenty-four hours a day. As much as Henryka loathed Adolf Hitler's words and still-alive-ness, she refused to turn the television off. She was too afraid she might miss some vital clue.

The resistance wasn't dead either, despite the recovered Führer's best efforts. In the space of days, five countries had been reborn, claiming their place on Henryka's map: Great Britain, the kingdom of Iraq, Finland, Turkey, Italy (the southern half, boot heel to midcalf; north of Rome was still tangled with thin-yarn fronts, battles in progress). Henryka colored in their borders with much less joy than she should have. These victories did not surprise her. The British Isles and the Italian peninsula still held bitter memories of the initial war. Both were a hotbed of pins on her map. It hadn't taken much for the regions' wider populations to join the rebellion. Iraq, Finland, and Turkey had all been ruled by Reichskommissariats spread thin, where the National Socialists' infrastructure could not survive resistance without additional support from Germania.

Five countries won. Six, counting Egypt.

But these victories weren't enough.

The rest of the map was drowning in red chaos. Death plotted out with thumbtacks and string. The resistance in Paris had taken a vicious blow. Its leaders captured, defamed, executed on the spot. Once-Poland and once-Austria's uprisings were floundering, if not completely dead. Moscow's resistance was locked in grid-tight urban warfare, its attempts at breaking into the Kremlin and arresting the Reichskommissar continually rebuffed. But the biggest of Henryka's worries loomed much closer to home, just a few meters above, tearing apart Germania's streets. The moment the Führer's declaration of not-deadness had appeared on people's televisions, the city spiraled into pandemonium.

General Erwin Reiniger was still alive. (Thank God.) As soon as Henryka had radioed the news of the Führer's survival, Reiniger and his men had retreated from the Volkshalle to a more defensible position, north of the river Spree. Many of the other conspiring generals followed. Others, upon learning of Hitler's survival, lost heart, shifting their allegiances before their names could be pinned to any conspiracy. In the end, the divide was strangely matched. Waffen-SS and fealty-bound Wehrmacht men fought against the rebels. Germania's citizens hunkered inside old air-raid shelters as the city tore itself apart.

There were no bombs yet. The Luftwaffe remained grounded, in part because its commander-in-chief, Hermann Göring, remained in Reiniger's custody. The main airfield, in the northern town of Rechlin, was under National Socialist control, as were many of the planes and their pilots, but Henryka doubted Hitler was foolish or desperate enough to raze half of his own capital.

Germania was a line drawn in the sand, festering violence. There was no clear offensive. No solid defensive. Just building-to-building combat. Streets taken, blocks lost. On some corners, the swastika hung high. On others, it was burning. Even now Henryka could hear gunshots, staccatoing between the crackling radios. Reiniger had ordered her to evacuate the map room, but Henryka refused. Without this communication center, the resistance would fall apart altogether. She'd labored too hard, too long, to let something like death frighten her away.

She presented this choice to Kasper, Brigitte, Johann, and Reinhard: Stay or go, live or (probably) die. All four remained at their posts, sleeping only a fraction of the hours and subsisting on stale slices of bread and food that came out of cans.

As for Adele...more than once Henryka considered releasing her, but it couldn't be denied that the girl was a liability. She'd seen too much of their base of operations, and who knew *how* many things she'd heard through that door. They'd gone this long without being discovered. (None of the movement's defectors had been people privy to the beer hall basement's location.) They had to keep every advantage they had.

So Adele remained trapped inside a closet while the calls kept pouring in: victory, defeat, victory, defeat. The Third Reich was crumbling away at the edges, yet becoming more concentrated at its core. Among the incoming reports were those about the Waffen-SS units moving through the countryside, quelling any resistance they could find. Henryka marked their locations on the map with tiny double *Sieg* rune pins. The capital was ringed in a noose of black lightning. One that was drawing tighter day by day.

Germania's bloody stalemate could not, would not, last.

Kasper and Johann kept answering the radios. Brigitte and Reinhard kept tapping away at their cipher machines. Both tasks were Sisyphean. Transmissions were coming in a relentless stream, too many to answer, let alone rest from.

Kasper, in particular, was exhausted. Out of all the map room's operatives, he'd slept the least, receiving report after report, dictating strings of code to Reinhard in a flat voice. But something about Kasper's current call seemed to spark him: The young man's face went electric when he read Reinhard's unscramble. He tore off his headphones, held them out for Henryka.

"You're going to want to take this," he said. "It's from the Muscovy territories. The cell in Molotov."

Molotov. Henryka had to double-check her map to confirm what she knew of the city. It lay a couple of hundred kilometers west of the Ural Mountains and was one of the last significant settlements before the Lebensraum faded into a no-man's-land of massacred villages and struggling potato farms. The resistance there consisted of slave laborers and disillusioned settlers—men and women forced out of the central Reich by lottery.

"Good news?" She hoped.

"I think it's Yael."

———

"Volchitsa? Is that you?"

While Yael's breath hitched at the sound of Kasper's voice, she actually burst into tears at the sound of Henryka's. The woman was exhausted, her syllables wavering the way they did when she forgot to sleep. Too often Henryka favored the resistance's cause over self-care, too often Yael had seen the Polish woman's hairline edged with brown roots, eyes bruised with countless waking hours.

"It's me," Yael managed. "I'm here."

I'm here. We're all still here. The knowledge stole Yael's oxygen away and kept stealing it, replacing air with saltwater tears. It wasn't until this moment that she realized how strong the fear of her friends' deaths had grown. How like a shadow it followed her…

"We shouldn't—" Was Henryka crying, too? It certainly sounded that way. A series of sniffs managed their way through the speakers. "We should go back to code. We don't know who might be listening."

Encryption codes weren't meant for flowing conversations. It was infuriating, really, how slowly their exchange crawled. But the information being passed between Molotov and the beer hall basement was too precious for enemy ears.

Yael offered her own report first, trying to cram the past six days into as few words as possible:

REAL FÜHRER IN GERMANIA. BALLROOM HITLER WAS SKINSHIFTER DECOY. EXPERIMENT 85 STILL ACTIVE. NOVOSIBIRSK ARMY INVADING MUSCOVY. INTENDS TO RECLAIM FORMER SOVIET LANDS.

Et cetera, et cetera.

Miriam was doing her due diligence as Comrade Mnogolikiy, translating the messages into Russian for the Soviet officers. The men stood in their red-star uniforms, scattered constellation-wide throughout the front room. Yael could see them cataloging the furniture, trying to determine how many of the Förstners' possessions originally belonged to slaughtered Soviets.

The minutes stretched. Yael kept finding things to say. Adolf Hitler's television speech started anew at least half a dozen times. Irmgard continued tapping answers out of the Enigma machine. Ernst made a tray of tea, complete with biscuits. Luka ate his share with great relish. ("Have you tried these?" He tossed one to Yael, which clipped her shoulder in a spray of crumbs. "*Worlds* better than veggie goo!") The Soviet officers grew increasingly restless, shifting their weight from boot to boot.

Comrade Commander Pashkov was the first to speak. "Ask what's waiting for us in Moscow. That's the reason we allowed this radio exchange, no?"

"Patience!" Yael snapped in Russian, even though her own supply was running short. She, too, wanted to know everything, but keeping Henryka informed was her priority. Who knew where her discoveries on Experiment 85 and Novosibirsk's army might lead?

But eventually she ran out of information to thread through the Enigma machine. It was time to

REQUEST A STATUS REPORT ON GERMANIA AND MOSCOW.

Henryka's messages began leaking in, painting a picture of a tipping-point landscape. Everything was on edge: pessimistic failed putsch, optimistic civil war. Hitler's resurrection had spooked a good number of Wehrmacht soldiers back into the National Socialists' ranks, but not enough to abandon all hope.

"What of the road to Moscow?" Comrade Fox Brows asked once Miriam finished translating the details of Germania. "How many National Socialist forces can we expect to encounter?"

It took five minutes to encode these questions, along with tactical facts. Another ten minutes passed before they received Henryka's best guess: Novosibirsk's army—with its numbers and equipment—should have no trouble reaching Moscow. Storming the Kremlin and demanding Reichskommissar Freisler's surrender would be more difficult, but possible.

"It's not the seizure of Moscow I'm worried about," one of the nameless comrade commanders offered. "None of this is of consequence if the National Socialist regime survives. Hitler won't suffer Moscow to remain in our hands."

"I agree with Comrade Commander Chekov," Pashkov said. "What chance does this revolution really have of succeeding?"

This same question was trapped with the biscuit crumbs

in Yael's teeth, looping alongside all of Irmgard's handwritten notes. There were so many different ways to word it: *Is victory possible? Can you hold out for six more days/weeks/months? How much red will it take?* Yael chose to transmit the most succinct option.

CAN WE WIN?

The pause was shorter than normal. When the Polish woman answered, she used codeless, full-flesh words: "I don't know. W-we weren't prepared for this. A putsch, certainly. A revolution, somewhat. But Hitler still alive, on the Reichssender, telling people they'll be crushed if they resist..."

Hitler's survival changes things. That's what Miriam had told Yael in the graveyard village. That's what Yael could see here, cast in the television's sickly glow. He'd always been monstrous, but now when Yael watched Hitler looming on the screen, she was reminded of the many-headed hydra she'd read about in a book on Greek mythology. Cut off a head and two more sprang back. Try to kill him once, twice, fifty times, and he only grew stronger, crippling entire nations with a single speech.

Hitler wasn't supposed to be the person who *changed things.* That had been Volchitsa's calling, the one Yael had tried—so hard—to fulfill with 20,780 kilometers of race and a ballroom bullet. But what had changed? The wrong man was dead, an even worse one was alive, and Yael sat beneath a chordless piano, feeling more helpless than she had in Tokyo's streets, running as the putsch ignited and exploded half a world away.

Back to code:

REINIGER PUSHING NORTHWEST TO OPEN NORTH SEA PORT FOR SUPPLY LINES AND BRITISH AID.

SS CALLING IN REINFORCEMENTS FROM SUBDUED
TERRITORIES. FÜHREREID DIVIDING WEHRMACHT.
DESERTION RATE GROWING.

"What is a—a *Führereid*?" Comrade Commander Pashkov
asked.

"It's a fealty oath," Yael explained in swift Russian. "Every
soldier in the Reich is required to swear unconditional obedience
to Adolf Hitler himself. One of the main ideas behind both the
first and the second Operation Valkyrie was that Hitler's death
would free the Wehrmacht soldiers from the *Führereid* and allow
them to choose new allegiances."

"Who would've thought the Germans would be so honor-
bound to their horrors," Pashkov muttered.

"Not all of them," Yael said. Not Erwin Reiniger. Not all the
other Wehrmacht officers who'd tossed away their Iron Cross rep-
utations for this plot. Not all the thousands of soldiers who'd made
the choice to stay and fight on the resistance's side of the Spree.

More letters were pouring in. A final diagnosis. Two
questions.

VICTORY IN GERMANIA REQUIRES MOMENTUM
SHIFT. IS NOVOSIBIRSK OUR ALLY? CAN TROOPS
BE SENT?

Yael held her breath as Miriam translated. The Soviet officers exchanged shorthand glances, *D-O-U-B-T* spelled out with
brown eyes and blue.

"Moscow is our priority," Comrade Commander Chekov
began. "We simply don't have enough resources to storm Germania *and* maintain our control over Muscovy. Even considering
the companies we're scheduled to meet in Novgorod."

Miriam's forehead furrowed, still ridged with piano-key indents. "What of the armies on their way to reclaim old Leningrad? Perhaps if we diverted them—"

"Is it even a feasible option?" asked one of the unnamed commanders. "How many weeks would it take our army to fight its way through the central Reich? Does General Reiniger have the resources to hold out that long?"

"What are they clucking about?" Luka's elbow mashed into an old photo of himself, 1955 issue, as he pushed himself up from his newspaper perch. "Am I the only one who could go for more biscuits? A wash would be nice, too. I'm all for natural musk, but this Eau de Muscovy Wilderness Trek is a bit much."

All seven Soviet officers stared at the double victor, Reich's face on top of *Das Reich*'s face. The room's very air was alert—as if electric charges had slipped away from their machines, into eyes and ears and veins.

"What did he say?" Comrade Fox Brows growled.

"He wants a bath," Yael explained. "You shouldn't worry. Victor Löwe doesn't understand Russian."

"But you do." The officer's red eyebrows twitched. "Forgive me, comrades, but I don't think we should be discussing such things in front of the prisoners. Nor is there any point in debating this until we've established an open line with Novosibirsk."

Several of the comrade commanders nodded. The radio crackled—Henryka waiting for an answer. The room's static anxiety started migrating onto Yael's skin, stiffening her arm hairs, wreathing through her wolves.

"Agreed," Chekov said. "Have one of the radio units brought here. Comrade Mnogolikiy will take over the communications with Germania. Contain the prisoners to the rear of the house. Allow them food and baths, but under no circumstance should they be permitted near this room."

Prisoners. After all this, they still thought of Yael as a threat. Yael, too, felt threatened, the adrenaline under her skin buzzing.

—DON'T LET THEM LOCK YOU AWAY—

She couldn't just sit here—captive to red tape and politics— while her friends died. "No! Let me stay and—"

Miriam stepped in front of her: a fresh scent of lilies, chin set to the side. Something in the way she moved—so deliberately in front of the comrade commanders' stares—killed Yael's argument, leaving its corpse right there in her throat.

"Remember what I told you," Miriam whispered in German. "Be careful. Play the prisoner. Let me take care of this."

Her third wolf was protecting her, the way she always had.

Slowly, slowly, Yael nodded.

————

PLEASE HOLD. MATTER IS BEING DISCUSSED.

CHAPTER 26

Felix was listening.

He lay on the floor between slanting towers of papers, pretending to be asleep. (It wasn't so difficult with the morphine weight against his lids.) He kept his eyes closed and his breathing light in order to eavesdrop on the radio conversation. Russian was beyond Felix, but the German parts—read aloud by a woman named Irmgard—were easy enough to understand. Felix clung to every detail he could. (Names: *Erwin Reiniger.* Plans: *Pushing northwest to a North Sea port.*) He'd need as much information as he could squirrel away to prove his loyalty to Baasch and ensure his family's safety.

If they were still alive.

If. Was there a more torturous word? A more free-fall feeling?

Felix wanted a solid *yes/no* answer to ground him. He wanted to walk over to that radio and make the call to SS-Standartenführer. He wanted to hear Papa's voice, Mama's weeping. He wanted to explain to Baasch that he was still trying to fix things....

A peek through hazed eyelashes showed Felix that the radio was in touching distance, but there'd be no reaching it. The girl and the others kept talking. German and Russian swirled through the musty ink air like a pair of dueling sparrows: all clatter and chat. Voices rose and fell and rose and fell until finally Luka said something about a wash, and Felix's stretcher was carried out of the room and into the hallway.

Taxidermy animals glared down with glass eyes and useless fangs. Crooked frames—holding not portraits but honest-to-goodness insects—punctuated the wall space between bookshelves. And...

Was that a telephone?

Felix couldn't be certain. The stretcher-bearer guards were carrying him too fast—already they were turning a corner, setting him down on the floor—but it sure looked like it. Squat-toad shape, black as some of the beetles pinned in those pictures.

If the guards left him here alone. If Felix could get out into the hall undetected. If the telephone was actually a telephone. If he could spin its rotary dial through the number Baasch had made him memorize. If he could connect with the SS-Standartenführer's office and explain. *If, if, if...*

But as soon as the guards' boots scuffed away, Luka's burst in. The victor flopped onto the bed and started sloughing off his shoes. The first boot hit the ground, its open end and...fruitful...smells too close to Felix's face.

The mechanic coughed.

Luka paused. "You awake, Wonderboy? Need any morphine?"

The drug *was* starting to wear off. Felix's pain, both phantom and real, refused to be killed. He felt it flickering in the empty space above his right hand, swelling, hotter and hotter, against his bandage. Soon it'd be searing enough to make him sweat.

Another dose of morphine might take away Felix's pain, but it would also make him sleep. He couldn't risk missing his chance to reach the telephone just because some of his nerve endings wouldn't accept their own death.

"No."

"Suit yourself." Luka yanked off the second boot, dragged the first a civilized distance away from Felix's face, and set both by the bed. "I'm going to scout out the kitchen situation. I'll bring you back a ham or something."

Felix watched the victor's blistered heels slip out the door. He waited a moment, then another, and another... but no one else came into the bedroom.

He was alone.

It was impossible to tell, simply by sound, if the hallway was empty. This house had an old man's body—creaking and groaning at every joint. Were those guards pacing the floorboards outside? Or years of arctic winters making themselves heard? Or wildlife ghosts trotting beneath their stuffed heads?

The image of Eurasian lynxes pacing down the hall, of moose knocking stacks of novels to the floor with velvet antlers, made Felix smile. The expression felt strange, almost cracked, against his cheeks. It vanished as soon as he rolled from the stretcher (PAIN) and used the bedpost to pull himself up (MORE PAIN). Felix could tell as soon as he stood that he wasn't supposed to. His legs were jelly, and the floor slanted at odd angles beneath his every step. The bedroom was small—three, maybe four, full strides across—but what should've taken seconds became a journey of minutes. His route was roundabout, making use of whatever support his good hand could find: walls, wardrobe corners, a side table with an unfinished game of chess.

Felix was just half a step away from the door when his balance faltered. His arms flailed, trying to find something, anything, to steady him, and caught the edge of the chessboard. Thirty-two pieces—kings, queens, knights, pawns—clattered across the floor. Felix fell with them. The ground's impact tore his breath from his lungs. He lay stunned, amid chess-fall and boot-stink.

"Felix?"

He looked up to find the girl—Yael—standing in the doorway, freshly bathed. Wet hair fell, near-translucent, around her face. The bloodstains and dirt of days were gone, as were her scabs. Her bruises had taken on a less violent greenish tinge. Even her clothing was softer: a lumpy, knitted sweater that looked like something Felix's mother might have made. Back in the time before. Its sleeves were too long, dragging across the girl's knuckles as she helped Felix into a sitting position.

"What happened?" Her eyes darted through the chess-piece casualties, landed back on Felix. (So sad. So bright. Too sad. Too bright.) Could she *see* him? Did she know what Felix had done? What he planned to do?

Don't look at the door. Don't think about the telephone behind it. Easier thought than done. Had it been this difficult for her—a liar in Wolfe's clothing—hiding in plain sight? What had been going on behind Adele's face, Adele's eyes, when they camped in the evening sands, when he'd told her how much her family needed her? When she lifted her P38 and lashed it—red-hard—across his skull?

Felix clenched his teeth. Echoes of both pistol-whippings gathered at the edge of his jaw. "I tried walking."

"Oh, Felix—" Yael's lips pressed together, full of emotion he could only guess at: Stress? Suspicion? *Sorry?* "You've just experienced a major trauma. You should be resting."

"It's hard to rest with...everything that's happened." *Don't look at the door. Don't think about SS-Standartenführer Baasch waiting for your call.* "I don't like sitting on my hands. Never have."

"I've gathered that. Though I'd hardly call recovering from an amputation sitting on your hands." She studied him. Her lips stayed tight. "Your face is looking better, at least."

"Yours, too. If it *is* yours." These last words stung, a little too true to what Felix felt inside. Gloves off, primal temper. He mustn't let the girl *see* such raw emotions. It was his turn to take these things and twist them into something she wanted to hear. "It's not the easiest to keep track of."

"This face isn't mine, but it isn't anyone else's either." Yael cleared her throat. "I know I have a lot of explaining to do. How much did the SS tell you about me?"

"Only that you can manipulate your appearance. They weren't much for chatting," Felix recalled. "The interrogation was pretty one-sided. None-sided, really. They kept trying to kick answers I didn't know out of me. All I had to give them was the dogs, and I—I didn't want to"—*lies, lies, all lies*—"but it hurt so much, and I just wanted the pain to stop."

"Dogs?"

228

"On your arm." He nodded at her sweater sleeve. "The tattoo."

Yael pushed the tangled knots of yarn up her forearm to show him. "They're wolves."

So they were. He could see that now that he was closer.

"Wolves are Hitler's favorite animal," Felix told her. It was a vomit fact, spouted out of habit. When they were younger, Adele used to convey the knowledge to anyone who'd listen, her chest puffed with pride that the Führer's sacred creature was also her surname. The coincidence inspired appropriate awe from their classmates, who *ooh*ed and *aah*ed in the school's play yard.

Yael did no such thing.

"We see different things in the creature." She tugged her sleeve back down.

"Sorry." Another reflexive, bile word. (Why should *Felix* be sorry?) "Adele used to brag about that fact a lot. But I suppose you already knew that."

"I'm a skinshifter. Not a psychic." The girl finally dropped her eyes from him and began picking up chess pieces. "That would've made the mission a whole lot easier. I studied your sister for a year: memorized all her school papers, her habits, her Hitler Youth records. I learned every single fact I could about you and Martin and your mama and papa. I know more about your family than I know about my own."

Martin. Mama. Papa. The girl's voice had changed—it was huskier than his sister's—but she still said these names with the twist of the real Adele's accent. As if she, too, were a Wolfe.

It was the wrong sort of closeness: one-sided, none-sided. It made Felix bristle.

"I learned everything I could about Adele so I'd be able to take her place in the race." The girl kept talking, collecting pawns and bishops and rooks. "The night before the Axis Tour, I snuck into your sister's flat, knocked her unconscious, and changed my face to match hers. Adele was taken back to the resistance's headquarters. She's been held there ever since."

Felix felt his heart skip, then rev as sudden as a fuel-flooded engine. His sister at least was alive!

Yael went on. "When you showed up in the Olympiastadion, I thought for certain my cover was blown. That's why I tried to knock you out of the race before Cairo. You were endangering yourself just as much as the mission. If you'd gone back home to Frankfurt, you would've been taken with your parents to a safe house by some resistance operatives after I shot the Führer."

At this, Felix's pulse swerved, crashed. Everything he knew and everything he hoped were colliding, exploding in an irreconcilable ball of flames.

Gestapo torture → BOOM ← Resistance safe house

It took every ounce of Felix's discipline not to let the shock reach his expression. He kept his face very, very still while taking stock of hers. "A-a safe house? Mama and Papa are in a safe house?"

"Of course. They're with my friend Vlad. There's no safer place in Europe. Trust me." Her gaze looked true. Her words sounded earnest.

They would, Felix reminded himself. *She's an excellent actress.*

But Yael had no reason to lie about this, and Felix had every need to believe her.

Trust me or his own eardrums? Papa's voice, Mama's tears. He'd heard them, as certain and devastating as the pain in his fingers....

"I tried so hard to make you go home. I didn't want to leave you behind in the Imperial Palace, especially with the SS swarming everywhere." There was that sorrow again: Sadness with more facets than a diamond glinted behind Yael's stare. She was looking at Felix's pink oozing bandages, the ugly gape after his middle finger.

Maybe it was not *all lies*. Maybe she *was* sorry....

But was she right?

Felix didn't see how she could be. (Papa had talked to him on the telephone, for God's sake!) The tricky thing about hope, however, was that it was an emotion immune to logic, and now Felix was hooked, dangling on the end of its thin string.

If the resistance had his family...that changed things. A lot of things.

"You had the world to worry about," Felix said slowly, recalling their conversation. How much was broken, what could and could not be fixed. How many times would he revisit that room, see it afresh?

1: Adele, too stubborn to listen. Felix, trying to keep things from breaking.

2: The girl, not giving a *Scheisse* about the Wolfes. Felix, trying to save them.

3: Yael, trying to fix the world. Felix, the one too stubborn to listen.

God, he missed the auto shop—spark plug swaps, straightforward engines. Nothing nearly as complicated as this: trying to sort right from wrong and truth from lie and what the hell would keep his family safe in this bloodful world.

"If I'd known about the safe house, I wouldn't have tried to stop you." Was *this* the truth? Maybe. Maybe not. It was what Felix needed Yael to believe.

It also seemed to be what she wanted to hear. "You're a good brother, Felix. A good son, too. Your family is fortunate to have you."

"Can you take me to them?" Even if his parents weren't in the safe house, Adele was definitely in the resistance headquarters— the exact place Felix needed to be. All *ifs* aside. Salvation or damnation.

Yael frowned. "I don't know."

"I know I'm a…burden now, but I'll earn my way," he said. "The resistance needs mechanics, don't they?"

"It's not that. Technically, we're the Soviets' prisoners. My friend Miriam is negotiating on our behalf, but I have no idea when or *if* they'll decide to release us."

"Please," Felix pressed. "Just promise me you'll try."

Yael said nothing. She set all the gathered chess pieces on the floor between them. Her hand dipped into her pants' pocket, came back with something silver and heartbreaking. Martin's pocket watch—beaten and battered and finally broken. When she set the timepiece in Felix's palm, he didn't try to open it. His left hand did not feel strong enough, and he already knew what he'd find if he did: hands frozen in place behind cracked glass, trapped in a time that no longer existed.

How had it come to this?

How had *he* come to this?

"Felix Burkhard Wolfe." The way the girl knew his full name (and used it) sent shivers through Felix's spinal column. "I promise I'll do everything in my power to get you to Germania. I will get you back to your family."

CHAPTER 27

It was well into evening when Yael was summoned back to the front room. The place was even more cluttered than before; several newspaper stacks had been shoved aside to accommodate the Soviets' radio unit, along with its operators. The pile of papers next to the Enigma machine had grown fivefold, all covered in Miriam's handwriting: Henryka's back-and-forth negotiations with Novosibirsk. Yael was too far away to see what they said.

The aimless/fidgety/lost feeling tailed Yael as she entered the room. She had no idea where to stand, and it didn't help that all seven Soviet officers were staring her down in that nerveless way of theirs. Yael's eyes were quick to seek Miriam's. Her friend stood by the piano, hands folded, face firm as she nodded.

Be brave, that gold gaze seemed to say. *Anything is possible.*

Comrade Commander Chekov was the first to speak. "Have a seat, Comrade Volchitsa."

Comrade. Not prisoner. Yael took note of this as she sat down on Luka's old *Das Reich* dais. The newspapers sagged under her weight.

Once she was settled, Chekov continued talking. "As you can see, we've been in contact with Novosibirsk and Germania, trying to decide on a course of action that would be beneficial for both contingents. It took some negotiating, but we've agreed on a solution.

"You and Comrade Mnogolikiy are to return to Germania and assassinate Adolf Hitler."

The room went silent. Yael realized that the television had been switched off. The electronic Führer was gone, and so was the buzz, buzz, hate of his words. Yael saw herself reflected in the screen: a girl cramped down by the shock of this announcement. The circuitousness of it.

Again. They wanted her to kill Adolf Hitler again.

"The resistance's main obstacle to victory is the desertion of its Wehrmacht fighters," Chekov went on. "If the Führer were eliminated, as originally planned, the *Führereid* would be lifted, and General Reiniger's forces would grow. Not only this, but your resistance friends have Hermann Göring in custody. He's second-in-command in the National Socialist Party, Hitler's natural successor. Once the real Hitler is dead, Göring will be forced to announce his resignation and appoint Reiniger in his place, a position he could claim with the Wehrmacht's full support. The National Socialist government would be dismantled from there. Novosibirsk's claim on the Muscovy territories would remain unthreatened.

"All this is in the transcripts if you wish to see them," Chekov added, gesturing toward the Enigma papers littered at the piano leg's base.

Yael didn't need to read the notes. This might not be the

verdict she'd expected, but it made sense. Novosibirsk would only sacrifice one of its soldiers (as opposed to thousands upon thousands). Erwin Reiniger's transition into power would be seamless, backed by the full weight of the Wehrmacht. Even the SS would be rattled....

Hitler's survival changes things.

So change it back.

It wasn't helplessness that filled Yael's veins, weighing her down as she stared darkly through the television glass. Not this time. No—what rose through her blood was the wolf-fierce, the Valkyrie-calling, the clang of her iron voice:

—ALL OVER AGAIN TAKE THE SHOT KILL THE REAL BASTARD HIS DEATH CAN END THIS—

"Yael?" It was only after Miriam spoke that Yael realized she'd been staring at the screen, wordless, for a while now.

"We need to make sure we kill the right Hitler, the real Hitler. We know now that the Führer's been using skinshifter decoys for public appearances. He wasn't shot in the ball-room. He probably wasn't even shot in the Grosser Platz." The thought of Aaron-Klaus firing those four shots (all for nothing) tore through Yael's every word. "If we manage to infiltrate the *Führerbunker,* we're probably only going to get one shot at killing the man himself. We need to be one hundred percent certain our target is the genuine artifact. Not a skinshifter."

"You're absolutely right." Miriam nodded. "Which is why we need to retrieve as much information as we possibly can on Hitler's face-changer decoys before we go forward with any assassination plans."

"But where would we..." Yael's mouth went dry, and there

was a burning under her skin not so unlike the one those needles had placed there over a decade ago. *How are you feeling?* she could hear Dr. Geyer asking through his too-stretched smile. Instead of listening to the girl's answer, he flipped through the notes of his clipboard: all of Yael's suffering reduced to letters and dates.

She knew exactly where they'd find information on the Führer's decoys. In the heart of the red lands, where the train tracks ended and the stacks of smoke began, behind layers and layers of barbed-wire gates, along the path lined with poplar trees, inside the building made of neatly stacked bricks, down the hall, and into the office where the Angel of Death had been laboring all these years, waiting for her to return.

There. The place she did not want to go again.

Miriam had come to this conclusion as well. "If anyone knows the details of Hitler's face-changing substitutes, it will be Dr. Engel Geyer." She stated this in her military voice: bullet-proof, every emotion bouncing off it. "Henryka looked through her records. The doctor is still working in the camp."

Of course he was still there, cutting children open with no remorse, and oh, how Yael's blood boiled to think of it!

"Once you and Comrade Mnogolikiy gather all the intelligence you need on the other face-changers, you'll return to the resistance's headquarters and use the resources there to sort out the final details of the assassination," Chekov told Yael. "I trust we have your full cooperation?"

—*CHANGE THINGS HOPE HOPE FIGHT*—

Boil, boil, up and over, hot-froth anger, spilling into Yael's words.

"When do we leave?" she asked.

CHAPTER 28

Yael's first mission had taken an entire year of planning: The intricacies of racing across Europe, Africa, and Asia to assassinate the Führer had been ironed out over months. Drawing up the details of this new mission had been reduced to a mere thirty-six hours.

Forging citizenship papers was easier than ever with Molotov's Reich office at their disposal. All it took were a few minutes of typing and a few photographs cut out of old identity papers and pasted into the new ones. Yael and Miriam created aliases for every territory they planned on passing. A collection of faces, names, birth dates, and hometowns that would be plausible for any area where a patrol might stop them.

Getting the boys through the Muscovy territories and the central Reich undetected was a different matter. Adding Felix and Luka to their roster made things infinitely harder. Miriam opposed the addition—vocally, vehemently—but Yael stood her ground. Even though Miriam insisted the boys would be safe in

Molotov, Yael could not get the sight of the executed soldiers out of her head. Piled mountain high. Weeping blood in streams. If she left the boys here, she would not rest easy.

Besides, Yael had a promise to keep.

Luka wasn't quite as immediately recognizable with his face half covered in beard, but even facial hair couldn't disguise that he was the double victor. Poster boy. Wanted the Reich over.

Felix's face wasn't that far behind in notoriety, and even after eight razorless days, it looked as hairless as before.

A solution to the boys' very recognizable, very unchangeable appearances presented itself in the form of a truck. It was the sort of vehicle you didn't look twice at: body pocked with rust flecks from harsh taiga winters, meant for transporting crops and other goods between cities. It had also been used by Molotov's resistance cell to transport less legal packages (and people) in a hollow compartment beneath the truck bed's boards. The space was shallow, and smelled overwhelmingly of engine grease. It was a testament to how much Felix wanted to get back to his family that he was willing to hide in the space.

When Luka saw the truck's cracked windshield, he made a face. When he saw the compartment he'd have to share with Felix, he groaned. "And I thought the ZIS-5 ride was rough."

"You can stay here if you want," Yael told him.

Luka raised his eyebrows. "You trying to get rid of me, Fräulein?"

"It's going to be dangerous." Crossing 3,300 kilometers through war-strung territory with only a rusted truck and a few pages of papers was insanity. Not to mention their..."pit stop"...as Yael had come to think of the first portion of their mission. Stealing the identities of female overseers, walking back inside death's jaws, and prying out a few teeth...

More than dangerous.

Deadly.

Too many things could go wrong. Would, if statistics had any say in the matter. Luka was smart. The boy must've known this, but all he did was shrug. "Staying here with a bunch of soldiers who want to shoot me on sight doesn't seem much safer. Besides, someone has to keep sticking Herr Wolfe full of morphine so he doesn't scream again."

Sensible reasoning aside, Yael was happy that Luka was coming. She'd grown used to the victor's company. His deflective remarks, his sneers, all those faint, shimmering threads of emotions kept snapping and restringing between them.

"I'm sure you'll be a wonderful nurse." She bit back a smile.

It was a good thing Felix was acrophobic instead of claustrophobic. Miriam insisted they fit as many munitions as they could into the gaps—just in case. Both boys lying together in the hidden compartment was a tight squeeze. Shoulder to shoulder inside a nest of rifles, pistols, and boxes of bullets swaddled in a waterproof tarp. The sight was unsettling.

Even more unsettling was when Yael had to slide the wood paneling shut, drawing a dark, dark shadow over the boys' bodies. She hesitated at the very last moment, letting her stare linger with the light. Both boys met it.

Felix nodded.

Luka winked.

They filled the truck bed with sacks of potatoes. By the time the transport was fully loaded, it bowed a few extra centimeters from the weight. Yael eyed its worn tires, hoping they'd be able to handle the muddy back roads she and Miriam would be favoring. Herr Förstner assured her they would.

"Ten years and this beauty hasn't failed us. She'd carry you all the way to the heart of Germania and back if you wanted." He gave the truck a solid pound with his fist.

Luka thumped back in double time.

Miriam stood by the cab door. She hadn't changed faces yet, but she already looked like a different person. Her Soviet uniform was gone, replaced by Mary Janes and hosiery and a fine knit sweater. Clothes more suited to a Lebensraum bride. Yael, too, was wearing a skirt, fighting the scratch of the stockings against her leg. The outfit Irmgard had scrounged up for her was far from comfortable, but at least it was lumpy enough to conceal the old TT-33 pistol Miriam had given her. There was makeup, too—skin-colored powder dashed all over Yael's ebbing bruises. She was the picture of Aryan health.

"Are you ready?" asked her third wolf in the flesh.

Ready? It was the same question Kasper had posed to Yael in the van outside Adele's building. She'd laughed at the operative and said *More than* before plunging into the victor's flat.

Yael was not laughing now. Her own sweater sleeves hung a little too far down her arm, tickling her knuckles; other wolf memories prickled beneath them. Mama, Babushka, Aaron-Klaus. She did not know if she was ready to return to these outside of Vlad's exercises. Enduring nightmares was so different from stepping back into the past. Foot to stone. Heart to hurt.

Yet it was not just the dead and their memories who depended on her, but the living. The Wolfe who needed his family. The general who needed an army. Countless countries that needed to be reborn.

Because of these, Yael hitched up her skirt and climbed into the cab of the truck.

She was not ready, but she was going.

She was going back to the beginning to find an end.

She was going to find the Führer. The *real* Führer.

She was going to finish what she'd started.

INTERLUDE

THREE PORTRAITS OF
APRIL 2, 1955

I

Early April saw the cemetery as a cold, unsung place. Its trees were more bare than not, clawing at an overcast dawn. The gray of the stones had bled out across the rest of the landscape. Grass, gravel, ground ... even the air felt dimmed as Felix breathed in.

He was early this year. Usually when he came to visit Martin, spring had a firmer hold on the world. May 2's warmth and flowers made the whole visit bearable. But today the weather leeched the life from Felix's bones as he walked through rows of angels and crosses. Some stones were worn beyond reading. Others tumbled to the ground altogether.

The marker Felix was looking for was still standing, still readable. The summation of his brother's existence etched into its granite:

MARTIN WILLMAR WOLFE
BELOVED SON. REMEMBERED BROTHER.
15 OCTOBER 1934 — 2 MAY 1950

When Felix reached it, he stopped, fingers curled into fists in his pockets. Martin's absence was always there—leaning alongside Felix as he worked on Volkswagen engines, cramming into the Wolfes' church pew, hovering around the rare family dinner. But the gravestone always hit Felix with the finality of it.

Martin. Beloved. Remembered. Gone.

He liked to think that (somewhere, somehow) his brother could hear him. So once a year Felix came to talk.

"Hello, Martin."

His brother said nothing.

"I know you weren't expecting me today, but this year has been different."

Different. The least inflammatory word he could think of to describe his twin sister trimming her hair into a perfect imitation of Felix's curtained haircut with their mother's sewing scissors and father's razor. It was eerie how much he felt as if he were staring at himself when Adele held out her hand for his papers.

"I'm racing in the Axis Tour," she'd told him. "If anyone comes checking for me, Papa can tell them I'm ill. You'll need to stay hidden to maintain my cover."

He'd wanted to tell her no. He should have. But that had never been the way things were between the twins, so Felix gave Adele his documents and promised to keep out of sight.

For the majority of the Axis Tour, Felix had stayed indoors—blinds shut, shadows heavy—watching himself race across the world. Reichssender footage tended to highlight the race at its best and its worst. During the first few days, they hadn't focused much on Felix Burkhard Wolfe, the sixteen-year-old from

Frankfurt with fair times. He was neither a victor nor an underdog. Plus, he was oddly camera shy.

As the days passed, the number of Axis Tour racers dwindled, as it always did, but interest in Felix Wolfe began to climb. The racer had managed to stay at the head of the pack, keeping pace with Victor Löwe and Victor Tsuda through accidents, alliances, and attempted sabotage.

By the third week, the race was tight, and as a result, the wrecks grew nastier. Just a few days ago, outside Hanoi, one of the German racers (seventeen-year-old Georg Rust) had been edged off the road into a rice paddy, an accident that cost the rider his leg. The incident had been caught on camera. Georg— a black-and-white blur—flying along with his Zündapp before being crushed into the mud. The first time Felix saw it, he was breathless. The fifth time, he felt sick. By the tenth showing, all he could see was the past and the future:

Martin flying, crushed on the Nürburgring racetrack.

Adele flying, crushed on the road to Tokyo.

Felix's insides flew with the fear of it all, crushed by the weight of his own helplessness.

It would all be over soon. The racers had left the *Kaiten* and were navigating the final leg. A few more hours and a winner would emerge to claim the victory of 1955. The Reichssender was abuzz with projections. A severe stomach flu had knocked front-runner Tsuda Katsuo out of the race. Victor Löwe was ahead, set to claim the tour's first double victory, but Felix Wolfe was close on his tail.

"Anything can happen," one of the Reichssender hosts had said, "when racers are desperate enough."

This was exactly what the real Felix, watching from the tiny family room in Frankfurt, feared. He knew he should keep his promise to Adele, stay inside just a little longer. But his nerves were getting the better of him, and he just couldn't. Three weeks of watching, waiting, not knowing whether his sister was dead on the road had worn Felix thin. He needed a distraction that wasn't the Reichssender, so he'd come at the loneliest hour to the loneliest place, where only the crows might see him. Where only the dead might hear . . .

Though it was not May 2, Felix kept to the other tradition of his annual vigil: talking. He sat by Martin's grave and told his brother about every Wolfe and the year they'd had. There was Mama's sadness—shut-door days that piled into themselves—and long pre–Axis Tour hours in the garage with Papa, who could no longer hold a wrench like he used to. In the wake of Adele's departure, both symptoms had grown worse. Neither of his parents would look at the television screen, for fear of flash-forward ghosts, though every night at supper, Papa asked for news of Adele's standings. His voice was quiet, his eyes crinkled with pride.

Felix—tender-treading ambassador that he was—offered his parents the highly edited version. He left out the sudden drop in Adele's time on the road from Hanoi to Shanghai. Georg Rust's ruined life and severed leg were *definitely* not mentioned. . . .

All these things he saved for Martin. "She's somewhere in Japan now, second only to Victor Löwe."

Anything can happen. . . .

Felix needed to keep talking, stay distracted, not think about it. But the only Wolfe left to talk about was Felix himself.

And—as it happened every year—when Felix reached his own story, he never knew what to say. He supposed if Martin really *could* hear him (somehow, somewhere), then his brother knew everything already.

In fact, he was probably watching Adele now. Seeing everything Felix couldn't.

"Keep her safe." It was not the dead's job, but Felix tasked it anyway. His words climbed up into air, sky, nothing.

Not even the wind answered.

II

Japan in the springtime was breathtaking. Its skies wiped clear of clouds and roads lined with flowering cherry trees, pink and white blossoms dusting the pavement like snow.

The Axis Tour of 1955 marked Luka Löwe's fourth drive down this very stretch of asphalt. But it was the first time he'd *really* noticed the beauty of the trees. Maybe this was because he was going a touch slower than normal, keeping pace with the racer beside him.

Felix Wolfe. This was how the rest of the competitors (and officials and the Reichssender) knew him. But—as Luka had discovered so abruptly in a washroom at the Rome checkpoint— he was a she. Adele was her name, and a beautiful one at that. It rolled off the tongue so easily, and Luka loved saying it. He couldn't, mostly, because of Adele's secret (the one he swore to keep), but at night, when it was just the two of them camped out under the stars, he said it as often as he could: *Adeleadeleadele.* Until his tongue was tired and the sound of the name lost all meaning.

But it was still beautiful.

Beautiful name. Beautiful girl. Beautiful world full of cherry trees.

Luka was not driving as fast as he had during the previous years, but something inside him felt like it was flying. The joy of getting a red bicycle times ten. Ever since discovering Adele's secret and agreeing to keep it, ever since forging an alliance with her, this emotion had been building inside him. Up, up, up, to the point of bursting.

He couldn't not feel it. He tried everything he could not to show it, but it was almost impossible to stop the twitch of his mouth—smiles the mere thought of Adele conjured. Whenever Luka sat down in front of the Reichssender cameras, though, he imagined his father was watching. That kept the filmed grins to a minimum.

There were no cameras on this stretch of road. Hardly any other racers either. (Most had stopped for rations over an hour earlier.) Nothing to stop him from grinning ear to ear like a sloppy drunk as he rode alongside this girl, who was so very different from any of the fräuleins he'd known in Hamburg.

Adele revved her engine just enough to pull a few meters ahead, one hand free, gesturing to the side of the road. Then she slowed her Zündapp to a halt, parking it in a fairy-tale landscape of spent cherry blossoms.

He didn't *need* to break, but a deep part of Luka wanted to. They were on the outskirts of Osaka, a little over five hundred kilometers from the finish line—hours away after weeks of riding—and he was far enough ahead of the other racers that a short pit stop would do no harm. Even Adele was a good ten minutes behind him in cumulative time. Luka would have to part ways with her soon, pulling ahead just enough to make sure his entrance into Tokyo was a triumphant one.

Everything would change, once he won. The Reichssender would be all over him, and Adele Wolfe would be forced to melt silently back into her Frankfurt life. It might be weeks, months before he'd see her again, which was why Luka decided to pump his brakes.

He parked his own Zündapp just a meter from the road, unclipping his helmet and uncramping his legs. Adele stretched her svelte frame as she hopped off her motorcycle, removed her own helmet, and gave her short Hitler Youth hair a shake. Luka couldn't help but stare (beautiful girl, moonstruck thoughts) and wonder how he'd ever thought those bold cheekbones and comet-trail eyebrows belonged to a boy.

Adele caught him staring and grinned at him through her racing goggles. The smile was contagious. Luka couldn't help but return it.

"You wanted to stop and smell the sakura?" he asked.

"They are pretty." Her gloved fingers reached up to the nearest branch, twisting a flower free. Its petals quivered as she held them up to her nose. Inhaled. "Not much of a smell, though."

Luka watched the blossom, so close to her lips, and wished he could be in its place....

Adele blew an extra-hard breath out, which sent the cherry blossom tumbling to the ground. "You got any of that jerky left? All I have are protein bars."

Luka knew he did, somewhere in the depths of his panniers. He turned to unbuckle them.

"I could use a little extra fuel before Tokyo," Adele explained.

Tokyo. If Luka shut his eyes, he could feel it: the cheering crowds and smooth tarmac. The ripple of his Zündapp's wheels as he rolled over the finish line, repeated his triumph of 1953.

Luka Löwe. Double victor. Hero of the Third Reich. Tough as leather, hard as steel. Worthy.

He was so busy imagining this scene, digging through his possessions for the jerky packet, that he didn't give a second thought to the footsteps behind him—*SMASH*. PAIN. Bluuuuuuuuuuuur.

BLACK.

When Luka woke, the cherry tree branches smeared above him: a windless pink haze. His temple throbbed, and when his hand ventured to the back of his skull, there was a stinging that made him string together several non-mother-approved words. The fingertips returned weeping red.

He hadn't known a head could hurt this much.

When Luka finally stood, the spinning above him moved into his stomach. And back up again. He was still wiping bile from his lips when he found himself looking for Adele. (Was she okay? Had she been attacked, too?) But there was no fräulein behind him. No motorcycle either. Just tender-colored blossoms, crushed by the tread of Adele's tires. Luka stood still for several minutes, taking in the emptiness of the roadside. Trying not to move. Trying not to vomit again.

He hadn't known a heart could hurt this much.

III

Yael crouched in the barn loft, body pressed to a hay bale. Knife in hand. Still, still as she eyed her target: felt fedora and black trench coat. There was a five-meter drop and a two-meter leap between them. Enough to put even her hardened muscles to the test. She edged as quietly as she could to the ledge, her blade curved downward.

—BE SILENT BE SWIFT BE SOARING—

She jumped.

It was a full leap, calculated to exact degrees of strength and distance. Yael landed a breath away from the coattails, knees unlocked and forgiving. The knife kept moving as the rest of her stopped, plunging deep into the fabric. One, two, three quick strokes to her target's vitals: kidney, liver, heart.

The dummy fell face-first. Straw innards poking from the holes she'd put there. Yael gave its gut a sharp, rustling kick and looked over at Vlad. Her trainer leaned against the cow stall, arms crossed. His face was as stony as he'd taught hers to be.

"It was a good jump," he grunted. "You hit all the right marks. Technically flawless."

"But?" Yael could sense the word coming—in the brevity of his sentences, the clip of his stance—so she decided to preempt it.

Vlad stepped forward. "Straw is just straw. Blood is a different matter."

Yael sheathed her blade and looked down at the dummy, trying to imagine the *different matter* spilling out at her feet. "You think I'll freeze up? I've seen blood before."

(Blood, too much blood. Rivers, floods, and seas of blood.)

"I know." Her trainer's voice went soft.

"I won't hesitate, when it comes to it." Yael's eyes lingered on the swastika badge Vlad had pinned onto the dummy's coat for effect. "You've trained me too well for that."

And he had. Vlad was a master at killing—he'd done it time and time again over the course of two wars and three decades for two different governments. During her three years on his farm, the ex-operative had taught Yael everything he knew about the art. Shooting, stabbing, strangling. The last thing she expected him to say was this: "Don't be so eager. It's no easy thing, killing a person."

"The National Socialists have no problem with it," Yael said, voice harsh with blood thoughts. The ones she tried, so very hard, not to dwell on. The ones that always caught up with her anyway.

"Do you really want to be like them?"

Vlad's question stung almost as much as the blows he'd dealt her in their first-year sparring sessions. It took all of Yael's training not to flinch or bristle or yell at her trainer for asking something like this. For even *thinking* something like this.

Like them. She was not like them. She was never like them. Wasn't that why there were numbers on her arm? Wasn't that why she was fighting?

Yael gestured down at the dummy instead. "Then why teach me any of this?"

Late-morning sunlight slanted through the barn walls' gaps, filled in the faults and scarps of Vlad's features as he knelt down, propped the dummy up. "Because this land is ruled by National Socialists. And you, Yael, were never meant to be a sheep."

She knew that. She'd known that ever since she cracked open Henryka's encyclopedia to the entry on Valkyries. Winged shield maidens. Powerful warriors who did not die, but were bearers of death. Who stood in the smoke and ruin of men's battles and chose the living from the damned.

Those were the women Yael wanted to be like.

"You're one of my best students, and you are going to be an even better operative. I'm only telling you this because I wish it was something my trainer had told me. Living by the sword catches up to you. One way or another." Vlad's good eye tightened; his empty eye socket (the scar he never talked about) twitched alongside. "All these skills I've taught you—they're burdens. Not gifts. Taking a life takes something from you. When you choose to kill, make sure it is for the right reasons. Make sure the decision is something you can live with."

Yael didn't know what to say, so she merely nodded. Vlad nodded back and pointed to the hayloft: "Again."

Wisdom imparted. Death made heavy. That was that.

That should have been that. But Vlad's words kept tumbling inside Yael. Jump after jump. Stab after stab. They

stayed with her through evening chores and their supper of
bread and stew. They lingered above her as she lay awake in
her bunk, nursing the day's collection of bruises and burning
muscles.

Taking a life takes something from you.

Do you really want to be like them?

But Vlad's were not the only words standing watch. There
were heavier ones. Spoken by the dead, a boy who'd once slept in
this very bunk.

*Someone has to do it. Step up and change things. Kill the
bastard.*

She'd come here, to the farm, to learn of life/knives/
bullets/death because of what Aaron-Klaus had said. Her friend,
her martyr, was right. How else would this terrible kingdom of
death fall unless someone stepped forward? Put an end to it.

But Vlad was right, too. Death was not her ally. Yael needed
rules to set her apart from the National Socialists. Guidelines
that would keep her akin to the Valkyrie.

It took some hours of lost sleep (Yael knew she'd pay for it
during her morning run), but she finally drew up a plan.

- No innocents.
- Those who tried to stop her would be stopped.
- Those who had information she needed and refused
  to give it to her would be hurt.

Everyone she fought would be weighed against these rules.
All except one. Because Yael already knew that when she came
face-to-face with the Führer, she would kill him.

It was a choice she would live with.

PART III

LAND OF ASHES

CHAPTER 29

"Papers, please."

The SS-Schütze who rapped on the window and held out his hand did not look particularly suspicious. Why would he? Two small blond women in a rusted farm truck overloaded with potatoes was the least-threatening thing he'd seen all week.

Yael knew their situation could change in a heartbeat. One wrong word, one too-loud whimper from Felix, one slip of her sweater sleeve, one smudge of her makeup, and all would fall apart. She was careful to—*KEEP SMILING MOVE SLOW*—as she rolled down the glass and reached into her sweater for her alias's papers, fingers brushing the TT-33's cold metal.

"Of course." She handed the documents over.

There was an SS-Schütze at Miriam's window as well, combing through her papers. Two more manned the traffic blockade. Yael could see another in the rearview mirror, circling the truck bed. He'd already cut open one of the potato sacks and was impaling the rest with his knife. Stab, stab, sharp, sick sounds.

The man reading Yael's false papers frowned. For a moment she feared she'd given him the wrong set (wrong face, wrong name, wrong birthplace, wrong, wrong, wrong), but all he said was, "There's been a lot of fighting going on. Two young fräuleins traveling alone—it's not safe."

"We haven't come far."

Not Yael's first lie or her biggest, but still untrue. The odometer had slotted new numbers into place close to three thousand times since departing Molotov. Nearly seventy-five hours had passed. Seventy-five agonizing hours of constant, trade-off driving on Yael's and Miriam's part. All *go*, little sleep. Felix and Luka hadn't fared much better. The boys were just as jostled as their potato cargo. The drive should have been faster—under average circumstances, the trip would've taken only two days.

But nothing about this journey was normal. Muddy back roads, strings of refugees, countless detours, battles unfolding... With Henryka's instructions, Miriam's map of back roads, and a bit of luck, they'd managed to avoid the larger cities, where bullets were still flying. Some of the smaller towns were unavoidable, most draped in the same chaos that had befallen Molotov: burnt buildings, smoke hazing the streets. Ruin reigned. Results varied. In some towns, their vehicle was ushered through, waved past smoldering swastika banners by resistance fighters. In others, it was stopped with a "Halt!" and a *"Heil Hitler!"*

Checkpoint after checkpoint. Lie after lie. They'd crawled out of the Muscovy territories and were now deep in the central Reich, where all the checkpoints belonged to SS, who were scrambling to maintain some semblance of order in this turbulent landscape.

Here discovery meant death.

"These roads are dangerous," said the soldier examining Yael's papers. "Most of the uprisings have been quelled, but there's some fighters unaccounted for. Just yesterday a unit was ambushed not twenty kilometers away."

So the resistance here wasn't completely crushed. Still fighting, despite the dismal reports Henryka had received about the region. This thought made Yael's smile less of a strain to hold.

"You're not going to Germania, are you?" The SS-Schütze jerked his chin at the line of vehicles stacked up behind them. Many were crammed with families and their earthly possessions: stacks upon stacks of suitcases weighted down with heirlooms. One car had a basket of live poultry pressed against its back window. "A lot of people from the territories are heading toward the capital, thinking it's safe. But I hear it's like the Battle of Moscow all over again. Nasty street fighting. You don't want to get caught in the middle of it."

"We won't be on the road much longer," Yael told him. A true statement. The safe house Henryka had pointed them toward was less than an hour away. The farm would serve as their base for the first portion of the mission. A place for the boys to hide while Miriam and Yael . . . completed their pit stop.

"We're transporting potatoes for my uncle," Yael rattled off the story they'd told at the last ten checkpoints. "Prices are high because the fighting has delayed shipments."

The frown stayed on the SS-Schütze's face. Yael gripped the steering wheel, kept smiling, and fought the growing fear that something was about to go wrong.

Miriam leaned over. She was just as skilled as Yael at playing the role of innocent Reichling. Her long yellow braid tapped the gearshift. Her eyelashes—just as yellow, not nearly as long—fluttered. "If you could point us to where we might be able to buy some gasoline, we'd be grateful."

The soldier shut Yael's fake papers, slipping them back through the window.

He was going to let them through.

It never ceased to amaze Yael, the moment when she realized she'd gotten away with her lies. The truck's engine shuddered as she tucked her papers away. It'd been doing that lately. (Three thousand kilometers and counting was a lot to ask of a twenty-year-old machine.) The SS man had just finished giving them directions when the motor sputtered, stopped.

Dead.

The SS-Schütze motioned toward the hood. "Car trouble?"

"It's an old truck," Yael told him. She could hear her own pulse inside her eardrums. "This happens a lot."

"I can take a look at it for you if you want."

Having SS prodding beneath the hood of their smuggling truck was the last thing Yael wanted. Felix was due for another round of morphine and antibiotics soon, and she wouldn't be able to signal the time to Luka without the patrol noticing. With the engine cut off, things were so quiet the soldier would hear a cough. Much less a scream.

She twisted the key, desperately hard. The ignition churned… several agonizing seconds… before it caught and held. The SS-Schütze waved them through the blockade.

—*GO GO GO*—

But the truck wasn't going. Yael's foot had to pump the gas

pedal several times before the acceleration finally kicked into first, then second gear. She couldn't tell if the ride's roughness was due to the cobblestone street or the ailing engine.

Don't die. Don't die. Please, don't die. Her prayer hung—unsaid on harp string breath—as they crawled through the town.

"That was too close." Miriam cranked up her window. "What if it hadn't started?"

Yael's eyes darted to the rearview mirror, watching the SS men watch her. Their black uniforms and silver badges pulled—*TOO SLOW*—into the distance.

—TOO CLOSE NOT FAR ENOUGH AWAY—

The sight through the webbed-glass windshield wasn't much more reassuring. Yael supposed that the town could have been charming, but it was impossible to tell. Its peak-roofed buildings were overwhelmed with swastika banners. Even more sinisterly strung were the bodies. Partisans and their boots dangled over the streets, hung from any available post. Mostly men, a few women. Some had crows on their sagged shoulders. All had the same handwritten sign looped around their bloating necks: I AM A TRAITOR TO THE REICH.

Yael tried not to count the corpses, but fifty-six was too many to ignore. Fifty-six lives and fifty-six deaths. Fifty-six signs meant to drain the hope and fight out of all who read them.

Even though all of them said the same thing, Yael read as many as she could. Each new declaration pressed her foot harder on the gas.

—HOPE HOPE FIGHT GO—

The engine kept coughing and smoothing out with each new injection of fuel, while they crawled through the morbid streets. At last, the motor managed to chug to the other side of town, onto what promised to become a quiet country lane. Within minutes, the townscape was already melting back into fields. Farmlands interrupted by lakes and bursts of trees. These passed in shades of silver and green as the speedometer gained momentum.

It was almost peaceful, this land. But no matter how quickly the truck's wheels spun in their corroded wells, no matter how much Yael opened her window to let the spring air rip into the cab, the *death* they'd passed lingered. Spoiling her nostrils, curdling her mouth dry.

"Do you really think this truck is going to make it all the way to Germania?" Miriam asked a few kilometers later, when the vehicle began shuddering again. Yael somehow knew her old friend wasn't talking about the engine.

This truck: a bunch of useless stabbed potatoes + Luka + Felix.

Yael frowned. They'd been over this. And over this. "Let's just focus on getting to the safe house first. We can get things sorted there."

But Miriam kept pushing: "All we'd have to do is drop them off outside one of these settlements. We can find a city with a medical facility for the Wolfe boy."

"They're in as much danger as we are. The SS arrested them in Tokyo because they thought the boys were a part of the assassination. Luka and Felix were being flown to the People's Court—"

"Do you really think the People's Court would choose to execute their double victor?" Miriam asked.

"Hitler executed thousands when the first Operation Valkyrie failed. Some inside his closest circles. There's no reason a victor would be spared. Besides, the boys know our plan. If we dumped them on the side of the road, how long do you think it would take for the SS to punch it out of them?"

At this, the older girl relented. "We never should have brought them."

Yael wished the smell of rotting flesh wasn't so unforgettable. She wished she wasn't driving toward hundreds more bodies. She wished that she didn't have to keep throwing herself between her past and her present, Miriam and the boys.

Yael wished that, just for once, her life could hold a shade of normality.

"Tell me about your flat in Novosibirsk." Yael had never lived in one. Basements and barn lofts and barracks, yes, but never a flat. "What color are the walls?"

It was a sudden shift in topic, but Miriam understood. (Of course Miriam understood.) "They were white when I moved in, but I found a can of bright blue paint and remedied that. It's small, one room. I got a discount because I'm on the seventh floor and there's no lift in the building. I have a brilliant view of the city *and* t-toned c-c-calves—"

This time, when the engine's shaking peaked and Yael pumped an extra burst of fuel into its systems, it did not smooth out. It cut off instead, rolling to a standstill in the middle of the dirt lane. When Yael twisted the ignition, it groaned and wheezed and did not catch, did not catch, did not catch.

This time, it really was dead.

CHAPTER 30

Luka was along for the ride.

It was not pleasant.

Bathroom breaks (or any break, for that matter) were a luxury on the Fräulein Express, and whizzing into an empty canteen while lying on your side on roads rougher than smallpox skin was no easy feat. It didn't help that Herr Wolfe was less than a lick away. Constantly crammed against Luka's shoulder, breath annoyingly hot as he slept the days away under the influence of morphine. Luka was tempted to stick himself with the drug, just to escape this jumbling, diesel-filled misery, but the number of syrettes was limited, and they couldn't afford to let Felix scream again.

He didn't. Even when the mechanic's morphine dose thinned and he woke, he was a man of few sounds. There was one constant question, though, whispered every single time: "Are we close?"

"Closer," Luka always answered. He had no idea *how* close. The truck's hidden compartment swallowed all sense of time. The slats in the wood were thick enough to let oxygen in, but too crowded with potato sacks to allow for any light. The paper-check patrol stops were becoming more frequent. Once or twice he thought he'd heard gunfire.

They were stopped now. The engine was running rough enough to wake Herr Wolfe from his sleep. "Something's wrong," he mumbled. "Don't you hear it?"

"I hear you." Luka scowled back through the dark. "And unless you want to become a bounty prize for some SS-Schütze, I suggest you keep the talking to a min—"

The engine cut off. And Luka's words along with it.

Scheisse! He had no more breath in his lungs as he listened to the exchange between the fräuleins and what he figured was a patrol of some kind. It was a brief affair, ending as soon as the truck started again.

"This isn't good," Felix muttered when the vehicle began rolling. "It's going to die again."

Verdammt if that mechanic wasn't right. His prophecy didn't play out immediately—it took an entire half hour before the hum of gears shut off again. This time, there were no patrol voices. Just the churn of an ignition catching, stalling, dying all over again. A car door squealed open.

"Do you think we can get it farther into the trees? We're sitting ducks out here in the lane." This voice, this logic, belonged to Yael.

"Not with all this extra weight in the back," Miriam countered.

Miriam and Yael pulled the potato sacks away in record time, prying the false floorboards back so Luka could finally, *finally* breathe in air that didn't smell like gasoline, piss, and

269

wound juice. Neither fräulein mentioned the stench as they crouched over the opening. Both had changed their faces to look like local girls, and their sleeves were long enough to cover up any ink, but Luka found he could still tell them apart. It wasn't the shades of the sweaters so much as their eyes. *Windows to the soul*, he'd heard them called once. Yael's soul, whenever he looked into it, did not seem to hate his guts. Miriam's was a different matter.

It was Yael who reached down to pull Luka out of the compartment. Their hands clasped, callused palms aligned. Her touch was all warmth against Luka's skin, raising him up. He felt it long after she let go.

Not nothing, then.

Luka shoved his hand inside his jacket pocket and took a look around. They clearly weren't in Muscovy anymore. Gone were the endless, edible pines, replaced by a country lane lined with beech and linden trees—leaves thin with spring. *Not very good cover,* Luka noted. *No matter how deep we push.*

"Felix?" Yael knelt over the truck-bed opening. "Can you examine the engine?"

The mechanic looked as if he could do nothing more than go back to sleep. Luka had seen dead houseplants with more perk. Somehow Felix found the energy to nod, managing his way into daylight with wincing movements.

The truck was a beast to move. It took all of them (minus Herr Wolfe) to shove it off the road, where, under Yael's key-turning and Felix's examination, it died another dozen noisy deaths.

"Engine's not getting fuel." Felix's words were extra slow, fighting the opiates in his system. "That's why it's stalling."

Yael slipped out of the cab, moved to join the rest of the group. "Something wrong with the lines?"

"Dirty carburetor is my best guess. I'd have to take it out and clean it to be sure."

"You don't need to be scrounging around an engine with your wounds," Yael said. "I'll do it if you tell me how. What do we need?"

"Tools. Time."

"How long?" Miriam asked.

"Half a day." Felix frowned. "Maybe more."

Miriam looked at Yael, jaw square. "You and I can't spare half a day. The safe house should have tools. Luka can help Felix patch up the truck while we finish our errand."

"It's only a few more kilometers up the road," Yael said. "Will the truck make it that far?"

Felix shook his head. "Even if we can get past the hard start, it's going to stall again. We won't be able to limp it far."

"How many kilometers is a few?" Luka asked.

"Five." Yael thought for a moment and then added, "Or so."

"No towns between here and there?"

"There shouldn't be." Her eyes met his. They were green this time. Fresh like the spring leaves around them. "Why?"

Luka pounded the truck with his fist. "Let's push it."

———

Oh, how he came to regret this suggestion. Bitterly. Sweatily.

Luka was perspiring from places he didn't know had pores. New blisters nagged his heels, and he was working up a wicked

271

thirst. One of his few comforts was that Yael was pushing alongside him. Hands to the bumper, sweater sleeves shoved high.

It was the first time he'd seen her markings in daylight. They were mesmerizing. Each wolf was unique. They ran at different gaits. One had its ears laid flat. Another was snarling. He could tell they meant something, but he was too afraid to ask. Afraid because he wanted to know. Afraid because there was still something massive and unsaid between them.

Afraid because it was not nothing.

He kept pushing instead, packing all the fear and frustration of the past few weeks into his shoulders, shoving it away into the truck. More than a few times, they were passed by cars laden with fleeing Lebensraum families. Luka turned his head the opposite direction each time, and Yael tugged her sleeve to her wrist, but the vehicles' inhabitants hardly spared the travelers a second glance. Nor did they stop to offer help. They had enough problems of their own.

It took two and a half hours to reach the farmhouse lane.

"This is it!" Yael yelled to Felix, who'd been in the cab steering while the other three pushed. "Turn here!"

"How can you tell?" To Luka, the turnoff looked like every other drive they'd shoved past. Gravelly. Lined with eager April weeds. Sloping up a *verdammt* hill.

"Henryka told me to look for those." She jerked her chin to a pile of stones at the corner. They'd been stacked with careless care—strewn enough to be natural. Unusual enough to signal those who were looking. "This farm has long been a haven for U-boats."

"Submarines?" Luka didn't even have the extra energy to quirk his eyebrow. "Aren't we a bit far from the ocean?"

"Jews in hiding." It was Miriam, to his left, who said this.
Oh.

With the end in sight, Luka shoved extra hard. His shoulder blades were wings of fire by the time Felix pumped the brakes. It didn't take long to realize something was wrong. The farmyard was too quiet—and there was that *smell*. Wet leather *Scheisse*. Fingers filled with pus. City squares filled with bodies.

Death.

Yael bristled and let go of the bumper, producing a pistol from who-knew-where. Miriam matched the motion, and the two women swept up the sides of their vehicle. Luka leapt into the truck bed, grabbing his jacket and the pistol it held. (Not his Luger, but an older Russian gun. His hands felt odd on it.) He hunched down by the cab, waiting for the first shot. The first yell.

It wasn't what he expected. "All clear!"

Luka leapt out of the truck bed. Slipping on his jacket. Keeping his gun close.

The odor was coming from the front yard, beneath a cloud of flies. It was an Alsatian dog—stiff limbs, matted fur—wreathed in weeds. Luka only ventured close enough to the decaying animal to tell that it had been shot through the skull.

The farmhouse was a larger carcass. The front door hung on its hinges like a child's loose tooth. Inside was a mess of things broken just for the hell of it. China smashed. Bookshelves overturned. Mattresses upended. Floorboards plied. Luka couldn't step anywhere without crunching glass as he followed the sound of Yael's voice into the foyer.

"This is the safe house?" he asked.

"It was." Yael knelt on the floor, examining a family portrait that had been dashed there. The Alsatian from the yard sat in the corner of the photograph. A family stood above him: father, mother, son, son, daughter, son. Faces framed by jagged glass.

"That dog is days dead." Yael placed the picture back where she'd found it. "The Gestapo are long gone."

"That's no guarantee they won't be back." Luka looked out the window, as if the secret police were driving up the lane now. Trench coats and treacherous Lugers. All he saw was the fly cloud and Felix, still sitting in the truck's cab.

"It's not," Yael agreed. "But we're only a few hundred kilometers from Germania. SS and Gestapo are everywhere. This farm is the best chance we have of hiding you and Felix while Miriam and I complete the first part of our mission."

What *was* the first part of their mission? Luka knew the bits-and-snatches answer: labor camp, doctor, Experiment 85, changing faces, something about fake Führers. But nothing his imagination could cobble together could explain the expression on the fräulein's face: Real fear. White fear.

Seeing the emotion on someone as steel strong, leather tough as Yael made Luka's stomach churn. "Exactly how long is this side trip going to take?"

"Stay in the barn. Help Felix fix the engine. If we're not back in twenty-four hours…" Yael didn't have to finish her sentence. Not when she was surrounded by smashed shelves and pictures of missing children.

"What do I do then?" he asked.

"You're a survivor." Yael rose to her full height. Her words weren't cruel, just pointed enough to sting. "You'll figure it out."

"I don't want to. I mean..." Luka paused. What did he mean?

Why was he here, in the middle of this ruined safe house?

The answer stood in front of him. Green eyes, straw hair, face in the shape of a heart. Some of her makeup had sweated off while pushing the truck. Luka could see hints of bruises beneath; faint yellows and browns were all that remained from SS-Standartenführer Baasch's hits. "Tell me you're coming back," he said.

Yael's lip twitched. "You worried about me?"

Yes, actually. It was more than worry. The thought of Yael *not* returning was unbearable, and not because there were SS sharks and wilderness wolves circling, but because the fräulein was making his cardiac muscles *feel*. (Even now Luka wanted to reach out and run his fingertips along the edge of her jaw, the way he had that night in the cabin.)

"Just...tell me. Please." His hands hung—too leaden, too fearful—at his sides. "I need to hear you say it."

"I thought all Double Victor Löwe needed was a cigarette." It felt like a test, the way Yael said this, stringing out each syllable on a whisper.

Had that ever been the case?

Not behind Herr Kahler's shop. What eleven-year-old Luka needed when he took that first (terribly bitter) swallow of smoke was to be himself. What about all those evenings with Adele, when the air around them was filmy with chain-smoking haze and tickling with laughter? All he'd needed then was to be heard, understood, known in a way ten thousand *Sieg heil* posters could never display.

Cigarettes were just tar-stick crutches, and, Luka realized, he hadn't been itching for a smoke in days. Maybe Baasch had burned the craving out of him. Or maybe, just maybe, he'd found something better.

Someone better.

"I—" he started to say, when Miriam appeared in the doorway.

The young woman was still holding her gun, and even though she was wearing the same skirt-and-sweater getup as Yael, she looked every centimeter a soldier. "Barn's clear. No animals. We should move the truck in there so the boys can start cleaning out the carburetor. You and I need to head out soon if we want to make it to the camp by sundown."

"We're coming." Yael nodded, then looked back at Luka. "What was it you were going to say?"

"Nothing." At least, nothing that could be spilled with Comrade Jumbly Name listening. Nothing he couldn't tell Yael later, when they were alone, because she was going to come back. She'd always come back. (Her bruises, his being here, were both testament to that.)

Luka rolled his still-burning shoulders and started toward the truck. "Let's get this over with."

CHAPTER 31

Felix's good hand was almost as white as his bandaged one as it gripped the steering wheel, driving without going anywhere. He stared at their destination through the mud-flecked windshield.

When Yael first explained they were stopping at a safe house on the way to Germania, Felix's hope grew an extra centimeter. It was a tiny, seedling thing, but he clung to it anyway. The idea that his parents were alive, unharmed, that Felix might see them soon, that not everything was broken (except perhaps his hearing) was too tempting not to believe.

"Not the one your parents are staying in," she'd explained after seeing the look on his face. "It's just a way station while Miriam and I retrieve information on Experiment Eighty-Five. You and Luka should be safe there."

But there was nothing safe about this house. The place was a shambles: hinges hanging, beams splintered, glass everywhere. Darkness that did not belong to shadows streaked through long grass, rose up in the form of fly clouds. Yael gave this spot a wide berth as she marched back to the truck. She stopped by the open cab door.

"What happened here?" Felix knew the answer. He knew, he knew, he didn't want it to be true.

"Gestapo."

Some men came to the house. Gestapo. They took us....

Ears did not lie, nor did his eyes. The farmhouse's windows looked hungry for daylight: all ragged glass teeth and dim shadows. The home had been gutted.

Yael was wrong. No place was safe. Mama and Papa weren't safe.

(*If, if, if* they weren't already dead.)

"We're going to push the truck into the barn so you and Luka can get to work repairing it. What do you need?" Yael asked.

"Assuming it's the carburetor? A screwdriver, a rag..." There was only one item Felix really needed, though he couldn't list it. All he could do was squint at the farmhouse and hope that somewhere in its squalor was a functional telephone.

"I'll see what we can find," Yael told him. "If all goes well, we should return from the camp around midnight. Can you get things fixed by then?"

Could he? The engine shouldn't pose much of a problem. It was everything else that made Felix doubt. "I'll try my best."

———

His mechanical intuitions proved correct: the GAZ-AA's carburetor was clogged with dirt, messing up the fuel flow. With two functional hands and his auto shop, Felix could've had the motor running again in a few hours.

It was going to take much longer than that.

He'd refused the latest dose of painkiller. Repairing an engine with only an *Arschloch* wielding a rusted screwdriver required clear thoughts. These came at a price: Felix's not-there fingers throbbed as he redirected Luka's attentions from the radiator. "*Not* that one!"

The screwdriver Yael found in the tractor shed might as well have been a sledgehammer the way the victor clattered through the engine. Indelicate to the max. "That's the one you pointed at."

"That is a radiator. Not a carburetor."

"They all look the same to me." The other boy scowled.

Felix didn't see how every engine part could possibly look the same when they looked so very, very *not* the same. He shut his eyes, lids fluttering with the pain of yet another headache. "How did you ever get through five Axis Tours without learning basic engine parts?"

"It's easier to fix stuff when you have a fleet of mechanics catering to your every whim."

As opposed to just one mechanic? Felix bit the question back. If they were going to sit here and argue, they wouldn't get anything done.

Not that their current progress was looking so stellar. It took twenty minutes before Luka had a grasp on where the carburetor was and how to pry it free. With the way the victor was handling the tools, Felix estimated the task would take another fifteen minutes. At least.

Normally, such roundabout workmanship would've nursed a twitch in Felix's temple (So much time wasted! So many screws scattered on the floor! *Bah!*), but now he welcomed it. Yael and Miriam had left the farm on foot over an hour ago. Luka's preoccupation with the screwdriver afforded Felix an opportunity to search for a telephone without an audience.

"We're missing some tools," he told the victor. "I'm going to see if I can find some down at the farmhouse. You keep working on that. Try not to trigger any explosions."

The clinking stopped. Luka looked up. "That can happen?"

Not really. But the clanging noise was worsening Felix's headache. He was glad to leave it behind as he made his way across the overgrown farm. Days of rest and antibiotics had left his steps steadier than they'd been since…well, since Tokyo. Felix shuffled as quickly as he could past the plague of flies in the front yard, as well as the garden hose they'd need to siphon fuel from the GAZ-AA's tank to clean the carburetor with. (He'd forgotten to request that tool, preoccupied as he was. No matter. He'd come back for it later.)

The inside of the house was worse than Felix had imagined. The way it had been torn apart—with such intentional, Gestapo wrath—added a frantic charge to his search. There was no phone in the foyer, just snapped table legs and glass shards that threatened to impale Felix should he fall. He kept close to the wall as he entered the kitchen. No phone in there either, only an abundance of flies, spoiling fruit, and a drawer of cutlery that had been yanked off its tracks—silverware everywhere.

Felix found the phone in the hallway, perched on its own shelf, intact, cable connected. He stopped and stared at the rotary dial. The house was horribly silent around him, reminding Felix that SS-Standartenführer Baasch was not his ally. The SS officer wasn't even the lesser of a select number of evils. He was just the man with an iron heel above Felix's family.

Because of this, Felix felt no guilt in picking up the receiver. Simply sheer terror. His stomach relived those fifteen terrifying seconds before the parachute: flip-flop falling as he spun through the numbers Baasch had given him. Salvation, damnation, *for Adele*, for any Wolfe who was left...

It was a direct-dial call, free of sweet-voiced operators. The person who answered was snapping. Brusque. "Yes? Who is this?"

"Sorry." Felix had no idea why he was apologizing. He folded into a stutter. "I—I need to speak with Standartenführer Baasch. Is he available?"

"Who is this?" the voice on the other end repeated.

"Felix. Wolfe. He told me to call—"

"A moment."

A grandfather clock sat at the end of the hall. Its glass plating had been smashed, and its weights had almost finished their long-wound, eight-day course, but the pendulum kept swinging, hands plodding around an elegantly scripted face. Felix watched its motion, mesmerized.

At least something still worked.

When the SS-Standartenführer got on the line, there were no *hello*s or *how are you*s. Just a single wheeze of breath before he asked, "Are you in position?"

"I want to speak to my parents." Felix's voice sounded much stronger than it felt. "I'm not telling you anything until I know they're alive."

There was a pause. Long enough to make Felix fear that Baasch would hang up the phone, sever their connection for good. Instead the SS officer grumbled, "Your father's alive. I had him transferred to Germania as soon as I arrived so I could be more... personally invested in his questioning."

"What about my mother?"

"You did not keep to the plans of your mission," Baasch reminded him. "For that there are consequences. I can't say she didn't suffer."

Falling, falling. Everything inside Felix was falling. His heart ached high in his throat. All he could think of was Mama—standing over the kitchen sink, potato peelings clinging to her wrists as she hummed an absent tune. Mama—ever so patient, trying to teach Adele how to loop yarn over the knitting needles. Mama—who, even though she was never the same after May 2, 1950, still smiled when Felix brought her cups of tea in the evenings, walking slowly so as not to spill the scalding liquid on his coveralls.

Mama—gone.

"No," Felix whispered, as if one word could make this untrue. But what was done could not be undone. What was broken could not always be fixed. Especially when death was involved.

"Your father is still with us, however. In fact, here he is now—"

"Felix? Son?" Papa's voice, again. It sounded even more

282

broken than before. Vocal cords unoiled, ground to pieces with grief. "Have you done what they asked?"

"I'm trying, Papa. I'm on my way to Germania now. I'll be there soon. I'll do what I have to do. You'll be safe."

"You need to hurry," his father rasped. "These men——"

There was a rattling on the other end, the phone passing hands.

Back to Baasch: "Need I remind you, Herr Wolfe, this is not a negotiation. Are you in position?"

"Not yet—I—we jumped too early. But we're coming. We'll be in Germania in a day or two if your patrols don't stop us——"

"My patience is wearing thin, Herr Wolfe. As is the Reichs-führer's. Take much longer and the deal will be off."

"No! No, please!" Felix's good hand tightened around the receiver. Tendons so frayed they felt ready to snap. "One of their leaders is named Erwin Reiniger. He's a general——"

"I don't need just one name, Herr Wolfe. I need all of them. Heads on a platter. This resistance needs to be stamped out so thoroughly it has no chance of ever rearing its head again. Do you see the time?" Baasch didn't wait for an answer. "Mark it. You have thirty-six hours to get in position and contact me. Fail to do this, and the lives of your father and sister are forfeit."

Felix was hurtling toward the earth. Terminal velocity: two hundred kilometers per hour. Salvation, damnation, salvation, damnation. He'd do anything, say anything, to stop it. "They have a plan. Something about a camp and retrieving information on Experiment Eighty-Five——"

"Herr Wolfe?" The voice that cut Felix off this time came from outside the tinny telephone speaker, accompanied by the crackle/clatter/crash of Luka Löwe's boots through the foyer wreckage. "You in here?"

"I'm coming," Felix whispered into the receiver. He'd just managed to set it back on the switch hook when the victor blundered into the hall. There was a large snub of grease on his nose.

"Nothing's exploded. Yet," Luka added. "What are you rooting around for?"

Nausea, shock, thirty-six hours sat on the tip of Felix's tongue. His mother was gone, and the rest of his family would be next if he didn't swallow these things back, lie through his teeth. "I need a toothbrush."

"I appreciate fresh breath, but I don't think it's our priority right n—"

"We'll need it to scrub out the carb bowl. I figured a toothbrush would be more thorough than the rag we have."

The victor's eyes narrowed at the dim hallway. "And you decided to look for one in here?"

"I was on my way to the bedroom." Felix waved toward the grandfather clock—which was poised to chime the five o'clock hour. He hoped there actually was a bedroom back there. "Walking's not exactly my strongest skill right now."

Luka shoved his way down the hall. Within moments he was back. Frazzled red toothbrush in hand. "Anything else?"

"We need the garden hose," Felix said, a little too loudly, trying to drown out the SS-Standartenführer's threats in his head. They clamored anyway: THIRTY-SIX HOURS against his MIGRAINE. Thrashing like a man without a parachute.

"Right." The victor tucked the toothbrush behind his ear. "Let's go fetch it. The sooner we get this truck running the better."

Felix couldn't agree more.

CHAPTER 32

Dusk. Floodlights clashed against growing shadows. Death's workday was coming to a close. Yael lay belly-down in a pine forest, eyes on the gravel road that snaked along the perimeter of the camp. Eleven years ago she'd walked this path as Bernice Vogt, hand in hand with Dr. Geyer's nurse. Eleven years ago she'd run into these very trees, heart full of holes.

Yael wanted to run now. Even though she'd spent most of the afternoon pushing the truck and walking the long road here, her legs were twitching to the tempo of her iron voice.

—*NOT SAFE RUN KEEP RUNNING DON'T LOOK BACK*—

But she had to stay still. She had to look back.

Yael had to ignore the instincts that had kept her alive so many times.

How else would the world survive?

There was movement in the woods beside her. Darkness streaking through darkness, materializing into an *Aufseherin*—

female overseer. The mere sight of her uniform—wool blazer and skirt, impractical cap, eagles everywhere—sent Yael's insides into a tailspin, even after Miriam told her: "It's me."

As many times as Yael had looked into the mirror and seen a stranger, it was still unnerving to see the shift on her friend. She wondered if this was how Miriam had felt all those many years ago, when she'd discovered young Yael wearing her dead mother's face.

"Success?" Yael asked, mouth dry.

The only way inside the camp was through the front gates. To walk this path, they needed aliases—convincing ones. Names and faces that belonged to actual guards. Miriam had gone to fetch these. It'd taken her a little under an hour.

Her friend nodded and began pulling smuggled clothes out from under her jacket. Shoes, hat, even hairpins…everything needed for a second *Aufseherin* outfit. "It's a good thing these blazers are baggy."

Night air nipped at Yael's skin as she stripped the Lebensraum bride wear and pieced together the overseer's uniform. Trading stocking for stocking. Skirt for skirt. "Who are we?"

Miriam fished a set of papers from her breast pocket. "My name's Ingrid Wagner. Yours is Elsa Schwarz. Looked like this. *Sounded like this.*" Her voice box went squeaky thin, face shifting in the same moment. When Yael opened the woman's booklet, she found that exact visage staring back: Stark cheeks. Eyes limpid, tinged with cruel.

Usually, when Yael changed, she tried to imagine the life of the skin she was wearing, letting it settle into her thoughts and speech. But Elsa Schwarz did not fit. Everything inside Yael squirmed against this woman.

"Can you see my bruises?" she asked, once the transformation was complete. She'd freshened her makeup before the trek here, but it was a delicate balance: powdering her face enough to hide Baasch's battering, yet not so much as to look cakey.

"Your makeup's fine." Miriam melted back into Ingrid's face as she smoothed Yael's collar, pinned Elsa's mousy hair just so. "Pinch your lips a little more. Make your eyes harder."

"I know!" Yael snapped. Nerves. Too many nerves. Her guts felt akin to the camp's fences—barbed and electrified. "I've been doing this longer than you have!"

Her friend's hands froze. "You don't have to do this."

"We need this intelligence, Miriam. If we make a mistake and assassinate the wrong man again—"

"No." Miriam swallowed. "I mean *you*, Yael."

The buzz in Yael's stomach jagged and leapt.

"You didn't leave me, Volchitsa. I made you go. You were six years old. *Six.*" Her friend spit the number. "And I sent you out alone to face wolves so much larger than yourself. Lying to the guards, lying to Dr. Geyer...I can only imagine how terrifying that was. I won't ask you to face that again. I can gather the intelligence myself."

Wait and watch in the pines. Leave Miriam without moving. Let someone else hold the torch for a while. These were such strange thoughts, because for so many years Yael had been the only one who *could* do the impossible. Changing things was her job, her burden to bear. Hers, hers, hers alone.

But she wasn't alone anymore.

Yael shook her head. "I'm coming with you."

"Are you sure?" Seeing so much concern on the face of an *Aufseherin* was eerie. It was all *Miriam*. Her sister. Her guide. No uniform or Roman nose could change that.

"Two sets of eyes and ears are better than one," Yael told her. "As are two sets of pistols and knives. We go together."

———

Walking back through those gates was the hardest thing Yael had ever done. Nothing in Vlad's training had prepared her for this: returning to the edge of devouring, staring back at it, stepping in.

There wasn't so much smoke this time. It crept out of the stacks, wreathing into the night sky with phantom fingers. The killing machine's supply of bodies had thinned. By the turn of the decade, the central Reich had been officially declared free of Jews, but it wasn't just Yael's people the crematorium fires hungered for. Romani, Slavs, and other groups Hitler designated as *Untermenschen* kept the train cars clattering, though such transports were rare these days. According to Henryka's documents, most of the camp's current inmates were Aryans—homosexuals, political prisoners and their families, anyone the Führer deemed a threat to his New Order— condemned to a lifetime of hard labor. The furnaces remained to greet their withered end, once-roaring flames now a dull glow. Guards stood in their towers, high above, seeing all. Yael felt every one of their eyes and crosshairs on her changed skin. Marking her.

Miriam did not flinch when the SS-Sturmmann by the gate nodded at them, nor did she shudder when the Alsatian dogs growled and tugged at their leads.

—KEEP WALKING HEAD HIGH DO NOT FEAR—

The iron voice had finally shifted, determined to make the best of Yael's decision.

—THEY DO NOT SEE YOU—

No one stopped the two *Aufseherinnen* to ask them questions. They walked through the swing of the gates, past the dogs' teeth with ease. The tower guards turned their gazes elsewhere. Every corner Yael turned she expected to see the doctor in his white, white coat. Arms outstretched, needles in hand.

But Dr. Geyer was not around the first corner. Or the second. He was not standing in the broad poplar-lined avenue by the medical block. He was not sitting on the stone steps to the infirmary.

The medical block's hallway was smaller than Yael remembered. The whole place was caustic with bleach: a scent that scoured her stomach as she walked past the room that held the examination gurney. That door was mercifully shut.

Shades had been drawn over the hall-side glass of the observation cell windows, and Yael did not have the courage to raise them. Were any victims within? Any children from the last transport, routed especially to this camp on Dr. Geyer's whim? Even if there were, she could do nothing to save them. Not without jeopardizing the mission. If Yael glimpsed their faces now ...

Miriam's thoughts appeared to be similar—past playing into present bleeding into future, rehearsing at the edges of her borrowed *Aufseherin* face. Her hand did not reach out to lift the shades. She kept walking down the hall.

The door to Dr. Geyer's office was also closed. Miriam stood watch as Yael slipped two bobby pins from Elsa's hair and tricked the lock with them. Her heart slammed hard as the door swung open, but the Angel of Death was not sitting at his desk. He was not welcoming her back with his gap-toothed smile.

Yael let out a long breath. They'd planned for both eventualities: the doctor here, the doctor gone. Using pain to wrench the information they needed out of Dr. Geyer, or ferreting whatever intelligence they could out of his office documents.

She was glad that—for now—it was the latter.

The place was soulless but not empty. There was a small television in the corner. A bowl of hard candies sat on the desk, beside a black rotary phone. Metal filing cabinets besieged the walls, stacks on stacks of information trapped behind locks. They were all marked with handwritten labels, experiments clustered into groups of ten.

Yael locked the door, tugged the blinds over the windows, and went straight for the cabinet marked EXPERIMENTS 80–90, using her pins to jimmy its center drawer open. A series of carefully marked manila envelopes rolled out. Dr. Geyer's cataloging system was much more organized that Henryka's. His papers were filed according to experiment number, ordered by date.

Miriam flipped through these, muttering aloud, "Eighty-four, eighty-four, eighty-six..."

Where the documents of Experiment 85 should've been was a seamless transition from Horror 84 to Savagery 86. Yael worked the other drawers of the cabinet free. Neither held proof of Experiment 85.

"There can't be nothing," she said, scanning the collection a third time. Experiment 85 did not exist in these cabinets.

"They're sensitive documents." Miriam pushed the center drawer back into place. It *schnick*ed shut with a lock. "Dr. Geyer's notes were probably relocated."

Or renamed.

The Angel of Death had been busy in the years since they'd escaped. His experiments climbed into the high hundreds—an overwhelming number of labeled drawers. Yael was beginning to fear they'd never end when they gave way to cabinets branded with letters instead of digits.

DP.

She broke open the top drawer of the first cabinet. Like the others, it held neat rows of manila envelopes, crammed according to date. When Yael grabbed the foremost one and tore it open, a series of photographs slid out: a dozen versions of the same girl. She was young in every picture, too small to fill the portraits' negative space. Her stare was made of bronze, clashing with the camera. Paleness crept in as the pictures progressed—peppering her hair, patching her skin. Erasing all markings. Only her bones stayed the same.

Yael picked up the oldest photograph, with dark eyes and shadowed hair. She flipped it over to see the writing on the back.

Yael Reider. 121358ΔX. Preinjection.

It was her.

Yael Reider. A girl who had been lost for so many years. A girl who was not DECEASED, as the clotted red stamp on the back of the manila envelope stated, but very much alive. Alive and here, seeing herself as she was for the very first time.

I'll bet you had the most beautiful dark hair. You seem like a girl who would have had curls.

Henryka was right. This first picture had been snapped before the processing scissors. Yael's hair was dark and long, spiraling at the ends in a way the Polish woman would call "gorgeous."

"This is it." Yael slipped the picture into her *Aufseherin* jacket pocket and turned the envelope over, label side up. **Experiment 85** had been crossed out, replaced with: **Doppelgänger Project.**

"There are drawers of these." Miriam took in all the **DP** cabinets with a sharp breath. "So much…"

She was right. Yael's own file was not thin, and it was only the beginning. Papers on papers followed papers on more papers. Yael tried not to think of how many lives (how many deaths) they symbolized as she pulled the next folder out.

"Just look for what's important."

"It's all important." There was devastation, drowning in Miriam's voice. One Yael heard only because she felt it. The ocean of grief always there, under everything. Threaded with currents of rage.

"It is," Yael agreed. Her own throat squeezing. "But right now we need information on the Führer's decoys."

Miriam said nothing else. She tugged the second folder free. Began reading.

Years of sneaking peeks at Henryka's resistance intelligence had trained Yael in the art of skimming files. Her eyes whipped through words, brain snatching up facts it deemed significant, stowing them away for later.

From August 1946: **Modifications to the compound following test group 12's autopsies have yielded a 75% survival rate among test group 13.**

Yael shut this folder and moved on to the next drawer.

From December 1946: **Reichsführer Himmler's interest in Experiment 85 has increased since the last presentation. He has agreed to pass along findings to the Führer.**

From June 1948: **Survival rate continues to hover at 95%. The Führer has signed off on the Doppelgänger Project. The first SS candidates are due to arrive tomorrow for injections. Reichsführer Himmler has assured me only the fittest men have been selected as a part of this detail.**

An SS detail! Of course. Hitler's bodyguards all held *Schutzstaffel* ranks. It made sense that his decoys belonged to this ruthless force as well.

Yael kept skimming. The survival rate held true. Ten SS men had successfully undergone the "Doppelgänger Treatment," as Dr. Geyer was now calling it. They were kept under strict observation for a year—their mimicry abilities tested and retested and retested—before they were cleared to return to Germania. Ten more SS men were sent in their place. In the summer of 1949, the cycle began anew. Injections, observation, testing and retesting and retesting...

But these notes were seven, eight years old. Yael needed the complete picture. How many SS skinshifters were they facing? Seventy? Eighty? More? Where were these men posted?

Perhaps it'd be best to skip ahead to the most recent documents. Work her way backward...

Yael opened the sixth drawer. Grabbed the final manila envelope. Her breath caught at its label: **SS-Maskierte-kommando des Führers**.

The Führer's Masked Detail.

The file began with a roster: a list of twenty soldiers. Men of every blood type (A, B, AB, O), but all of "pure" blood. These subjects had been allowed to keep their names, along with their SS ranking. Most of them were SS-Rottenführers and SS-Unterscharführers. Numbers had been added to the end of their obligatory blood-group tattoo: A1, A2, A3, B1, B2, B3, and so on.

There was a DECEASED stamp on this document, too. Its ink looked much fresher, overlapping the information of AB4. ~~Unknown skinshifter~~ had a name: SS-Rottenführer Gustav Lohse.

SS-Rottenführer. Men who joined the SS did not lead innocent lives, did not die blameless. The man might have been a skinshifter, but he was nothing like her. The lines held true.

The blood on Yael's hands felt a shade thinner as she handed the roster to her friend. "This is a start. There are separate profiles on each member of the detail."

Miriam's fingernails made dimples along the document's edge. She scanned it. "Dr. Geyer marked them all."

"He'd have had to," Yael reasoned. "Otherwise it would be impossible to determine the real Führer from the skinshifters."

"Tattoos on their left inner bicep," Miriam read. "Not a very noticeable location. Can't say I'm exactly relishing the thought of ripping off nineteen National Socialists' shirts to find the real Führer."

Nor was Yael. Nineteen remaining SS skinshifters. The number was both relievedly low (at the rate of Dr. Geyer's earlier notes, she'd been expecting quadruple that) and dreadfully high. Nineteen men who could wear Adolf Hitler's face at a moment's notice... How many could Yael and Miriam handle discreetly before finding the real Hitler, ending him?

Was assassinating the real Führer even possible?

There was still so much they didn't know. Yael looked to all the files she'd skipped in her haste to reach the end and wondered how many more secrets they held. Was Hitler's *Maskierte-kommando* the only one? How much had the compound evolved? Was skinshifting still the only side effect or had the Angel of Death managed to coax more sinister impossibilities from the human body?

"Do you ever wonder what you would have been like if..." Yael kept staring at the open cabinets, thinking of the first-face Reider girl inside her pocket. "All this... hadn't happened?"

"Dead." Miriam looked up from the roster. "Why?"

"You don't feel as if..." Yael hesitated. Maybe the poison she felt inside her hadn't come from Dr. Geyer's syringes at all. Maybe she was still alone in this....

"As if what?"

"He made monsters of us." It was the first time Yael had let the fear inside her take the form of words. Her voice had never felt smaller.

"It doesn't matter how many drugs Dr. Geyer put into our

veins. He didn't make us. We've made ourselves. We've fought tooth and nail for the right to live." There was a certainty lining Miriam's sentences that Yael ached for. "Monsters cut children open and call it progress. Monsters murder entire groups of people without blinking but get upset when they have to wash human ash from their garden strawberries. Monsters are the ones who watch other people do these things and do nothing to stop it. You and I are not monsters. If anything, we're miracles."

Maybe Miriam was right. Maybe Luka was, too. Maybe a monster wasn't made out of a few drops of blood or a mother's fevered cries ("It's a monster!") or the *monster, monstre, монстр* whispers from Barrack 7's terrified women. Maybe Katsuo's motorcycle death was truly an accident. Maybe SS-Rottenführer Gustav Lohse was a death that could be pardoned....

Maybe she *was* a miracle.

The miracle it would take to *change things*.

Her first wolf had always seen it. *(You are special. You are going to change things.)* Her second wolf had hissed against the *monster, monstre, монстр* rumors until the very end. Her third wolf was here, saying it to her face. Her fourth wolf had shot a skinshifter, and Yael knew in her heart that Aaron-Klaus was not a monster. Nor was Vlad, fifth wolf, master of killing.

Her wolves knew her.

And now, Yael Reider was beginning to know herself.

The office flooded with noise—bright and terrible. Not an alarm, but the telephone. Ringing. Once. Again. Too loud. People would hear the sound if they hadn't already. Yael reached out to yank the connection cord from the wall.

"No!" Miriam stopped her. "If the line goes dead, that will raise suspicion!"

Yael eyed the door; panic knotted her stomach. "We can't just leave it ringing!"

A third ring. A fourth. Miriam's hand lifted the receiver. Her voice dropped several octaves, as close as her gender-bound vocal cords could manage to the timbre of Dr. Geyer as she said, "Hello?"

CHAPTER 33

It was not like Dr. Engel Geyer to let the phone ring more than once, Reichsführer Heinrich Himmler mused as he held the receiver to his ear. He supposed, though, that their conversations hadn't been particularly pleasant lately. No one's were. How could they be, when everything they'd worked so hard to achieve was under attack, eroding away territory by territory....

The scene from the Victor's Ball had left Himmler as shocked and reeling as everyone else in the Reich. That, combined with over a dozen different uprisings all over the map, had caused him to panic. Panic had caused him to sign off on SS-Standartenführer Baasch's release-retrap plan. One that was turning out to be fantastically unhelpful and unnecessary, as Himmler realized only after the *Immelmann IV* landed three passengers lighter. He didn't need some mechanic from Frankfurt bumbling around at espionage when he had an entire detail of doppelgängers at his disposal. Well, not an entire detail now. There was the initial death in Tokyo, and another member of the *Maskiertekommando* had been shot trying to cross the front. Three others, on the same mission, had breached the resistance's lines, only to go radio silent.

The silence did not bode well, nor did the news from Baasch's snitch.

Ring, ring, went the telephone. Himmler was just about to hang up when the doctor answered, "Hello?"

Geyer's voice sounded off, as if clogged by a head cold. Perhaps it was, but Himmler didn't take the time to ask. This wasn't a cordial call. "Dr. Geyer. This is the Reichsführer. I know it's late, but I have a matter that needs your immediate attention. We've been informed that the resistance might attempt to access information on the Doppelgänger Project. Under no circumstances can this be allowed to happen. Alert the perimeter guards to be on the lookout for intruders. Destroy everything connected to the project. Documents. Compound samples. I want all of it gone."

"But it's my life's work—"

"There is far more at stake here than your work, Dr. Geyer! Or your life!" Panic. Again. Making him snap. Himmler paused, inhaled, exhaled, until he was sure he could speak again without yelling. "Those files contain sensitive information. If it falls into the wrong hands, it could unravel everything."

The doctor's hesitation oozed through the phone. The Reichsführer couldn't fault him for it. Experiment 85's research and results were remarkable, truly the work of a lifetime. But none of it was worth what those documents could cost them.

"Who informed you of this possibility?" Everything about Geyer's question—the wording, the nasal-drip haze in his voice, the lack of *respect*—grated on Himmler. All pity evaporated.

"Need I remind you, Dr. Geyer, it was your carelessness that allowed for Inmate 121358ΔX's survival in the first place. This mess is on your head, and I am currently the only soul standing between you and the Führer's wrath. You'd do well not to question me. Destroy all evidence of the Doppelgänger Project. Now. Do I make myself clear?"

"Yes. I'll take care of it right away."

CHAPTER 34

"Yes. I'll take care of it right away."

"Who was that?" Yael asked after Miriam set down the receiver. The conversation had lasted less than a minute, but whatever had occurred on the other end of the line was drastic. Ingrid Wagner's face was tile white, corpse white, filled with anger and colorless fear.

"We've missed something...." Miriam's voice returned to its normal octave, clenched as tight as her jaw. She turned back to the filing cabinets.

"What are you talking about?"

"There's something here, something important." The meticulous order of the **DP** drawers crumbled as Miriam began pulling out envelopes, stacking them on the doctor's desk. It was a random pile, containing a few files from every single drawer: early 1945 all the way to the *Maskiertekommando* profiles. Anguish abridged. "We need to take these. As many as we can carry. Find something we can use to secure them beneath our jackets. Hurry!"

Yael wanted to keep pressing for information, but her friend's urgency was contagious. She searched the office's other drawers and came up with two rolls of medical gauze. "This should do the trick."

Miriam was already unbuttoning her jacket, shoving up her blouse, pressing as many envelopes as she could against her bare torso. Their block shapes, so crammed together, reminded Yael of explosives. The amount of gauze used to secure them was only excusable for a surgical patient.

Yael constricted her body a dress size in order to pack more papers between cotton and ribs. They managed to tie the entire pile from Dr. Geyer's desk onto their bodies, plus some extra envelopes retrieved for good measure, before Miriam nudged the drawers shut. One by one they locked back into place, each a little emptier than before.

"We have to leave," Miriam said. "Right now."

"What do you—" Yael was still tucking her blouse back in, yet her friend was already at the door, peering between the shades' slats into an empty hallway. "Miriam, your jacket isn't even buttoned!"

The other girl's fingers twisted the overseer uniform back into place. Her hidden papers crinkled.

"Careful! If you move too fast, they'll hear you," Yael reminded. "What's going on?"

"Questions later." Comrade Commander Mnogolikiy was back. (In spirit, if not in face.) Barking orders. "We need to get out of the camp."

Miriam pushed open the office door before Yael could argue, conquering the hallway with clipped steps. Yael followed; scores of concealed pages rustled against her rib cage as the two made

303

their way out of the medical block, leaving the drawn shades and scent of bloodless bleach behind.

It was night in full now, pressing down against poplar branches and barbed-wire barriers alike. The groans of barrack suffering from Yael's childhood had thinned alongside the smoke, faded to the point that the camp almost seemed quiet. This made Miriam's rush all the more noticeable.

"Slow down!" Yael struggled to keep stride with her friend. "If you move like prey, you get noticed."

It was a quote from one of Vlad's many lessons. One that had stuck with Yael through the years. One that rang true with Miriam now. Her steps slowed, though Yael could still see the throb of some emotion (Anger? Fear?) in Ingrid Wagner's neck veins.

Yael grabbed her friend's sleeve, pulled her to a stop. "We're almost out, but you can't walk through the gates looking like this. Breathe."

Miriam did the opposite. Lungs seizing. Freezing. Pupils flaring as they fixed on the path ahead. Yael turned and felt her own lungs freeze, seize at what she saw.

The Angel of Death moved through the lamplight, white coat winking in and out of shadows. Like everything else in the camp, the years had made him smaller. Yael knew, logically, it was because she'd grown taller, but the thought that something inside Dr. Geyer had shriveled helped her.

—KEEP BREATHING—

In the ballroom, when Yael stood face-to-face with the man she thought was the Führer, the only emotion she'd felt was fury. Even then, surrounded by the enemy on all sides, it hadn't occurred to her to be afraid.

She was now. This fear was far different from what she'd felt after Luka's truck-bed confession. It was a child's terror. Clawing through her stomach, up her throat, demanding to be felt.

The path's crushed bricks and granite griped under Dr. Geyer's shoes as he walked. Downcast stare. Arms tucked behind his back. He was only three steps away when he noticed the *Aufseherinnen* beneath the poplar tree.

—*DON'T LOOK HIM IN THE EYES HE'LL SEE YOU HE'LL KNOW*—

"Good evening, Fräuleins." The doctor smiled and dipped his head in greeting. There was still a gap between his two front teeth. Yael found herself falling back into old habits, fixing her stare on this space instead of the eyes above.

He did not make me. He did not break me either, Yael thought so she might keep breathing. But with the files bound so tightly to her chest, all she could manage was "Evening" before her lungs crumpled.

Miriam couldn't even manage that. She nodded.

He did not make me.

—*KEEP BREATHING*—

He did not break me.

Dr. Geyer passed them by without another word. His coat flared against the light of a second lamp, tapering off into darkness as he veered toward the medical block.

He was going to his office, Yael realized. They'd left in such a hurry . . . there was no way they'd put *everything* back exactly as it had been. The doctor would notice something out of place; an alarm would be raised.

This time, when Miriam broke into an almost jog, Yael

305

joined, ignoring the rustle of papers under her wool blazer, putting as many steps as she could between herself and what had just passed. When they came in sight of the gate, they slowed. Light was everywhere, cutting details into vicious silhouettes. The muzzles of the guards' rifles, tips of the dog's fangs, barbed-wire edges—all looked extra sharp under the floodlamps. Waiting to impale her.

They did not make me.

—KEEP WALKING—

They did not break me.

Yael stamped her fear down, keeping every detail of Elsa Schwarz's face calm. She did not look to Miriam to see if her friend was doing the same. Instead she nodded at one of the guards, gave him a half smile.

The gates swung open.

Yael took one step, then another and another, her *Aufseherin* shoes sinking into the tire grooves made by supply trucks. This tread kept her steady: past the *pant, pant* of the Alsatians' hot breath, past the *sizzle, sizzle* of charged metal lines. Even when the electric fences and canine enamel were paces behind, Yael still felt the impossibility of escape at her heels. Death's jaws following her, ready to snap and swallow.

But the *Aufseherinnen*'s way out was as easy as the nurse's had been. There were no commands to "Halt," no storm of guard-tower bullets, just the clang of the gate as it shut again. Miriam and Yael and their *Aufseherinnen* faces walked all the way to the fringe of the spotlights. Only here did Yael let her half smile slip. Achy hollowness took its place.

Once they were well out of sight of the gates, they melted

back into the trees, returning to their cache of old clothes and passbooks. Miriam dismantled her overseer uniform all the way down to envelopes and gauze, remasking her features into her farm-girl face. Yael did the same, clenching against the breeze that whipped through the trees. Ash stale.

"Miriam?" she asked. "What happened back there?"

"These files are valuable." The other girl was shoving the pine needles into piles. Small funeral mounds for their *Aufseherinnen* outfits. "Very valuable."

Yael plucked her first-face photograph from her pocket before adding the jacket to the rest of the clothes. The image called to her, begged to be looked at, but she slipped it into her sweater pocket along with the thumbtack and the smallest doll and the TT-33 and everything else she carried. "Who was on the telephone?"

"It doesn't matter," her friend said. "We need to get these documents to Germania."

"We need to go back to the safe house. I'm not—"

"Leaving Luka and Felix." Miriam stopped tossing vegetation over the shallow grave and rose. "I know. I was planning on getting them anyway."

"You were?" Yael couldn't hide her surprise. It was the first time the subject of the boys had come up without a fight.

The night shadows of the forest shifted when Miriam began walking, settling all at once—dark and grim—across her face. "We need to get things sorted."

CHAPTER 35

It had taken hours and more than a few swear words on Luka's part, but the truck no longer sounded like an asthmatic horse. The victor stood over the open engine, listening to it purr for a good minute before Felix gave a thumbs-up from the cab.

"About time." Luka slammed the hood shut. "How can you do this all day?"

"It usually doesn't take me all day." Felix switched the engine off. His expression matched the smell of a forgotten milk bottle, growing more and more sour as the afternoon turned into evening. Whatever side of the secret compartment Felix woke up on, it was clearly the wrong one.

"Relax," Luka told him, though he was far from taking his own advice. It was well past dark, and the fräulein patrol wasn't back yet. The twenty-four-hour mark was still some time off, but this didn't stop the victor's eyes from finding the barn door every five minutes. "Everything's fixed now."

"Fixed?" Some color was coming back to the mechanic's

face. His body must be making up for all that lost blood. "You call this fixed?"

"I don't know what else you'd call a running engine."

The boy slid out of the cab, wounded hand brushing the door. The curdle of his lips broke into agony. Luka supposed that amount of pain would make anyone grouchy. He tugged a spare syrette out of his pocket, decapped it with his teeth. "I think someone needs more pain-be-gone juice."

Felix—amazement of amazements—took the needle without argument. He leaned against the truck, eyes shut, giving a guttural sigh as the morphine slid back into his system. His hair was a mop of sweat and grime, clinging to his face.

Adele had often looked like that, after long days on the road, when she removed her helmet, held her hand out for a cigarette. Her cheeks had the same weary crease of smile lines.

"I didn't attack your sister, you know." Luka surprised himself by saying this. Felix's opinion of him had been formed long before they met. Just like Miriam's and most other people's. "Just kissed her. A few times."

"That's almost worse," Felix grunted.

Luka tossed the emptied syrette into the straw. "I can assure you the spit-swapping was consensual."

The mechanic's spoiled-dairy expression was back. When he opened his eyes, their pupils were screwed pinhole tight—the drug taking hold. "Spare me the details. Please."

The details. Luka's fingers wandered up to the back of his head, touched the pearly scar-skin there. He'd never told anyone the details. (Not even when he petitioned government officials for a longer hairstyle so he could hide the mark.) He wasn't about to start now. "Adele knows how to handle herself. She'll be okay."

"Did you give me a double dose?" Felix asked after a moment.

"No. Why?"

"Morphine makes you much less of an *Arschloch*."

"I could say the same of you," Luka retorted.

"Ah. There it is. Never mind."

The barn door slid open. Luka watched as the fräuleins slipped in: quieter and quietest. Both looked heavier . . . not just in lumpy-sweater kilograms, but in the eyes. Yael seemed close to tears. Miriam looked as if she wanted to eat Luka alive and use his bones to pick her teeth.

"Find what you were looking for?" he asked as lightly as possible.

Yael nodded.

"And more." Miriam stared an armory's worth of daggers when she said this. Tonight they were uncommonly sharp.

Yael went straight to Felix, taking his wounded hand in hers and examining it before asking, "Did you get the truck fixed?"

"*I* fixed the truck. Thank you very much." Luka snagged the frazzled toothbrush from his ear and waved it like a war trophy. The thing was so loaded with grease it bore more than a passing resemblance to Hitler's mustache. "Though," he conceded, "Felix did help."

"It's running," the mechanic said. "It should get us to Germania."

"Good. Let's get it loaded up—"

"We're not leaving yet."

They all stopped and turned to Miriam. She was reaching under her blouse, bringing back handfuls of medical gauze and envelopes. She chucked one after another onto the barn floor.

"Miriam, what are you doing?"

This wasn't the plan. One look at Yael's face told Luka that. An uneasy feeling began to pick at the bottom of his stomach. Nothing good was in those files. Nothing good was in Miriam's stare. The envelopes kept coming, but the second skinshifter didn't let him out of her sight. "We've missed something. I intend to weed out what."

Yael watched the pile of files grow, slapping against the straw. "We're in danger here. We can organize the papers once we get to Germania."

"Everywhere is dangerous," Miriam replied. "This needs to get sorted now."

The final envelope landed on the pile. Miriam crouched down and began opening them. Yael stood to the side, looking worn in every sense of the word, doing nothing to stop her. Luka could not tear his eyes away from the papers as Miriam arranged them into neat piles.

The one she shoved closest to him had a photograph clipped to the front. Young girl. Terrified smile. She wore a six-pointed star on her shirt.

Luka's stomach dropped and kept dropping.

He'd seen such a star before. It was one of his earliest memories: being young and toddling on Hamburg's sidewalks, seeing an older boy with a star stitched to his coat and wanting it. When Luka told his mother, she scolded him. "That's not for people like us."

This only made Luka want the star more. He looked for

them every time his mother took him out on errands. But the bright yellow scraps of fabric grew fewer and fewer, until the stars disappeared altogether. When Luka asked his mother where they went, she frowned and said, "Away."

Away made Luka imagine far-off lands. Boat journeys to skyscraper cities like New York or to South America's heaving jungles. In school, his teachers explained that the Aryan race needed room to grow, so the Lebensraum's *Untermenschen* populations were relocated or put to work in labor camps.

He'd believed them.

Mostly.

There was a part of Luka—one that grew larger with age— that knew these answers weren't right.... They were too glossy. Too simple. They did not fill the emptiness of the sand-scoured Saharan towns. They did not speak to the tangled skeletons of the Muscovy territories. They did not still the winds that sometimes slunk through the streets of Luka's childhood, filling Hamburg with a smell that singed his insides, a smell his mother and teachers and neighbors all went out of their way to ignore.

Ignorance was not quite bliss, but it was easy. Much easier than the alternative...

(Why choose to get crushed when you can survive?)

Some of us don't have that choice. This had been Yael's answer in the back of the truck. This was the truth unfolding in front of him now, spread across the barn floor by Miriam's steady hand. *Away* was not a thriving metropolis or lush tropics. It wasn't a slave's life.

Away was this: pages' worth of lives and deaths and pain. The things Luka found himself reading were brutal, unbelievable.

Scrawls about chemicals and injections and pigment levels. Daily reports on blood pressure and core temperatures. Detailed notes on dissections.

There were more pictures. More children. *Gottverdammt* children—some on the verge of adolescence, others too young to even be in school—stared at the camera, their eyes all shades of solemn dark. Hair just as black and brown. The photographs were divided into series. Luka shuffled through these with a growing sense of horror, one that gnawed an open pit in his stomach. Each collection of pictures, each *child* ended the same way—a postmortem snapshot clipped to an autopsy report. All looked eerily the same: chalky skin; empty, water-pale eyes; hair the color of nothing; left arms bare and turned out, inked with numbers.

Miriam's numbers. Yael's colorlessness.

All Luka could manage to think as he stared at the files was *This is not possible.* No person could endure this. No person could *do* this.

But it had been done. And done and done and done. It was only a fraction of suffering, he realized as he stared at the many papers. There were more hidden beneath Yael's outfit. More left behind in the camp. And the crime itself... hadn't they called it Experiment 85? There were eighty-four experiments before it. And how many after?

"This..." Felix sat on the floor, looking nearly as wan as the pictures. His head shook. "This... this can't be real."

"It is." Yael was the only one in the barn still standing. "This is where skinshifters come from. This is how Hitler has cheated death so many times."

"They're children," the mechanic whispered.

"Yes. We *were* children." Miriam crouched in the middle of the files. Her voice was all this suffering and more—bound into a finite vocal box. "Children of the Third Reich's *Untermenschen*. Jews, Romani, Poles, Slavs, so many others...It was Adolf Hitler's intention to wipe us off the face of the earth. National Socialists have murdered entire nations of people. Are you really so naive to think that a few years of life would make a difference?"

Felix buried his face in his one good hand.

Luka could not look away. Not anymore.

Entire nations. Murdered.

Miriam's eyes lit on him. "What do you see, Herr Löwe?"

Luka did not know what she was asking, but he knew his answer. He saw what he could not unsee: the work of devils, executed by the hands of men. Men like the hundreds of brownshirts *heil*ing in the Grosser Platz, who looked to the Führer and nowhere else. Men like Kurt Löwe.

Luka's teeth felt like they were rotting in his mouth. Bile. A mist rimmed his eyes. Not even a scrape of a sleeve could keep it back this time. *Don't you ever show emotion,* came the clanging refrain. Shouting through his snow of thoughts. *A German youth must be strong.*

What good was strength if all it did was this?

Miriam kept asking, questions changing. "What are we missing? Hmm?"

Missing? What is she talking—

Luka wasn't prepared for the leap. Miriam was as spry and strong as her old army uniform had suggested. She was on him in a flash—papers flying, knife from nowhere pressed to his throat. In any other situation, any other time, Luka would've fought. But he stayed, spine to floor. All shock. Wishing the acid decay would leave his mouth.

"Miriam, what are you doing?" Yael yelled, but it made no difference to the pointed pressure on Luka's larynx. He was positive that if he swallowed, his skin would split open—bile, blood, life everywhere. Not a millimeter of movement could be spared, so Luka stayed on his back, meeting Miriam's stare.

"How much have you told them?" A snarl. The blade edged tighter.

"W-who?" he rasped.

Miriam's lips curled. She had very sharp incisors. "You might have Yael fooled, but my heart isn't clouded with your charm."

"Clearly." As soon as Luka said this, he knew it sounded like a stupid, petty thing. *Scheisse*. Why was he always saying stupid, petty things?

"Miriam!" Yael flashed into his periphery. Her hands on the other skinshifter's shoulder, trying to pull her away without accidentally slitting Luka's throat. "Get off him!"

Miriam sheathed her teeth and looked to Yael. "Let me take care of this."

"Take care of *what*?" Yael asked.

Luka's pulse flickered three beats against the blade before Miriam answered, "The SS knew we were coming."

Another two beats: "Who were you talking to on the telephone?"

"The Reichsführer. He thought he was ordering Dr. Geyer to destroy all traces of Experiment Eight-Five. He was scared, Yael. There's something in these pages. . . . 'Sensitive information,' he called it. Sensitive enough that the SS would rather wipe the Doppelgänger Project out of existence than let its records fall into the hands of the resistance."

"That's why you wanted to take the files," Yael whispered. "But... how could Himmler know about our mission?"

"He said they'd been informed. We need to know what else has been leaked."

"What makes you think Luka told them?"

Miriam's laugh had no humor in it. "What makes you think he didn't? How many lies has Herr Löwe told to get his way? Didn't he betray you before just so he could win the Axis Tour and the Führer's approval?"

His revenge against Adele. God, it all seemed so petty now. So stupid and petty.

"Victor Löwe is the Reich's hero, and now he has a chance to save it. An opportunity you've practically handed him."

"I disagree," Yael said.

"You can't just go blindly trusting this boy—"

"I'm not."

"We need answers," Miriam shot back.

"We'll get them, but Luka can't talk with your knife at his throat."

When Miriam pulled back the blade, it was rimmed with red.

Luka's throat burned. His investigative fingertips came back crimson. "If I'd wanted a shave..."

Stupid. Petty. Stop. Miriam needed no extra stabbing incentives.

Yael stepped between the two and locked her stare into

Luka's. There was no love (or hate?), no ice (or burning?) in her gaze. She was even better at cutting those things off than he was. She reached out to take Luka's pulse, touch heavier than ever against his wrist as she launched into her control questions.

"What is your name?"

"Luka Löwe," he managed through his traumatized larynx.

"How old are you?"

"Seventeen."

"Did you tell the SS about our mission?"

Luka shook his head. "No."

"Have you had any contact with Reichsführer Himmler or his men?"

Again, "No."

Yael held his stare another second. She dropped his wrist. "He's telling the truth."

"You don't know that—"

"I do," Yael said. "Look at his eyes."

"Tears are easy to fake." It was only after Miriam said this that Luka realized he was still crying. Full tears now. Too much for even a soft leather sleeve to sop up.

"His pupils are constricted. If he were lying, they'd be owl wide," Yael explained. "His pulse is steady. He has none of his traditional tells."

"He's fooled you before."

The *Kaiten* kiss.

"Yes, well." Yael cleared her throat. "I was distracted."

Luka had lied many times in his life. But not then. Not now.

Miriam wasn't convinced. The second skinshifter's hand was

married to the hilt of her knife as she turned back to Luka. "If you're not here to get information, then why *are* you here?"

Luka had nothing left. He'd been bled of blood and defenses and stupid, petty remarks.

"Because of Yael," he said.

Both fräuleins watched his pupils. Both saw the pinprick truth.

Miriam sheathed her knife. Yael turned away.

It wasn't just Luka's heart that hurt. He could only hold his nausea back long enough to run out of the barn, into the yard. He braced against the weathered wall as the heaves came, and came, and came. Lasting long past the contents of his stomach.

His face was all tears and bitter beard-bile. Luka smeared this away with his sleeve, gagging on the smell of wet *Scheisse* leather. Or was it the dog—still buzzing with rot, not ten meters away—he smelled? The scents were the same.

They were all dead.

Another heave (dry, full of nothing) overcame Luka as he reached for the dog tag around his neck. Blood of himself. *I want to be like you, better/stronger/more.* War hero. Loyalist lemming. Murderer. He pulled and kept pulling, until the line of fire on the back of his neck matched the front. Until the links snapped, not so strong after all.

What good is it?

For most of Luka's life, the jacket had been too large. Dragging past his fingertips, rubbing his knuckles, weighing him down. Only in the past year or so had it truly begun to fit. Father's shape, Father's form. It felt too small now. Suffocating his skin as he pried it off. He shoved the dog tag in its pocket, took his pistol out and reholstered it in his waistband. He didn't bother holding his breath as he walked to the still Alsatian. Its stench was everywhere. With two hands he took Kurt Löwe's jacket and draped it over the carcass. Brown leather covering blood-matted fur.

Luka couldn't go back to the barn. Not just yet. Not now that all of him knew—the choice Miriam and Yael and oh so many others never had. The choice he'd made not to ask more questions, find more answers, because he'd seen the cost of true resistance at the Grosser Platz (inferno in the skin, Luger to the skull, *BANG*).

I was afraid.

Still am.

Guilt crushed Luka anyway, pressing down with a galaxy's weight. All those stars. All those hundreds of thousands and millions of stars...

He made his way through the patchy weeds to the farmhouse steps, where he sat, head in arms. Feeling everything.

CHAPTER 36

The pictures couldn't be real.

That's what Felix told himself as he stared at the photographs. Kids laid out on cold tables—white hair first—their stillness seeping through time and ink. Most of them had been...dismantled. Cut open. Insides spilled out. Someone with bent crab-leg handwriting had sorted through these pieces, taken inventory. Bone density, urine samples, blood analysis, all glands and organs measured. Thyroids—there were lots of pictures of those—spread out like fleshy butterflies before being sliced, diced.

Crustacean writing on the photograph by Felix's foot told him that particular thyroid belonged to Inmate 125819ΔX. Not a criminal, but a girl. He knew this because the numbers matched a different picture: **Anne Weisskopf. 125819ΔX. Preinjection.** She looked close to Felix's own age. She looked scared. Her eyes reached through the camera lens, pleading.

In Tokyo, he'd wondered how face-changing worked. What

made it possible? Now the answers were spread at his feet, and all Felix could do was cover his eyes. It was easier not to look at Anne Weisskopf and her insides, so he sat in the straw, his good hand over his face. All he could feel was the morphine Luka had just given him, glowing through his arteries, veins, capillaries. Taking the iron in his blood and making it shine.

A scuffle and a yell made Felix peer through his fingers. Miriam was on top of Luka, knee to chest, knife to throat. Yael was trying to intervene. A drama unfolded. Even though the scent of motor grease mixed with golden-sweet horse feed inside Felix's nostrils, it seemed as if he were watching a show on the Reichssender. Yells, tears, knife-wielding...all of it went through an extra filter of detachment.

"Who were you talking to on the telephone?" Yael asked Miriam.

"The Reichsführer. He thought he was ordering Dr. Geyer to destroy all traces of Experiment Eight-Five...."

Felix's phone call to SS-Standartenführer Baasch had made the rounds, all the way back to Miriam. But how had Miriam convinced Reichsführer Himmler he was talking to this Dr. Geyer fellow? Unless...

Unless ears *could* lie...Doppelgängers could change their vocal cords to sound like anyone. Yael had shifted her own to sound like Adele. What was to stop one of the SS doppelgängers from impersonating his father?

Real, wrong, false, right, what was truth, twisting, everything was twisting...

What if the Gestapo never had his parents at all? What if Mama and Papa really were at Vlad's safe house, alive and unharmed? What if *Felix*—not Yael—was the rat, scrambling as frantically as he could toward SS-Standartenführer Baasch's trap?

All these realizations hit Felix at once. *Slam, slam, slam* as he watched Miriam lower her knife from Luka's throat. As he listened to Yael question the victor. Information had been leaked, and both women were on the hunt. It wouldn't be long before their attentions turned to Felix.

Should he run? (Out of the question. Fleeing on morphine legs wouldn't get him very far.) Should he tell Miriam and Yael the truth, beg for mercy? (But what if Papa's voice really had been Papa's voice? What if Felix only had a day and a half, less now, to save him?)

Already they were walking around the pile of dead paper children. Yael knelt in front of Anne Weisskopf's file, her skirt flowering over hay and hellish things. She grabbed the inside of his wrist, pressed her fingers to his pulse.

Good, lesser, evil, lies, death, so many shifting skins…there was so much to focus on. Too much. Felix had to narrow his sights. The one thing he knew for certain was this: He could not, would not risk Papa's death. Lying was his only option.

"What is your name?"

"Felix Burkhard Wolfe." Felix stared at the powdered bridge of Yael's nose as he answered. The *not real* feeling filmed his insides. He clung to it.

"How old are you?"

"Seventeen."

"Felix, did you tell the SS about our mission?"

One of the few useful things SS-Standartenführer Baasch

had given Felix was a list of things to avoid when telling a lie. Body language basics: no swallowing, no looking to the left, no hesitating. There wasn't much he could do about the shape of his pupils or the rate of his pulse.…

"No, I didn't," he said.

Miriam loomed nearby, watching his eyes with hawklike intensity. Yael's face was a blank slate as she read Felix's own. Could they *see*? Was his body betraying him, inkblot pupils spreading out? Pulse peppering—*lies, lies, all lies*—through his skin?

"Have you had any contact with Reichsführer Himmler or his men?"

"The last time I saw the SS was when they shoved us in the *Immelmann IV* to fly us back for our trial," Felix told them.

"That didn't answer her question," Miriam pointed out.

"No, I haven't contacted Reichsführer Himmler, or any of his men. Why would I? All I want, all I've ever wanted, is to get back to my family. Adele, Mama, Papa, all of them are safe with the resistance." *Were they?* Yael seemed to think so, which was all that mattered for this lie. She couldn't possibly know about the leverage Baasch had on him, because that leverage might not even exist.

"No pupil dilation. No pulse variation," Yael declared after a moment.

Felix blinked and wondered *how*. Maybe it had something to do with the surrealism of everything.… Even his body couldn't tell the difference between true and false, pain and drug, Wolfes and doppelgänger ghosts.

"Someone did it." Miriam was still suspicious. Still watchful. "Who else, if not these boys?"

"It could've been anyone." Yael dropped Felix's wrist. Her fingers migrated to her temples, pressing either side of her head as if she could squeeze a solution out. "It must have been someone from Molotov. Or Germania. Or the National Socialists discovered our Enigma code and managed to listen in."

"If that's the case…" Miriam's breath was more of a hiss. "What else does the SS know? Yael, if they're aware of our assassination plans, they could be waiting for us in the *Führerbunker*. The real Führer could be transferred anywhere. The Kehlsteinhaus. The Wolfsschanze."

"We don't know that," Yael said.

"That's right. We don't know!" Miriam kicked at a tuft of straw. The woman's knife was put away, but she still looked ready to stab someone. "We could be walking straight into an ambush, and we'd have no idea!"

Only then did Felix notice the lump behind Miriam's foot. It was the syrette Luka had just used, emptied of its morphine. Morphine now soaring like a golden sunrise inside Felix, turning pain into peace, lies into truth.

The drug! It was the drug that had spared him—calming his heartbeat, tightening his pupils. Yael must've thought Felix was still abstaining from the painkiller. If she saw the crumpled syrette, realized how it was affecting him…

"We do have one advantage." Yael waved her arm, indicating the files and photos. "Though it'd be better to get these records sorted in Germania. Henryka and Reiniger need to be informed about the leak as soon as possible."

Miriam's foot kept scuffing the barn floor, kicking up enough straw to cover the syrette. Out of sight, out of suspicion.

"I'm going to find Luka," Yael said. "As soon as all this is cleaned up, we can depart for Germania. Agreed?"

Scuff, stamp. Miriam nodded. Yael ducked through the half-open barn door. Felix sat; the drug in his veins climbed higher, shone brighter as Miriam started collecting the Doppelgänger Project documents. He considered the straw mound, wondering if he should try to dig up the empty syrette, pocket it. But no. Felix picked up Anne Weisskopf's papers instead—brittle hair, brain matter, *help me* stare—and tucked them back into their manila envelope.

Some things were better left buried.

CHAPTER 37

Luka hadn't moved. He sat on the farmhouse steps, cradling his face inside his elbows, and kept sitting. The dead dog hadn't moved either, but its stench was starting to fade. It was amazing what olfactory nerves could adapt to, what levels of denial the human body was capable of....

"Luka?"

Yael. He hadn't heard her approach. Everything in Luka wanted to look up and greet her. Everything in him dreaded it. But when he tried to move, he found that he couldn't. The crush of skies remained. Who was he to slough it off?

Yael settled on the step beside him. Her sweater brushed his bare arm. She said nothing. The silence squirmed inside Luka, twisted, twisted until he could no longer keep it.

"I'm sorry, Yael. I didn't know about the experiments. I thought the camps were for labor. I thought..." Luka stopped. He couldn't imagine what he'd thought now: *away* and all. There was no excuse. Not for murder this massive. Not for all the suffering that had happened while he was off smoking cigarettes.

He lifted his head. Most of the moon had decided to take the night off; what little remained hung as thin and useless as a fingernail clipping. Yael was but a sketch beneath its light—hair dripping silver down her shoulders, washed-out face. Her eyes were the focal point: dark as danger, whet by emotion.

"You didn't know. Is that the truth?" she asked finally.

The truth. That's what sat between them now. Not a wall of unknowns, but a chasm, bottomless, without end.

How could things ever be even between them?

"Yes. And no. I never knew, but I was too scared to know. But fear isn't an excuse, and I—I don't want to be a coward anymore." Luka rubbed his hand through his hair—over the pearly scar (which felt like nothing now), down to the base of his neck (so empty without the dog tag links). "Is it too late to join?"

"What?"

"The resistance. Can I still join? Is there some list I add my name to? A blood oath? Or something?"

Yael watched him for another moment. Her stare could not be more different from Miriam's, but Luka still got the distinct feeling he was being judged. Every word weighed, every flicker of his pupil noted.

"Consider yourself a member," she said.

"That's all?" It didn't feel like enough. (Why did it never feel like enough?)

"I already did your background check. Luka Wotan Löwe. Born February 10, 1939, in Hamburg to Kurt and Nina Löwe."

Wotan. The wince-worthy name belonged to Luka's grand-father. Antiquated even then. "You certainly were thorough."

"I had to know what I was getting into."

"So what am I getting into?"

Yael's arm drew away from his and pulled something from her sweater. She placed it in Luka's palm. It was paper, he realized. Another photograph. He had to tilt it toward the distant barn light to see what he already knew was there: another young girl. Her portrait was made of opposites. Dark hair. Light skin. Terrified lips. Eyes that looked ready to make something flint, catch, explode. These held a different kind of strength. Something far deeper, far truer than the blitzkrieg brutality his father upheld.

"It's you, isn't it?" The picture felt so very rippable against Luka's palm as he turned it over to read the faint words on the back. "Yael Reider."

"I found it in the Doppelgänger Project files with all the others. I'd forgotten what I looked like. Until today."

"I can't imagine," Luka whispered. There were so many things he couldn't imagine.

"For years I just kept drifting. Face to face. Name to name." Yael rolled up her left sleeve until her arm was bare next to his. "These tattoos were all I had to hold on to who I was."

Luka's eyes struggled to adjust with the view, just as they had with the photograph. They focused first on the light parts: spots of star-kissed skin. It was only after a few seconds that the black lines seized his focus and would not let go. Wolves he couldn't unsee. Marks that meant something.

328

Luka was still afraid, but what good was it? His jacket was gone, and the truth was already between them, and he wanted to know who the hell this girl was and what made her so strong.

"What do they mean?" he asked.

CHAPTER 38

Telling truth from lies was simple, once you learned the science behind it. Yael was having visions of *veritas* everywhere tonight.

Truth: Luka wanted to join the resistance.

Truth: Luka was afraid.

Truth: So was she, still.

Knowing when to trust someone wasn't so cut-and-dried. It was a mysterious equation, made of heartstrings and gut feelings. So when Luka's stare fell to her wolves and he asked "What do they mean?" Yael could not rely on a pulse or a pupil. There was only her iron voice:

—TELL HIM WHO YOU ARE—

Beginning to now. It was a long story, and at times hard to convey. Yael tried her best to do each wolf justice. The Babushka's magical, miracle words. Mama's fever-soothing fingers. Miriam's bravery. (At this point in the narrative, Luka interrupted. "*That* Miriam?" he asked, rubbing the swollen knife memory on his throat.) Aaron-Klaus's assassination attempt. (A second interruption: "I remember him. His face was on fire. I mean—not actually on fire. More like...lit." Yael knew exactly what he meant.) Vlad's training.

Look straight ahead. Fight with your weak.

At the end of it all, Yael realized, it did not feel very much like an ending. There was still so much more to her story. One of the larger pieces sat beside her in his undershirt. Arms speckled with goose bumps. Jaw made of edge. Though she'd finished talking, he kept listening with an intensity that set the skin on her own bare-wolf arm alight.

She watched him through the silent dark and thought of the next chapter.

"Yael Reider," Luka said after a moment. "You're impossible."

"So are you, Luka Löwe."

"I think we're using the word differently, Fräulein of Infinite Faces, who speaks six languages and identifies poisons by smell."

"A few months ago, I found the idea of a National Socialist poster boy with a heart just as absurd." Yael placed her hand over his. The picture of her oldest self was still caught between Luka's fingers. "But here we are."

His touch tightened against hers. Goose bumps flared across both of their arms. This was no *Kaiten* kiss. No heaven and earth moving beneath her feet and passion torching her lips while the sun shone overhead. It was no train kiss either.

It was just a touch: skin to raw to skin. The simplest thing.

It was real.

She stared at their fingers: hers slender with neat oval nail beds, his crusted with engine grease, both made of fingerprints and cuticles and nerve endings that shot signals to their brains. *(We're touching!)*

(What now?)

"I don't want to be their poster boy," Luka said in a husk of a voice. "I never wanted that."

"Then why did you race?"

"My father."

Kurt Löwe. Kradschützen. When Yael first read Luka's file, she assumed the racer was carrying on a legacy, taking up the chrome handlebars of his father's mantle. But there was an edge in the victor's words that spoke otherwise.

"When I was growing up, all he ever talked about was the war: riding motorcycles through the Muscovy territories, killing commies. I thought he was a hero. He thought I was a weakling. I started racing because I wanted to prove him wrong, make him proud. But he had too much *verdammt* pride to share it. No matter how many races I won, it was never enough for him. I was never enough. I needed to be faster, stronger, better. Nothing made a difference. Not even becoming a poster boy." His hand tensed under hers, as if he was about to pull away. "Sorry."

"Why are you sorry?"

It was Luka's turn to look down at their hands and the picture between. "You've been through so much, and here I am complaining about my father...." He drifted off. "It must seem so small to you."

Yael started at her young self. "No person's life is small," she said.

"Yael." Her name was gruff and velvet off Luka's tongue: all at once familiar. "I don't just want to be a member of the resistance. I want to do more. Fight. Stop this"—his fingers trembled over her photograph—"from happening."

"That's always been the goal," Yael reminded him. "The National Socialists aren't making it easy. I found a roster in Dr. Geyer's office. There's a whole detail of skinshifters dedicated to protecting Hitler. The *SS-Maskiertekommando des Führers*. The doppelgänger I shot in the ballroom was one of them. There are nineteen others."

"Nineteen?" Luka gave a low whistle. "*Scheisse*. That's some hefty survival insurance."

Nineteen men who could vanish into a crowd, reappear on the Reichssender at a moment's notice. Hydra heads, all of them. It wasn't just a matter of weeding through the doppelgängers to find the real Hitler, but making sure none of them could spring back....

"Then there's the matter of the leak," Yael went on. "Getting access to the Führer was difficult enough when the National Socialists weren't expecting us. Now the SS could be waiting at any turn."

"So turn a different way," Luka said. "If the SS is expecting you to hunt down the real Führer and kill him, don't. The odds of success sound a bit stacked anyway. Hitler could be sipping mineral water on some tropical beach right now for all we know."

"Novosibirsk isn't sending any reinforcements, and Reiniger's only hope of winning Germania is to increase his army. That won't happen unless we assassinate Hitler and lift the Wehrmacht's fealty oath." Not to mention the dance of politics with captive Hermann Göring. "The plan was perfect."

"Best-laid, I know." The starlight above was fit only for ghosts, but every centimeter of the victor's face was shining as he went on. "What if you don't have to kill Hitler again? What if all you need to do is destroy the idea of him?"

Yael stopped breathing. "What do you mean?"

"The *Führereid* makes soldiers swear unconditional obedience to 'the leader of the German empire and people, Adolf Hitler.' Not his nineteen decoys. Proof of them alone would be enough to nullify the oath in some men's minds. If we copied these files and printed them in *Das Reich*, if we found a way to expose the Doppelgänger Project on the Reichssender, it wouldn't just be Wehrmacht soldiers rallying to General Reiniger's cause." The lit-ness of Luka's brow and cheeks spread to his voice. "*We* know Hitler's been using skinshifters, but the rest of the Reich has no idea.... Show the Reich what you showed me— get all that 'sensitive information' out there—and we're sure to get more than a few civilians in the mix."

Das Reich? The Reichssender? Civilians? Yael's head spun with possibilities and oxygenless sparks. She took a new breath in, let the thoughts settle.

It wasn't a terrible plan. It wasn't even a bad one. It could actually be good. (After all, what better way to kill a hydra than by severing all its heads at once?) With the evidence of the *Maskiertekommando* and its origins out there, all trust in the Führer as a figure would be broken. Hitler's unquestionable hold on the masses would, in fact, be questioned. (Real? Or doppelgänger?)

"That would cause chaos."

"Exactly." Luka grinned.

Breaking into the Ministry of Public Enlightenment and

Propaganda *would* be easier than infiltrating the *Führerbunker*. Possible, at least. "Accessing *Das Reich*'s printing press would be too time-consuming. We'd be better off using the Reichssender, but…"

"What?"

The truth Yael carried under her sweater, beneath her skin, was shocking. For most it would not go down well. Even with paper-and-ink proof. Even if she showed the world who she was, what she'd endured. "Who's going to believe me?"

"It doesn't have to be just your word against the National Socialists. Let me present the information on the Reichssender with you." Luka was a candle unto himself. Face and words and faith: bright, bright. Alive and burning. "Before you shot fake-Führer, the entire Reich watched him give me a toast. They've watched me race for the past five years. They know me. Hell, some of them might even trust me. If I'm going to be Hitler's *verdammt* poster boy, then I might as well use that status to hamstring the *Saukerl*."

His fingers danced under hers. Nerves shouting louder than ever: *WE'RE STILL TOUCHING! WHAT NOW? WHAT NOW?*

"Luka, the Reichssender station is in the middle of Germania—"

"I know where it is. In the Ministry of Public Enlightenment and Propaganda. At the Ordenspalais on Wilhelm Street. SS central. Shares cups of sugar with the Chancellery. I've been there plenty of times for interviews. The front-desk girl has a collection of my autographs."

Of course she does.

"I know you love sporting the jacket as a hat, but that won't cut it this time," Yael told him. "Walking down Wilhelm Street with Victor Löwe would be the equivalent of pasting a bull's-eye to our backs."

"The Ministry of Propaganda can't be the only place with filming equipment," Luka reasoned. "If we find a camera in Reiniger's section of Germania, we can prerecord the presentation, the way they do with *Chancellery Chats*. All you'd have to sneak into the Ordenspalais is the film reel."

"It"—if there was another argument, Yael couldn't think of it—"could work."

"It *will* work." Luka's confidence was contagious. Spreading like fever-heat through his fingertips into hers until Yael's insides were brimming. Nerves mixing with iron voice and hope that was not heavy.

What now?

—NOW WE MAKE OURSELVES—

Yael was not a monster. Luka was not the next generation of National Socialism. They were what the Reich would come to fear the most. A Jewish girl and a German boy holding the future and the past in their hands—together.

They sat this way for as long as they could—her wolves to his skin—until the barn door opened wider, bathing the yard with light. Miriam called them back.

Luka squinted at the brightness. "She's not going to stab me, is she?"

"Not tonight." Yael didn't want to let go of his hand. "One last thing."

Her picture was clearer under the new light, full of finer details: eyelash swoops and the frays of thread peeking from her collar. Yael stared eleven years back, took all the buzz and brim and feelings inside, and changed.

Into herself.

It wasn't an exact replica, but a reimagining. (Adolescence left much room for interpretation.) Her forehead was high, with an oblong bone structure. Brown hair grew long, curling at the ends, tickling the insides of her elbows. For the eyes Yael chose a color to match her mother's. Pine-forest dark: made of cool shadows and rich earth. Altogether such a far cry from Adele Wolfe or Elsa Schwarz or the many other skins she'd spent her life slipping into.

This one fit.

A mirror would have been nice, but Yael didn't really need one. She knew this face was right. She could see it in the way Luka was staring at her. His eyelids were raw from tears, and the fire of an idea, a plan, *changing things* still roared behind his indigo irises.

"It's your best face yet," he said.

CHAPTER 39

The road to Germania was not straight. They backtracked to retrieve their abandoned potato sacks before navigating the route Henryka had advised. North first—up bare-bones country lanes. It was Miriam's turn to drive, and though the purple beneath her eyes was beginning to match the dawn sky, she did so without complaint. Exhaustion had made itself at home in Yael as well, but between the discomfort of the files wrapped to her torso and the thought of what lay ahead, she could only sleep in snatches.

Westward, the roadblocks and the lines of refugees grew thicker, as did the urge to—*GRAB YOUR GUN ARM YOURSELF*—every time a patrol rapped on Yael's window. Every time she fought it back, reciting the same "transporting potatoes for my uncle" story (the one that felt thinner and thinner with every telling) as she listened to the sacks receive more knife wounds, waiting for someone to ask her to roll up her sleeve.

It never happened. Always they passed.

"The informant must not have known about this truck.

They would've stopped us by now," Yael reasoned. "That rules out any leak from Molotov."

Miriam grunted. Most of the morning had been quiet—interrupted only by the motor's steady hum and patrols' questions.

"I wish you'd told me about the phone call, back in the office."

"I was trying to protect you."

"I know." Yael's hand slipped back into her pocket, found the smallest doll—uncovered so long that it was worn down to the grain. "It just takes some getting used to."

"So does Herr Löwe."

"You should call him Luka."

Miriam's lips pinched.

"So does Luka," she relented. "If it had been him…would you have done what needed to be done?"

"You mean torture?" Vlad had trained Yael in this art as well. The practice stayed within her lines, but it was far easier to imagine breaking an SS-Schütze's kneecaps than turning a knife on Luka. "It wasn't him."

That's what I thought was written all over Miriam's face.

The day turned grayer, cloaking most of the sun. The muddy back roads disappeared, giving way to pavement. (All smooth, asphalt autobahns led to Germania.) Their truck fit right in with the flood of Lebensraum refugees: common *Volk* crammed into Volkswagens, boys on bicycles, women walking in mud-stained dresses, even a few horse-drawn wagons. People were going to any lengths they could to avoid war.

All while running straight toward it.

It was well past noon, and rain had started slapping at the

cracks in their windshield when the flow of feet and wheels slowed, forcing Miriam to downshift. They'd arrived at a cross-roads, where a bouquet of white road signs shaped like arrows told them GERMANIA was close. Keep going 20 KM.

But the way was blocked. Barbed wire curled across the pavement—hastily strung. The SS soldiers next to it weren't checking papers, but pointing to the alternate route with the muzzles of their Kar.98Ks.

"You can't go this way!" Yael heard one of them yelling as she cranked down her window. "There's a skirmish—"

A rumble—low, deep to the point of feeling—dipped out of the sky, cutting off the soldier's words. Yael's first thought was thunder, but there was no jagged light above, and soon she heard two more bellows: distant, close together.

Tanks.

If panzers and other armored vehicles were involved, then what lay ahead wasn't just a skirmish. They'd reached the front lines. *Or side lines,* Yael corrected herself as she reenvisioned Germania's battlegrounds as Henryka had described them to her over the radio. North of the river Spree belonged to the resistance. General Reiniger was still pushing beyond the capital's borders, toward the North Sea.

But the SS were directing them south, back into the depths of their own territory. The refugees obeyed without question. Only fools would want to drive into battle.

Fools and Yael.

Her heart twisted left with the steering wheel as Miriam followed the rest of the traffic. She drove only a few kilometers—south, south, farther south—before pulling to the shoulder and cutting the engine. "This is as far as the truck's going to go. Any roads west will be blocked. If we want to cross over to General Reiniger's territory, we'll have to do it on foot."

If only it were so straightforward. But there was nothing simple about navigating their way across an active front with a convalescent and no intelligence on where units were placed, all while trying to avoid becoming target practice for Reiniger's own men…

"We should wait until it's dark," Yael said. She hated to delay, but they needed the darkness. So far no one from the passing stream of refugees had spared their truck a second glance; once Luka and Felix climbed out from under the potato sacks, this anonymity would be short-lived.

"Night's better. Get some rest. We'll need it." Miriam slid back into her seat, eyes shut.

Yael did the same, listening to the sounds of rain tapping glass and distant battle song. Mausers spitting, panzers booming, death descending along with the storm. It was strangely lulling.

She slept off and on. There were not so many nightmares. Instead of aiming a gun at Adolf Hitler's face, she held her picture up to a camera lens. All her wolves sat beside her in the Reichssender studio while she introduced them one by one to the all-hearing glass. An ON AIR light hung red above them. She was just introducing Aaron-Klaus when Miriam nudged her awake.

"Time to go."

Twilight made the whole world heavier. Rain kept falling, and semiautomatics rattled the air. The sounds were terrible, but

Yael took heart in their consistency. It meant Reiniger's forces remained strong enough to hold their ground.

Now their merry band just had to get to it.

She climbed into the truck bed and wrenched the holey potato sacks aside one last time. Miriam had parked the truck far enough off the road to avoid the displaced Reichlings' head-lamps. Shadows were their ally as Yael opened the hidden compartment.

"How are you feeling?" was her first question to the pair.

"Wet." Luka was, indeed, sopping when he sat upright. His hair plastered over his face and into his beard. Madman chic. At least there was no rice this time. "We there yet?"

"We have to take a walk first." Some kilometers away, another round of bullets punctuated Yael's sentence for her. "We're going to try and reach Reiniger's men on foot. Felix, can you keep up?"

"Do I have a choice?" he asked.

"We could try using the stretcher."

"No." Felix winced as he propped himself up. "You don't have to drag me. I can walk."

More shots in the distance. "If we're spotted, we're going to have to run."

"Then a stretcher is definitely a bad idea." Felix was emphatic. The boy was just as soaked as Luka. Blue-lipped and miserable in a way that made Yael want to wrap him up in a blanket.

"Are you sure?" she asked.

"It's his fingers that are gone, not his feet. He was trotting around the barn yesterday like a prize pony," Luka told her. "How far do we have to go?"

"No idea. Could be we only have a few kilometers to crawl. Could be there's an SS patrol waiting in those trees." She nodded to a huddle of pines, drooping with the day's rainfall. It was hardly large enough to hold a person's attention, much less a patrol. *But*, as Vlad had told her, *sizing up your enemy means accounting for every possibility. Underestimation gets you killed.*

"Pass those up." Miriam appeared, motioning to the guns.

Together, Luka and Felix delivered the arsenal. They had a sufficient amount of weaponry: a rifle and a handgun each, along with enough bullets to hold back a sizable onslaught. The ammunition pouches had been covered and were still dry. Yael strove to keep hers that way as she strapped it to her person.

The Doppelgänger Project papers were even more precious. They couldn't muck their way through such a wet night without damaging them, so both girls stripped the documents from their bodies. Yael took the waterproof tarp that covered the ammo and swaddled the files (along with her own portrait and pocket talismans) three times over before stuffing them into a pack. This she handed to Miriam, who, they'd agreed, would take the lead. If she fell, Yael would be more likely to reach the bag.

"Weapons are a last resort," Miriam said as she swung the pack over her shoulder, flanking it with her Mosin-Nagant. "You start shooting and your chances of getting killed jump up by a hundred. Understood?"

All nodded.

"Know this"—Miriam's quelling-soldiers-to-their-knees stare shifted to both boys in turn—"If I think either of you are turning your iron sights on me or Yael, I'll shoot. I will not hesitate. I will not miss."

Luka took the warning in stride, securing his own gun to his shoulder. "Trust me. You're the last person I want to pick a fight with."

"That's the problem," Miriam pointed out. "I don't trust you."

"Let's get moving," Yael urged, eager to have this conversation, this night, done with. One at a time they slipped out of the truck. Yael brought up the rear, wishing hard for her not-Lebensraum-bride outerwear as she squelched through soggy earth. Hosiery and Mary Janes made terrible tactical gear.

Rainfall meant cover against enemy detection, but it also meant *Scheisse* visibility. No moon, no stars, all clouds. Yael's twenty-twenty vision strained to keep up with Luka's back as their group slunk through the dark, managing only a few yards before Miriam signaled a halt. It took a few flashes of artillery (far off, in the direction of the town) for Yael to gather why. The trees had ended, a field stretched out in their place: mud as far as the night would let her see. Yael noted a few hedges dotted the ground—large enough to take shelter in, thick enough to cloak an ambush. Dangers out here would vary by kilometer. SS patrols on this side. Reiniger's men on the other.

Miriam readjusted the cinches of her pack. "Let's take it slow. No talking. Follow my lead."

With the gunfire so distant, and the rain falling so fully, and the darkness so hard, there was no need to crawl. Miriam guided them out into the open, followed by Felix, then Luka, then Yael. Every step into the field the mud grew worse: toes to ankles to shins. Yael's flimsy shoes didn't last long. (Good

344

riddance!) She squelched stocking-first into the marks Luka's boots left.

They reached the first set of bushes without incident. No helmets or Kar.98Ks melded into the leaves. To their right, the contested town lit bright. Its silhouette was ravaged, as if a dragon from lore had swooped from the clouds and taken great bites out of its gabled rooftops. They were still some kilometers from drawing even with the lines of battle. Only a few more kilometers after that and they'd encounter Reiniger's men.

The field was an eyeless, soulless wasteland. Miriam forged the way to the second, third, fourth hedges. A few times Felix stumbled—palm-first, face-first—protesting Luka's attempts to help him up. (The victor did anyway. Back muscles clenching through his soaked undershirt.)

Yael hoped, very much, that they would not have to run.

By the fifth set of bushes, she was beginning to think they wouldn't. Most of the field was behind them now, and they were parallel with the town's war-lit center. Soon they'd be out of SS territory.

Miriam must have been thinking the same thing. Their march became bolder.

Too bold.

The sixth mound of foliage wasn't empty. When Miriam burst onto the scouting party, both sides were stunned. Black uniforms flinched in front of the storm-drenched fräulein, not knowing what to make of the sweater clinging to her hourglass waist, the blouse whispering around her breasts. They hesitated a moment too long.

Miriam swung her rifle forward and fired.

There was too much rain and chaos to count their opponents. All Yael could make out was the *Sieg* rune badge on the sleeve of the closest soldier. SS. These men had killed and killed and killed to earn their rank, and they would kill Yael if she didn't end them first. This was the ugly, unforgiving truth. This was why Vlad had taught her to fight.

Yael was not a monster. She was a survivor.

Life or death was not a question this time.

—FORWARD FAST FIND HIS THROAT—

Yael lunged, stockinged feet screwed into the mud as she twisted around, grappling the nearest soldier in a choke hold. She held and held. Shots darted this way and that. The dragon devouring the town roared. Yael could feel its fire—hot against her side. The man's breath rattled into her inner elbow, thrashing.

More shots. One of the bullets found the soldier. He went limp in Yael's grip: no fight, all dead. She dropped him. Next target. A helmet and a set of wide eyes. This soldier was ready, turning along with Yael as she leapt, using his strength to throw her to the earth. She hooked her legs under his as she fell. Gravity dragged the second soldier into the mud alongside her. Yael grabbed her pistol and fired.

The shot was hasty, but true.

She kept her finger on the trigger, searching through the downpour and shadows for a third target. All her sights found were more bodies and Luka.

"It's me!" He threw his arms over his head. "No shooting!"

Miriam was close by, scraping tendrils of hair from her cheeks. "Everyone alive? Uninjured?"

"Yes and yes." Luka dropped his hands. "Glad I have a gun now, m'lady?"

Miriam grunted.

"I've been shot," Yael told them. The firefight's adrenaline was ebbing, and the burn against her rib cage had worsened. A dozen red bees all wriggling to get through her pores. Yael fully expected when she bunched her blouse away to find a hole—as open and pouring as the ones from her nightmares. When she looked down, she saw the soles of the dead man's boots, so close to her toes.

Taking a life takes something from you.

It had taken flesh this time. Not a hole, but a line of absent skin, carving along Yael's side. The wound throbbed, but the bleeding seemed minimal. She pronounced it "Just a graze."

"Are you sure?" Both Miriam and Luka asked this, stepping toward Yael in the same moment. Each looked at the other as if they were intruding.

"Yes." Yael let down her shirt. "Where's Felix?"

"Here!" Adele's brother was a meter away, face full of mud, rifle flung to the side. Rain streaked through his electric hair, washing dirt away. "I couldn't work my gun left-handed. Lay low to make myself less of a target."

"There might be other scouts around," Miriam warned as Luka hoisted the other boy to his feet. "We need to move."

They kept slogging through the field. The bees in Yael's side turned into hornets—angry, nest-stepped ones. She ignored them, fixing her stare on Luka's back. Every few steps, the victor looked over his shoulder, as if double-checking her very existence. Every other few steps, he stopped and pulled Felix upright by his shirttails. The mechanic's stumbles were getting more and more frequent.

They should have brought the stretcher.

Yael's rib cage hive whipped into a fury. How long had they been walking? Where was the morning? How much colder could the rain get? Hadn't they gone far enough?

(Hadn't *she* gone far enough?)

Luka looked to her again. Through a flash from the town, Yael saw that his face was as translucent as his shirt, stripped down to emotions and veins. Blue, blue, shock and fear. "Behind you!"

When Yael turned, she saw movement in the direction of the bodies they'd left. The gunfire must have drawn the attention of another scouting group. Yael couldn't tell how many, there was too much rain-blurred distance between them. A good thing— for the second SS patrol hadn't yet spotted their group.

But sight went two ways. If she could see them . . .

—HIDE RUN FIGHT—

Yael had no time to decide which was the best course of action.

"There!" A wail pierced through the rain. Hounds of bullets followed.

Shots spit into the ground by Yael's feet. The rainfall made for sloppy aim, which she discovered when she hoisted her own rifle to return the favor. Fighting in these conditions was out of the question. They were too exposed for a bullet not to land in the second or third volley.

Hiding was also out of the question. They'd already been spotted, and Yael saw no hedges nearby.

Their only chance was to "RUN!"

She screamed this as she squeezed the trigger.

The others obeyed. Miriam paused to add her own *BOOM*-ing protest to the mix. Felix slipped. This time Luka didn't just lug him upright. The victor lifted the other boy over his shoulder with a Herculean scream, becoming a stretcher of sinew and bone. His footsteps plunged deeper than ever as Yael trailed them.

She ran, waiting for another thousand bee stings to ram through her back. But the death that always lingered there did not fold forward. She ran and ran, until the pain in her side became nothing, and the field suddenly ended. Trees and their witch-claw twigs snapped up Luka and Felix. Yael barely had time to shield her face as she dived into the underbrush. Bullets clamored at their heels, hit the bark with sullen thuds.

Hercules was done, collapsing into the vegetation with Felix and the rifles.

—TIME TO FIGHT—

Luka grabbed a Mosin-Nagant, pressed the buttstock into his shoulder, and spun around to face the field. Miriam did the same, using a trunk for cover. Yael hunkered by her own tree, pulling back her rifle's bolt to free it for another shot. She could tell by the number of bullets and their steady onslaught that this patrol was larger than the last. Much larger.

She peered into the glistening rain, waiting for the next flash. It came, bringing with it the outlines of their approaching enemy. Ten fleet-on-their-feet shadows. Yael let the image burn against her eyelids, aimed from memory at the nearest man, and fired. She did this three more times, though the next flash revealed she'd only stopped two of the ten. Her Mosin-Nagant needed reloading, but there were eight men charging the trees and seven bullets left in her TT-33.

A shot from Miriam brought one down. Luka's bullets were wild cards. Felix was trying his best to bring his hands and his pistol to a truce. Yael fired another bullet. The trunk by her face splintered with a close call.

Three men down. Seven descending. The patrol was only yards away, closing in fast. The artillery flashes weren't coming quickly enough for Yael to pick out her marks.

When she fired the next bullet, it sounded as if every tree around her had decided to fall. SO MUCH NOISE. Too much for a single handgun. Or even a handgun plus Luka's rifle. It was coming from behind them. Shots being fired *from* the trees!

The next jag of light showed the SS patrol stopping, uncertain.

The one after that painted them in full retreat.

Yael looked back into the trees to find shadows that hadn't been there before. Several gathered around Felix and Luka. Their uniforms were nondescript—neither black nor swastika-ed. It was too dark to tell, but Yael was certain, if she looked, there would be frays and tears identical to Ernst Förstner's.

These men were resistance fighters.

They'd reached Reiniger's line.

She was just about to exhale her thanks, when the men lifted their Mausers again, aiming their guns straight at Luka's and Felix's heads.

CHAPTER 40

"Pass code?"

The gun was barrel-first in Felix's face, such a small circle evoking so much fear. His mouth had gone dry, and his tongue felt nailed to his teeth. He held his hands up. The others were doing the same. Weapons down, arms high.

"The wolves of war are gathering! They sing the song of rotten bones!" Yael tore at her sleeve, unleashing the tattooed wolves. "I'm Volchitsa, and these three are with me!"

The Mausers didn't move.

Was it normal to sweat when you were this cold?

"All of you take off your shirts," said the fighter whose rifle was prepped to blow Luka to the heavens. The man's left sleeve had been ripped off at the shoulder. (In fact, all of the soldiers' left sleeves were gone.)

"What?" Miriam asked sharply.

"If you are who you claim to be, it shouldn't be a problem. Shirts off. Now."

They obeyed, stripping down to their underthings. A fighter by Felix grabbed the mechanic's bare arm, wiping the mud off his left bicep. Wiping still, until the skin became prickly and irritated.

"He's clean!"

"This one, too," Luka's inspector declared.

The soldier studying Miriam paused, staring at her numbers as if they were a safe combination he couldn't quite crack.

"It's not a blood-group tattoo," she told him, "if that's what you're looking for. I'm a face-changer, like Volchitsa here, but I'm not SS."

"They're with me," Yael said again. "General Reiniger and Henryka are expecting us. Now, may we please put our clothes back on?"

It was an affirmative. Rifles lowered, shirts were restored.

"Apologies," the fighter closest to Yael said. "New protocol. We've had a few breaches the past few days."

"Breaches?" Yael winced when she stood, hands clutching her side. "Enemy skinshifters?"

"Four that we know of. One got shot trying to cross the front. He went frosted postmortem. When we examined the body, we found the blood-group tattoo. Higher-ups figured he was a skinshifter. Another almost killed General Bauer, trying to take his place. He had the blood-group marking, too. That's when General Reiniger ordered everyone to destroy their left sleeves. We discovered two more that way."

"Sneaky *Saukerl*s," Luka muttered.

"When was this?" Yael asked.

"First one got shot a while back. Didn't ferret out the rest of them until two days ago."

"Explains our leak," Yael said to Miriam, who just frowned.

Felix was grateful no one was looking too carefully at his mud-caked face as he listened in. His morphine armor was long gone, and Baasch's deadline was a noose around his neck—drawing in, in with every passing minute.

There were only a few hours left to reach the resistance's headquarters, ask them to radio Vlad's safe house, dig into the truth of things. What was real? Mama's death or Mama's life? Felix's hearing or his hope?

When the SS-Standartenführer first spoke of the resistance, Felix imagined a few hundred men with rifles holed up in a city block. Eavesdropping on the radio conversation in Molotov had only reinforced the image. But as the patrol led them to a transport—passing tank tracks and command tents and men barking orders—Felix realized this was a serious underestimation.

This was more than a few hundred men. Much more.

This was the Wehrmacht.

Everywhere Felix looked, he saw some version of his father's uniform. All National Socialist badges were gone, and the brown fabric soaked, but the resemblance was unmistakable. Generations of men wore them—some sporting Papa's gray hair, others closer to twenty-one. The age Martin would have been. Felix spotted one or two soldiers his own age, their Hitler Youth uniforms stripped to barest buttons and seams. Boys who could so easily be him.

Papa, Martin, himself, Papa, Martin, Papa, Martin.

Felix pressed his good hand to the watch in his pocket and wondered what his brother would do in the face of all this.

Would Martin have called Baasch from that farmhouse telephone? Could Martin sacrifice all these people to the SS for the Wolfes' safety?

Could Felix, if it came to it?

The ground was slick with mud—just like the many miserable kilometers they'd slogged through. Only here, the earth had been stamped down by scores of boots, slashed through with tank tracks. Extra-treacherous landscape, perfect for stumbling.

Felix didn't stand a chance.

Papa, Martin, Papa—face full of mud, teeth pressed into tread. Grit scratched shapes beneath Felix's eyelids. The ground peeled away before he could even try to push himself up.

Luka—the *Arschloch* who'd just saved his life—was helping him to his feet again. "You all right there, Wonderboy?"

Not really. He was losing focus, getting distracted by a picture too huge to process. These soldiers passing in dizzying numbers were not Felix, nor his family. They weren't who mattered, and if Felix allowed himself to think any differently…that's when doubt crept in. That's when the choice Baasch gave him would be too horrible to make.

"I'm fine." Felix tried to wipe the grit from his eyes, but his arm was just as filthy, and he only succeeded in smearing more between frost-colored eyelashes.

He was glad when they finally reached their transport: a Kübelwagen. The car was too small to fit the four of them plus a driver, but it was the only vehicle the front could spare. They crammed into the seats, slipping on account of mud everywhere. Felix couldn't tell if the girls had shifted their hair into darker colors or if they were simply that caked in dirt.

"We look like golems," Miriam muttered as they settled in.

Felix had no idea what a golem was, but Yael laughed as she climbed into the front passenger seat. The sound was so at odds with its surroundings, so...hopeful.

"We'll be clean soon enough," she assured them, then turned to Felix. "You'll be reunited with your sister. I'm directing the driver to Henryka's office."

Almost there.

Battle sounds faded as their vehicle pulled away from the front lines, but they returned within minutes. Germania was smoldering. Felix smelled the city's ashes through the open windows, mixing with rain. They drove farther and farther into the city, past standstill streetcars and buildings pocked with bullet-hole constellations. It was hard to reconcile these streets with the bustling capital Felix had visited only a month before. Gone were the housewives carrying freshly wrapped baked goods under their arms, the schoolchildren thronging along sidewalks. Cafés usually cluttered with coffee cups and congenial conversations were gutted clean.

Felix kept expecting the Kübelwagen to pull to a stop—in front of an imposing house with a brass door knocker, by the steps of a stately marble structure—but the driver kept going, until the gunshots were a deafening distance away. He could almost *feel* the heat of the battle when the engine cut off.

Yael slid out of the car, waved for them to follow.

He was here. He'd made it! To...a beer hall?

Of all the locations Felix had imagined the resistance

leadership might meet, a bierstube with swastika banners draped along its walls was not among them. Places like this were hives for National Socialist officers. Baasch himself might've even enjoyed a pint here once or twice.

"The headquarters have been here this whole time?" Felix wrinkled his nose at the smell of stale beer as they followed Yael inside. Like most places they'd passed, the beer hall had been abandoned in a hurry: lights out, tables scattered with half-empty glasses.

"We moved when Aaron-Klaus shot the doppelgänger," Yael explained. "But we've always used a beer hall for cover. Any National Socialists loyal to the resistance could frequent a beer hall without attracting attention. If we'd operated out of a private residence or a warehouse, the Gestapo would have noticed."

"You hid beneath their pint glasses," Miriam grunted with appreciation. "Smart."

"*Verdammt* smart," Luka echoed.

They walked to the rear of the establishment and descended a set of stairs. To Felix's eyes, the cellar was just as empty as the hall above, but Yael led them through a series of hidden doorways. The final one was made of reinforced steel, locked from the inside. They stopped in front of it. Yael rapped her knuckles to the metal—two sets of sharp, double knocks—and waited.

The first thing Felix saw when it opened was a cloud of hair, frizzed and floating. There was a woman under it, brandishing an uncapped marker in her fist. "Yael?"

"Henryka!"

They were waved into the headquarters, the door bolted

behind them. Henryka and Yael lost no time embracing. A hug that reminded Felix this was her homecoming.

Some home. He scanned the basement. Several people huddled around a pair of radios and Enigma machines. Bookshelves flanked a hallway opening. The Führer glowed in the corner, mouthing "You will be crushed" from the television screen. A typewriter lay on the floor, smashed. There was no sign of his twin sister.

"Where's Adele?"

Henryka let go of Yael. There was a small flock of marks on her right cheek—cuts that had recently shed their scabs. These collided into each other when she frowned. "She's—"

"FELIX?" The shriek was muffled, but there was no doubt in Felix's mind it belonged to Adele. He *felt* his sister's franticness—punching along with her fists against a second reinforced door.

The room was too small for the way Felix ran through it. His own body met the door—hard. Nothing budged except his bones. "I'M HERE, AD!"

"LET ME OUT! PLEASE LET ME OUT!"

Felix reached for the handle. Locked. He slammed his right hand against the metal, remembering only too late that it was injured. PAIN shot through him: phantom and real.

The others stood in a semicircle, watching his efforts. Henryka crossed her arms. "Unless you're a howitzer or a man with a key, you're not getting through that door," she told him.

Felix clutched his hand to his chest, fighting back a scream. "W-what is she doing in there? She's just a girl—"

Every female in the room gave him a withering look.

Luka snorted.

"Your 'just a girl' sister can do a lot of damage." A dark-haired young man tore off his radio headset and rolled up his sleeves to show welts tangling with his inner arm veins. The work of nails. "She fights like a drowning cat."

"Because you've kept her LOCKED UP for a month!" It was his sister's worst nightmare: being trapped with no way out. No wonder steel rattled at Felix's back, pounding with kicks and fists and whatever else Adele could throw. "Where's the key?"

Henryka's arms stayed crossed. "We've kept Adele in there for everyone's safety. Hers most of all. It's a war zone outside, and she's wearing the face of the girl who shot Hitler."

The face YOU stole! Felix swallowed the accusation back. He mustn't let his rage build up, mustn't let them see. "Where is the key?"

Henryka leveraged freedom as effectively as Baasch. The unlocked door came with conditions: Felix assumed all responsibility for his sister. If Adele harmed anyone or damaged anything, both Wolfe twins would go into the closet.

Understood?

Understood. (Anything to get her out.)

When the door swung open, Adele threw an arm in front of her face, hissing at the brightness. Both he and his sister had been born pale creatures, but a month without sunlight had left Adele translucent. The only color was in her hands, which she'd pummeled raw against the door. When Felix looked above her for the closet light, all he saw was a pull chain. No bulb.

They'd trapped Adele alone in the dark.

Alone. In the dark.

All this time.

"Felix?" Adele dropped her arm, blinking as she tried to reconcile the basement's light with the sight of her brother. "How—what—"

Adele's shoulder blades dug like stunted wings into Felix's forearms when he hugged her. Had they always been this sharp? Or had the resistance been starving her, too?

Felix's wound burned, and his sister squirmed (she'd always been averse to hugs longer than three seconds, further proof that Adele was, indeed, Adele), but he held her tight, afraid of what might happen if he let go.

"Ow, Felix!" Adele managed to weasel out of his grip. She looked ready to punch something—fists bunched, lips knotted—as she took in the rest of the map room. Her stare froze on "Luka?"

"Fräulein." The victor nodded, but the rest of his body stiffened, as if Adele were a grenade with the pin pulled and he was fighting the urge to flee before she exploded everywhere. "I'd say it's been too long, but—"

"What is this?" Adele jerked forward, only to find her collar caught in Felix's grip. "Revenge for Osaka?"

Felix had to use both hands to hold Adele back. He knew her rage, he *felt* it. But Henryka was watching the exchange with pressed lips, and the young man with clawed-up arms tensed, ready to hurl both twins into the closet.

"Let me go!" Adele twisted around, blouse tearing, and grasped at her brother's hands, stopping only when she saw the bandage. "Your hand! Oh, God. Felix, your fingers..."

"It doesn't hurt anymore," he lied.

"What the hell is going on?" his sister whispered.

Felix wished he knew. A clock by one of the shelves told him it was just a shade past midnight. Thirty-one hours had passed since his call to Baasch. Only five remained before... what?

What was going to happen? It all depended on Felix's next question. Henryka's next answer. "Yael told me my parents are in a resistance safe house. With a man named Vlad. Have you heard from them?"

"Kasper, have you had any messages from Vlad's farm?" the older woman asked. The man with the clawed arms shook his head. "Johann?"

Johann sat with his headphones half on, immersed in conversations both verbal and electrical. It took him a moment to answer. "No. Nothing."

"That's not unusual," Yael assured Felix. "Vlad's something of a hermit."

"Can we contact him? I want to speak with my parents, to make sure they're okay." *Please let them be alive. Please let them be them.*

All traces of warden-Henryka had vanished, remolding into a motherly smile. "Of course you do. However, it's quite late. In all likelihood they're asleep—"

"Please. Can we just try?" *YOUR LIVES DEPEND ON IT*, he wanted to scream, but Papa's life might depend on Felix's discretion, so instead he took a breath and explained, "It's just, I'd like to talk to them as soon as possible. They're probably worried sick about Ad and me."

After a moment, Henryka relented. "Kasper? Reinhard? Would you try hailing Vlad?"

Exhaustion toned Kasper's eyes as he twisted the radio dials to the right frequency. Another man—older, middle thirties—was typing into an Enigma machine, jotting its results down in a notebook, passing them to Kasper, who read it aloud into the transceiver. Gibberish letters—not unlike the conversations Felix had overheard in Molotov.

The rest of the room went about its business. Johann and a girl whose hair served as a pencil pincushion operated a second communication station. Luka leaned against a bookshelf, his eyes never straying far from Adele. Miriam began arranging the Doppelgänger Project files on a card table, photographs on top. Felix shifted to an angle where the television glow drowned their images out.

Yael began speaking to Henryka in near whispers. "I'm afraid we've run into some complications. There's been a leak—"

Kasper's radio was a mechanic's gold mine: cords and gauges and switches and red lights. The Enigma machine was simpler on the outside—not so very different from a typewriter. It held two sets of alphabets. A keyboard version plus a lamp board, which lit up with a letter's code double when the regular keys were pushed. The code was unbreakable without the exact rotor combination.

Felix moved as close as he dared to the operator's shoulder, and even then he had to squint to make out the letters on the rotor markers: w-l-s.

Three tiny letters were all that stood between the resistance and their foe.

Three tiny letters and a phone call.

Felix hoped he wouldn't have to. He hoped his parents were alive, safe. But this hope was shrinking while Baasch's noose tightened. Seconds ticked into minutes, and from the look on Kasper's face, no one had answered his hail. When the young man caught Felix's eyes—looking, looking—he shook his head.

"Keep trying," Felix urged.

Kasper repeated the letters into the radio. The room buzzed around them. Henryka and Yael's exchange was picking up steam—growing hotter and hissier when Miriam joined their conversation. The television emitted a pitch that would drive dogs mad. Pencils scratched. Keys clacked. But the sound Felix needed to hear most never came: Vlad's end stayed silent.

Kasper sighed. "No answer. Sorry. Like Henryka said, it's late and Vlad's the early-to-rise type. He's probably asleep. I can't keep jamming the radio waves with all the other transmissions trying to get through. They're important."

NOTHING'S AS IMPORTANT AS THIS! "Doesn't he have a telephone?"

"No. We're fortunate he has a shortwave, to be honest." Kasper was already readjusting his radio's channels.

"But—"

"Leave Kasper to his duties." A hand settled on Felix's shoulder. Its fingers were bird-bone delicate, but their grip was made of metal. Henryka spun him around, nodded at his filthy bandages. "For now you have other things to tend to. There are medical supplies in the washroom. Go get cleaned up."

"I'll show you where it is," Yael offered. "You and Adele can catch up in my old quarters."

The beer hall's subbasement was an entire warren of rooms. Its hallway was lined with more bookshelves, full of titles Felix had never seen before: *The Metamorphosis, The Call of the Wild, The Biology of Desert Wildlife, Les Misérables.* Well-loved books with creased spines. The whole place had a well-loved feel. A chocolate smell haunted the kitchen, and three of the four sleeping quarters were stuffed with record players, lamps, quilts, photographs, fire extinguishers, plush rugs, art stranger than anything Felix had ever seen—as if the painters had dropped their subjects, splintering them almost beyond recognition. In one of the rooms—he noted—sat a telephone.

Yael paused by the fourth, starkly empty room. Its doorknob hung in pieces, the wood around it beat to pulp. "I assume I have you to thank for this?" she asked Adele.

"And I assume I have you to thank for all of this?" A month's worth of unburned energy charged Adele's words as she fired back. Felix didn't have to turn around to know his sister was gearing back up for a fight.

The last thing he needed was to get locked into a closet. "Ad—"

"Don't 'Ad' me! I've just spent a *gottverdammt* eternity locked up in the dark, and you're acting like everything's FINE?" His sister spit bullets. "A girl came into my flat, Felix. She attacked me the night you left—"

"I know."

"YOU KNOW?" Adele's shriek was too large for the hallway. "You know and all you're going to do is take a shower?"

"It's"—how could he tell his sister he'd gone to the ends of the earth and back for her? That he would go farther still?—"complicated."

"Then uncomplicate it."

Yael—strangely enough—came to his rescue. "You have every right to be angry, Adele, but Felix is the last person who deserves your yells. Let your brother clean out his hand. You'll have plenty of time to talk."

Adele sniffed and walked through the broken door without further fuss. Cease-fire. For now. Felix was grateful. The longer he stood here wearing mud-crusted bandages, the more he imagined a new infection rooting, spreading.

He still had so much to lose.

The washroom sat at the end of the hall—as lived-in as all the other rooms—there was buildup on the showerhead and a family of toothbrushes by the sink. Yael raided the towel cabinet for gauze and antiseptic—and though Felix had seen enough of both items for a lifetime, he grunted his gratitude when she handed them over.

"I know you're good with first aid, but"—she nodded at his right hand's missingness—"can you manage?"

"Adele can help me," he said pointedly.

"Right." Yael dug more of the same out of the cabinet. When she got all she needed, she nudged it shut with her knee, started moving back toward the hall. She stopped suddenly. "Felix, I'm sorry you had to find your sister like that. They shouldn't have kept Adele in the dark."

Sorry. As if the word hadn't been watered down to the point of meaninglessness between them. It was as useless as the sopping wrapping Felix unraveled from his fist and tossed into the wastebasket.

Yael disappeared to tend to her own wounds. Felix wrenched the showerhead on.

It would take a lot more than *sorry* to fix things.

CHAPTER 41

Luka wasn't about to let the lady Wolfe sneak up behind him again. He kept his back to the wall whenever one was available. When it was his turn to shower, he did so with the curtain open, never letting his eyes leave the washroom's lock as the freezing water trickled in a dozen X's down his shoulders. He did shave with his back exposed, but that was only because there was a mirror involved. The door's reflection stayed motionless; the straight blade scraped against Luka's jaw.

She cut him without trying.

He didn't notice at first. The cut didn't hurt, just bled: red and less red as it melded with the lather. Luka cleaned it as best he could, keeping his full attention on the removal of hair from skin thereafter.

Adele Wolfe wasn't worth his fear. Or his bloody throat.

She was waiting for him in the hallway—in plain sight and every bit as striking as Luka's memories of her dictated. He halted, unsure if he should approach or lock himself in the bathroom again.

"What are you doing out here?"

"Waiting for you," she said coolly. "*I* don't barge in on people when they're bathing."

Their sparring match had begun. This initial jab was aimed at the first time they'd met, when Luka had walked into the washroom at the Rome checkpoint and saw ... well ... nothing short of everything.

"Got any cigarettes?"

"No." Luka decided to try stepping around the girl, but the hallway was small enough for Adele to block his path.

Eleven months of his life, nearly one year out of seventeen. That was how much time Luka had dedicated to planning out the moment he'd face Adele Wolfe again. Now that it was here, all he wanted to do was keep walking.

"C'mon." Her chin tilted up in the same way it had their first night out of Dhaka, when the jungle sang symphonies around their camp, and they smoked nearly an entire pack to keep the mosquitoes at bay. That was the night they shared their first kiss. And second. "You always had a few stashed away. Behind your ear? In the hem of your pants?"

She reached out to search these places. Luka dodged. "I've got nothing for you."

Adele's eyes narrowed. "Are you still sore about Osaka?"

"Sore? Try scarred."

"I might've hit you a little too zealously," she admitted, "but don't pretend you wouldn't have done the exact same thing if you were in my position. In fact, I already suspect you *did*. Felix told me all about how he found fake me drugged on the *Kaiten*.

"So how did you do it?" Adele pressed. "Slip the stuff into her *kake udon* when she wasn't looking? Shiv her with a syringe?"

367

"I don't sedate and tell."

"You had no problem doing that when we rode together."

"Things have changed since then." The Axis Tour of 1955 was closed off in Luka's mind, encased like some museum display. When Luka thought of the boy who'd sat in the jungle heat, kissing the girl with a cigarette burning between her knuckles, he did not feel angry or vengeful. He felt . . .

"Changed." Adele frowned. "Answer me this, then: Why did you invite her to the Victor's Ball?"

"Why do you care?"

The girl's chin tilted higher; she stepped closer. "She was *me*, wasn't she?"

No, Not-Adele was not Adele. She'd always ever been Yael—a girl who, when she touched his fingertips, made his heart beat a dozen times faster than it ever had in this fräulein's arms. Yael, who believed that no person's life was small. Yael, who made him want to be *more*, but in a way that mattered. Yael, who was in the main room, waiting for him to return so they could start plotting the Reich's death blow.

"The two of you could not be more different. Now, if you'll excuse me—"

For spending a month locked in a closet, Adele was surprisingly agile, matching his next side step as well as a shadow. "I know that look. You *like* her. You *more* than like her."

"Is that a crime?" Luka asked.

"Some might think so." Adele blew her angel hairs out of her face. Once upon a time, Luka thought they were cute: all white and frayed, like some ice-princess crown. Now, magic-less, they just looked like hair.

Luka pushed—gently—past Adele. His shoulder met hers, and it truly was nothing. The vague melody of Yael's voice from the other end of the hall held more electricity.

"Are you sure you don't have a smoke?" Adele didn't try to stop him this time, just watched as he stepped around, away.

"I've never been more sure of anything in my life," he said.

CHAPTER 42

Yael sat in front of the operations map, taking in all of its revisions. Egypt, Great Britain, Iraq, Finland, half of Italy, Turkey. Some of the indigo ink was fresher: the Iberian Peninsula, Greece, and a good portion of the Muscovy territories. (Novosibirsk's army was closing in on Moscow, sweeping through the surrounding countryside with gray-yarn fronts.) Fledgling countries had been marked in dotted black lines. These crisscrossed through continents, cutting them into smaller parcels of land. Many formed shapes Yael had seen in the pages of Henryka's 1931 World Atlas.

It was such a vast and colorful difference from the map Yael had studied only a month ago. Old order was being restored. Forgotten countries made new.

"It's beautiful," she said, reaching out to touch Egypt's borders.

"Keep still!" Henryka *tcht*ed from her side, brandishing a needle tailed with surgical thread. "This isn't exactly embroidery."

Yael settled back into the chair. The bullet graze, for all its stinging, was small. The resistance leader had spent an inordinate amount of time fussing over it, flushing out every speck of dirt with at least three different rounds of antiseptic. There'd never been a cleaner wound.

"I'm glad to see you, too, Henryka."

The smile lines in the corners of the Polish woman's mouth weren't as deep as they should've been for her age. The needle paused as she eyed the ink-heavy map. "It is a beautiful sight, but I fear much of it won't matter if we lose Germania. These new governments have the structural integrity of a seeding dandelion. It wouldn't take much to scatter them, should Hitler and his government survive to reclaim the territories."

"Reiniger's forces seem to be holding their own." Yael nodded to a second map—one that showed Germania's streets in winding detail. Pins pocked the blocks closest to the Spree, surrounded the holes of ground gained and lost.

"It's centimeter warfare." Henryka's smile vanished as she kept sewing Yael's flesh back into place. "Not enough to make a real difference. The SS has us surrounded on all sides, and our supplies are dwindling. We might not even have enough to reach the North Sea...."

"Cue the cavalry," Miriam said from the card table. Her appearance was back to what Yael now considered normal—dark hair threaded with silver, eyes flecked with gold. She sat, elbow high in documents.

The Doppelgänger Project files had survived the front crossing in better condition than any of them—dry and unbent. They weren't the only papers on the table. With the leak in play, all options were laid out. Blueprints of the Chancellery and *Führerbunker* sat alongside a map of the Ministry of Public Enlightenment and Propaganda. The latter had been hand-drawn by Luka himself. He was, Yael noted, quite gifted at sketching: showing poise in even the shortest of strokes. His knowledge of the Ordenspalais building was partial, covering only the halls he himself had trod, but it would be enough to guide an infiltrator through the annexed wing that held the Reichssender studios. Enough to sneak an exposé film reel on Experiment 85 and Hitler's *Maskiertekommando* into the control room.

The plan was received with much less fuss than Yael had expected, especially on Miriam's part. She and Henryka listened to Yael's reasoning—fifteen hydra heads, chaos, poster boy posterity—without interruption, if only because their initial assassination plan was (more or less) impossible.

At the end of it all, Henryka nodded. "We'll have to consult Erwin and the other officers. But I agree. Revealing this information could invalidate the *Führereid* and cripple the National Socialist forces."

Miriam's sole objection was to the idea of Luka's presenting. It wasn't his influence the other girl questioned so much as his right. Seeing a few photographs, shedding a few tears did not an advocate make. Who was he to speak for them?

Not *for,* Yael had reasoned, *with.* It had taken several rounds of head-butting to sway Miriam from the "absolutely not" into the "maybe, fine" camp. The subject was now a bruised, tender thing between them.

Speaking of tender... Yael grit her teeth as Henryka sewed the last of her stitches. Needle piercing skin—even for healing purposes—set her on edge.

"Has the cavalry found anything?" she asked Miriam.

"Just more of the same." Apart from a shower and a quick bite, Miriam had been inseparable from the files, scanning every single page once, twice, thrice, as many times as it took to make sense of the panic she'd heard in Reichsführer Himmler's voice. "No silver bullets, yet."

Yael thought what they had—proof of the experiment, a roster of the *Maskiertekommando*, Luka's word—was enough. Still, it made sense to sort. Whichever one of them infiltrated the Ministry of Propaganda would only have a few minutes to air the reel before being discovered. Their program needed to be brief enough to fit inside this window, powerful enough to spark change. Only the most relevant files would do.

Henryka cut the thread, padded Yael's side with antiseptic, and smothered the sting with a bandage. She nodded at the map of Germania's streets. "Maybe your time would be better spent studying ways in and out of the Ordenspalais."

In paper terms, they were only a finger's length from the Reichssender station—a half-hour stroll over the Spree, down to Wilhelm Street. But the double-lightning pins of the SS units between the two points resembled a spider's nest. Yael stared so hard at the *Sieg* runes that they blurred into one hairy arachnid blob. Infiltrating the area would take stealth and luck. Escaping would require even more of these things.

It wasn't as impossible as a mission into the *Führerbunker*, but it was nearly as dangerous.

"Luka will help with that once we plan out the presentation.

Any news on camera equipment?" she asked Kasper, who'd just signed off on a transmission.

He ground the heel of his palm into his eyes, as if sleep deprivation were something that could be pummeled away. "Nothing yet. But they're telling all units to keep an eye out. If any of our men find filming equipment, they'll contact us."

Yael made her way to the card table. Though it was late, the day's sleep and the adrenaline from the crossing left her with too much energy to call it a night. Time to start reading—Reiniger's approval pending, cameras or not.

Luka emerged from the hall, freshly showered. The victor's wet hair was slicked back, and he'd shaved so tightly that Yael noticed angles on his face she hadn't before. The architecture of his cheeks reminded her of a cathedral—vaulted, somewhat Gothic, base of stone.

Funny, how even completely unmasked, he could keep showing new sides.

Yael's heart revved—autobahn fast—as Luka settled in the chair next to hers. She had to glance down at the floor to make sure her own chair wasn't floating. She needed to be grounded, now of all nows. She'd made the mistake of letting Luka distract her at the end of her last mission, and it had cost her the race.

Yael tried to push these feelings back, but it was like swallowing sunshine. Bright yellow rays shimmering inside her. Had they been alone, she would've reached out to touch him again. Not the hand this time. Someplace closer. The ridge of his shoulders. The nape of his neck . . .

"You cut yourself," she said.

"Oh. Right." Luka's hand scouted out the spot on his lower jaw, stopping when it smudged red. "It's just a nick."

"You are *not* getting blood on these files," Miriam warned.

"Wouldn't dream of it, Comrade Mnogolikiy." Luka wiped the blood off on his shirt, pronouncing Miriam's Russian name so flawlessly that she did a double take at the boy.

"Your Russian's improving."

"*Nyet.*" Luka shook his head. "Just my manners."

Miriam's smile was faint, but Yael didn't miss the pinch of future crow's-feet. She pointed to a stack of autopsy reports by his elbow. "If you're going to give the presentation *with* us, you should familiarize yourself with Experiment Eighty-Five. Start by reading these."

Luka set himself to the task. Opening up the first folder, setting aside the photographs with careful fingers. Yael delved into her own pile. It was taxing work, wading through life after life, reliving Experiment 85 through: Anne Weisskopf (125819ΔX), Edith Jacobson (137992ΔX), Talaitha Mirga (143026ZX).

Longer, longer ran the names. Higher, higher climbed the numbers.

But something about the numbers was off where the *SS-Maskiertekommando des Führers* was concerned. It was a discrepancy Yael had first noticed reading through the notes in Dr. Geyer's office. If the Doppelgänger Project officially started in 1948 and ten SS candidates went through the injections every year with a 95 percent survival rate, basic math dictated that there should be seventy-six SS skinshifters.

So why could they find evidence of only twenty?

"Good question," Miriam said when Yael posed it. "There

could be other *Maskiertekommandos*. Ones that aren't assigned to Hitler."

"Wouldn't their rosters be in here?"

"We had to leave a lot of papers behind," Miriam reminded her. "And we haven't read through everything yet."

"Fifty-six more skinshifters running around?" Luka grunted. "Cheery thought."

Wasn't it, just?

All of this stretched Yael's soul a bit thinner, but she didn't want to miss anything, so she kept reading. Every word on every page. Whenever the numbers and names and memories became too overwhelming, she would look to the operations map and its defiant wash of indigo. What hope Henryka had, marking these reclaimed lands with ink—permanent, unchangeable. Yael stared at it as long as guilt would allow, but the ink from the Angel of Death's fountain pen—just as permanent, just as unchangeable—kept calling her back.

She'd reached 1952. An entry from June: **Reichsführer Himmler has ordered the cessation of new SS subjects due to the Führer's recent decision to remain out of the public eye.**

Yael shared this with the group.

"That explains the numbers." Miriam frowned. "Somewhat."

"But that was only a few weeks after Aaron-Klaus tried offing the Führer," Luka pointed out. "Why would they halt the doppelgänger conveyer belt if one just saved Hitler's life?"

Yael read on, summarizing. "There *were* other *Maskiertekommandos* for some high-ranked National Socialist officials. Bormann, Göring, Goebbels, Himmler. It says here all their

members were eliminated to reduce the risk of the Doppelgänger Project's exposure."

"Himmler and Hitler must've known the panic it would
cause," Miriam reasoned. "After the Grosser Platz shooting,
they passed the Führer's survival off as a miracle and erased as
much evidence of the doppelgängers as they dared. Now history
is repeating itself."

"Not really." Yael shook her head and set the page full of
Dr. Geyer's penmanship aside. Next to Anne and Edith and
Talaitha. By the fury of her five wolves. "Some things cannot be
erased."

And these things were about to be aired on the Reichssender
for all the world to know. Everything the Führer had tried to
hide would blaze like dry brush in the wilderness, burning both
the *Führereid* and the people's trust to ash.

Hitler, Himmler, and Geyer—they did not make her.

They would not unmake her either.

But Yael would try with everything that was in her—
sunshine and suffering, stolen lifetimes and death at her wing
tips—to destroy them.

CHAPTER 43

Never had time dragged so slowly. Never had hours passed so swiftly.

━━━

Four hours: Felix should've felt better after the shower. Mud gone, muscles loosened. Instead he was as exposed as the wound he held aloft for his sister. On-fire raw. Both sat on the bunk in Yael's sleeping quarters. Its plain white bedding became littered with bandages and bottles as Adele performed first aid, casting aside whatever she didn't use. Martin's pocket watch lay among them.

"I'll look at that next." This meant worlds beyond worlds, coming from Adele. She looked at Martin's pocket watch as often as she visited their brother's grave: rarely, never. "We'll need something to keep track of time, and they might get suspicious if we keep popping in and out of the map room."

He'd told Adele everything he could, fitting a recap of the Axis Tour, the Tokyo torture, Baasch's plan, and everything that had come of it, into fewer minutes than did the tale justice.

"Those *Saukerl*s!" his sister said once the story ended.

"Which ones?" Felix wondered.

"All of them!" Adele's hair hung bright around her face, but days of darkness roiled beneath her words. "Baasch, Yael, the whole *verdammt* lot!"

Felix remembered that anger—red, revenge rage. How it covered the floor in Tokyo, filled the cracks inside his mouth. Some of it still throbbed under his fresh bandages, but the absoluteness of the feeling had evaporated. Baasch's mission no longer felt like his right. It was all a muddy mess of lives and deaths and wrongs, and by God if Felix didn't want to wash his hands of it!

"Do you really think Mama's dead?" Pitch-black emotion seeped through Adele's teeth.

"If she's not, if she and Papa are really at Vlad's…" What good had *if*s ever done him? Best to go with a more solid answer. "I don't know. I don't know what to do, Ad."

His sister palmed Martin's broken watch. "Don't you?"

━━━

Three hours: Adele told her side of things as she fixed the watch, using tweezers from the medical cabinet (she'd had to wait for Luka to leave the washroom to retrieve them) and Felix's instructions. In the end, there wasn't much to either the tale or the repair. Aside from Yael's attack in the flat and Adele's three escape attempts, her month had been reduced to bruised toes and lightless noise. She'd overheard quite a bit through those layers of steel. Enough to know that the resistance's chances of overthrowing the Führer were dismal.

"Even if your SS-Standartenführer doesn't have Mama and Papa, what will happen when the SS takes back Germania?" Adele asked. "We'll be captured and beheaded regardless. They'll torture the location of Vlad's farm out of someone, and Mama and Papa will die, too."

When the watch started working again, they set it to the time kept by the map room clock: 2:43 AM (Central Reich Time). Martin's timepiece counted seconds steadily, ticking with the exact urgent volume it had used in the Imperial Palace's guest quarters.

You know what you have to do, it seemed to say. *Don't you? Don't you?*

Two hours: Adele was right.

One hour: He crossed the hall with leaden steps, into the sleeping quarters with the telephone. The others were in the front room, voices jumbling together while they discussed the Doppelgänger Project papers. As if those files could actually make a difference.

What if they could? The question followed Felix through the door. It slithered around his neck as he walked to the chest of drawers, where the telephone sat. It flared inside his phantom fingers as he lifted the receiver, trying not to think of Yael or the hundreds of Wehrmacht men who could be Papa, Martin, himself.

The thought reared its head anyway. Doubts—a dozen, hundred, thousand different faces' worth—crept through the tendons of Felix's good hand. Stilled it. But there were hands that kept moving: Martin's watch itched in his pocket. Reminding Felix that his life—the lives of all he held dearest—would be much shorter unless he kept his focus, reached out, and dialed. And really, what faces was he thinking of? Yael was the faceless girl. The men of war were faceless, too, soldiers destined to die no matter what Felix did.

The only faces that mattered were the ones he *could* save.

This was it. The last piece.

Salvation, damnation.

Felix dialed.

Despite the predawn hour, it took only two rings before the call was answered, then transferred. Felix hardly had time to second-guess his decision when Baasch got on the line, sounding half asleep as he growled his greeting. "Yes?"

Felix's breath quivered in his throat.

There would be blood.

There had to be blood.

But it would not belong to the Wolfes.

"I'm in position," he said.

CHAPTER 44

Still no news on the camera setup, but this didn't stop Luka from reading until his vision blurred all letters into one. Until even the mug of black coffee by his wrist (which had been drained and refilled multiple times) couldn't help keep the words straight.

But he wasn't just reading, was he? His job was to tell. Words were Luka Löwe's forte, but taking mass murder and human experimentation and Hitler's largest lie and cramming all these things into a speech was testing even his oratory abilities.

He spent the better part of an hour with a pencil in hand—trying to think of the best way to say the worst thing. Graphite pressed to paper in bursts, the skeleton of a speech took shape.

> People of the Third Reich. This is Luka Löwe, your double victor, and I am here to

tell you the truth. The Führer Adolf Hitler has been lying to you about a great many things. Peace. Purity. Progress. This is what Hitler tells us our empire has attained. "The Aryan race is great," he tells us. "The Aryan race is strong. The Aryan race is meant by God to rule."

Lies.

I am going to tell you the truth. The truth I think most of you already know: We are not great. We are not strong. We are murderers, stained in the blood of innocents. Hundreds, thousands of

He stopped. Pencil stabbing so hard into the paper it made a little hole.

The words did not feel like enough.

"Where's an eraser?" he asked the room.

Yael grabbed the paper, skimming over his writing instead. "This is good!"

She passed the speech to Miriam before Lúka could snatch it back.

"Numbers are easy to dismiss. That's why they marked us the way they did." Miriam tapped her forearm. "Numbers don't hurt. Numbers don't bleed. Choose one of the autopsy reports. Air *that* on the Reichssender if you want them to face the truth. Show people a child's picture, give them a name, a birthday. Show we're flesh and blood. Not digits."

Luka spent another half hour rereading the files. Flesh and blood and bone.

Choose one.

How could he choose just one when there were so many?

So many...

It wasn't just the words blurring together, but the pages themselves. Luka stared at them until his eyes crossed and the stack melted into a blur. There was an ache in his shoulders that trickled all the way down his spine. Who knew paper could be so heavy?

Yael's chair scraped out. "I think we could all use a bit of fresh air. Miriam? Luka?"

Fresh air. Did that even exist anymore?

Miriam waved the pair off, not even glancing up from her share of the documents. Dedication: legendary. If only there were a way to bottle up that kind of energy and disperse it across the whole of the resistance. Their victory would be won in days.

Their victory. This thought didn't surprise Luka, only confirmed what he'd felt twisting inside him for so long. As fierce and fiery as the feeling behind Aaron-Klaus's face that morning in the Grosser Platz. As frantic as that sable.

This was his fight, too.

Yael led him into the cellar. Instead of heading back to the beer hall, she took a second set of steps that wound up to the building's rooftop. Sometime in the past few hours, the rain had let up. Clouds peeled back to show hints of the morning to come: A soft glow began to play off the rooftop's many puddles.

It wasn't a quiet dawn. Below, the city rumbled, not with the normal electric streetcars or delivery trucks, but a not-so-distant firefight.

"I wouldn't wander too far from the door," Yael warned Luka as he stepped out. "There could be snipers."

He stopped just beyond the threshold. She stood next to him. "What a night."

"What a month," Luka murmured back.

Yael smiled. She looked more herself than ever in the gentle light. She'd changed into old riding gear, and her fill-in-the-Aryan features had vanished, reclaimed by the face she'd shown him on the farmhouse steps. Jawline resolute. Black eyelashes so thick they might have been kohl. Eyes that made Luka feel as if he were back in the taiga forest running through wolf-patched snow—green so dark it was brown, brown so fresh it was living. Her hair was still in soft curls, but she'd knotted it into a bun. Some wisps had come free, licking her forehead in the poststorm breeze.

One strand tickled the edge of her lips.

Luka wanted to kiss her. Now more than ever. Instead he stood with his back to the doorframe, breathing in air faint with burning.

"I have a feeling this will all be over soon." Yael stared out across the rooftops. The city was scarce with lights, which made the silhouettes of the buildings that much more stark. Across the Spree, the Volkshalle caused the rest of the skyline to cower. "It's all about to crumble. One way or another."

Luka wondered what amount of explosives it would take to raze a mammoth like the Volkshalle to its foundations. Not much. Take away a few key pillars and the weight of the building would bring itself down.

"What will you do, when all this is over?" he asked.

"If I'm alive..." she prefaced. "If I'm alive, then I'll live. I'll wear short sleeves. When people ask what my name is, I'll tell them the truth. I won't have to check my face every time I step outside."

What simple things to dream of.

"What about you?" Yael asked. "Still fancying becoming a poet?"

"A poet?"

"At the Rome checkpoint, you told me maybe you'd become a poet after all this."

"Did I?" All Luka could remember about Rome was how much he wanted to win. To take back from Adele the victory she'd wrenched from him. He'd sat at that dining room table, seething in cigarette smoke while she slurped her noodles.

"You told me we needed each other. That was when I first started seeing you..." Yael's voice drifted off, but she was watching him.

He stared back into the evergreen wilderness of her eyes.

"I lied to you, Luka," she whispered.

"Which time?" he asked.

Both of them smiled, because the lies they'd exchanged were too many to count.

"In the ballroom." Yael's voice was as tumbling as their waltz had been.

That was a moment Luka remembered perfectly; he'd

spilled out the true truth straight from the heart: *There is no one else.* And Adele (who was not-Adele but had always ever been Yael) had yanked his cardiac muscle straight from his chest and shredded it to bits with pointed canines: *I do not love you. And I never will.*

His heart was in her teeth again. Luka stood frozen, waiting for her truth.

"When you won the Axis Tour, I thought you'd ruined everything. When you followed me to that alley in Tokyo, I thought you'd ruined everything. But you've surprised me, Luka Löwe. Again and again, you've surprised me in the best of ways."

Yael Reider drew close. Closer than they'd been in the Tokyo alley or on the deck of the *Kaiten* or on the train to New Delhi. So near that Luka thought he could feel her heart fluttering beneath her chest, just off sync with his.

"I do love you," she said, and kissed him.

———

Him. Her. Lips meeting without lies. It was the purest, strongest, most heart-clenching thing.

He loved her, too.

Scheisse, he loved her. It wasn't just a feeling, but a *knowing*, hot inside him. Love like burning.

Luka kissed her back. Until he couldn't tell where he ended and Yael began. Until her fingers raked through his hair and past his scar, and he did not care because they were both alive, and this was the truest thing he'd ever done. Until the world burst into flames around them.

For a moment, Luka wondered if his emotions had simply taken flight. But when Yael pulled back and gasped, he opened his eyes to see that there was no phoenix, no magical incarnation of the feelings roaring inside his chest.

These flames were very, very real. Below them, the street was on fire.

CHAPTER 45

All thoughts of snipers and life-changing kisses vanished when Yael ran to the building's edge. The burst of flames that had pulled her out of sheer bliss belonged to a grenade, now only a spot of char on the sidewalk. Fighters (all Reiniger's, Yael could tell, because they were missing their left sleeves) were falling back, using parked cars and storefronts to protect themselves from the fire of the advancing enemy.

War had come to their doorstep.

SS soldiers rounded the corner, moving with boldness that meant numbers. Their bullets hailed through the street. Shattering glass, wounding stones, flaying flesh. Yael watched, transfixed, from the rooftop—a Valkyrie over battle. Unable to choose: *Life or Death?*

Death ...

Death ...

It was all death beneath her. More SS and loyalist Wehrmacht flooded the street. (And more and more and more.

Until Yael wondered if there were any double-lightning pins left south of the Spree.) Reiniger's men didn't stand a chance. What could so few do against so many? The remaining resistance fighters retreated, but the National Socialists gave no chase. Instead they pushed straight into the entrance of the beer hall.

They knew about the headquarters.

It was the only building they entered, and their jackboots strode toward it with such *purpose*. There was nothing to stop them. Not even a locked door…She and Luka had left the entrance to the basement unbolted for an easy return.

—*MIRIAM HENRYKA KASPER FELIX ADELE JOHANN REINHARD BRIGITTE MOVE MOVE MOVE*—

But when Yael turned for the staircase, she found Luka barring her way, hands stretched across the door, frame to frame. When she tried to push past, he wrapped his arms around her, not a hug, but something fiercer.

Yael pushed. Luka held. He was strong, and even her hardest strain didn't budge the pair a single centimeter.

"If you go down there, you'll just get captured, too." Luka's voice rumbled from his chest to hers. "What good will that do anyone?"

There was a way past the victor—but it involved hurting, really hurting him. Yael might have considered it if Luka hadn't been so *verdammt* right. She could not save her friends. Not this time. Even if she flew down those stairs in a Valkyrie fury, how many men could she manage bare-handed? She didn't even have her gun…Like a dummkopf, she'd left it downstairs on the card table. Next to the files.

Oh, *Scheisse,* the files!

—DESCEND AND YOU WILL NOT ASCEND DOWN IS DEATH—

Here was death, too, Yael realized. SS soldiers were already swarming the building's bottom levels. How long would it take them to find their way up to the roof?

Luka seemed to realize this, too. His arms loosened, so that Yael could lean back and see the fear on his face, tangling with disheveled hair. His eyes stormed the stairwell. "What do we do?"

Miriam, Henryka, Kasper, Felix, Adele, the other operatives…

She didn't have *room* for that many more wolves.

"Yael!"

"Do—do you have any weapons?" she asked.

"Aside from my irrepressible wit and charm? No. You?"

"My knife." It was tucked in her boot, force of habit, but a fight was out of the question. Only one option remained.

The rooftops.

She pulled Luka away from the door, spattering through puddles made molten by the rising sun. They ran to the roof's edge, where the gap between buildings required a leap. Yael ignored all her pain—the wail of her wolves, the stitches in her side—and jumped. Luka made the mistake of looking down instead of across. He halted at the brink.

"Any chance you saved that parachute?"

Yael didn't know if the sound leaving her throat was a laugh or a sob. Probably both. Unbelievable, absurd, irrepressible boy. He wasn't *really* scared of the fall. (She could see that in the way he loped over the gap, morning gold flaring through his stare as he landed next to her.) He was just trying to keep her afloat. Laugh, sob, while her life got shot to pieces beneath her.

Together they ran, lunging across a block's worth of buildings before reaching a gap too wide to cross. When they entered the building beneath, it was quiet. The doors to the flats were locked. Yael threw herself at the nearest one.

It was an artless lunge, doing more damage to her than the door. Yael still had hairpins, but her hands shook too hard to pick the lock. She couldn't stop thinking about what was happening in Henryka's basement. There was only one way out of the headquarters. No chance of any of them escaping...no chance...

"Yael?"

Her body couldn't keep up with her need to—*BREATHE JUST KEEP BREATHING*—and she began choking on her own air.

"Yael? Yael?" Luka's voice sounded like the train: *yah-ell, yah-ell, yah-ell.*

Dead. Oh God. They were all dead.

How had this happened? How was she on the floor, on her hands and knees, crying until she retched and still crying? How was Luka next to her, still saying her name as if it would help something?

"Yael, we can't stay here. We have to go."

"Go where?" She laughed, sobbed.

North? Where Reiniger's forces sat hamstringed by the loss of their headquarters?

South? Where the Volkshalle loomed and the immortal Führer lurked, writing a victory speech for the Reichssender cameras?

East? Where Novosibirsk's army clawed toward Moscow, unaware of the crushing blow the resistance had just been dealt?

West? Assuming the Americans let them in. Their desire for political neutrality left them little tolerance for refugees. Many had fled there in the last war, only to be sent straight back into the fangs of the Reich.

Any of this was assuming they could leave the building. Even if Yael and Luka raided one of these flats for civilian disguises, they wouldn't get ten steps through the besieged block without being spotted.

"We're trapped—"

Five stories below, a door crashed open. Luka held a hand to her lips. Hobnails clattered against the stairwell's polished wood.

The SS were coming.

CHAPTER 46

Felix knew the SS were coming. He'd even made sure the door was unlocked for them, but this didn't make SS-Standartenführer Baasch's entrance any less terrifying. The blitzkrieg was loud, for one thing. So many metal-edged boots stomping across the concrete floor. So many bullets biting bookshelves and walls. Miriam grabbed a gun from the card table and used it to take down three of the first advancers before getting shot herself. The radio operators had their own weapons, but instead of using them to remove a few more SS from the earth, they turned their sights on the communications equipment. The girl with the bun full of pencils dispatched her cipher machine, twisting its rotors into a useless combination, before smashing it onto the floor. Henryka ran for the map, managing to rip the Muscovy territories from the wall, all the way down to the Mediterranean before the invaders reached her. The older woman did not go down gently. Her limbs thrashed with wiry precision, breaking one SS-Sturmmann's nose, crushing the larynx of another. In the end, only a bullet could stop her. Kasper and Johann managed an even higher cartilage-crunch count before being forced to the floor at gunpoint.

It lasted only thirty seconds—a supernova of bone dust and noise. Half a minute, and the room turned to ruin. Reinhard was slumped over his Enigma machine, dead. Henryka looked smaller than small on the floor—surrounded by scattered thumbtacks—life's largeness shot out of her. Pink misted her cloud of hair.

Felix stood in the hallway entrance, deafened. His hands trembled above his head and kept trembling as one of the SS soldiers yanked him into the kneeling line of resistance fighters. Felix's kneecaps cracked against the concrete, not far from where Henryka fell. Her body was facing him. Felix couldn't tear his eyes away from the violence of color around it.

What had he done?

Technically, SS-Standartenführer Baasch's boots sounded no different from those of any of the other men clattering around the basement. They were made of the exact same material: heel plates and hobnails of iron. But Felix *knew* Baasch was coming before he entered the map room. *Tap, tap, tap* to reveal gray eyes (still dead). The sight sent chills up his not-there fingers.

"This is it?" The officer paused and took in the map room. "Quite simple, for a rats' nest."

"There are more rooms in the back, Standartenführer Baasch," an SS-Sturmmann informed him. "They're being searched as we speak."

Baasch removed his hat and tossed it onto the table, over the Doppelgänger Project documents. Felix kept waiting for the SS-Standartenführer to acknowledge him. Instead the officer collapsed into one of the chairs and continued issuing orders to his men. "Check the radios. See if any of them are still working."

"Unhand me!" They'd found Adele. Felix's sister was back to the wildcat version of herself as the SS-Sturmmann wrangled her into the map room. "I'm a victor of the Third Reich! Commended by the Führer himself! There's been a mistake! My brother—"

When Adele caught sight of the kneeling row—Lugers to temples, Felix among them—her words dried up. She stopped twisting. Baasch waved her over to his chair.

"Victor Wolfe, I presume?"

At the officer's signal, Adele's left sleeve was peeled back. No wolves.

"I am myself, thank you very much," his sister told Baasch coolly. "Now, if you'll please tell your men to stop bruising my arms—"

Baasch didn't. "Check the others! She could be passing for anyone!"

One by one they tore back the prisoners' sleeves. No wolves. No wolves. They paused when they found Miriam's numbers—braided with blood from her gunshot wound. "How did she get rid of the dogs?"

"It's not her," Felix told them. He needed to get the Luger away from his head. He needed the SS to let him and Adele go. Safely. Just like they promised they would.

"But she has an *X*—"

"Herr Wolfe is right. The numbers don't match. So where *is*

396

Inmate 121358ΔX?" Baasch's stare landed on Felix. Narrowed. It made Felix feel as if he were back in the Imperial Palace. Thirteen days, twenty thousand kilometers ago. Nothing was fixed. Everything was falling to pieces. Salvation, damnation, damnation, damnation.

Felix examined every face in the map room, saw none of Yael's. Luka was missing, too. "She—she's not in the sleeping quarters?"

"Only Victor Wolfe was back there," explained the soldier who still vised Adele's arm. "We can check again."

"No." The SS-Standartenführer waved at his sister. "Put Victor Wolfe with the others."

And so Adele was shoved to her knees, held there by another gun. As soon as the hammer clicked back, Felix knew there was no deal. SS-Standartenführer Baasch had never intended to let them go. His sister was a scapegoat, and Felix was a fool. A treacherous fool with a Luger to his head.

What had he done?

"You said Adele would be pardoned," Felix croaked at Baasch. "You gave me your word."

The SS officer stayed silent as he pulled out his handkerchief—spotless again, freshly pressed into eighths—and began unfolding it.

"You snitch! You *przeklęty* coward!" Felix *felt* Kasper's snarl. The curses were mixed with actual spit, sticking to the side of the mechanic's face.

Johann and the blond girl said nothing. They didn't have to. Their *stab, stab* murder stares communicated all. And Miriam... if looks could kill, her gaze was a massacre.

But there was a worse death inside Felix. A revelation: He was not just broken this time, but the breaker. All of this—tendrils of Henryka's hair clawing at his pant leg, smashed radios, and the blood, blood everywhere—was his fault. HIS.

Adele kept addressing the SS-Standartenführer in an imperious tone. "When the Führer hears about this—"

"The Führer ordered this. I'm sorry to say his word overrules mine, in the scheme of things." *Sorry?* Whatever the SS-Standartenführer used that handkerchief for, it obviously wasn't tears. If anything, he looked quite pleased with himself. "Personally, I think it's a waste, eliminating stock as good as yours, but stabilizing the population after such widespread rebellion requires a very . . . public spectacle."

Adele blinked. "What are you talking about?"

"They're going to execute us on the Reichssender," Kasper said, his voice already dead.

Retaliation in kind. Blood being paid at the guillotine blade. Heads tumbling across the Grosser Platz's stones, cameras rolling with them.

"Execute?" His sister gave a strangled cry. "But—I didn't do anything!"

"Start searching the documents. Look for communiqués, rosters, anything that will help us understand how deep this movement goes." Baasch pulled his Luger from its holster and began using his handkerchief to polish it. "The answers are here. We just have to know how to flush them out."

Felix couldn't take his eyes off the weapon.

WHAT HAD HE DONE?

"You promised my father wouldn't be harmed," he managed through the scream in his head. "Honor that at least."

The kerchief stopped sliding. The gun beneath was so bright it looked liquid.

"Honor..." the officer repeated slowly. "Honor and blood. 'Blood and honor.' None of those things will really protect you, Herr Wolfe. I've been a member of the National Socialist Party since the early days of Munich. I've watched men rise through the party ranks and fall just as quickly. Honor and an Aryan pedigree will only carry one so far. To excel, to *truly* excel, you must be cunning. Ruthless. You must crush those beneath you and claw those above—"

"This radio is working, Standartenführer!" The man examining the equipment pointed to the set in the corner. Kasper's bullets had only grazed its display—cracked glass here, a dented knob there. A faint voice flickered through its headset, reciting nonsense letters. "The messages are encoded."

"Try the cipher machines," Baasch ordered. "Use the combination Herr Wolfe provided us over the phone."

It took two soldiers to shove Reinhard's body off the Enigma model. The initial examiner clicked its rotors into place and pecked a few keys before declaring, "It works!" He paused to translate the rest of the message. "Some of the retreating resistance fighters alerted their brass that we took this street. They want to know if the headquarters are still secure."

Baasch stood. "If we keep radio communications open, we'd know their every move. We could have General Reiniger himself by sundown."

Tap, tap, tap—a sound that made Felix want to curl into himself and never leave. But the SS-Standartenführer wasn't walking toward the mechanic this time. When he lifted his finely polished Luger, it came nose-to-nose with Adele.

"Who operates the radios?" he asked Felix.

Felix nodded at Kasper and Johann.

The Luger shifted lanes, parking in front of Kasper.

"You'll send a message to General Reiniger, assuring him the headquarters are secure," Baasch told him. "Then you will continue to operate the radio as you would under normal circumstances. They mustn't suspect we're listening in."

The dark-haired young man stared down Baasch's gun without so much as a twitch. "You think I'm not ready to die?"

"Your men are circled with limited resources. Even if you don't operate the radio for us, we'll wear your army down to bones by sheer force." The officer nodded at the papers that filled the map room's every nook and cranny. "We're sitting on all of your movement's deepest secrets. Every operative. Every name. Entire notebooks filled with the messages you've encoded and decoded thus far. What point is there in withholding this information from me? What hope do you have?"

Baasch cocked his shiny, shiny gun.

Kasper said nothing.

The Luger began to wander, drifting from forehead to forehead as Baasch's jackboots beat out their terrifying rhythm. *Tap, tap*, Felix's temple. *Tap, tap*, the bridge of Miriam's nose. *Tap, tap*—Johann's rock-hard jaw. *Tap, tap*, Adele—*NO, NOT MY SISTER, NOT AFTER ALL THIS!*

"Operate the radio or one of them dies."

"You think the National Socialist war machine hasn't devoured every single member of my family?" Kasper asked him. "You think I haven't lost more friends than I can count to the guns of the SS? Preying on sentimentality will get you nowhere."

The pistol kept drifting.

"I am going to count to three," the SS-Standartenführer said. "One, two…"

Adele was trying to put on a brave face, but her shoulders shook. A sob half lodged in her throat. The other resistance operatives knew their fate: caught by the SS, a bullet to the head would be a mercy. They stared straight ahead, stone silent, all still. Miriam watched the officer pace through heavy lids. Felix shut his own when the Luger passed him a second time.

All this blood, and no one had been saved.

What hope did any of them have?

"Three."

CHAPTER 47

Yael could not stop her tears, but she could make them silent. They streamed down her face as the jackboots climbed. First floor, *STOMP STOMP*, second, *STOMP STOMP* ... They made so much noise Yael couldn't tell how many men there were. A dozen? Three? Fewer? More?

Not that it mattered. There was no way off the block. It was over. All dead. All for nothing.

Luka's hand fell from her mouth. "Give me your knife!"

The blade slid cleanly out of Yael's boot; she handed it to the victor hilt first. He took it like the weighty thing it was, testing the swipe of the blade against the air as he stood. Then he pulled Yael—gently—to her feet, and pressed the knife's edge against her throat.

"Keep crying, be ready," he mouthed before spinning her around to face the stairs.

"UP HERE!"

Three floors below, the jackboots paused.

"HERE!" Luka's second yell rattled Yael's eardrum. She dared not flinch. (The blade on her skin was beyond acting. One slip and the slice would be all too real.)

The SS soldiers *STOMP*ed up the final flight of steps, weapons drawn. Yael counted four of them through her tears: two SS-Schützes and two SS-Oberschützes. When they caught sight of Luka, they paused, a dazed look filming their faces. None of them knew quite what to make of the double victor, the knife he held, the girl beneath it.

Four.

Not an impossible number.

—*BE READY*—

"Victor Löwe?" the foremost SS-Oberschütze asked.

"This is her!" Luka's knife twitched against her jugular, as close as their kiss had been. "The inmate you're looking for."

The men frowned, their weapons drooped. The nearest SS-Oberschütze climbed the rest of the stairs, and the others followed. All within striking distance. "Inmate 121358ΔX?"

"Show them your marks!" Luka's breath was vicious against her ear.

—*DISTRACT THEM*—

Yael tugged up her sleeve. Everything inside her tensed.

Four pairs of eyes looked at five running wolves.

Luka's wrist flicked. The knife whipped off her throat—

—*NOW*—

Valkyrie unleashed.

Yael's wolves sprang forward with her, lunging at the SS-Schütze closest to the stairs, seizing his pistol by the grip and shoving him back. The gun was already primed for *death, death,*

death. Three shots in quick succession became three corpses on the floor. One of the SS managed to fire, but his bullets veered into the ceiling. Luka had overpowered the first SS-Oberschütze, his blade finding another throat.

At the end of it all, plaster trickled like hourglass dust from the ceiling. The stairwell was silent. Yael knelt over the men she killed, shards of battle adrenaline slicing her veins. Her tears had stopped; she had a clear view of their faces. Noses, mouths, eyes, sparkless corpses.

How was it they looked so human?

"This one—" Her fingers wandered to the SS-Schütze she'd sent down the steps. She plucked the man's cap from his head and tossed it to the victor. "You could pass as him. Keep your brim low and your face down."

For her own alibi, Yael selected the uniform with the least blood. The second SS-Oberschütze. Her imitation couldn't be exact (it never was with males). All she could do was make her breasts as small as possible, mimic the man's broad facial bones, and hope no one would look too closely at her throat, where there was a conspicuous lack of an Adam's apple.

It was the most temporary of disguises.

Luka's SS uniform was too small on him—its buttons strained as he bent down to collect the guns, padding already stretched fabric with a second Luger. He offered the third pistol to Yael.

"Seconds? You can never have too many guns. Especially considering what's down there." He nodded past the half-stripped bodies on the stairs.

She shook her head. "If we get into a firefight downstairs, we're dead."

With a shrug, the victor claimed the gun as his own. "So we'll use your super spy skills to get the hell off this block.... Then what?"

"I'm going to the Ordenspalais." Yael didn't know this was her intention until she said it, but when she did, it felt right. It was her end. Her only end. "I'm going to give that speech on the Reichssender."

Luka's hands froze over the third pistol, tucked halfway into his waistband.

"I know we've lost," Yael said. "But I can't let Hitler erase Experiment Eighty-Five and the lives it cost."

"But the SS has the files..." Luka faltered.

"I'll be the evidence. I'll tell the world who I am, in my own face this time." Change or no change, Yael would leave her mark. Anne, Edith, Talaitha...all of them would leave their marks. "I'll show them how simple it is for a skinshifter to imitate the Führer. Perhaps that will be enough to cast doubt on his leadership. You—you should go east. Seek asylum in Novosibirsk and carry on the fight from there."

Luka stared at her—eyes more black than blue in their intensity. In them, Yael could see the forty thousand kilometers they'd traveled together. The three kisses they'd shared. The lifetimes of stories and emotions that bubbled between them.

He knew her.

No matter what face she wore, Luka knew her.

"I'm not leaving you." He crossed his arms, wrist bones peeking out of his too-tight uniform. "Someone has to man the filming equipment, and I doubt you'll find many eager volunteers at the Ministry of Public Enlightenment and Propaganda. You need me."

Luka was right. She needed him to film. She needed him to help navigate the building. She needed *him*.

But the cost?

"Luka, I—" The truth, so hard to tell. Through labored breath, Yael managed it. "I don't think I'm coming back."

"I know." Luka took both of her hands in his. "I know, Yael. I'm with you."

———

The enemy was everywhere. More than half the men occupying the street belonged to the Wehrmacht—sleeves and badges intact—bound by oath to the resurrected Führer. SS *Totenkopf*s winked past in the morning light, bobbing with soldiers' steps. It almost looked as if the skulls were laughing.

Yael tugged her own cap down and walked south. Luka stayed a half step behind, using her broadened shoulders as a shield. They kept a decent pace: slow enough to look unhurried, quick enough to keep eyes from lingering. None did. The men they passed were engulfed in their own duties: searching buildings, hauling in artillery, securing the block.

The river was only a few streets on. The closest bridge across was blackened with SS traffic, flowing both ways. Yael and Luka encountered no barbed wire or blockade when they walked across. The Spree rushed beneath them, as unyielding as it had been the day Aaron-Klaus caught Yael trying to pick his pocket. As fresh and old as the grief inside her. Every death Yael had ever faced was welling up to the surface of her skin. Babushka, Mama, Miriam, Aaron-Klaus, Katsuo, Felix, Adele, Kasper, Reinhard, Johann, Brigitte, Henryka, Miriam again…

Dammed tears ached behind her eyes.

Not for nothing.

They reached the south bank without interference. Yael knew they were close to the Reichssender studios when she spotted the broadcasting tower—its skeletal heights clambered into the sky. (Apart from the pillars of smoke rising from the northern horizon, the morning was blue, all blue. A perfect day for ruination.)

Wilhelm Street. The heart of things, where swastika banners hung so thick from buildings that their very stones were hidden. The enemy was thick here, too, but Yael and Luka blended in. Their stolen uniforms and quick waves of their passes were enough to get them past the first checkpoint, in view of the Wilhelmplatz. The park was ordinary enough. Looking at its trees and gravel paths studded with memorials, one wouldn't guess it was a playground for beasts.

On one end: the Chancellery. Opposite that: the Ordenspalais. The former palace's facade was cobbled—old stitched into the grotesquely new. After the war, when radio broadcasts gave way to the Reichssender as the foremost means of propaganda, Joseph Goebbels had his ministry expanded, adding an annex large enough to hold filming studios. There were stages for the terribly scripted shows about Lebensraum families, along with desks for the evening news (just as terribly scripted). It was a sprawling place—halls twisted around nonsensical corners, and every door looked the same. The main entrance bristled with security, far too much for their imperfect disguises to dupe.

This didn't seem to bother Luka. The victor took the lead, veering them to the ministry's newer end.

"Where are we going?" Yael asked, trying to keep her steps confident when she was anything but.

"Filming propaganda is long and excruciatingly boring," Luka explained. "I had to find all sorts of places to sneak smokes between interview takes."

One of these *sorts of places* was a service entrance. The heavy door opened to a gravel lot full of vehicles from the Reichssender's camera fleet. It was too much of an afterthought to be guarded, locked from the inside. Yael knelt in front of the lock, retrieving the bobby pins she'd stowed in the SS-Oberschütze's pockets. Her hands had steadied over the last half hour, but it took a good deal of tooth-grinding and lip-licking to work the lock free. It slicked back like a sigh of relief, hinges creaking, door cracked.

They were in.

No one noticed. There was no one *to* notice. The annex was strangely deserted, but, Yael supposed, there was no need to go on filming *Story of a Perfect Lebensraum Lie* when most of the Lebensraum settlements had been wiped off the map. There was no need for news either when the Reich wanted to keep its people in the dark. The Führer's speech was enough.

The granite hallways stretched and stretched. Decades' worth of propaganda posters lined their walls. Goebbels's finest work. Many were from the war: impossibly tall soldiers with impossibly strong jaws, swastika flags billowing like storms behind them. There were old watercolor advertisements for the League of

German Girls, including the one with the face Yael had borrowed so long ago.

And then there was Luka.

1953. *Sieg heil!*

Yael had seen the poster before, but this time it made her stop.

His jaw was just as impossibly strong as the others. He stood in front of a Zündapp KS 601, saluting something beyond the painting's reach. An Iron Cross hung around his neck. In the background, a swastika flag melted into a map of the Axis Tour's path.

The real Luka paused next to her, giving an unimpressed grunt. "I had to pose for the painter—Mjölnir—for hours. Goebbels kept yelling at me every time I twitched. You wouldn't believe the places that start to itch when you're not allowed to move. Earlobes, pinky toes, unmentionables…Whenever Goebbels wasn't looking, I'd try scratching with the motorcycle handlebars."

Yael couldn't help but smile at this image: fourteen-year-old Luka using a parked Zündapp to dismiss his epidermal urges. Such a very different portrait of the boy, far removed from this *Sieg heil!* swastika-everything picture.

Luka wasn't smiling. His eyes narrowed at the poster, sharpened in a way that made Yael wonder what he saw when he really looked—past paint and into memory.

"That's not Luka Löwe," she whispered. "That's the boy Hitler and Goebbels and Mjölnir tried to make. You could have become him, but you chose to be more."

Something about this last word tore the victor's stare away from his watercolor rendering. This time, he did smile. It wasn't the half-cocked grin Yael was so used to. Nor was it forced. The expression was toothless. A soft, genuine emotion.

"We should keep going, before our luck dries up," he said. "I've never seen the place this deserted before...."

It was eerie, how their footsteps echoed past a dozen more Mjölnir paintings. How they turned a corner to find yet another empty hall, all its doors shut. Luka led the way to the nearest one.

"This is the studio where they conducted my more formal interviews," he explained. "It should have what we need to film a presentation."

The victor reached out, opened the door to the studio.

It was not empty.

CHAPTER 48

I am not going to die.

But Miriam knew she might, at the end of Baasch's countdown. Simple process of elimination told her this. He needed Kasper's and Johann's voices. He needed Adele's face. The Wolfe boy was too full of easy information to shoot. Yael, thank the fates, had escaped.

Miriam and Brigitte were the outliers, and unless Kasper talked, one of them was going to catch a bullet. She'd already taken one to the shoulder today—which was more than enough. There were smarter ways to go about this situation. If Baasch needed Kasper's voice, that was what Miriam would give him: "I'll do it. I'll operate the radio."

The officer did not lower his gun. His signet ring shimmered. "I didn't ask you."

"I'm a face-changer." Miriam dropped her voice into a gravelly imitation of Kasper's. It worked well enough. The operative's voice was already hoarse from days of nonstop talking. "They won't be able to tell the difference between my voice and his over the radio. That's all you need, right? A convincing lie?"

Baasch's lips twitched. Miriam couldn't tell if the motion signaled disappointment or pleasure. The expression might be hard to read, but the man wasn't. She'd known many like him: ruthless creatures who enjoyed watching their prey dance before they devoured it.

The trick to dealing with them?

Be the prey and dance, dance until they licked their lips.

Then strike.

Pretending to be prey was not difficult. Miriam was a wounded Jewish woman—all properties that discounted her in the SS-Standartenführer's mind.

"Just how many lab rats did Dr. Geyer let loose?" The officer tutted, then nodded to the radio stool. "Very well. Take a seat.

"Gag the others," he ordered his men. "We don't want them making any unnecessary fuss. And someone else tie up this inmate's wound. We don't need her bleeding out midmessage."

The loss of blood had made Miriam dizzy. She swayed her way to the communications station. Kasper called her some colorful words just before the gag silenced him, but Miriam pretended to be deaf to his insults. She also pretended that passing the traitorous Wolfe boy didn't boil her insides down to their linings. She should've known he was the leak, should've questioned his motives further, should've never let the wretch out of her sight. Not that it mattered now. He was going to the same guillotine they were if Miriam couldn't pull this off....

She wasn't even fully sure what *this* was as she sat down to the radio, wincing. One of the soldiers began patching up her wound and not gently.

"What should I say?" Miriam kept her eyes down, scanning the room as she did so. Thumbtacks, two stiffening bodies, a dashed typewriter, the television (which had somehow survived the firefight) still flickering behind the desk...none of these things would help. The SS-Standartenführer's men were sacking the place, ripping books from shelves, and tossing documents they didn't need to the floor.

The whole process was making an awful lot of noise.

"Tell them the headquarters were overlooked and all inhabitants are safe," Baasch said. "Then we'll ask for an update on Reiniger's positions."

"I wouldn't dive straight into that," Miriam advised. "Let them volunteer the information. If you want to establish a longer repertoire, then the conversation needs to flow at a natural pace."

It was only when the SS-Standartenführer's stare narrowed that Miriam realized she'd lapsed back into her commander tone. Abrasive syllables had become old habit when she was confronted with men and uniforms.

"I am in charge of this exchange." Baasch's words danced on toothpoint. "I dictate the message."

So he did. A dutiful soldier spelled out the message on the back of one of Henryka's discarded files and typed it through the cipher. Miriam recited the encoded letters in Kasper's husky voice, letting her finger linger on the transmission button as many seconds as she dared, hoping that ears on the other end might catch snippets of the SS's office sacking.

The process felt life-drudgingly slow. Minutes passed as their message was ironed out, a response cobbled, jumbled, recited back, put through the cipher.

THE WOLVES OF WAR ARE GATHERING.

"The wolves of war are gathering?" Baasch read it aloud. "What does that mean?"

It could mean a number of things. Perhaps the pause between the initial transmission and Baasch's response had been too lengthy. Or maybe Miriam's warning had been received, caught in the smack of a jackboot or the crash of a book.

"It's a pass code," Miriam told the officer, recalling Yael's frantic yell to resistance fighters the night before. "They want us to verify our identities."

The SS-Standartenführer's lips set. (Angry or resigned? Impossible to tell.) He walked over to where Felix Wolfe knelt, pale hair dripping into a paler, sweat-sopped face. The boy flinched at every one of the SS officer's steps. Miriam had to remind herself she didn't feel sorry for him.

"What's the response?"

"Something—" Felix gasped when Baasch jerked the wadded cloth from his mouth. "Something about r-rotting songs and bones! I don't remember the exact wording."

Miriam did. *They sing the song of rotten bones* crooned through her memory. Rotten, rotten. This was all rotten. And if they could make it clear to the resistance that their communications had been seized without the SS knowing...

"'Their song of bones is rotten,'" Miriam told the SS-Standartenführer. "That's the counterphrase."

Kasper's cheek twitched against his gag. Brigitte and Johann maintained their stonewall stares. Well-trained, all of them.

None of the SS had bothered securing their limbs yet. Why would they, when the operatives were stripped of weapons and so clearly outnumbered? Pistols to their skulls were enough.

"Is that it?" Baasch asked Felix. "You swear on your sister's life that's it?"

Play, play. Watch the prey dance.

If the Wolfe boy went any paler, he'd be invisible. He nodded. "Yes, yes. That's it!"

It was a groveling answer, so convincing that Miriam couldn't tell if he was lying for their sake or if he truly believed the response was accurate. So convincing that Baasch swallowed it whole.

"Send it," ordered the SS-Standartenführer.

——————

THEIR SONG OF BONES IS ROTTEN.

CHAPTER 49

They'd walked into the middle of a speech. No—not a speech, Luka realized as he halted in the doorway. A *Chancellery Chat*. The very same swastika standard that appeared on every screen in the Reich hung from the studio ceiling, providing a backdrop for the high-backed chair and the Führer sitting in it.

The *gottverdammt* Führer. Or, at least, a version of him. Any blood-group tattoo that might prove otherwise was covered: The man wore his shirt buttoned all the way to the collar and a jacket over that—charcoal gray, military cut. A golden eagle party badge had been sewn over the breast pocket; the bird blazed beneath the stage lights.

Hitler wasn't alone. There was a camera with the scantiest of production teams camped out behind it: a cameraman and a boom operator. Four SS guards stood to the side of the room in a schoolboy row. None of them seemed alarmed by Luka's arrival. (Then again, he *was* wearing their uniform. Between the slouched cap and the dim studio, no one had recognized him. Yet.)

"We have dealt the enemy a mighty blow, but the battle is not yet won. I call upon you now, people of the Reich, to—" When Hitler spotted the pair, his speech withered in his throat. "What are they doing here?"

A fifth man bearing the SS insignia turned to face the newcomers. Luka recognized Reichsführer Heinrich Himmler immediately. A pair of round spectacles that served to make beady eyes beadier, a thin excuse for a mustache, a dippy chin. None of these traits added up to a very impressive appearance, but there was something else, something...predacious... beneath the man's skin. It was ill matched to his calm expression.

"I gave explicit orders we were not to be disturbed," the Reichsführer said.

That explained the deserted halls.

Fight? Flight? Take a bow? Luka was at a loss for what to do next, so he just stood on the threshold. Something was off.... Every single interview he'd ever given in this building guaranteed two things: lights so hot they made you sweat and Joseph Goebbels in attendance, taking in every detail with a face that looked as if someone had served him a plate of dog feces. Not a word or a gesture escaped the Ordenspalais without the propaganda minister's express permission. He wouldn't be absent for something as significant as a *Chancellery Chat*.

So where was he? Where were the extra guards? Where was the rest of the production staff? A studio like this should be swarming with people: lighting assistants, producers, set managers, multiple cameras and microphones....It was almost as if Himmler wanted the room to be as bare bones as possible.

Yael pushed past Luka, her steps powerful. Shadows spooled

out of her as she strode to the stage. Dark hair, daring eyes, becoming *herself*. "I have an urgent message for the Führer, concerning the recent assault on the traitors' headquarters."

"All messages to the Führer are to be conveyed through me," Himmler began, but Yael was in front of the camera, beside the chair, pistol out, pressed to Hitler's head.

Breathing became a forgotten pastime. Luka stayed where he was—uncertain. The skeleton film crew didn't move; camera lens and microphone stayed on the unlikely pair: Hitler, speechless. Jewish girl in death's uniform. The real SS soldiers kept their formation; all four looked to Himmler for direction.

"You're she, yes? Inmate 121358ΔX. The girl from the gurney? I remember you sitting in the examination room, so very small." Reichsführer Himmler moved into the haze of studio lights. Their brightness turned the rim of his glasses into mercury.

"Don't!" Yael swung behind the chair, gun still anchored to Hitler's head. "Unless you want the Führer to get shot on the Reichssender a third time."

"This will never air on the Reichssender," Himmler assured her. "I think it's safe to say that after Tokyo the Führer will no longer be appearing on live television."

It wasn't just the room's emptiness that niggled at Luka, but the way the Reichsführer filled it. Why wasn't the head of the SS on his knees, begging for Hitler's life? Why did messages to the Führer have to be conveyed through Himmler?

...

...

Holy Scheisse!

"Which doppelgänger is this?" The earth's very orbit fell still, throwing Luka into motion: out of the doorway, onto the stage. The rush knocked off his cap, popped a button from his too-tight uniform, but Luka didn't care. The thing was suffocating him, so he tore it off. Back to undershirt. There was no need to hide now anyway.

Luka drew out one of his Lugers as he moved, lining his sights on Reichsführer Himmler. Just above the facial hair abomination, just below the spectacles. "A1? B3? O5?"

The gun's appearance rattled the Reichsführer much less than Luka had expected. He stood nose-to-nose with the malicious metal. His lips did not twitch. His eyes did not blink.

Hitler's mustache trembled. Not out of fear, but anger: "I'm not a doppel—"

Himmler held up his hand. The Führer's mouth snapped shut.

That clenched it.

The man in the chair was a skinshifter. Through and through. But he wasn't just a double or some fleshed-out version of target paper. He was a mouthpiece.

He *was* the Führer.

"Victor L—" the Reichsführer began.

"How long?" Luka asked. The end of his pistol quivered.

Heinrich Himmler wasn't the sort of man who was often interrupted, especially at gunpoint. He was at a loss for how to respond. "Excuse me?"

"How long have you been controlling the Reich, Reichsführer Himmler?" It seemed so obvious, now that Luka thought about it. "The *SS-Maskiertekommando des Führers* isn't a security detail. It's not even a placeholder for public appearances.... You have a whole list of skinshifters under your command who can wear Adolf Hitler's face at a moment's notice. This whole regime is a puppet show, and you're its *verdammt* master."

Luka was right. The silence told him that.

The cameraman shifted on his stool. The microphone shivered at the end of its boom pole. The four SS guards didn't so much as blink. Yael's gun vaulted from the skinshifter's temple, seeking a new target in Himmler. False Hitler wrested the Luger from her grasp before she could squeeze the trigger, moving with far more speed than a sixty-six-year-old could muster. His face melted back into that of a much younger, fair-haired man as he turned the weapon on her. Yael stared down the barrel, lungs heaving.

Luka's trigger finger was starting to ache, but he wasn't ready to shoot. There were still so many answers he needed to hear, so many things he wanted to say. "The Führer's dead. Isn't he?"

"That's the beauty of the Doppelgänger Project. The Führer cannot die." Heinrich Himmler gestured at the four SS guards. Each blinked into a vision of Hitler—bristled mustache, bewitched blue eyes. "The Führer is immortal."

"But Adolf Hitler wasn't." Memories—new and old— were coming together in Luka's mind. Notes from the Doppelgänger Project fit seamlessly into the scene from the Grosser Platz. *Reichsführer Himmler has ordered the cessation of new SS subjects*—Aaron-Klaus's gun firing, red unfurling under, into Hitler's shirt—*due to the Führer's recent decision to remain out of the public eye.* Hitler collapsing to the ground, three holes in his chest. SS swarming his body. Luka unable to move while every-thing fell apart around him.

He'd seen the truth all along.

"Hitler didn't cease making public appearances after the New Germania rally because he feared for his life. He died that day."

"Aaron-Klaus"—the noise Yael made was at joyful odds with the gun in her face—"he did it."

Luka's accusations kept flowing: "You, Reichsführer Himmler, were trying to control the narrative. That's why you wiped out all the other officials' *Maskiertekommandos* and ordered the doctor to stop creating doppelgängers. It wasn't because Hitler feared the project's exposure.... You did! You wanted to blind Hitler's potential successors. If Bormann, Göring, and Goeb-bels believed the Führer terminated the Doppelgänger Project, they wouldn't suspect you of using it to slip behind the curtain of power."

"Well done, Victor Löwe." Heinrich Himmler's face re-mained clinical. There was a coolness to the droop of his lids, something chilled in his voice. "Four whole years and not even Dr. Geyer came close to guessing the truth. You were wrong about one thing, though. The *Maskiertekommando was* a secu-rity detail, in its earliest years. Hitler himself came up with the idea when I presented the results of Experiment Eighty-Five to him. Whenever a situation was deemed high risk, one of the doppelgängers took Hitler's place. He'd write the speeches and run through them until the doubles perfected every single inflection.

"May 16, 1952, was different." Himmler's chin tilted on its axis. His glasses glimmered. "The Führer wanted to give his own speech at the New Germania rally. The rehauled capital was the fruit of *his* labor, and Hitler thought he should be the one to present it to the *Volk*. After the shooting, he bled out on the stage, but the *Maskiertekommando* whisked the body away before his death was declared. I replaced him with a doppelgänger who had less severe wounds. Those few who knew about the Doppelgänger Project assumed it was a double who died. Everyone else simply assumed the surgeons of Germania were miracle workers."

"So you and the *SS-Maskiertekommando des Führers* took over the Reich. No fight from Göring. No protests from Bormann. Just a seamless transition of power." Luka laughed. The sound was sparse, accusatory. "Cutthroat work, Reichsführer Himmler. Really top-notch."

The production staff was fidgeting again, but the microphone kept hanging above them, and the cameraman hadn't taken off his headphones. The film kept rolling. Its feed wasn't live, and the reel would probably never leave this room.

Luka had the very distinct feeling that they wouldn't be leaving the studio either. Himmler's confession did not come free, and five Lugers to Luka's drawn one spelled out a rotten ending. (He wasn't *that* good of a shot.)

Surviving was a lost cause.

He might as well give his *verdammt* speech.

He'd hoped for a larger audience—more in the millions than the singles. But if eight sets of ears was all Luka got, then hell if he wouldn't make them listen. He held his pistol high and started talking.

"My father was in the Kradschützen. Did you know that?

When I was a kid, I used to pedal around Frankfurt on a rusted bicycle pretending it was a motorcycle and shooting imaginary communists because I wanted to be like him. I wanted to feel as if I was a part of something that mattered.

"When that feeling is inside you ... when you're so *hungry* to matter and that missingness is all you are, you'll believe anything, won't you? If some lunatic stands up on a beer hall table and tells you you're the best thing that's ever happened to humanity because you were born to the correct set of parents, you won't tell him he's wrong. You might even begin to hope he's right."

"Victor Löwe. We really don't have time to entertain one of your monologues." Himmler's jackboots creaked as he shifted his weight. Four SS-soldiers-turned-fake-Hitlers mirrored the movement—restless.

"Consider this my Victor's Speech," Luka snapped back. "It was only after I met Yael that I realized what my father, what *I*, what every single citizen of the Reich has been part of: wiping out entire villages—no, *countries*—of people. The populations who were cleared to make room for Lebensraum weren't just sent away. They were murdered in masses. Used for sick, twisted medical experiments. I've read the files on the Doppelgänger Project. Experiment Eighty-Five is made up of hundreds of dead children."

"It was a most difficult task." The Reichsführer did not flinch. "Most difficult, but I carried it out for the love of our people. In the pursuit of progress, sacrifices must be made. They were only *Untermenschen*—"

"They were innocent children with names." Words were not enough, not nearly enough, but Luka kept trying to say them because he needed to make himself heard. He needed to make all those children—their silence—heard. "Abel Topf. Mary Grausz. Naomi Hirsch."

"Quiet." Finally, the Reichsführer was starting to look unsettled. His tweedy eyebrows knit together. "That's enough."

"Anne Lehrer." Luka raised his voice louder. "David Mandel."

"I said enough!" *Now* Himmler was yelling. "ENOUGH!"

Stand your ground. Make the silence heard.

What good was strength, unless it helped Luka do this?

The skinshifter closest to the Reichsführer pulled out his pistol, pointed the barrel at Luka. There was no time to think, no chance to shoot, and still the names kept spilling out: "Esther Reuter. Levi Wexler. Charani Weisz."

The list was endless, but it ended there. (Not with a whimper, but a *BANG*.)

Luka didn't feel a thing. The bullet had missed. He was still standing....

But then he heard his own name being called: "Luka! Luka! NO!" and Himmler was staring at him, horror molding his doughy face. Both of these things caused Luka to look down at his chest.

A neat little hole had appeared in his undershirt. It was red all around.

Huh.

The feeling came a few seconds later. Luka's nerve endings caught up to his shock: a rush of pain. Like burning, like burning. The world bowed up to meet him. He fell with his back to the floor, unfired pistol spinning away. Studio lamps glared from above.

Bright white light. What a verdammt cliché.

Yael appeared, pressing her hands to his chest. Her dark hair spilled everywhere: blocking out the lights' sharpness, flowing with the plea in her lips. "Nononono! You *Arschloch*! Please! Don't leave me!"

Luka didn't want to, but he didn't think he had a choice. Already he could feel whatever made him himself ebbing. It took all the strength he had to bring his hand to Yael's face. She was warmth and *life* beneath his fingertips.

"Y-Yael."

"Yes?"

His hand slipped. She caught it in her own. Her palm was slick with his blood.

There were so many things he could say to her. (*I love you. I'm not afraid anymore. I guess this makes us even. I don't want to go. Yaelyaelyael.*) But Luka's words were becoming scarce, and he wanted the last of his to make a difference.

"T-too many g-guns," he whispered, hoping she understood.

Yael stiffened, then nodded, her eyes glowing through tears. Luka fixed his stare on them, staring and staring until he was back in the taiga forest, running through wolf-patched snow—through green so dark it was brown, brown so fresh it was living.

Running...

running...

CHAPTER 50

Yael didn't just see the life leave Luka Löwe's body. (Indigo eyes shining, dimming, snuffed. Jaw pulled tight, then going still. His final mask stripped away.) She *felt* it: Luka there. Then not.

How could someone so *there* be so gone?

It tore her—into yet another piece—with a pain not even the loudest scream could capture. Yael stayed silent, bowing over Luka's body, letting her dark curls create a mourning veil around them. No one had accounted for the victor's other guns, which, she supposed, was why he'd used his dying breath to remind her of their existence. Yael's blood-coated hands found his second Luger, gripped it tight.

Six men was an impossible number to shoot without being shot.

Taking a life takes something from you.

—YOU HAVE NOTHING LEFT TO LOSE—

Yael flicked off the safety.

"The blood. I can't—" Reichsführer Himmler's voice was

oddly warped, as shrill as an out-of-tune violin. "Get this mess cleaned up! All of it! I want all of them gone!"

The skinshifter from the *Chancellery Chat* chair was the first to approach Yael. Her gun was in his hands, and because of this, he moved with lazy steps. Yael stayed crouched, gauging all the room's marks through a part in her hair. If she timed her shots just right, she could take at least two, maybe three, of the *Saukerl*s with her. Himmler among them, if she was lucky . . .

CRASH! The microphone clattered to the floor; the boom operator, fearing for his life, made a dash for the exit. The cameraman wasn't far behind. Two versions of Hitler ran after them, guns drawn. Shots *CRACK*ed through the studio, and both members of the filming crew fell—backs pierced with lead.

The skinshifter closest to Yael looked up at the wrong time.

She didn't shoot him, but this wasn't a merciful action. In his non-Hitler form, the *Maskiertekommando* officer was a muscley mass of a man—perfect for catching rounds. Yael swung behind him: Luka's Luger out, exhaling death. The sound was the shattering inside her amplified. Bullets tearing tissue, biting bone. She fired around the skinshifter (who was already crumpling under his cohorts' shots) at the pair of Hitlers by the stage.

Shot, change.

Shot, change.

They died, turned white, stayed dead.

The two skinshifters by the door turned from the production team's bodies. Robbed of her human shield, Yael ran for the next closest thing: the *Chancellery Chat* chair. Within seconds it went from regal to ragged. The wood was heavy enough to take most of the shots. Yael was still alive as she pushed herself up against the shredded velvet, made the remaining ammunition in Luka's Luger count.

She caught the fourth skinshifter in the chest; he fell.

The fifth and final Hitler dove behind the camera. Yael held her fire, realizing for the first time that she just might survive this, and if she did, she needed the film to be undamaged. She'd have to shoot the skinshifter from a different angle.

Yael lingered behind the chair, hoping he'd whittle away the rest of his cartridges at the splintered throne. When it became clear that he wouldn't, she scouted the rest of the room. Apart from the chair and the camera, there wasn't much in the way of cover. The only other shield she might use was sitting among the bodies of the *Maskiertekommando*, his bespectacled face just as ashen as theirs. The sight of so much blood had undone the Reichsführer.

Blood, of all things. That was why the floors of the medical block had been scoured clean for Himmler's visits. The man who'd overseen the murder of nations was afraid of blood. Her hands were still covered in Luka's—and when she reached Himmler, the man gagged. Yael crouched behind the Reichsführer, pushed her own pistol into the base of his neck.

"Get up!" She did not recognize her own voice. It was more than snarl—it was iron, forged by grief upon grief. It brought Heinrich Himmler to his wobbly feet.

She shoved him forward by his silver-threaded collar, scanning the shadows for the fifth skinshifter. She hadn't heard him move, and he hadn't managed a shot during her dash from the chair to his commander. Perhaps he'd been wounded....

"D-don't shoot!" Himmler ordered in his broken-strings

voice. It echoed through the studio. Yael heard a rustling behind the filming equipment.

The skinshifter was still there. Waiting.

She hooked her arm around the Reichsführer's neck and tilted her gun toward the camera. It was not Hitler who whirled out. It wasn't even a stranger. It was Luka. Beautiful, dead Luka. His lion-gold hair burst into the light. His lips twisted into a snarl as he fired at Yael, hit her new human shield instead. His eyes were black, black as wrath in their sockets, but it was nothing compared with what Yael felt rising inside her.

The *Saukerl* had stolen the victor's face in the hope that it would disarm her, make Yael hesitate long enough for the *Maskiertekommando* soldier to get a clean shot of his own.

It didn't.

She knew her ghosts.

Yael pulled the trigger just as the Reichsführer collapsed beneath her. She watched a bullet pierce Luka's chest a second, heart-splitting time. She watched the white wash him away; the final skinshifter fell to the floor.

Shot, change.

All of Yael's senses roared. She stood in the center of the room, and the Luger was still in her hand, but there was no need for it. The only sound remaining was her heavy breath. Her noiseless scream.

The first body Yael checked was the one at her feet. The last enemy's shot had shattered Heinrich Himmler's spectacles and skull in turn. His was a quick, indelicate death.

Yael did not turn to where Luka lay, because she knew that if she did, she would not be able to keep going. She'd sink to her knees and sit there in her too-real nightmare until the other SS in the Ordenspalais overrode Himmler's standing order "not to disturb" the *Chancellery Chat* filming.

No, Yael had to keep going. These five skinshifters were dead beyond doubt—features frosted, limbs already stiffening—but they only made up a third of the remaining *Maskiertekommando*. There were still ten men who could wear Hitler's face and use it any way they pleased.

The Führer could not die. Would not die.

Unless Yael showed the world he already had.

CHAPTER 51

The film wasn't difficult to remove. Yael had watched the Reichssender crew do it plenty of times after her on-the-road interviews as Adele Wolfe. She tucked the reel under her arm and started for the door. Her steps shook, from the very marrow out, not because she'd been wounded, but because the room around her felt less than real. *She* felt less than real, a hollow girl among corpses.

White men smeared in so much red. The truth spooled tight under her arm.

Was this enough to change things?

Adolf Hitler was long, long dead and Aaron-Klaus had made a difference. Not such a useless death after all. But what about all of this? What about Luka? What was the use? Why did he have to die?

Why was she always the only one left?

The film crew had almost made it to the door before being shot down. The boom operator had been hit in the neck.

Instantaneous. The cameraman was...not dead. The man stared at her. A low groan left his lips: pain.

Pain meant *life*.

Yael stopped and knelt down, turning the man over to appraise his injuries. He'd been shot—once—in the back. The bullet had passed through, leaving an exit hole in the camera-man's right shoulder. Bleeding was a problem, but if Yael helped stanch the flow, he just might make it.

"Do you want to live?" Again, her voice felt apart from her. As if another being were forming the words just above Yael.

The man nodded.

"The only way that might happen is if we air this on the Reichssender. If I patch you up, can you help me?"

He nodded again.

Life. Yael needed it now. *Life* and the truth out there. Which was why she tore off a portion of the dead boom operator's under-shirt, wadded it into a ball, and pressed it to the cameraman's wound.

His name was Dietrich. Dietrich Krauch. He'd been a cameraman since the war, one of the Reichssender's first em-ployees, which was why he'd been chosen as one of the select few to record the reclusive Führer's *Chancellery Chats*. It was the highest of honors, veiled in unusual amounts of confidenti-ality.

"We never actually filmed in the Ch-ch-chancellery," he explained through chattering teeth (shock setting in). "The lighting is n-no good there, can't get the same picture q-qual-ity. But the Führer encouraged the rumor that he was a recluse, s-said it was safer if no one knew he came to the Ordenspalais to film. Hitler always had his SS guards clear extra personnel out of this wing for productions. Didn't even want Goebbels p-present."

So that was why they were still alone. Ever since the last shot, Yael had been listening for the footfall of SS, but reinforcements never came. Himmler had cleared this area of the building so thoroughly that no one had heard the firefight. The Reichsführer had buried himself in his own crypt of secrecy.

And he was about to take the Third Reich with him.

"Now you know why." Yael crammed the cloth against Dietrich's shoulder. "Himmler and the *Maskiertekommando* wanted as few witnesses as possible in case they were exposed. The Reich needs to know this, too. We need to get Himmler's secret on the air."

"Werner and I were supposed to deliver the film to the master control room once everything wrapped," the cameraman explained. "It was to air immediately."

"How many men are in the control room?"

"There's just one operator. His name is Bernhard. But the control room is on the other side of the annex." Dietrich frowned. It was clear even to the cameraman that he was in no condition to walk that far. "Bernhard won't recognize you...."

"That won't be a problem." Yael surveyed the boom operator's face: chicken pox scars, a dash of gray on the eyebrow, lips of average plumpness. Through the glaze of death, his eyes shone blue.

Dietrich's shock grew twofold as he watched Yael adopt his dead cohort's features. She stripped the boom operator, trading in her SS-Oberschütze uniform for his outer garments. There was a bloodstain on the back of Werner's collar. Still wet. It stuck to Yael's neck as she bent down to retrieve the film reel.

"Keep pressure on the wound," she instructed the cameraman. "Don't let up, or you'll bleed out."

Once the *Chancellery Chat* aired, the studio would be swarming: Dietrich's help, her doom.

The halls were empty, empty, echoing. In order to reach the master control room, she had to go back the way she came, pushing past Luka's 1953 poster. The boy he never was. The boy she'd never speak with, laugh with, cry with, see again.

But why, why, why?

So much loss demanded an answer. All of Yael's insides ached for it. Her fingers went white against the film casing, and she kept walking, past the service entrance, all the way to the master control room. She found Bernhard in a rolling chair, legs propped on the control console, nose deep in a book. He leapt to his feet when he saw Werner, reading material flying. "*Scheisse!* Sorry, Werner. Didn't hear you come in."

Yael grunted. She kept her back to the door, hiding the dark splotch left by the boom operator's death. Bernhard was too flustered to notice. He held his hand out for the reel. "Finished, already? That was fast."

—*ALL READY TO FINISH*—

She passed him the film.

CHAPTER 52

The warning of rotten bones had been sent.

Felix knelt on the floor, kneecaps slowly breaking against concrete as he listened to Miriam imitate Kasper's voice. The mimicry sounded so close to the truth, it filled Felix with agonizing doubt. It would've been simple for SS-Standartenführer Baasch to put a doppelgänger on the phone. Had Felix ever talked to his father?

He would've asked, except he'd been gagged again. Tongue-tied to keep the resistance from finding out what they already knew: Their map room was compromised. Baasch's men seemed determined to strip the place, but the task proved arduous. The number of papers they found stuffed in filing cabinets and wedged in gaps between bookshelves seemed miraculous. Pages multiplied before their very eyes. Rosters, blueprints, notes on operations, forged passbooks, transcripts of the 1955 Axis Tour, maps...it was a fire-hazard collection of information—enough to burn the resistance down to the roots.

SS-Standartenführer Baasch took all of it in with a strange sort of glee. No doubt the officer was envisioning the promotion he'd garner from this: SS-Oberführer Baasch. Gorget patches on his collar threaded with not one but *two* silver oak leaves each.

Whenever Baasch's men showed him a new document with a new name, the SS-Standartenführer's eyes glinted brighter: steel, sterling, titanium. "Excellent. Set it aside to present at the People's Court."

The pile grew. Miriam continued the radio exchange. Felix's knees kept aching, breaking. Henryka's hair had faded from pink to rust, stiffened curls clawing at him. So many had died, were dying, because of Felix's words, and he couldn't undo it. He wondered if his *yes, yes* lie would make a difference at all. Maybe now General Reiniger wouldn't walk into the rattrap. Maybe—

"What's that?" One of the men raiding Henryka's desk paused, caught by the glow of the television. The Führer sat on-screen, and this time he wasn't alone.

Yael hadn't just escaped...she'd made it to the Reichssender studios! Felix couldn't see her wolves, but he could place the face as hers. The anger was hers, too—blazing alongside her gun as she pressed it to Adolf Hitler's temple. The pistol that edged Felix's own skull slackened, his guard transfixed. The man by the desk twisted the volume knob, and the entire map room froze: eyes open, ears listening, unable to pull away as the truth unfolded from the speakers. A drama that was so very obviously *not* scripted. Yael, Reichsführer Himmler, Luka, whoever the man in the chair was...all of them were made of emotion so real it seeped through the Reichssender, cramped the map room.

Confusion: "Wait, the Führer's dead?"

Fear: "Is this true, Standartenführer? Did you know?"

Anyone staring at the SS-Standartenführer would realize he hadn't. Baasch's skin had gone waxy—glistening pale. His handkerchief hung limp at his side, stained with Luger oil.

Luka was listing the victims: flesh and memory versions of the paper under Baasch's hat. Felix waited for Anne Weisskopf's name to be spoken. The loss inside him kept piling— vertebrae shattered, finger bones lost, gravestone past and guillotine future, ghost woman and her ghost curls, all those names and still not Anne's—higher and higher, turning into something HOT.

The room exploded.

Sometime during the broadcast, Miriam had unplugged the radio headset, wrapped its cord around her hands in the style of a garrote. She drew this around her guard's throat, lining the life out of him.

The resistance operatives moved as one. Brigitte snatched a pencil from her hair—bun tumbling free as she lodged the writing utensil into the nearest SS leg. Kasper grabbed the gun near his head, diverted its shot at the guard who loomed over Adele. Johann's move mirrored this—just as fast, just as fluid.

All this happened before most of Baasch's men could tear their eyes from the television. The operatives were outnumbered, three to one, but their willingness to die, their need to live, was equal to the SS's confusion.

Felix had fought before, but never like this: tooth and claw, your life or his, his, his. The room blurred and sharpened all at once. Trapped moments sped by: Brigitte managed to pull down a bookshelf for cover; Miriam abandoned her garrote for a gun; papers flew off Henryka's desk as SS fell behind it.

The odds kept shifting. Four to one when Johann was shot in the sternum, fell, did not get up. Two to one after the SS took a wave of bullets and the Wolfes joined the fray. Felix's hits were far less powerful than Kasper's, but they were effective. He even used his bandaged hand, striking with cornered animal rage. Again and again and again. Until he couldn't tell if the red on his knuckles was from within or from the face of the SS-Schütze he was beating.

The fight evened. One to one. SS-Standartenführer Baasch's handkerchief fell to the floor as the officer made a graceless retreat for the exit.

NO.

It wasn't desperation to survive that drove Felix to his feet. It wasn't anger or vengeance that made him lunge after the SS-Standartenführer. The HEAT inside was a different beast, unleashed.

For the first time since Felix had met the SS-Standartenführer, he wasn't trapped. Now they met on Felix's terms: shoulder to spine to concrete. They hit the floor together.

What had he done? Something a *yes, yes* could not undo. Something Felix could never take back, though this didn't stop him from trying. He used both fists: the broken and the breaker.

Baasch wasn't a slight man, nor was he one to lie back and take a beating. Their fight was more than even; it was vicious. Crush below, claw above. The SS-Standartenführer's punches caught Felix in the jaw, ribs, chest, anywhere he could reach. Felix didn't even try to avoid the blows.

"Did you—ever have—my—parents?" Iron edged his words, and he was bloody, all bloody, and Baasch's face was drowning under his fists, but Felix didn't care. "Answer—me!"

The SS-Standartenführer's mouth gaped: broken teeth, airless answer. There were too many ricochets ringing through the map room to hear it.

"LOUDER!" Felix roared. Only now did he realize that the SS officer's hits had stopped. Baasch was beaten, but it did nothing. The coals kept searing Felix's chest. His right hand was a torch, hurt worse than ever.

Pain mossed over Baasch's eyes. He drew a breath.

"Your—" was the only word he managed before his skull opened. The hole was small, only 9mm, but it was large enough for death to worm through, claiming the SS-Standartenführer for its own.

These eyes were dead. Hindsight proof that the SS-Standartenführer had had at least a glimmer of a soul, however hardened. Felix turned to find Miriam only a few steps behind him, still holding the gun. The soul in *her* eyes was overflowing— lightning bright and luminous.

Miriam aimed the pistol at his heart.

Felix didn't throw up his hands, the way Baasch's surviving men were doing under Brigitte's and Kasper's guns. He did not try to plead or beg. He'd done what he had to, and now it was time for him to pay.

Felix stared back at Miriam—blue eyes to blazing—and nodded.

Adele ran to her brother, lodging herself in front of him. She faced Miriam. "No! Please! I told—I told Felix to do it! He was only trying to protect me! Baasch was going to kill our family."

The gun didn't move.

Neither did Adele.

"Ad," Felix whispered, "get out of the way."

"NO!" his sister spit, with every ounce of stubborn, angry love in her body. "No! This isn't *right*! Baasch *forced* you—"

"I still made the call," he said, hoarse. "I still chose."

A hush had fallen over the map room, allowing for new noises from above: gunshots, heavy machinery churning against asphalt. So that was why reinforcement SS hadn't come. They were engaged in another fight. Had Reiniger's men managed to rally back for the block so quickly? It seemed unlikely.... But then, who was on the other side of the battle?

Miriam heard the sounds as well. She waited another beat. Artillery rumbled. Adele stood in front of her brother. Arms outstretched, as if another few lengths of flesh and bone might protect him.

"Get out."

What? Felix couldn't believe what Miriam had just said.

"Take your sister and *go*!" Miriam waved her Luger at the main door. "If I see you again, Herr Wolfe, you're a dead man."

This time, Felix believed her.

Adele hooked her arm around her brother, pulled him off Baasch's corpse. They walked into the cellar together. The

SS-Standartenführer's two remaining men followed: stripped of their weapons, dazed with their intact lives. The door locked shut behind them, sealing Miriam and the other two operatives in with a mound of corpses.

Why was it that this side felt more like a tomb?

CHAPTER 53

The dance of prey had come to a close.

Miriam locked the door to the cellar, hoping the SS wouldn't get a chance to test their howitzers on its reinforced steel. Hoping the battle above would swing out of the National Socialists' favor.

It was impossible to avoid the dead; stepping around one corpse simply led to another. Miriam had to tiptoe her way to the communication station. Her garroting move had ruined the headset cord. Not much had been spared in the second firefight, though the radio still seemed to be working.

Kasper and Brigitte were another exception. Well-trained though they were, the pair looked overwhelmed by the sheer number of bodies. Miriam wondered what it said about her that this carnage wasn't shocking, had not been shocking for a long, long time.

What *had* shocked Miriam was what she'd witnessed on the Reichssender: Luka Löwe not just playing the hero but being one. Himmler's on-air confession. Yael among wolves...

Miriam hadn't seen the end of the tape, as busy as she was fighting for her own life. The television was as much a corpse as the others: screen shattered, circuits laid bare. The Führer's face was finally gone, but so was Yael.

It was easy to worry about her friend and harder to hope. But neither of these things would do much good, here among the dead. What *would* be helpful was a line of communication with the world above. Miriam tested the headset from Johann's busted radio in Kasper's machine. Someone was still transmitting on the other end, listing letters faster than Miriam could memorize.

"Do you have a pencil, Brigitte?"

The operative patted her hair only to remember that her pencil was half javelined in one of the bodies below. "I had extras. Somewhere..."

"It's still broadcasting?" Kasper approached the stool.

Miriam nodded. "After what just happened on the Reichs-sender, General Reiniger needs this map room more than ever. Do you have protocols to tell them the crisis has been averted?"

"Well, yes——"

"Good. Use them." Miriam handed him the headset and joined Brigitte in the search. She looked on the card table, where the Doppelgänger Project files lay undisturbed by the chaos. Luka had been using a pencil to write his speech, hadn't he?

SS-Standartenführer Baasch's hat crowned the top of the pile. Miriam swept it off. There was nothing she regretted about squeezing that trigger. It was the final aim that lingered with her—unfired.

Had it been smart to let Felix and his sister go? Probably not. Had it been right? Miriam didn't know. This mercy went against everything the Soviets had taught her: *We will destroy the murderers of our children/comrades/friends.* But she'd been learning new lessons as of late, and the way Adele had flung herself between Felix and the gun reminded Miriam of Yael and the Molotov firing line. Reminded her that killing the Wolfe boy would be foolish.

In the end, his wasn't her life to take.

Luka's pencil lay where the victor last set it, wedged against his speech: half written, now finished. Miriam handed the writing utensil to Brigitte. "Here. This will do."

The operative righted a fallen stool and settled in front of the Enigma machine. Two bullet holes speckled its unhinged lid, the machinery within untouched. After a few unjumbled letters, more than enough exchanged pass codes, communication between the resistance map room and the forces above was reestablished. Miriam left the operatives to their radio exchange and moved toward the far wall, where Henryka's map folded into itself. The back of the paper was heavy with indigo ink, bled through. All Miriam could see were new countries. Upside down, piecing themselves together in a sea of white.

She knelt to the floor and collected fallen thumbtacks until her hands couldn't hold any more sharpness. One by one, she used them to pin the world back into place.

CHAPTER 54

"Werner, what the hell—" Bernhard twisted in his chair when the screen version of Yael appeared on the monitors. Fear swept across his face. "Goebbels will have our heads for airing this."

The operator reached for the control panel. Yael reached for her gun.

"Don't touch anything!" she barked.

Bernhard stopped. The terror of his expression went a shade darker. "W-Werner? What's wrong with your voice? What's going on?"

Yael didn't answer. He'd find out soon enough.

The whole world would.

Something on the monitors caught the operator's attention. Kept it. "Is—is that Victor Löwe?"

It was. Yael's eyes teared as she watched Luka standing in front of Reichsführer Himmler. He looked so vibrant in front of the cameras. So *verdammt* alive.

But she knew what was coming.

Yael held her Luger aloft, keeping half an ear toward the hallway. Nothing yet. But the SS had seen her on the screen. Phone calls were being made. Jackboots would come running. There was only one door into the master control room from the hall. Yael locked it behind her: a small defense. Metal (one jammed handle + four bullets + a blade in her boot) wouldn't stop an SS unit.

There's always a way out. One of Vlad's lessons. Her trainer had taught her to look for every possibility inside a room: windows, lies she could weave, faces she could steal. But now Yael wasn't so certain she wanted to find it.

Life or death?

Never had the second option been so tempting. It had claimed everyone else—why not her? For so long Yael believed she was chosen. Spared to do what others could not: kill Hitler, destroy this kingdom of death. The deed was done, and the sword Yael had used to do it was catching up to her. Outside, the hall exploded with sound: shouts, boots, louder shouts. They'd found the studio. Hydra heads, Himmler, Double Victor Löwe, blood everywhere, and Dietrich.

Not long now.

Luka was reciting the names. Bernhard was beyond speech; his mouth was slack, all lines of dread gone. Hearing not just a list of victims but an entire new vein of history. Watching not just Victor Löwe take a bullet but an entire frame of existence fall back, shatter, die.

But why? Yael's heart rended. *Why, why, why?*

She watched herself run to him. She heard other steps—real

ones—outside the control room door. The handle rattled. There was a shout. On-screen Yael was pleading, trying to stop what could not be.

Question: Why?

Yael stared at the Luger in her hands. The very same gun she was smuggling off Luka's body in a dozen monitors. The weapon that had brought her here.

Answer: Luka died to get the truth out there.

And now it was.

Answer: Luka died so Yael could *live*.

And now she would.

—GO GO GO—

The hall door shuddered and splintered. The lock held, barely. Yael snatched a wool coat from a nearby stand, throwing it over Werner's blood mark as she made for the rear of the control room, scanning its ceiling tiles, screens, buttons…looking, looking…

—THERE'S ALWAYS A WAY—

The place had been divided into segments by load-bearing columns, some as wide as walls. It was larger than Yael first thought. Consoles stretched into consoles stretched into consoles nearly half the length of the Ordenspalais annex. Yael dodged rolling chairs and countless images of her past self, putting as many columns as she could between herself and the view from the hallway door.

Shots sounded. New bullets? Or her own, long fired? Yael didn't stop to investigate. She kept running with all the strength and speed and need to live left in her.

—THERE'S A WAY—

The room ended with daylight. A window! Its glass sluiced from ceiling to floor: the rigid, grand signature of Albert Speer's architecture.

—TWO WAYS—

To her right was a door. The plaque read ARCHIVES. When Yael cracked it open, she was greeted by the smell of mothballs mixed with dust. A sliver of darkness.

—DEAD END—

The window wasn't much better. Its panes looked out onto a street lined with government buildings, alert soldiers. In Werner's bloodied civilian clothing, Yael wouldn't make it half a block before being stopped.

The SS would expect her to try. Yael counted on this as she used her final bullets to crack the window, kicking a sizable hole in the glass. She slipped into the archive room. There was a brief second of light to memorize the space: large, stretching with shelves upon shelves of old *Chancellery Chat* film reels.

The door eased shut. Darkness fell over the graveyard of the Führer's words.

Yael didn't trust herself to go far without stumbling, but she had to get away from the door. Ginger steps guided her to the end of the first stack of film. She slipped past it—second, third, fourth row of reels.

Her pulse was everywhere, scattering with every raw-meat beat of her heart. The SS men were all noise outside the ARCHIVES door. Glass crackled as they broke the window even wider, following Yael's supposed path.

"To the street! Quickly! She won't have gotten far! The

control room operator says she's wearing civilian clothing. Black coat. Spread the word! Alert the checkpoints!"

More glass crackled and snapped. And then, nothing.

Yael's diversion had worked—

The door to the archives room swung open, bathing the place in light. Darkness shrank into shadows on the wall, gathering in the form of a single man. He paused—silhouetted—in the doorway. Yael kept her back to the stacks, breath going stale in Werner's throat.

The overhead lights flickered to life. The shadows vanished, but the man didn't. Yael heard his every step as he moved along the first stack of reels. She twisted into the length of the fourth stack. Out of sight, crouched low.

Her hunter paused at the end of the stacks. Just three rows, two meters away. Air became acid in Yael's lungs. She gripped the knife in her boot. Her fingers trembled against its hilt.

The jackboots resumed their beat: iron heel to linoleum. They sounded hungry, prowling past the second stack and the third, closer, closer....

One more step and he would raise the alarm.

One more step and Yael's life would be over.

Yael leapt out before he could take it, using Werner's hefty frame to slam her opponent into the linoleum. The floor cracked the wind out of the soldier's lungs, snuffing his half-formed yell. This didn't stop him from thrashing, wild blows that Yael dodged with automated precision. Her blade was in her hand. One swipe, one strike was all it might take.... But...

The SS-Sturmmann's uniform was pristine. Perfectly tailored

to an escape. Knives were, by nature, messy tools of killing, and if Yael used hers, it would sabotage her future alibi with blood blotches and stab holes.

Not by the blade this time, but by her fist.

Bone to flesh to flesh to bone.

One blow to the temple and the storm trooper went limp. Yael lost no time peeling off Werner's clothing, studying the SS-Sturmmann as she did so. Brown hair, pristinely trimmed. His lids, when she peeled them back, revealed blunt blue eyes. Mole on the edge of his jaw. Bottom teeth slightly overlapped.

Yael moved in a flurry of buttons, stripping the SS-Sturmmann of his outer garments and dressing herself in the storm trooper's insignia: skulls, eagles, runes, all silver. The official papers in his uniform pocket told Yael she was impersonating Otto Gruber.

The SS-Sturmmann wasn't dead, just lifeless. Yael couldn't bring herself to cut his unconscious throat (there were still *some* lines left), so she used strips of Werner's clothing to secure him in the archive's far corner, well away from any stacks of reels Otto might be able to thrash against when he woke. It should be some time before he was found.

Yael straightened the collar of Otto's uniform, returned the knife to the SS-Sturmmann's jackboot. She walked to the exit, switched off the light, and shut the door. Yael paused by the blasted window; the scene beyond it was just as jagged. Frantic street, milling with SS uniforms.

She blended right in.

SS-Sturmmann Otto Gruber walked down the lane, just

as much a hunter as the others. His stale blue eyes searched doorways, glossed over vehicle windows. Every time someone asked if he'd seen a man in a black coat, he shook his head. The question grew rarer the farther he walked, replaced by different rumors.

Adolf Hitler. Heinrich Himmler. Dead.

These names, combined with this word, exposed an emotion Yael had never before seen on the faces of the *Schutzstaffel*— fear. They were doubly orphaned. Leaderless, leaderless. From the lowest SS-Schütze to the highest SS-Oberst-Gruppenführer, none were spared this panic.

For the first time, Yael walked among them as the only fearless one. She carried on the search for herself, circling the shrubs of the Wilhelmplatz, even stopping to peer through the gated entrance of the U-Bahn station. (The place was impassable.) She moved as subtly as she could to the checkpoint. Its guards were being bombarded from both sides. Concerned National Socialist officials wanted to see evidence of the dead Reichsführer and his *Maskiertekommando* puppets with their own eyes. More officials wanted to leave the Wilhelm Street area to tend to urgent matters. One of them had the great misfortune of wearing a black coat.

The guards still had the wherewithal to stop her, check for papers. Yael obeyed, holding out Otto Gruber's passbook, keeping her chin tilted to disguise the fact that she lacked an Adam's apple. Only a few meters away, the official in the black coat was spluttering into the barrel of a gun.

One more step and she could melt away into Germania's cityscape, borrow a dozen faces, find Reiniger.

One more step and she would live.

The guard pressed Otto Gruber's papers back into Yael's palm. Gestured her forward with a wave.

One more step…

Yael took it.

CHAPTER 55

The truth was in the signal.

The signal was everywhere.

Across the continents, television screens flickered and changed. From Führer's face to Führer's face. At first, most viewers couldn't differentiate what they were seeing from the loop. It was a chair, it was a flag, it was a Führer giving a speech they could recite in their restless sleep.

Then the girl with the gun appeared. Volume knobs cranked from zero to ten. Silence to NOISE. Loud was Heinrich Himmler's confession. Louder was Luka Löwe's Victor's Speech. Loudest, the shot meant to silence him.

The clip played only once. Not everyone saw it.

Not everyone saw it, but everyone heard. News of Adolf Hitler's death—and the incredible deception surrounding it—spread faster than a wildfire in drought. It tore through air-raid shelters and Wehrmacht units, lighting up the ears of SS and partisans alike. Victor Löwe's death followed, close as smoke, flushing out any illusions that blood kept them safe.

Momentum shifted. Everything changed.

It wasn't just the resistance that rose up this time. Loyalist Wehrmacht no longer found themselves bound by the *Führereid*. Revolutionaries rose out of the population's woodwork. General Reiniger's army grew double, triple, tenfold as the remaining National Socialist leadership tore at one another's throats—shredding themselves apart from the inside. The swastikas of Germania burned and burned until the skies went black and the New Order became a thing of the past.

General Reiniger's bolstered forces made the push northwest, securing the Luftwaffe airfield and opening supply lines to the North Sea. Ammunition, fuel, heavy machinery, all the troops reborn Britain could spare…all came pouring in, carving out a new kingdom with the capital—reclaimed, renamed Neuberlin—at its core.

Out, out the indigo spread. The red bled away, away.

For months, the fighting raged. Scores more battles. Thousands more lives. Reiniger's forces hammered the remnants of the National Socialists and the Waffen-SS south until their backs were to the Alps, and there was no more retreat. The last major battle was fought at the base of the mountains. The National Socialists were a wave dashed upon the rocks, and dashed and dashed, until, finally—surrender.

January 5, 1957. A snowy Innsbruck evening. General Erwin Reiniger met with Führer Martin Bormann, a man as ragged as his self-proclaimed title. Pen was put to paper. Bormann's name was signed in ink.

The war was over.

What now?

PART IV

LAND OF PROMISE

CHAPTER 56

This tattoo session was different. There was a needle, yes, and there was pain (more than enough), and there were memories. Yael sat in the cracked leather chair in the artist's back closet on Luisen Street. It had been almost a year since she saw the man last, yet he looked so much older. His glasses were too big on his face. There were lines around his cheeks that hadn't been there before.

He wouldn't take Yael's money, even when she thrust two tattoos' worth of marks at him.

"It's the least I can do. After what you and the others did... I can sell art again," he said in a quiet voice as he began prepping the needle. Gathering the ink. "What are two more wolves compared to a new start?"

Two more wolves. That wouldn't do. Henryka's memory belonged in the pack, but Luka... Yael's thoughts filled with a brown jacket and cigarettes. Things Luka Löwe used to set himself apart because he wasn't like the others. Never like the others.

Luka Löwe—the boy she hated, the boy she loved, the boy she lost—was not a wolf.

"Just one more wolf," she told the artist. "Then I want a different animal."

The man's fingers were a ballad of movement, setting the needle down, picking his sketch pad up. He grabbed a charcoal pencil from behind his ear and brought it to the page in a skillful rendering of Henryka's wolf. Lines that would cross the skin of Yael's elbow from the fangs of Vlad's wolf into...

"What's the second creature?"

Not a wolf, not a wolf, not a wolf.

Luka had always reminded her of something else. Predatory and proud, lounging across floors and desert sands. Looking at Yael with a dangerous, fierce emotion in his eyes. (Love, she knew now, love that was still clawing her heart raw.) Fighting when it mattered the most.

"A lion," Yael whispered.

The artist continued drawing—all concentration—his tongue poking out of the corner of his lips. Stroke by stroke, the lion took shape. Big mane, long lope, muscles of power—all conveyed by a collection of elegant lines. The creature would flow seamlessly from Henryka's wolf into the blank skin of Yael's left bicep, leaping between the old life and the new.

"Will this do?" The artist held up his sketchbook. Final wolf and only lion.

Yael didn't trust herself to speak. She nodded and offered out her arm one last time. The tattoo needle hurt like it always did, sliding deep into the layers of her dermis. The artist copied his lines from paper to skin with perfect precision. *Buzz, buzz,*

buzz. Tails, torsos, heads. *Buzz, buzz, buzz*. Pain with every line. Pain that meant life.

Some hours passed before the needle finally fell silent.

It felt very much like an ending.

The shapes of the wolf and the lion glowed hot as Yael sat up and examined the artist's work. The wounds were raw, red, exposed, but Yael could see what they were to become. Dozens of delicate, spidery lines connected the memory of Luka Löwe and Henryka to her other ghosts.

Babushka, Mama, Miriam, Aaron-Klaus, Vlad, Henryka, Luka.

The living and the dead.

The remembered.

The artist took just as much care in bandaging up the tattoo as he had in making it. The stinging smell of witch hazel wafted through the closet as he wrapped the gauze around Yael's arm.

"Make sure you change the bandages and clean it regularly," he instructed her. "It will take time to heal. Just like all the others."

CHAPTER 57

It was a warm morning—holding more than a few hints of spring, even some strokes of summer to come. Felix rolled his coverall sleeves as high as the auto shop entrance. He was elbow deep in a Volkswagen engine; its grease claimed every available part of his skin—cuticles, life lines, pores—some of it ingrained so deep not even a shower could lift it off. The only truly clean patch was Felix's right hand. Wound gauze and antibiotics were long gone, replaced by a black fingerless glove. Adele had stitched its last two openings together to cover the whorled scar.

It had taken Felix months to retrain his maimed hand to hold a wrench again, and even then the grip of the three remaining fingers wasn't what it used to be. His left hand grew stronger out of necessity. He and Adele had to eat, and food prices weren't kind—two fixed engines to a decent dinner. There'd been several weeks, in the thick of the war, where Felix felt as if hunger pains had flipped his stomach inside out.

It had ended, once the battles moved south and Frankfurt

settled back into a routine as normal as any routine could be in the wake of the Third Reich's destruction. People brought their broken things to Wolfe Auto Shop, and Felix fixed them. There was bread on the table, cheese, too, sometimes. Some rare days, Adele managed to barter their measly marks for meat or eggs.

Felix ate his meal every night wondering if it would be his last.

Yael was alive. He'd seen her on the television—tattoos hidden, unchanged face—flanking General Reiniger while he addressed Neuberlin and Germany proper on their future as a republic. All details of elections and restructuring a parliament were lost to Felix. He watched Yael and knew Miriam's mercy had only delayed the inevitable.

The wolves were coming. One of these days, they'd show up at Felix's door, demanding blood for the blood that was taken.

Every time a new customer ducked into the auto shop, every time he heard Adele scuffing her shoes against the doormat, Felix was certain his reckoning was at hand. But it wasn't. And it wasn't. And it wasn't. Winter thawed into spring, which flirted with summer.

Felix kept working. Always, the dead leaned over the engines with him. Martin, Mama, Papa. Luka Löwe (he missed the *Arschloch*, more than he'd ever imagined he could). Henryka and those radio operatives. Anne Weisskopf. Today's heat made their presence extra weighty.

"I didn't think you'd be here."

Felix dropped his wrench. It clattered through the engine. He didn't bother picking it up. His fate stood just outside the auto shop, by a stack of spare tires. Dark hair, sleeves short enough to show the left arm pack. He hadn't heard Yael approach. Of course he hadn't.

She was a feather-footed spy. How easy would it have been for her to whisk behind Felix, slit his throat?

He took little comfort in the fact that she hadn't. A debt such as this could only be settled face-to-face.

Felix straightened. He knew Yael had weapons hidden on her person, and he kept waiting for her to reach for one. She didn't. Instead she crossed her arms and craned her neck, reading the letters Felix's Papa's father had painted there in the thirties. WOLFE AUTO SHOP, white against black-coated cinder block. Time and weather had peeled most of the finer edges away. Papa always meant to refresh the sign, but it was a chore that kept getting bumped to the bottom of an ever-growing list.

Felix wished he'd thought to touch it up. He doubted Adele would once he was gone.

Yael stepped through the garage door. Her arms stayed crossed. "I thought you sold this place to Herr Bleier for an Axis Tour bribe."

"I did."

After the map room, the twins had spent several weeks in Germania, hopping from air-raid shelter to air-raid shelter as the street skirmishes would allow. They made their way to the capital's outskirts, where Adele's flat sat untouched. Felix and Adele stayed only long enough to pack valuables, photographs, canned food. Frankfurt, he'd convinced his sister, was where Mama and Papa would return if they were still alive. Frankfurt was their only chance to be a family again.

A journey that should've taken less than six hours lasted over a week. The roads were so bad that they were forced to go on foot, and, more than once, war interrupted their path. War had interrupted Frankfurt, too: houses abandoned, stores looted, families gone. Felix and Adele found the garage clammed shut, milk bottles crowded on the house stoop.

Herr Bleier never came to claim his real estate holdings. Felix found out later it was because "Herr Bleier was killed in the uprisings. With no family and no government to collect his property, the deed fell back to us."

Yael grunted and gave the place a twice-over, her gaze landing on the oil patch shaped like a lopsided heart. The one Felix used to sit on while he watched Papa work. "Looks just like the photographs."

Felix kept waiting, waiting for the bullet, the blade, but there was no stab, no sudden shot, and he couldn't stand just standing here anymore. "Have you come to kill me?"

Yael's eyes snapped up from the floor, holding all the elements Felix had expected: sharp anger, the flinch of the betrayed. Felix wondered what they saw in turn. (Not on the outside; mirrors told him often enough how unkind the months had been. Skipped meals had hollowed out his cheeks, grayed his lids. Even his hair had taken an ashen tinge.)

Could she *see* the dead crowded around his shoulders? The nights he couldn't sleep because he felt Henryka's curls coiling around his thyroid? The days that felt too long because Felix knew they were taken from those unwilling to give? People who had faces?

"I've thought about it." Yael's gaze broke from his, fell to Felix's glove. "We've been hurt enough, don't you think?"

He didn't know what to say to that. He didn't know how to breathe. "Then why—why are you here?"

"Is Adele home?"

She was. Felix knew if they entered the Wolfe house, they'd find his sister in the family room, trying to budget out the week's marks.

"Why?" he asked again.

"I made you a promise, back in Molotov," Yael said slowly. "I was only able to keep half of it. Today I'm going to see it to the end."

Is this real? The garage was going dizzy blue. Felix blinked, took a breath to push the sparks away. He thought it was. He hadn't had a dream this good in a very long time.

"I've come to take you and Adele to your parents."

━━━━━

Yael led the way on her motorcycle, another Zündapp KS 601. Adele drove, her fingers tapping nervously against the Volkswagen's steering wheel as they wound through the countryside. Felix stared out the window. The day was so pleasant he half expected to see families out picnicking. Baskets brimming with cheese, rolls, figs, and bottles of mineral water, blankets spread out over the grass. But most families had neither the time nor the extra food to spend on a picnic lunch. As for grass...

War had wrought its ruin on the land. Kilometer after kilometer of torched orchards and crater-pocked fields streamed through Felix's reflection. These scars were months old. Even the full force of spring wasn't enough to mend them.

But there were places the war hadn't touched. Where the road itself became more suggestion than fact. Where the trees grew with a rugged consistency that reminded Felix of the

Muscovy taiga. Where the mountains rose into grand things: rock, rock, snow, peak.

Their Volkswagen engine churned against growing slopes. The turnoffs became fewer and the drive longer. Felix began to wonder if Yael was leading them toward the end of the world. They'd certainly come close to the top of it: The sky's blueness looked near enough to touch. Felix rolled down the window. Was air supposed to smell this sweet? Was his chest supposed to feel so light?

The safest place in Europe sat at the top of a hill. Vlad's farm. Felix leaned forward to look through the windshield for a better view. He could make out a barn, a house—simple wooden structures. The first person he saw was...Mama! Alive. Out of bed. *Gardening*. She knelt among rows of infant seedlings. Her hair was wrapped in a plaid kerchief; she held a spade in her hand. When she glanced down the drive and caught sight of Felix's face pressed to the Volkswagen window, she started running.

Papa appeared next. He stood at the barn door, holding a pail of milk. This dropped, sloshed everywhere, when he realized whom his wife was dashing toward.

The car hadn't yet pulled to a stop, but this didn't keep Felix from opening the door, stumbling into the gravel, falling on his hands, pushing himself up again, running to his parents. The meeting was a sobbing embrace. Papa smelled like straw; Mama was all earth. They hugged Felix with a strength he didn't think they still had, pressing him against their chests until his earlobes hurt. Adele wasn't far behind, joining the tangle of arms. She didn't try to squirm away until her hair was practically soaking with their mother's tears.

"We thought you were both dead!" Adele said through tears of her own. Her eyes crinkled together, as if she was trying to squeeze the emotion back in. "We were in Frankfurt, waiting and waiting! Why haven't you come home?"

"We tried," their father explained. "A few times. But Vlad convinced us it was safer to wait here while the resistance tracked you two down."

Is this real? Felix had to be sure. These could be doppelgängers for all he knew.

"Mama, what color was the blouse you cut up for Adele's doll? The Christmas Papa came back from the front?"

"That was so long ago." His mother was taken aback by the question. Her soft eyes blinked several times before she answered, "It—it was blue? Wasn't it?"

It was.

Felix turned to Papa next. "What did Martin get that Christmas?"

His brother's name drew a veil across all their faces—something somber and gray. Something that made his family themselves, and Felix knew even before his father answered that the Wolfes were together again. As together as they'd ever be.

"A pocket watch," Papa answered. "He didn't put the thing down for a week. Even tried to bathe with it. Do you still have it?"

Felix plucked the timepiece from his coverall pocket. It sat, silver and shimmering, over his glove. Mama and Papa noticed his amputated fingers and gasped at the same time.

"Safe and sound." Felix handed the watch to his father, but it didn't stop beating.

You remember what you did, don't you? Don't you?

He looked over his shoulder to find Yael standing in the middle of the gravel drive. It was colder here. Felix's coverall sleeves were back to their original length, but Yael had already removed her riding gloves and jacket. Her arms were bare again, still crossed. Mountain light brought her wolves into finer sight. He now noticed there were more of them—no, just one more wolf.

Felix had never asked Yael what the tattoos were *for*, but as soon as he saw the lion, he knew. At least, in part.

The farm's third inhabitant appeared on the porch. Vlad. It must be. Even holding a cup of tea, the man looked dangerous: a gallery of gashes and missing body parts. When he caught sight of Yael, he raised his cup in greeting.

She began walking toward the house.

"Yael." Felix broke away from his family—three steps and pause.

Yael paused, too.

Sorry would not bring back the dead. *Sorry* would not fix things. But it was all Felix had to offer. "I'm sorry."

His apology felt so small. A feathered hawk speck against a wide-world sky, suspended on wind currents. No rise, no fall, just flight without motion, hovering between them.

Yael's arms loosened. Her lips parted, and her breath slipped out until she reached the bottom of her exhale. She had no words left, none for him at least. She gave Felix a nod so subtle he would've missed it if he blinked.

Something inside him landed.

Yael continued her hike toward the house. Vlad welcomed

469

her inside, shut the door. Felix stood on solid ground, staring at the cabin's rough-hewn wood.

"Felix!" Adele called his name. "What are you doing?"

He turned to find the Wolfes still there. Papa rubbing the bald spot on the top of his head. Mama holding her spade in one hand, gripping her daughter with the other.

Felix joined them.

CHAPTER 58

Vlad's kitchen was everything from Yael's memories: table covered in a chain mail pattern of mug rings, shelves lined with vodka bottles, teakettle simmering on the stove. Two years later and her trainer was just as unchanged, made of the same scars and scowls. Yael wasn't bearing her numbers, or any face he might recognize, but he knew her on sight.

"It's about time you showed up," the old intelligencer grunted in Russian. "Those two have been pestering me about going home since they got here. You know I don't like whiners."

"They can't have been that bad." Yael took a seat, clasped her hands over the battered tabletop.

Vlad swept to the other side of the kitchen. "Were at first. Even made a few escape attempts before I convinced them it was better to wait. They've at least been tolerable since I got them doing chores."

"I came as soon as I could." Part lie, mostly truth.

During the months of war, Yael had kept busy in the map

room. Joining Miriam and Kasper and Brigitte and a dozen fresh faces in an attempt to fill Henryka's role. (No one could, but they did their best.) The months after Bormann's surrender had been a haze—the ash of war settling, the dust of rebuilding republics rising. Only in the past few weeks had there been room to remember the Wolfes.

Time might heal wounds, but the scabs inside Yael were fickle, falling off in the moments she least expected, bleeding all over again. There were days on end when she could not trust herself to look Felix in the eyes and choose life. Even today, standing by the open garage door, watching the mechanic bent over his work, she'd felt her heart split into a mess of wounds and wants.

Murder or mercy?

On paper, a simple question. In the flesh, a different matter.

It was Miriam who told her the truth of what had happened in the map room. At first Yael would not believe it, could not wrap her mind around what Felix, of all people, had done. It did not match up with the boy she knew—dogged strength, inherent goodness. The one who'd fixed her motorcycle and bound her wounds, who'd said he was on her side no matter what.

No. Not *her* motorcycle. Not *her* wounds. Not *her* side.

Never *her* side…

Yael had known it would hurt, this inevitable break between them. But never could she have predicted just how devastating the rift would be: Felix's betrayal, his deal with SS-Standartenführer Baasch, the fall-through and the fallout. Every detail filled Yael with another layer of anger, a smoky ache, new yet so, so old, added to all of her many other griefs. Henryka hadn't even been buried yet. And Luka's body…she couldn't bear to think.

Life or death?

It was a choice Yael hadn't fully made when she walked into Wolfe Auto Shop. There was no cold blood. No lines of innocence holding her back. Even Felix knew it, asking *Have you come to kill me?* in the most matter-of-fact tone he could manage.

She was staring at the floor when he said this. At some dark stain that could've been blood but was probably something more mechanical. Her heart kept splitting inside her. Growing and breaking, rended and rendered, reminding her that she was so, so sick of death. All it carried. All it buried.

Felix deserved to die, yes. But Yael deserved to let him live.

She could hear the Wolfes' laughter—faint and full— through the cracks of the kitchen door. Again her heart grew and broke. Vlad poured her a cup of tea and slid it across the table. Sans the vodka he usually slipped in his.

A pity. Today Yael could've used it.

She cupped her hands around the warm china, let the heat crawl through her fingertips. Vlad settled in the chair across from her, one eye squinted and seeing all. "How are you holding up?"

Yael knew he didn't have to ask. She knew she didn't have to answer. "Barely."

"Better than not at all," Vlad grunted, took a swig of his own tea. "It's a wonder you're here after all those stunts Reiniger put you through. He got another job lined up for you yet?"

"There are ten remaining members of the *Maskiertekommando* still at large," she told her old trainer. "Reiniger thinks most of them have taken to the ratlines."

Though the boats departing from Europe's shores were being combed for fleeing National Socialists, it was impossible to catch all of them. These escape routes—ratlines—were crawling with SS. Uniforms tossed, monsters trying to pass as men. Most, their intelligence told them, were headed to South America, hoping the continent's vast mountains and jungles would be enough to swallow them.

It wouldn't.

"You're certain there are only ten?" Vlad asked.

Yael was. Not only did they have the whole of the Doppelgänger Project files at their fingertips, but they had an expert witness. Dr. Engel Geyer's escape attempt had not been as successful as some of his counterparts'. He was captured on his way to the coast. Several vials of the Doppelgänger Treatment were on the doctor's person, though Geyer's face was his own: gap teeth, sharp eyes. He admitted he was too afraid to self-administer the compound. Five percent was too high a risk for the Angel of Death.

Ten *Maskiertekommando* men. Miriam and Yael. These were the only skinshifters left. The rest of the compound had been locked away, preserved as evidence in the trial of Dr. Engel Geyer.

"Reiniger wants Kasper and me to track the skinshifters down and give them...more visible marks."

Long, long ago, an *X* had marked Yael as a survivor. But it would be a double *Sieg* rune that marked the skinshifting war criminals. A black jag on each cheek. Impossible to hide, no matter what face they ended up wearing when they were brought to trials of their own.

"Ten skinshifters. That should keep you busy."

"We have their files. Himmler kept extra-careful tabs on

them. He didn't want them slipping away either. He noted all of their familial attachments, significant places in their past. If they cling to any of these, we'll find them." Yael blew on her tea and took a sip.

Vlad's cup was empty. He made no move to refill it. "Have you stopped yet?"

Both of Yael's arms were on the table. Six wolves and a lion. Yes, she still faced them every sunlit day. Yes, she still stopped to recite their names every darkening night.

"I remember."

Where she came from, what she came through.

"The dead we will always have with us." Vlad's eye twitched as he leaned back in his chair. "But I don't mean taking time to reflect, Yael. I mean taking time. You've spent your whole life hiding and fighting. You've earned some rest."

"I am. Resting," Yael told him. "It's not all spy stuff. I have a place of my own now."

The residence was half Miriam's as well, a place for her sister to stay when she wasn't traveling to and from Moscow, attempting to balance a seesaw of politics. They'd painted the walls blue and were trying their best to keep a collection of potted plants watered. Nay, blooming.

Every day Yael learned more about herself. Not just her past, but the past before that: the history that ran through her blood. Miriam's memories of life before camp ran deeper than Yael's— after all, she'd had eight more years of them. She gave Yael what she could: prayers, stories from the Torah, Hebrew in parcel and part.

Her rest came in the form of Shabbat. Every Friday evening, no matter what hardship or grief the week held, Miriam and

Yael lit candles and said a blessing over a cup of wine. Miriam did not remember how to make the braided loaves of challah, nor did any of Neuberlin's bakeries, and so they had to make do with regular bread.

The National Socialists had tried to burn all traces of Judaism from the earth. Much had been scorched—synagogues, Torah scrolls, souls—destroyed on a scale almost too vast to comprehend. (How many, how many?) Yet it was not *all* ashes. There were survivors—men and women and children who'd managed to ride out the New Order years in Novosibirsk and its surrounding wilderness. Most chose to remain in these places, where roofs and jobs were plentiful, where a synagogue still stood, where they need not fear their neighbors' knives. For some, however, the call of the old-countries-made-new was too strong.

A woman named Shoshana was among the first to arrive in Neuberlin. Her fingers knew how to knead the challah dough, braid it just right. Now every week she made loaves for Miriam and Yael, for the five, ten, fifteen others who appeared. Among them was a rabbi by the name of Rosenthal, who had a Torah scroll in his possession, its Hebrew calligraphy more precious than gold.

They were a community on edge—constantly looking over their shoulders despite the protection promised by Reiniger's government. (The world was changed, yes, but it was far from perfect. There was a reason Yael kept her P38 close.) But their roots went deep, bound them together in collective memory. With each new arrival, they pieced together more of their past, built more of their future.

"I have the living with me, too," Yael told her fifth wolf. "What are you going to do, once the Wolfes are gone?"

"Weed the garden. Keep the cows alive." Vlad caught the look on her face, laughed. The sound was as growly as everything else that came out of his mouth. "Reiniger has new tasks for me, too, I'm afraid."

He did not elaborate, and Yael did not press, though she did wonder. Vlad's talents and resources were many. Exactly where would Erwin Reiniger direct them? Toward relations with Moscow? Or the situation in the Greater East Asia Co-Prosperity Sphere, where restlessness had gripped the populations, threatened Emperor Hirohito's rule?

"We'll survive." Vlad topped off both drinks. Without vodka, again, but this didn't stop him from raising his teacup, tapping it to Yael's own. "Who knows, maybe we'll even thrive."

CHAPTER 59

The camp was deserted. After Reiniger's victory, the place—and all the others, far, *far* too many others—had been seized, exorcised. There were no SS at the gates. No rifles resting on their shoulders. No bristling Alsatian dogs at their sides. The watchtowers stood blind. Weeds sprouted through the rocks between the railroad ties—the ones that had whispered Yael's name to her so many years ago. (*Yah-ell, yah-ell, yah-ell.*)

They said nothing now, adding to the silence that lay thick over the place. It hovered above smokeless stacks, walked the empty barracks, seeped through every brick and board, soaked into the souls of all who heard.

They were few; they were more than Yael could have hoped—the ones who'd come to pay their respects. Most of the community from Neuberlin made the journey, bearing candles and matches, stones and prayers. There were others, too, men and women Yael didn't recognize. Some spoke Russian. One couple had a baby. There was a young man whose face reminded

Yael so strongly of Aaron-Klaus that she had to stare at him a good three seconds before deciding that, no, she was not seeing ghosts, just visiting them. Some were already lighting their *Yahrzeit* candles, flames shivering against their palms as they coaxed their matches, set them to the wicks.

Yael's candle and matches remained in her pocket. She didn't want to light it alone, because she did not have to. Miriam was here, somewhere. They'd endured the drive from Neuberlin together, navigating the final stretch of gravel road, past the pines that grew along it. Again, Yael wanted to run into the trees, but as soon as they reached the gates where Rabbi Rosenthal and the others were beginning to gather, Miriam clapped her on the shoulder and said, "Stay here. I'll be right back."

So Yael stood, taking in the quiet. A wind rushed through the forest—carrying pine-needle whispers and a sappy scent she couldn't remember from her childhood. Evergreen had outlasted the smoke.

When Miriam returned, there was a strange look on her face: heavy and hard and hopeful. Soil was wedged into her knuckles and nail beds. She held her hand out to Yael, unfurled her palm.

Soft flesh, life line, grainy wood.

Yael couldn't speak when she picked up the doll. She could not cry when she twisted the biggest one open and found the next, and the next, and the next. Four faces, each different, all of them there. Aside from some loose clods of dirt, the set of matryoshka dolls looked untouched. Plucked straight from dark-night memories: the offering of the Babushka's wrinkled hands, Yael falling asleep with the family knotted against her chest, Miriam's promise to keep them safe.

They'll all be together again someday, she'd told Yael.

Neither of them believed that day was a real, tangible thing. That twelve years later they'd be standing outside the open gates, preparing to light candles for the dead.

Yael took the smallest doll from her pocket and placed it inside the rest. *Snap, snap, snap,* safe. Not ten steps away, Rabbi Rosenthal cleared his throat to greet the group and bring them into a more organized mourning. Those who'd been lighting their candles stood, and though they had all the space they'd ever need, their group drew inward, shoulder to shoulder, knit tighter than any. Miriam's hand found Yael's, squeezed hard. Yael squeezed back and did not let go. Her other hand held the doll tight.

Wind was still sweeping down from the pines when it was time to recite the Kaddish. It wrapped itself around the voices of Rabbi Rosenthal and the other men, gave their words wings. The prayer lifted up, up, out.

Yael shut her eyes and listened.

Here was a people. A family. A faith.

Her people. *Her* family. *Her* faith.

Here was a silence broken.

Yael's name was already in the history books (inked—forever and always—beside **Luka Wotan Löwe**), but this did not stop her from accomplishing more. She followed the ratlines to South America and marked every *Maskiertekommando* she could find. She stood at the end of the Avenue of Splendors and watched the Volkshalle's dome crumble to dust; the shock waves of its demolition shook the roots of her molars. She thought of the dead and fought for the living, entering the battleground of Neuberlin's politics to make sure the voice of her people was not lost, would never be lost again.

She ate challah. She laughed. She wept. She wore herself proudly: short sleeves, first-face forward. The wolves and the lion went with her, always with her, running across warm skin, under daylight. The sun kept shining, and there was nothing left to her that was a lie.

Happily, sadly, humanly ever after...

Yael Reider lived.

ACKNOWLEDGMENTS

I can't believe I'm writing this sentence, because it means, for all intents and purposes, that this book is finished! Done! *Finito!* I cannot count the number of times I stared at my messy Word document, doubting that I'd ever be able to turn it into a finished novel. And yet, here I am, at the series' end.

Telling a story as expansive as this one requires a lot of support. (A LOT.) I had plenty of expert cheerleaders and cheerleader experts. Jacob Graudin helped me plot Germania's downfall over pints of beer. Kate Armstrong read early chapters and gave me the encouragement I needed. Megan Shepherd and Anne Blankman provided excellent rough-draft feedback. Since I'm nowhere near as gifted with languages as Yael, Anna-Anya Spann aided me with Russian and Nora Leitz with German. Nagao and Wombat spent hours helping me brainstorm the breakdown and subsequent repairs of the GAZ-AA truck. Rick Zender of the College of Charleston Communications Museum faithfully answered e-mails. Matt Hunter fielded my medical questions. The amazing people behind the C&Rsenal YouTube channel let me pick their brains about firearms, battle tactics, and alternate war scenarios. I'm especially indebted to Lisa Yoskowitz and Judah Beilin for their cultural insights.

Publishing is a tough business, and I'm fortunate to have a grade-A team in my corner. Tracey Adams—agent extraordinaire—has put such faith in me and the stories I wish to tell. She also found me an amazing publishing home at Little, Brown Books for Young Readers. My trust in Alvina Ling's ability to edit my stories has become unshakable. (You really *are* a superhero!) Nikki Garcia,

Hallie Patterson, Kristin Dulaney, Andrew Smith, Megan Tingley, Victoria Stapleton, Danielle Yao, Emilie Polster, the NOVL team—thank you for all that you do to get my books into the hands of readers. Orion continues to do a stellar job publishing my books across the pond. Felicity Johnston took up the editing torch midseries and did so fabulously. Nina Douglas—thank you a thousand times for the blogger tea, Platform 9 ¾, and for just being brilliant.

This series has had *so* many avid supporters. Laini Taylor, Jackson Pearce, Amie Kaufman, Victoria Schwab, Megan Shepherd, Victoria Aveyard, Marie Lu—thank you for shouting from the rooftops about Yael's journey. I've continued to be astounded by the power of readers' love. It's one of the best things an author can ask for, really.

David, thank you for telling me over and over that I could write this book and for tearing up when you read Chapter 49 at Red Lobster. Dad, I know you didn't intend to lend me your World War II books for two and a half years, but thanks for letting me get away with it. Mom, thank you for being my first and biggest fan. Adam, you're in the acknowledgments now. (But for real, thanks for reading *Wolf by Wolf* instead of watching sportsketball. It means a lot.) If I listed all the family and friends who've helped me stay sane while writing *Blood for Blood*, this book would be much, much thicker. But all things must come to an end, and so I'll close out these acknowledgments the way I do all others. Thank you, God, for your gifts and grace. *Soli Deo Gloria*.

Once upon a different time, there was
a boy who raced through a kingdom of death.

Turn the page to start reading *Iron to Iron*, a thrilling
novella set in the world of *Wolf by Wolf*.

Once upon a different time, there was a boy who raced through a kingdom of death. He wore a brown jacket where all others were black, and it was said that his face could snare the hearts of ten thousand German maidens at first sight. His own heart? Hidden behind layers of leather and sneer and steel. Untouchable.

Until it wasn't.

———

CHAPTER 1

Nineteen fifty-five was going to be Luka Löwe's year.

He could hear the screams of the Reich pulsing through the walls of the Olympiastadion's changing room as he laced up his boots. The chant beat against his temple when he double-checked the safety of the Luger pistol hidden in his waistband. (The last thing he needed was to get his *Arsch* shot off by his own gun.) The yells roared, louder and louder with every passing minute. Feral volume, constant beat.

"Sieg heil! Sieg heil! Sieg heil!"

Hail victory.

It was not his name they were shouting, but it might as well have been. Two years ago, Luka had been the face of this phrase. After his astonishing win in 1953, posters of the fourteen-year-old victor had been plastered the Reich over: from the walls of Germania's U-Bahn stations to the alleyways of Moscow. It was a watercolor portrait by Mjölnir—one of Joseph Goebbels's favorite artists. The man had painted Luka in the style of a war hero: sharp jaw, tight-cut hair, black jacket, arm rigid in a salute as he stood by a Zündapp KS 601. A swastika standard billowed in the background, its red edges melting out into a map of the Axis Tour. Ten cities—Germania, Prague, Rome,

Cairo, Baghdad, New Delhi, Dhaka, Hanoi, Shanghai, and Tokyo—all connected with a scarlet line: 20,780 kilometers. Half a world of sand, sweat, mud, blood, and—on more than one occasion—death.

The Mjölnir version of Victor Löwe stood in front of these things: a conquering hero. The actual Luka hated him.

Pride. That's what the poster was meant for. That's what Luka should've felt surging through his veins every time he looked at the propaganda piece. He was the best of the Reich's racers, but being the best didn't fill him with a sense of glorious purpose. Instead it did the opposite. Whenever Luka saw the boy on the poster, he felt all at once smothered and drained.

Years of training. Days and weeks and months spent at the racetrack. Striving, striving, striving, getting dust in his teeth and road rashes up his arms and burn marks against his calves. All for this: SIEG HEIL! 1953.

Luka's face was on a poster, and he was the best of the Reich's racers, but there was still something crushing inside him. Something missing.

One victory was not enough. It certainly hadn't been for his father. When Luka first returned from Tokyo with his Iron Cross, all Kurt Löwe had to say on the matter was, "I bled on the fields of the Muscovy territories for my cross. I lost an arm for it, and now they're handing them out as prizes for a *gottverdammt* race?"

If being the best wasn't enough, Luka would just have to be the best of the best. Not even Kurt Löwe would be able to shrug off *two* Iron Crosses.

"Victor Löwe?"

Luka barely heard the knock on the changing room door, much less the official behind it. The screams for VICTORY had reached a drowning volume.

"Time...procession..."

Ah yes. The procession. Where the twenty racers were led out onto Olympiastadion's manicured grasses and presented like racehorses: trot and all. This part was always laborious to Luka. He hated pomp and circumstance, standing still when everything inside was chomping at the bit.

He shouldered on the final, most essential piece of his uniform, zipped it into place, and walked out into the stadium. The place—with its thousands of spectators and their lung-bursting *heils!*—was so loud that Luka could hardly feel his own footsteps. When the crowd caught sight of his trademark brown jacket, their yells swelled even louder.

"Sieg heil! Sieg heil! Sieg heil!"

The smell of gasoline soaked through the March air. Twenty factory-shiny black Zündapp KS 601s sat in a staggered row. Every lens the Reichssender television channel owned honed in on Luka's face as he led the line of Reich racers into the center of the stadium.

There were the usual pleasantries. Racing officials gave speeches about the importance of March 10 and the Axis's Great Victory and the providential destiny of the New Order and the Greater East Asia Co-Prosperity Sphere and on and on. Anthems were sung, and racers were introduced, while the sun beat down at the height of its afternoon strength. By the time they were allowed to mount their motorcycles, Luka could feel his skin sizzling—sunburn making itself at home.

His wasn't the first Zündapp in the lineup. That particular honor belonged to Tsuda Katsuo. *Victor* Tsuda Katsuo, a sixteen-year-old from Japan who'd cut Luka's 1954 victory out from under him. The boy was a good racer, an even better saboteur. If Luka wanted to win the Double Cross, he needed to be a better racer, the best saboteur.

Tsuda Katsuo was Luka's biggest threat, but far from the only one. There was Georg Rust from Munich, third in the starting line. Kobi Yokuto—the younger brother of Victor Kobi Eizo, who'd won the Axis Tour of 1951—was fourth. Both racers were seventeen, medal-less, and in their last eligible year of racing, which meant they'd be determined. Nay, desperate.

From there the threat level took a sharp decline. Of the three remaining sixteen-year-old racers only one—a slender boy from Frankfurt with the surname Wolfe—had qualifying times that came anywhere close to concerning. Max Kammler (fifteen, in his second year of racing) was another to watch. On the Japanese end there was Saito Jun, who'd impressed Luka last year with his ability to slip through tight racing formations, and Watabe Takeo, the boy who liked sharp knives.

The rest were wet-behind-the-ears first-years and boys whose qualifying times had no *drive,* no *oomph.* They were what Luka liked to call the "cataclysmic racers," whose only chance at the title lay in some force of nature coming along and sweeping away the rest of the competition. (See the flash flood of 1951.)

But all these boys were behind Luka. The only thing he could see was Katsuo's fender, blinding his eyes with concentrated chrome sunlight.

"Lovely day for a drive. Eh, Katsuo?"

The boy turned at the sound of his name. When Luka wiggled his fingers in a wave, the Japanese racer's expression hardened: as iron as the cross around his own neck.

Katsuo's many-worded response contained neither *konnichiwa* nor any of the choice Japanese curses Luka happened to know. But body language was universal, and there was no missing the disdain that coated Katsuo's syllables.

"Same to you!" Luka's mouth hooked into a half smile—more mock than not. He settled onto his Zündapp, testing the ease of its throttle. Everything seemed to be in place. "Enjoy the view of the open road while it lasts!"

The other victor's nostrils twitched. In one fluid motion he twisted around, kicked his bike to life, revved the engine. A wave of exhaust slapped Luka's face—pipe innards and angry asphalt. The smell stank, but Luka's smirk only grew. His words were wriggling under the Japanese victor's skin, making him emotional. *Good.* High emotions meant rash decisions. Rash decisions would not a double victor make.

Luka cranked his own motorcycle, all traces of a smile retreating as he glared at Katsuo's fender.

This would be the year of Luka Löwe.

"Take your marks."

Double victor. Hero of the Third Reich.

"Get set."

Tough as leather, hard as steel.

"Go!"

Worthy.

492

CHAPTER 2

The racers tore through the capital's streets, wheels spinning out as many kilometers per hour as their engines would allow. Germania to Prague was the shortest section of the Axis Tour: an afternoon of driving on Grade A roads. Luka had navigated this leg so many times during training that he figured he could drive it with his eyes closed. He almost wanted to. Katsuo's fender kept winking an annoying shot of sunlight at him. *Catch me. Catch me if you can!*

It was tempting bait. *Verdammt* tempting. But Luka knew better than to go for it.

Georg Rust didn't.

They were just past Dresden, where the grandiose cityscape of palaces and churches faded into cherry tree orchards still a month shy of bloom, when Herr Rust edged into the frame of Luka's goggles—pulling from third place into second. Luka didn't try to block him, watching as the boy passed and fell into line behind the wink, wink, lure of Katsuo's fender. Georg waited a few kilometers before he tried to overtake it. The move was sharp and fast, bold enough to succeed. He drew even with Katsuo, then passed him, rip-roaring down the autobahn.

Though the thought of falling behind made Luka itchy, his hand stayed steady on the throttle. Speed was important, but it was only a fraction of what it took to win this race. Victory was a complicated tapestry. Endurance, sabotage, knowing your competitors' weaknesses and strengths, careful alliances, sheer luck—racers needed to know how to thread all these things together just to finish the Axis Tour. Much less reach Tokyo at the head of the pack. You couldn't just barrel into the horizon like a Persian cat with its tail on fire and expect to win.

It seemed Georg Rust disagreed. The boy's maneuvering skills were nothing to scoff at. Five times Katsuo tried to reclaim his lead, and each time the seventeen-year-old from Munich cut off the victor's path with hair-raising precision, refusing to back down even when their motorcycles were centimeters from touching.

Georg was first over Prague's checkpoint line. Katsuo second. Third—it pained Luka to see his name etched in that place. *But,* he reminded himself, *there are 20,433 kilometers left to change that.*

Herr Rust hadn't even broken a sweat. The boy parked his bike and shucked off his helmet. A fine wave of sunburn marked the goggleless half of his face, and he was grinning through the pink. Katsuo's face was red—more emotion than burn—as he stared at the back of Georg Rust's fair head. It was a stare Luka knew well: stalking-tiger savvy. The stare he'd made the very grave mistake of ignoring.

———

1st: Georg Rust, 2 hours, 32 minutes, 14 seconds.
2nd: Tsuda Katsuo, 2 hours, 32 minutes, 16 seconds.
3rd: Luka Löwe, 2 hours, 32 minutes, 17 seconds.
4th: Kobi Yokuto, 2 hours, 32 minutes, 20 seconds.
5th: Felix Wolfe, 2 hours, 32 minutes, 24 seconds.

———

Hours had passed since the end of the leg, and Luka's soup was long gone, but the road jitters had no intention of leaving. Luka always got them after a day of adrenaline: that feeling of nerves flayed open like electric wires, jolting his insides to *go, go, go.* Cigarettes usually helped. They were illegal and tasted like *Scheisse,* but they whispered to the fears inside him. Brought all the chaos and noise and striving down to a quiet hum.

Luka was on his third of the evening, filling his corner of the checkpoint's dining area with rebellious haze. No one had come to reprimand him for the black-market smoke. No one ever did. It was one of the benefits of being a victor. Short of treason, Luka could do whatever the hell he wanted. *Petty laws need not apply.*

He smoked, he listened, he watched. You could tell a lot about a racer by the way he handled his road jitters. Herr Rust was all laughter and high spirits as he dug into his soup. Some of the younger German racers had swung by his table to congratulate him. Hans Muller, August Greiser, Walter Graf, Peter Schaub, Max Kammler. They clapped Georg on the back and asked him to recount the move for first. The story stretched a bit more with each telling. By the sixth version, Georg had nearly run Katsuo off the road while trying to claim his lead.

While Georg's tales grew taller, Luka's cigarette burned shorter. His eyes sought out Katsuo on the other side of the room. Like Rust, the victor had acquired a gathering. The boys around him were listening, nodding, and—Luka was willing to bet one of the cigarette packs he'd smuggled into his pannier—plotting. Katsuo kept shooting his glare across the converted warehouse, hitting the oblivious Herr Rust every time.

Let the competition take out the competition. Luka had better things to do.

Georg might have the ears of half the German roster, but he had no one to watch his back. Luka sat with his own back to the wall, exhaling a cool screen of smoke as he scanned the room.

It was slim pickings for allies this year. Language barriers and national loyalties prevented him from approaching any of the Japanese racers. Georg Rust was out of the question, and Luka had no use for the boys crowding around him. (If they were this awed by a simple pass, they wouldn't have the nerves to carry out what Luka had planned.) Kurt Baer and Dirk Hermann were hunched over a table, voices dropped to scratching whispers, making plans of their own. Perhaps they'd want to form a triumvirate....

There was one other racer: Felix, from the Nürburgring circuit. He too sat in a corner with his back to the wall. A lone Wolfe. The boy was slender. Had Mjölnir been tasked to paint him, the propaganda artist would've bulged out the jaw and beefed up the arms. The racer already looked half-statue due to the white-paste zinc oxide smeared— war paint style—from cheek to cheek. Sunblock.

Luka's own rosy nose stung. A glance at the scoreboard reminded him that Herr Wolfe had finished fifth for the day.

A smart, fast loner without vanity issues. Just the sort of ally Luka was looking for. He stubbed his cigarette out on the tabletop and made his way across the room. Felix was still eating, though when he saw Luka was headed his way, his chewing slowed.

Luka chose a seat on the wall side of the table, where he could keep his eye on the rest of the racers, and left a chair between them. The Wolfe boy froze, palms flat against the table. Mjölnir would have definitely altered those hands, painting harder knuckles and fuller veins, pumped with adrenaline and Aryan blood. The artist would've squared off the nails, too....

Felix slipped his hands under the table, saying nothing. His expression was stony under the cracked zinc oxide.

"You got any more of that makeup?"

At the last word the boy's face moved. A frown.

"The sunblock," Luka clarified. "Do you have any more of it?"

Felix didn't answer. Silence wasn't a response Luka was used to getting. Girls, press, fellow racers...Luka's presence often sent these parties into a frenzy. But this boy, with his wordlessness and eyes unmet, acted as if Luka weren't even there.

"Chatty, aren't you? Look, you want my advice?"

This time Luka was graced with a glance. Mjölnir would have a field day with those eyes. They were a rare strain of blue. The light, sparkly kind you'd find under the case at a jeweler's shop.

Luka pointed at Felix's soup, steaming into open air. "You better keep your food covered, especially when *Schweinehund*s like me come sniffing around. There's all manner of drugs floating around here that'll have you diving headfirst into a toilet bowl for days."

Felix hooked his arms around the bowl, pulled it closer to his person.

"Look," Luka went on, "I know this is your first tour, so I'll make it simple. You're not going to win if you play the lone ranger. You need to form an alliance. Find someone to watch your soup bowl when you can't. Someone to lend you zinc oxide when the sun gets too harsh."

"The sunblock isn't for you." Felix's words were brusque. Forceful enough to make his voice crack.

Rejecting a victor's offer to team up? Felix Wolfe was either the most foolish racer in the Axis Tour, or the smartest.

Triumvirate it was. Luka looked toward Kurt Baer and Dirk Hermann. Dirk was in his third year of racing. Too experienced to pass up the offer Luka was about to make him.

"Your loss," he informed Felix as he stood.

"You're the one with the sunburn." Herr Wolfe picked up his spoon with those twiggy fingers and dug back into his soup.

CHAPTER 3

Cigarettes before breakfast. Luka stood on the courtyard cobblestones of the Prague checkpoint, under a predawn sky, where the stars were only beginning to haze away.

Late to bed, early to rise. His had been a restless sleep. The road jitters never completely vanished—despite a fourth and fifth smoke over his discussion with Kurt and Dirk. The pair had welcomed Luka to their table without much ceremony, asking his advice about the next leg and discussing how to protect their places in the lineup, which, to be frank, weren't all that great at sixth and eighth. They were, Luka decided, an unimaginative coalition. Teaming up with them could be more pain than gain.

At the end of the huddle, he'd considered approaching Felix again, but the boy had already bunked up, spinning off a bunch of ZZZZZs under his black jacket when Luka poked his head into the dormitory. He was probably still snoring. Most sane people weren't up this early unless they had to be. Even the racing officials were asleep. It was just Luka with his cigarette ashes and the prickle under his skin that wouldn't go away.

He was stamping out his cigarette on the cobblestones when the checkpoint door opened. It swung slowly—as if whoever was behind it wanted to keep the hinge squeaks to a minimum. Luka stood motionless on his side of the courtyard, watching as a shadow slipped down the line of Zündapps, all the way to the one at the very end. Georg Rust's bike.

It was bold of Katsuo—trying something under the racing officials' sleeping noses. Sabotage was a traditional, if unsanctioned, part of the race, but it was almost always carried out on the road when witnesses were scarce.

The shadow halted, bending over the front tire. Not Katsuo, but Takeo. His favorite blade was in his hand, doing a delicate dance over the Zündapp's tire. There was no violent *hiss* of air or *woosh*ing tire pressure. Luka wasn't even sure the knifepoint had pushed through the tread at all. But Watabe Takeo seemed satisfied. He stepped away from Georg Rust's motorcycle and turned for the door, stopping short when he saw Luka in the courtyard corner.

"If you tell…" Takeo said in German. The boy's Higonokami folding blade was still open; he gripped its brass hilt meaningfully.

Luka shrugged. "I'm all for thinning the field. Though you should know I'm going to make a habit of checking my tire pressure before we leave every checkpoint."

Watabe Takeo flipped his knife shut and disappeared back inside.

Luka stared up at the lightening sky and lit another cigarette.

———

Georg Rust's front tire looked fine at the starting line. The racer flashed a million-Reichsmark grin at the Reichssender camera as he cranked his engine. Luka started his own motorcycle and braced for the road ahead.

If speed was the name of the game from Germania to Prague, then the leg from Prague to Rome was the first test of endurance. This portion was almost four times as long as the first—1,308 kilometers along a road that ran through countryside that swelled into foothills, jagged into the Alps, and then petered off into vineyards and medieval hill towns. Rome was at least an eleven-hour ride at top speeds. Longer still if you wanted to eat more than the odd protein bar crammed into your maw during the necessary stops to refuel.

It started out smooth enough. They zoomed through Prague's morning streets, past a Gothic cathedral that looked as if it had been ripped from the pages of a fairy-tale book, and quaint gas-lamp alleyways plastered with a decade's worth of Goebbels's propaganda posters.

Katsuo didn't try to pass Georg in these charmed city corridors. It was too dangerous. Narrow pavement had been made even narrower by the civilians who lined the road, cheering the racers forward.

"Sieg heil! Sieg heil! Sieg heil!"

Luka remained a steady third, never straying far from Katsuo's fender. They were three hours in—well into the Bavarian countryside—when Georg's front tire became noticeably tired. Its sides sagged, dark rubber puddling into darker pavement, until the racer could no longer ignore it. He was forced to pull to the side of the road and wait for a supply van.

First to last. Just like that.

Sabotage was in the air. The racers drove as close together as their times, and the thought that a few bullets might be enough to claim first was too tempting for Max Kammler. The fifteen-year-old was now running sixth, caught between Kurt Baer and Dirk Hermann. Felix Wolfe was doing an admirable job keeping these racers at bay, holding fourth place with iron-fisted technique.

They were between villages, well out of the range of the Reichssender cameras, when Luka heard the first gunshot. A glance in the rearview mirror revealed that the racing formation had become a panicked mess: wheels and wide eyes and Herr Kammler, waving his Walther P38 like he was a *verdammt* cowboy. The boy seemed to be aiming for tires, but even an expert marksman would find such targets impossible. There was too much movement, too many variables, for his shots to be sure. One flinted off Kurt Baer's Zündapp. Another bit the asphalt by Felix Wolfe's boot. It was only a matter of time before one of the bullets found flesh.

It was the sloppy tactic of an eager middleman—all aggression, no preservation—but that made it all the more dangerous. Luka's attention was torn down the center, half on the road ahead, half on the drama unfolding behind him. Dirk and Kurt were worse than unimaginative; they were at a complete loss at how to stop Herr Kammler, despite their perfect positions to execute a pincer movement. The pair dropped back instead, allowing Max to bully his way into fifth place.

Felix Wolfe was not so easily cowed. The boy's face was firmer than ever under the zinc oxide as he jerked his motorcycle in front of the oncoming troublemaker. Herr Kammler's reflex was to swerve away. The action required two hasty hands, and as a result, his pistol tumbled into the road and his motorcycle veered off it—causing the German rider to brake as the rest of the Axis Tour competitors rushed past.

Kudos to the Wolfe boy. And one more reason to keep an eye on him...though most of Luka's concentration shifted back to the road at hand. Katsuo tore ahead, and Luka stayed on his tail, always second, never passing. Never letting the fender pull more than a few beats ahead—a goal that became more challenging as the road climbed into the Alps.

They were well past the mountains and countless vineyards when evening stretched into darkness. Instead of chasing a spot of sunlight, Luka focused on the red flare of Katsuo's taillight. *Keep up. Keep up if you can!* The hours Luka had chain-smoked instead of sleeping gathered on his eyelids. His stomach felt like an alley-cat brawl—shriek and claw. The screams were even louder in his bladder and throat. How was it possible to be so *verdammt* thirsty and need to pee buckets at the same time? At least one of these problems could be relieved on the road, provided you were willing to sacrifice your dignity for several seconds of race time. Luka was willing to sacrifice much more than that.

(Hail a pissed-pants victory!)

Riding gear and urine did not mix. There was...chafing in rather unfortunate areas. When Luka reached the villa that served as Rome's Axis Tour checkpoint, the washroom was the first thing on his mind. But when he parked his bike and peeled off his helmet, he found himself besieged by a Reichssender reporter and accompanying camera.

"Tell us about today's leg....How do you feel about your time?...What happened to Georg Rust?...Do you have anything to say to your fans?"

If there was a medal for sitting on a motorcycle in a puddle of your own piss while offering tedious answers to equally tedious questions—Luka would've earned it. The interview couldn't have been more than five minutes, but by the end his legs were itching. Forget food and sleep! A clean pair of pants, a wash, and a smoke were all he really wanted.

Once filming wrapped, Luka paused only to scan the scoreboard.

1st: Tsuda Katsuo, 13 hours, 36 minutes,
43 seconds.
2nd: Luka Löwe, 13 hours, 36 minutes, 46 seconds.
3rd: Kobi Yokuto, 13 hours, 36 minutes,
52 seconds.
4th: Felix Wolfe, 13 hours, 36 minutes, 55 seconds.

The sixteen spots below were blank; the racers that would fill them were still out on the road, peeing into ditches and downing rations. This was when the gap between the top of the pack and the others became minutes instead of seconds.

Rome—kilometer 1,654—was when the race got interesting.

CHAPTER 4

The washroom door was shut. Luka rushed toward it without much thought—driven solely by the itch, itch of his pants and the need to get out of them. When he found it jammed, he pushed harder. It opened to the sound of running water, the sight of a back—svelte and bare. Luka stopped in his tracks. The back turned and became…

Breasts!

Luka dropped the clean clothes he was carrying, too busy staring to pick them up. Breasts. In all their curvy, magnetic, entrancing glor—

SNAP!

Pain shot across Luka's sunburnt face, sharp enough to make him swear out loud. He clutched his cheek and realized that the girl he'd stumbled in on was holding a towel. Instead of using it to cover up her bare chest, she'd wrung it tight and snapped it at his face.

Her face, Luka realized, belonged to the Wolfe boy. Well, not *boy*. (Obviously.)

"Stop staring!!" she snarled, readying the towel again.

SNAP!!

This time Luka dodged; the towel's end cracked the air by his ear.

"*Scheisse!* S-Sorry! I surrender!" He threw up his hands and shut his eyes, mind spinning.

Felix Wolfe was a girl. A girl with breasts. A girl who was most definitely not allowed to be competing in the Axis Tour.

"Don't they knock on doors in Hamburg?" Her question was soaked with sarcasm.

"It's a communal washroom!" Luka pointed out. "And you...you're not supposed to be here!"

"Don't tell me what I can't do!" the fräulein snarled.

"It's not me; it's the rules of the race." Luka stood still, waiting for the towel to snap again. He heard the click of a door handle.

"Because you're so concerned with the rules." The girl's hands dipped into the back of his waistband, yanked out the Luger hidden there. "'No weapons are allowed on racers' persons.' That's on page three of the Axis Tour rulebook. Rule Twelve, in case you were wondering."

The fräulein had his gun.

Luka opened one eye, half-squinting. The girl had thrown on some clothes. The zinc oxide had been scrubbed off her cheeks, revealing three dark freckles. Her hair was cut like Luka's...like all the other German boys: blond, curtained bangs slicked back, the hair by her temples and the nape of her neck shorn close. Features that had seemed so delicate the night before now looked sharp: cheekbones, nose, towering forehead. Whetted by the simple fact that they belonged to a girl.

"As Max Kammler made quite clear today, nobody follows Rule Twelve." Luka opened the other eye. He kept his hands raised. She'd flicked the Luger's safety off, but she wasn't pointing the pistol at him.

Yet.

"'Racers are only allowed to use riding gear that has been preapproved by Axis Tour racing officials.' Rule Eighteen." She nodded at his brown jacket.

"I got special permission to wear it," Luka explained.

"Did you get special permission for those cigarettes, too?" the fräulein asked.

This could go on for a while. Luka was tired. His pants were still stiff with pee, and the scratching cats in his stomach had grown ten sizes. The mirror behind the girl showed Luka the welt her towel had left. Nasty, puckered with blood, dangerously close to his eyeball. "Fine. Yes. I break the rules. But this… what you're doing? It's dangerous."

"Dangerous?" The fräulein's lip curled to show teeth. "I'm the best racer in the Nürburgring circuit. I can handle a motorcycle, even with ovaries."

"What do you think the Axis Tour officials are going to do when they find out you're a girl? Hmm? Give you a chain of daisies and send you on your way?"

"They're not going to find out."

The Luger swung up. Luka found himself staring down the barrel of his own gun, then into the eyes of the fräulein who held it. They were as fine cut and heavy as a crystal candy dish, filled not with sweetness but grit. Hard, yes, but not a murderer's eyes.

"You won't kill me," he said.

The girl shrugged and aimed the gun at his foot. "Maiming works just as effectively. Carrying a Luger around in your pants, where the safety can slip on your belt? You're just asking to get detoed."

She had oomph.

But he had her by the (metaphorical) balls.

"Don't think I won't tattle from my hospital bed. I'm not above petty revenge." Luka dropped his hands. "Listen. I think there's a way we can both come out ahead. You need me to keep your secret, and I need an ally to help me on the road. Zinc oxide, soup-guarding, all the things I told you last night."

"You want to team up?"

"Not want," he corrected her. "Need. You saw what happened to Herr Rust today?"

"The flat tire."

"That wasn't an accident. That was sabotage. Tsuda Katsuo can't stand for anyone to pull ahead of him. If you steal the lead without a plan under your belt, he'll take it back through less conventional means."

Those first-frost eyes narrowed. "I assume you have a plan under your belt."

"A few." Luka nodded. "Depends on how the race goes. Most of the plans require a set of helping hands, and I'd rather not have to rely on Dirk Hermann and Kurt Baer. They're slow. Unambitious."

"If I help you edge out Katsuo, you'll keep my secret?"

"I swear on my big toe, and all the little ones, too," he added. "But if you double-cross me, I'll have no problem letting Joseph Goebbels and every other Axis Tour official know what you're hiding."

"How do I know you won't do it anyway?"

"Look, love, I don't think you're in much of a position to doubt my honor."

Her eyes thinned even more. She jerked the pistol at him. "Call me *love* again, and see what happens."

"What's your name, then?" Luka asked. "It's obviously not Felix."

"Felix is my twin brother." The girl hesitated a moment before lowering the Luger. "I'm Adele."

"Adele." The name rolled smoothly off his tongue. "Adele Wolfe. I like it."

"Like it all you want," she told him. "You just can't say it where the others might hear."

"Certainly not, Adele." Luka held out an open palm. "My gun? If you please?"

Adele Wolfe switched the Luger's safety back into place and returned his weapon. Luka wondered if he was making a mistake, not turning her in to the racing officials immediately. But he needed her to help oust Katsuo from the running, and really, how much damage could one fräulein do? Even if she did get ahead of Luka, he could always expose her secret.

Luka's fingers closed over the gun. He tucked it back into his pants and smiled, ignoring the lightning stab in his cheek. "You and I are going to make an excellent team."

506

CHAPTER 5

The next day was straightforward: no sabotage, no subterfuge. Just an eight-hour stretch of road from Rome all the way to the edge of Europe—where the Mediterranean lapped at Sicily's shores and the racers were allotted an entire day of rest for the ferry crossing to Tunis. This boat trip was one of Luka's favorite parts of the tour. Over twenty-four hours without riding. No crowds screaming *Sieg heil!* His road jitters had faded into the backdrop, even though he was now technically in third. Luka had dropped back outside of Rome, allowing Kobi Yokuto to pass him. It was a necessary sacrifice. He needed the space to plot with his new ally, and riding close would afford them that.

Salt and wind lashed Luka's hair as he leaned against the deck railing. The sea unfolded beneath his feet. Shades of aqua and sapphire, echoes of the cloudless sky as far as the eye could reach.

The rest of the Axis Tour riders sprawled across the deck, letting their muscles mend just in time to be ripped apart again by unforgiving desert roads. (Luka's *least* favorite part of the Axis Tour: potholes, sand-clouded vision, dust in his teeth.) Even Katsuo was curled up in a chair, napping.

Felix—*oh, wait, Adele*—walked up to the railing, keeping a whole section between herself and Luka. Instead of leaning, she sat with her boots dangling off the side of the ship. She closed her eyes and lifted her paste-covered face to the sun. Again, the zinc oxide was very strategic, distracting the eyes from the fräulein's more feminine features.

"What's the plan?"

The volume of her question made Luka wince. There weren't any other racers in their vicinity, but boat winds had a habit of snatching words and spreading them. He stepped closer, lowering his own voice to a rough whisper. "The plan is not to talk about the plan where everyone might be eavesdropping."

"So when can we talk about it?" Adele's eyes snapped open. They were even more striking under daylight: clear as the Mediterranean shallows, something you'd want to swim in.

"We've got about three and a half days of riding to Cairo—provided the desert doesn't decide to play hide-the-road. Camps are longer in this stretch, since sand makes for *Scheisse* night visibility. Ride close, and we'll camp together."

"Camp?" Adele grunted.

"Trading night watches. Breaking bread—er, dehydrated meat. Trying not to cuss while figuring out how to set up those *verdammt* pup tents."

"I know what camping is." Her boots thumped the side of the ferry, offbeat. "I'm just not sure about camping with your ogling eyes."

"Worry not, Herr Wolfe. My intentions are completely honorable." Luka's fingers wandered to the welt on his face. It was mostly bruise now, set exactly where his goggles fitted. "Aside from plotting Katsuo's eventual demise, of course."

"Of course." She nodded, both feet drumming in agreement. "I'm glad we understand each other."

Did they? Maybe Adele thought she understood him (most people thought so, another hazard of being 1953 Poster Boy Wonder), but Luka was having a very hard time understanding her. The ladies in his life were his mother—a sweet woman whose shoulders had a habit of hunching every time his father walked into the room—and his fans:

girls with pressed blouses and pinned-up curls, who smelled like gardens and smiled as if they had something stuck in their teeth. They were perfectly pleasant, but uninteresting. There was no...*challenge* in them. All they did was listen to Luka's tales about the Axis Tour and nod, hoping he'd wrap up the story and kiss them. (Sometimes Luka did. Their lips were red and velvet soft, and—just like the first victory, just like his smokes—they did not fill him.)

Adele Wolfe wasn't like them at all.

Luka found it fascinating.

"Anything else?" Adele asked.

He'd been staring, he realized. Caught up in those drown-worthy eyes. Luka overcorrected, swinging his stare out to sea. "Make sure you've got a scarf for the next leg, to cover your mouth and nose," he told her. "That sand will shred apart your insides if you let it."

The desert road was just as terrible as Luka remembered. Worse, perhaps, because this year he wasn't leading the pack and Katsuo's wheels did an excellent job of spewing dust at Yokuto, who in turn flung it toward Luka. It didn't matter that he was wearing protective gear. The sand always found a way in, lodging between his molars and making the insides of his ears itch. His goggles acquired a fine film that made pothole spotting much more difficult than normal. There were plenty to spot. The road was a maze of them—so many that Luka wondered if the Axis Tour officials hadn't just gone ahead of the racers with pickaxes and chopped up the roads to make things more interesting.

Despite the constant swerving, Luka didn't let Katsuo and Yokuto get more than a few seconds ahead. Adele kept the pace, her fist hungry on the throttle. A few times she swerved the opposite way around potholes, pulling ahead of Luka and teasing Yokuto's flank. She had eyes for first: pushing, pushing into Katsuo's piece of road, trying to get her bike in position to pass the Japanese victor. The attempt could have been successful, except for Yokuto's sudden veer in her direction. Adele tapped her brakes, and Luka was forced to do likewise to keep them from becoming a tangle of metal and bloody limbs.

"Don't do that" were Luka's first words to her when they stopped to set up camp on the night-smothered sands.

Adele tugged down her mask. Dust marks slashed across her cheekbones. These plus the dark made her eyes ten times more cutting. "You wanted someone with ambition."

"Ambition!" Luka unstrapped his pup tent from the back of his bike, threw it into the sands. "Not stupidity."

"I saw an opening, and I went for it. How is that stupid?"

Let me count the ways. Luka fought the urge to roll his eyes, and did not win. "Never mind Katsuo's pride. Trying to make passes in pothole central is *pleading* for a wreck. Yokuto almost turned you into road jam."

The fräulein wasn't fazed. "But he didn't."

"Because you slammed on your brakes, which almost turned *me* into road jam and yet didn't because I slammed on *my* brakes, which took seconds off my time. I don't like seconds being scraped off my time." Luka tugged the tent parts from their bag and began assembling them. "This isn't some asphalt track. You don't just loop around a few times and win by muscling your way ahead. If you want to do well in the Axis Tour, you have to be in it for the long game."

"Fine, then. Let's talk the long game. That's why we're here, right?"

The tent came with instructions, but Luka tossed them aside. It was too dark to read anyway. "Our move, when we make it, will be after Hanoi."

"Hanoi!" Adele's breath hissed in, cut off. "That's thousands of kilometers away!"

"The long game is long. Katsuo's on his guard. If we make a move now, we're going to fail. You have to let your competition think he's winning. Let his pride put him at ease."

"So you just want to let him stay in first?"

"Yep. Why are there so many *verdammt* pieces to this thing?" The

510

poles and tarp were straightforward enough, but the stakes...there were supposed to be eight of them. Luka could only count seven. "Always something missing..."

"Why Hanoi?"

"The Li River," he answered, patting the sand for the escapee stake. "It's just a few hours outside of Hanoi. The bridge across it got blown to high heaven during the war, and the Japanese never replaced it. The ferry they use to cross it can only fit three riders at a time. If you're not in the first batch, you automatically lose ten minutes. If you're not in the second batch, you lose twenty. The area is a natural bottleneck."

Adele walked back to her bike. There was a rustling, and at first Luka figured she was getting out her own pup tent. She held up an electric lantern instead. *Let there be light!* It poured across her face and over the sands. Luka spotted the missing stake by his knee. If it were a scorpion, it would've stung him.

"You want to use the river crossing to squeeze Katsuo out of the lead?" She was quick. No denying that.

Luka snatched up a hammer and started driving the support poles into the ground. "Strategically it's the best place. Ten minutes is impossible to reclaim at that point. It's the second-to-last leg, and there's no more overnight camping after that for Katsuo to enact his revenge. He'll try something on the *Kaiten*, of course, but we'll be ready."

"Lull him into false security, stay on the defensive, strike at the end when he least expects it." Adele counted out the points of the conversation: thumb, forefinger, middle. "Got it."

"That's right, lo"—Luka caught himself, midhammer—"vely Adele."

The girl scowled. "If I'd wanted to be flirted with, I would've stayed in Frankfurt with a decent head of hair."

Both tents went up, ration packets were ripped open, canteens uncapped, and water guzzled. They were so close to the Mediterranean that Luka could hear the sea hushing as they dug into their food. It was a low, constant noise. Enough to mask the footsteps of any unwelcome guests who might come sneaking around at odd hours. Luka doubted Takeo would try any knife work so soon after Rome, but he didn't want to bet both tires on it.

"I'll take the first watch," he told Adele after dinner, reaching into his jacket pocket for the perfect pairing: cigarette and match. "I'm not tired yet."

Apparently Adele wasn't either. Her empty ration packets sat crumpled in the sand, but she made no move to switch off the lantern or return to her tent. Instead she nodded at the unlit cigarette between Luka's fingers. "Are those any good?"

"Not really. They're...an acquired taste."

"Then why do you smoke them?"

"Because I'm not supposed to." At least, that's why Luka tried them the first time, in the alley behind Herr Kahler's shop, at the tender age of eleven. Word was going around that the Führer wanted to outlaw cigarettes, which only made the demand for them even higher. His childhood friend Franz Gross had snuck one out of his father's pack to try. It took them five whole minutes to get it lit. One whole minute to inhale without spluttering. Luka coughed on and off the entire next week.

It wasn't until after his victory—three years later—that his smoking habit really set in. There were several reasons. He could get away with it as a victor. With his Axis Tour winnings, he could afford them at black-market prices. He needed something, anything, to prove that he was more than just a sketch on a poster on wall after wall after wall.

"They help me feel more like myself. Less like a lemming."

"Lemming?"

"You know...those little rodents that supposedly follow each other off cliffs in droves. They just run right off because the lemming in front of them did it. Tumble, *splat*, dead!"

"Let's have it, then." Adele held out her hand.

Luka stared at the fingertips. Against the lamplight, they had a plasterlike appearance. Breakable.

"What?" She frowned. "You think I can't handle it?"

"I—" Luka had no idea what to say. It wasn't a sensation that happened very often, but this fräulein and her un-fräulein-ness put him on needle points. His usual lines would not work with her.

Adele's palm stayed open. Luka handed her the smoke and light, then dove back into his jacket pocket for more of his own.

"Is that the story behind the jacket, too?" Adele struck her match against her biking boot. It fizzed to life, fluttering as she brought it to the end of the cigarette. A breath in, a fire caught, a smooth, smoke-spiral exhale. "Black leather is too lemming for you?"

"Something like that." Luka lit his own cigarette, let the tobacco hum through his veins. Good timing. Thinking about his jacket—the *real* story behind it—always put him on edge.

"How'd you get permission to wear it?"

"After my first victory, I convinced the tour officials to let me wear it in my father's honor. It was his prewar riding jacket. Motorcycles were his life. He was a member of the Kradschützen during the war, but he lost his arm on the eastern front. Couldn't ride after that. He gave this jacket to me as—as a reminder."

"And what does the jacket remind you of?"

"The kind of man I'm supposed to be." (Two-Cross strong. Not just hard, but unbreakable.) This was dangerous territory. Luka moved on quickly. "That was just an excuse. Really it's because I look much better in brown leather than I do in black. How's the cigarette?"

Adele smoked like a natural, wielding the cigarette without so much as a cough. "Full of ashy rebellion. I like it."

"So what's your story, Adele Wolfe?" he asked after a drawn-out drag. "Why aren't you back in Frankfurt, breaking all the boys' hearts with your decent head of hair?"

Her eyes lit up behind the cigarette's glow. "Racing's in the Wolfe blood. My father's a mechanic, owns a garage in Frankfurt, Wolfe Auto Shop. There were always racers from the Nürburgring tracks coming in and out of the place. My brothers and I begged our father to teach us how to ride. He did. We were all good. Good enough to start racing. Only I wasn't allowed on the tracks."

513

"I'm guessing this didn't stop you," Luka said.

"Ever wonder what it's like to be a female lemming?" She didn't wait for his answer. "If you aren't the daughter of an elite party member, when you turn eighteen you have only two options: find a strapping lad to marry and make babies with or get assigned to the Lebensborn, where you pump out babies sans wedding ring and schnitzel smashing.

"Husband, children, a life shackled to the kitchen...I don't want any of that. Never did." Adele let out a breath, watched its smoke curl into shafts of lamplight. "Motorcycle racing is a different story. Pulling out onto the road, feeling the asphalt rush beneath you, the adrenaline coursing everywhere...it's not just in my blood. It's *life*."

Luka knew what she meant. There was something about racing that pulled him onto his Zündapp again and again. It was the opposite of road jitters...a road *high*. Adrenaline at its purest. Tastes of fullness that only made the emptiness that followed more aching.

Life! Life! Is this all there is?

"What do your brothers think about you racing?"

"Felix has always supported me. He's let me use his papers ever since we were ten. Martin's dead," Adele said the last part quickly. "Broke his neck on the track four years ago."

The night suddenly felt a shade darker. "I'm sorry," Luka said. (And he was.)

"Life's short." Ashes speckled the sand as Adele tapped her cigarette. "It's getting shorter every day. I'm not going to waste mine fulfilling someone else's idea of who I should be. That's why I entered the Axis Tour. I want people to remember my name."

It doesn't help, Luka wanted to tell her. *Even when they're screaming it at the top of their lungs.*

"But you're racing as Felix Wolfe," he pointed out.

"Ever heard of Hanna Reitsch?"

"Who hasn't?" The aviatrix—with her waspish waist, fair features, and stellar flight record—had been a propaganda centerpiece for as long as Luka could remember. Goebbels gobbled her up, as did the rest of the Reich. "I met her once. We were giving interviews at the Ministry of Propaganda at the same time. She was nice."

"Hanna Reitsch was so gifted at flying that the Führer himself awarded her an Iron Cross. If Fräulein Reitsch can remain unwed and flying, then there's hope that I can be unwed and racing. If I prove I'm the best, they won't care I'm a girl."

"And by proving you're the best, you mean winning?" Luka asked.

"I didn't enter the race to lose."

At least she was honest.

"There our interests diverge." As they always did with these alliances. Nothing lasted forever, especially when it came to Axis Tour loyalties. Luka wasn't too worried. Adele knew her secret was unsafe with him if she tried anything underhanded.

"After we deal with Katsuo we'll part ways," he promised.

"Why do you need the Double Cross so badly?" Adele asked. "You already won the Axis Tour. You have everything."

He had everything, and it was too much. It was nothing at all.

Adele had so many words...so many *reasons*. And Luka? His Iron Cross hung heavy around his throat, and he struggled to even understand this hunger inside of him, much less verbalize it. He didn't *need* to win. Not the way this girl did. His previous victory assured him his choice of Lebensraum assignment. No lottery would force Luka to move to the never-thawing tundra of the Muscovy territories or to this godforsaken sandbox.

"There's always something more," he told her.

Adele was silent after that, nursing the last of her cigarette, staring up at stars or down at ashes. Luka made a study of her face in the lamplight. Striking cheekbones, comet-trail eyebrows, something beneath that was just as strong, far more blazing.

Life. Oomph. She was full of it.

He was more than fascinated.

He was hooked.

CHAPTER 6

They rode forth with the dawn. Warriors on steeds of steel, galloping across a land of endless dust. This was the part of the tour where Luka usually started reciting the alphabet backward in his head, so he wouldn't crash from sheer boredom. Sure, the sight of the glistening Mediterranean to his left was pretty, and sure, the Sahara desert was nice, too, but there was only so much water and sand you could see before wanting a change of scenery.

This year there was no need for *Z, Y, X, W*.... Luka had plenty to keep his mind off the thirst that jabbed at his throat between fuel stops. Adele kept snagging his eye, and not just because her rear end was nice.

Most people didn't talk to Luka Löwe the way this fräulein did: brass-tack sharp and to the point. Most people didn't listen to him the way she did either. Usually they shouted over him (*Sieg heil!*) or wanted him to say something different. ("Let's shoot that interview again. A bit less cursing in front of the cameras, please, Victor Löwe!")

Adele listened as if she actually cared what he had to say.

It was refreshing.

Verdammt refreshing.

When Adele asked for cigarettes the next two nights, Luka obliged, because he wanted to keep talking. Their conversation wound this way and that, meandering like a drunk booted out of a bierstube. It skirted motorcycle parts (as a mechanic's daughter, Adele knew far more about the click-and-clack innards of Zündapps than Luka), before landing on who their favorite Reichssender staff member was. (They both appreciated Fritz Naumann, a cameraman with wire glasses, and ever-wirier hair, who insisted interviews be kept as short as possible. "Film is precious," he'd say when other Reichssender staff fussed at him. "Do you want to radio Goebbels saying you ran out just as they reached the finish line?") Then they lamented the sad state of their on-the-road meal options: dried chicken/dried beef/dried cardboard.

"Give me some *grüne Sosse* with beef brisket and boiled potatoes." Adele fluttered her eyelids with phantom taste bud delight. "And a glass of *Ebbelwoi* to wash it all down. Real food."

"I have a theory that they provide such flavor-leached tack to make us go faster. Keeps us motivated to get to the checkpoint meals," Luka reasoned.

Adele laughed, a real, true sound that splashed into the canvas of stars above them. It wasn't until Luka heard it that he realized how much his life had lacked the noise.

"There's always the hunter-gatherer option. I saw Katsuo fishing out here last year." Luka nodded toward the ocean. "I have no idea if he caught anything. Or how he cooked it."

Adele shuddered. "I hate fish. All those slippery, slimy scales. Dead eyes just bulging out at you. They just taste like ocean vomit."

It was Luka's turn to laugh. He was surprised at how easily it slipped out. "You wouldn't fit in well in Hamburg. We love our fish. You can't pick up a fork without tripping over something of the piscine persuasion."

"I'll take the flavorless mystery meat, thanks." Adele tossed her third cigarette into the sand. It blinked out. She nudged the discarded butts with her boot. "I see why you smoke these things. They have a certain draw, don't they? Once you get past the initial taste."

Luka's cigarette was down to finger-burning length as well. He followed suit, very briefly considering a fourth before deciding he needed to slow down. *They* needed to slow down. At the rate they were smoking, his stash would be depleted before Shanghai, and his road jitters were always at their worst on the last leg.

"I'm surprised you like them so much," Luka said.

"You're surprised I tried them at all," the fräulein countered. "You shouldn't be. Fish affinities aside, you and I aren't so different."

"Yeah?"

"Yeah."

Luka waited for Adele to elaborate, but she didn't. Their conversation was winding down, and just as well, since the night was drawing long.

"We need to get up early tomorrow to make the push to Cairo," he told her. "Katsuo will probably be off at first light."

"You still want to let Katsuo stay in first?" she asked as Luka stood, stretching the affronted muscles of his wrists and rear.

"The plan hasn't changed, Adele."

"Felix," she corrected him. "I'm Felix at the checkpoint."

"We're not there yet, Adeleadeleadele." The name was a good one, as far as rhythms went. It flowed naturally into itself, tumbling off Luka's tongue like a frantic lemming herd. "Goodnight, Adeleadeleadele."

She laughed again.

A smile crept its way onto Luka's face as he ducked inside his tent.

———————

March 17, 1955. Cairo came.

1st: Tsuda Katsuo, 4 days, 1 hour, 56 minutes,
13 seconds.

518

2nd: Luka Löwe, 4 days, 1 hour, 56 minutes,
20 seconds.
3rd: Kobi Yokuto, 4 days, 1 hour, 56 minutes,
24 seconds.
4th: Felix Wolfe, 4 days, 1 hour, 56 minutes,
30 seconds.

Cairo went. March 18, 1955.

The desert continued, all flat. Luka found himself racing not just to keep up with Katsuo and stay cumulatively ahead of Yokuto, but also to get to the evening, when he could exhale words and smoke and feel his insides lift in a way that wasn't tangled with adrenaline or nicotine.

He didn't smoke as much the next night. This was the Valley of Thirst—the stretch of race that cut through desert so deserted it had no wells to refresh their canteens. Rationing sips of water was necessary in this two-day stretch, and too much smoke scratching Luka's throat always made him thirsty. Two cigarettes was plenty, but Luka stayed up talking long after the embers went out. He thought (feared?) they might run out of things to talk about, but the silences between them didn't stand a chance. Adele shot them down with rapid-fire questions. Some importantly strategic: "Will you help me guard the washroom in Baghdad while I get this road gunk off?" "Does the racing path always have so many potholes?" Others not so much: "Do you know what that star is called?" "Got any more cigarettes?" "What's your middle name?"

Hers: Valerie. Pretty. Fitting, seamless, into the rest of her. Adele Valerie Wolfe.

His: Wotan. Odd. Antiquated. The name of a grandfather who had probably inherited it from his grandfather before that. When Adele heard it, she laughed so hard that a piece of dried chicken/beef/cardboard got stuck in her throat and Luka had to smack her on the back until the offending meat slipped out.

Adele kept laughing until she cried. "Wotan?"

519

"You laugh now," Luka told her. All too aware that he was sitting next to her, close, close. Shoulders touching. This slight contact shot through him with all the heat of the desert day. "Just wait. It will make a surging comeback in baby names once I become double victor."

"A world full of little Wotans. God help us."

"Shhh!" Luka held his hand up.

Adele's laughter evaporated. The light on her face went hard, rage bright. A change so fast, so jarring, that Luka's breath rattled his throat. "Don't you *shhh* me—"

"No," he said, trying to keep his voice low as he reached for his Luger. "Listen."

Both Luka and Adele stared into the desert.

All was dark. All was silent. The Mediterranean was gone, along with its *hush, hushing* waves. There was no *shift-slide* of sand that meant footsteps. Had Luka's mind been playing tricks on him? He could've sworn he heard movement....

After several minutes Adele stated the obvious. "I don't hear anything."

They were still shoulder to shoulder. An odd pairing, if anyone was eavesdropping. Luka moved away, even though he wanted to do anything but. (Amazing, how such a small point of contact could pin you so heavily. He really had to *pull* to get the brown jacket away from the black.)

"Could be nothing," he said. "I'll take the first watch tonight."

Adele opened her mouth to respond when the desert screamed back. Luka leapt to his feet—pistol pointed forward. The darkness didn't budge, but the yells kept coming from some distance on, in the direction of Yokuto's or Katsuo's camp.

No gunshots. No death shrieks. Just Japanese.

"Sounds like a sabotage gone south," Adele said.

"You understand Japanese?" *That* could be helpful when it came to eavesdropping on Katsuo at checkpoints.

The fräulein shook her head. "Just the curse words. Whoever's shouting is using a lot of them."

Curse words: the most essential part of any foreign language learning experience. Now that she mentioned it, Luka could hear a few *kusos* and *baka kas* being tossed around. He wondered if Takeo's knife had slipped. Could be that it wasn't one of Katsuo's cronies at all. Maybe Kobi Yokuto had an ally no one had accounted for and was trying to sabotage his way into first....

The shouts faded. The desert plunged back into silence.

Luka and Adele stood apart. Listening.

Swish, swish! Darkness streaked in darkness, disappearing just as quickly as it came. Whoever initiated the attack had survived in enough shape to retreat, which was more than some racers from previous years could say (if the dead could talk). Luka kept his Luger high, in case the steps backtracked, but they didn't. And they didn't. And they didn't.

━━━━━

Katsuo and his Zündapp were still intact, as Luka was disgruntled to discover the next morning. They were better than intact. They were *fast.* Last night's events had thrust a bunch of stinging nettles beneath Katsuo's *Arsch.* His driving was daring, leaving no room for mistakes. It was an unprecedented pace. The Japanese victor was trying to shave off a half day of driving (and the night's camp along with it), risking life and limb to reach Baghdad by nightfall. Luka strained to keep pace through the constant screen of dust.

Kobi Yokuto—also intact—wove ahead of Luka, following Katsuo's line of drive: in, out, around, about. Yokuto's driving was jerky. There was a rage to his engines, one that built up and up as the afternoon pulled into the evening's golden hours.

Just as Baghdad's lights began blinking to life on the horizon, Yokuto made his move for first. His scarlet taillight swung to the side; his motorcycle bellowed up the road—faster, faster, furious—until he was even with Katsuo. The victor matched the frenzy of Yokuto's engines, refusing to let the other Japanese racer pass. Rpm for rpm. Grit for grit. Luka could keep up, but three years of racing this track warned him not to.

Rash speed + rough road = road rash.

Yokuto's taillight snapped up, as if the night had swooped down and snatched the bike in its talons. Luka clenched his brakes, swerving to the left as Yokuto's rear wheel arced impossibly high. The pothole kept the Zündapp as a prize, hurling its rider forward in a bomb cloud of dust.

It wasn't the worst wreck Luka had ever seen. Kobi Yokuto would live. If he was wearing his riding gear properly and landed just right, he might be spared the painful ooze of road rash.

Luka swung around the wreck, falling in line behind Katsuo's taillight. The other victor had slowed; the wide road next to him begged to be seized—heavy with dusk and dust and the promise of *go, go, win and be worthy.*

Pride before the fall. The proverb of lesser men, ones who had nothing to be proud of. **Stupidity** *before the fall* were the words Luka lived by, and he had no intention of being stupid enough to repeat Yokuto's fate. There were far smoother roads ahead, and so like any good predator, Luka Löwe would wait.

CHAPTER 7

There were two things Luka appreciated about the cataclysmic racers.

1. Someone had to be last on the scoreboard. Their slothy times ensured it wasn't Luka.
2. The longer it took for them to drag their wheels through the desert, the longer Luka got to sit on his *Arsch* in the Baghdad checkpoint—guzzling mineral water, making ashes of cigarettes, and watching March 20's sun drift up through latticed windows.

In many ways, days off were nice: sleeping in, taking showers to wash off the stink, eating actual food, using toilet facilities that weren't just a hasty dig in the side of a dune. Today, though, Luka didn't want to stay still. It wasn't because of his time on the scoreboard. (LUKA LÖWE, 5 DAYS, 12 HOURS, 2 MINUTES, 46 SECONDS. Eleven seconds behind Katsuo. Ten seconds ahead of ~~Felix~~ Adele.) It wasn't because Katsuo's stare was fixed back on him. Nor was it because his at-rest muscles were undergoing lactic acid mutiny.

It was because of Adele.

He wanted to talk more, but they couldn't do that here. At least, not the way they did in the desert. There were too many ears around, and whenever Adele spoke, it was with a boy's voice from a girl's throat: strange, husky.

Luka couldn't even really *look* at Adele without giving something away. His Reichssender interview was more distracted than most, because he could see Adele past the ends of Fritz Naumann's wiry hair, making a snowman out of the leftover mushed chickpeas on her plate. The sight (almost) made him smile, and not in the propaganda grimace/*cameras are watching* kind of way. This was an *I feel happy and my mouth wants to show it* reflex. One Luka had spent his entire childhood learning to iron out.

Don't show emotion. Don't you ever show emotion. Kurt Löwe's own voice had been flat when he said this, colder than the Christmas Eve snow falling around them. *I won't have any son of mine being weak.*

When Adele caught his eye, she smashed the sculpture with her fork and jerked her head to the camera. *Don't waste Fritz Naumann's precious film!* He imagined her saying this in her real voice, complemented with a laugh and a puff of smoke. It made quelling his smile that much harder.

What the hell was happening to him?

Luka was not weak, but it took all his strength to tamp down the edges of his mouth. He used thoughts of his father like nails. When Luka stared into the camera, he imagined Kurt Löwe watching the clip on the television—blue eyes as detached as the rest of his face.

Smile: deceased.

The Reichssender team usually spent twice as much time on Luka's footage as they did on any of the other German racers', asking questions that Felix Wolfe and Georg Rust were never expected to answer.

"Victor Löwe"—the interviewer cleared his throat—"I think many of our young female viewers are wondering, is there a sweetheart cheering you on back in Hamburg?"

This question. Luka was surprised they hadn't asked it sooner.

Last year it had popped up at nearly every checkpoint, as if Luka's answer would change if they worded their query differently.

"I . . ." He looked at Adele's eyes over Herr Naumann's shoulder. A blue so different from his father's stare. Voidless, holding a spark that set Luka's whole insides ablaze.

Don't smile!

The interviewer scrambled to save Luka's silence. "Or perhaps there's a fräulein in Germania?"

"No." Luka shook his head. "There's no sweetheart."

It wasn't the sweethearts that held his interest.

The interviewer was knee-deep into his next question when Yokuto strode into the main room, the whole of him patched in bandages. His face was furious through quilt-work gauze. He must've been in crippling pain, but this didn't stop him from stepping straight up to Tsuda Katsuo's table. The Japanese victor stood, unquailed by the few centimeters of height that Kobi Yokuto had on him. He did not flinch when Yokuto started yelling—a string of words bound together with a spray of spit.

Had the cameras not been on and the officials not watching, knives would've been drawn. Yokuto's hands thrashed through the air, pointing at Katsuo and then waving at a first-year racer. Oguri Iwao, fifteen, seventh place. Sporting not one but *two* black eyes. Luka hadn't made much of the injuries when the boy walked in. Bumps and scrapes were the Axis Tour's signature, but now it was clear the road had nothing to do with Iwao's wounds.

No. The first-year standing beside Katsuo had taken a beating. . . . His bruises were fresh, darkened just enough to match the shouts from two nights ago. Was he the saboteur in the sabotage gone south?

Probably, Luka thought as he watched the drama unfold. Katsuo did not return the yells. The Japanese victor just shook his head, his own hand held out to keep Watabe Takeo from snapping out his blade.

Kobi Yokuto reached into his jacket and drew out a small amber vial. Luka knew it on sight, if only because he had two very similar ones tucked inside the lining of his own jacket.

Drugs. There was no telling what kind. The liquid in Yokuto's hand could've been soporifics—meant to knock a racer flat for hours. Or it might be a poison too weak to kill, but strong enough to turn a stomach inside out for days.

Words kept flying. The rapid Japanese was beyond Luka's understanding, but a good deal could be inferred from the boys' motions. If the drugs belonged to Yokuto, he wouldn't be flashing them around so brazenly. Iwao winced at the sight of the vial—an expression so pained that Luka bet the first-year was its true owner. He must've been caught before he could empty the contents into Yokuto's canteens. That would explain the fine-pulp beating.

It would also explain Yokuto's sudden road rage, why he went for the pass on such a treacherous road. Katsuo had gotten under his skin—was still under it—judging by the way the boy smashed the vial to the floor.

Scores of tiny pieces glimmered by Katsuo's boot. Sleep or sickness spread out between the floor tiles, now useless. The victor smirked.

Yokuto spit at the floor and turned away.

For a long minute no one spoke. Fritz Naumann switched off his camera. Katsuo, Takeo, and Iwao sat down in unison. Adele smashed her fork into her chickpeas one final time. A servant came to sweep the glass from the floor.

Luka frowned.

The flat tire he had expected. It fit Katsuo's modus operandi perfectly. But sending a first-year to drug a racer who was technically in third place, eating Katsuo's dust? That was a wrench in the predictable, throwing off everything Luka thought he knew about his competition.

The long game was changing.

Was Luka the hunter? Or the hunted?

For the first time since he mounted his bike in Germania's Olympiastadion, Luka was not sure.

CHAPTER 8

The roads were better outside of Baghdad. They still weren't as smooth as the central Reich's autobahns, but this didn't stop Katsuo from blasting fourth-gear fast into the desert. It didn't keep Luka from following, fist tight against the throttle, teeth set on edge.

It might not be by blade or vial, but Katsuo was coming for him. With Georg Rust and Kobi Yokuto out of the way, there were no names on the Axis Tour roster that could possibly usurp the Japanese victor other than his own. Victor Luka Löwe—the greatest hope for the Third Reich's Double Cross—was next. He felt it with each turn of the wheel. *Next, next, next*, through the dried carcass of wilderness, past the watchtowers and fort ruins of long-lost kingdoms.

Luka rode ready: clenched muscles, adrenaline almost erupting from his ears. Fifty kilometers came and went. Then one hundred. By kilometer 250 and its accompanying fuel stop, Luka's entire body had turned into a giant cramp, muscles *burning* to do something.

But Katsuo was giving him nothing. The Japanese victor didn't even look over his shoulder, much less weave or brake in a way that might cause Luka to wreck. He drove straight through the hellish-looking landscape. (The land was literally on fire in places, as if Hades had risen up and taken its rightful place by the roadside. Cracked earth, flames and all. The sight was unnerving, until you realized it was simply oil fields.)

The first day out of Baghdad came to a close. Luka remained a knot of nerves. He sat by his pup tent, Luger on his knee, gnawing the last of his jerky with a jaw that had been in perpetual grit-mode all day.

"Cigarette?" Adele offered him his own fare with an arched brow. "You look like you need one. Or ten."

Luka dug the pack from his jacket and tapped it against his gun-less knee. One lone cigarette tumbled out. He handed it to Adele and moved to his motorcycle for a refill. They'd burned through over half of his stash, Luka discovered as he dug through his panniers. Too much, too fast to last until Tokyo.

Not that this stopped him from stuffing a whole new pack into his pocket.

The cigarette he'd given Adele was wedged between her lips. Unlit. "Match?"

"The Li River is too far away," Luka said as he handed one to her.

Adele struck the match against her boot: spark and blaze. "I thought you wanted Katsuo to get comfortable."

"Comfortable is one thing," Luka told her. "We're almost half-way through this race, and Katsuo has gone beyond the defensive. He's aggressive."

"So what's your plan? Sneak into Katsuo's camp and punch a hole in his fuel tank? If he's as aggressive as you say, he'll be as jumpy as you." She nodded at the gun on his knee. "You're going to get yourself shot."

"Wouldn't be such a bad thing for you, Fräulein Third Place."

He'd meant it as a joke, but Adele didn't laugh. "It would if you cashed in your blackmail currency from your hospital bed."

He wouldn't. Luka knew this. He almost said it, but then stopped himself. There was no need to go around baring all the dents in his armor. Let Adele think her *her*ness was still a liability.

"Your Li River plan is a good one," Adele went on. "You shouldn't just abandon it because Katsuo is getting a little narcotics happy."

"Bottlenecking Katsuo is impossible now that Georg and Yokuto are out of the picture. Even if we both pull ahead on that leg, he'd still claim the third space on the ferry."

"Then find a way to make the space count. You'll be a heartbeat away from his bike. Cut the fuel lines or slit his tire or something else knifey."

"He'll be watching," Luka pointed out.

"He can't watch both of us." Adele shrugged. "One of us can distract him while the other does the deed. If you take your hit at Katsuo now, we'd have to part ways. And, honestly? I'd miss this." She held up her cigarette, arm straight as a *heil* into the constellation-cracked sky.

This. Secrets, smoke, stars. *This.* The stir inside his chest, the way his nerves smoothed out and reconnected with new warmth whenever Adele looked at him.

He wondered if she felt it, too.

He... hoped?

"So would I." Luka's voice was so soft, so wrapped in layers of cigarette smoke, he wasn't sure Adele would hear.

The Wolfe girl puffed out her own smoke so hard that the little nubby angel hairs by her forehead danced. Lamplight and movement made them twinkle, a bit like a crown of frost. "We should keep riding together, stay the course."

Next, not yet, next, not yet.

He wanted to win. How long had he dreamt of that second Cross? How often had he imagined the look on his father's face when he glimpsed the sight: iron proof that Luka was far from weak.

He wanted to keep riding with Adele and, more than that, keep talking beneath starlight and smoke, watching the lamplight toss dramatic shadows across her face. Striking, all striking.

Why couldn't he have both?

There were no cameras, no prying eyes, and so Luka let himself smile. "We ride together."

"So." Adele leaned closer. "Tell me about all these sweethearts you don't have...."

They kept talking—long, too long—into the night.

———

Katsuo did not strike the next day. Or the next. Luka stayed the course—through the last of the flatlands, into the mountains that eventually tore themselves off the horizon and swallowed the road. He stayed the course even when the road whittled down to a series of cliffside paths barely wider than his motorcycle. He stayed the course through bare rock valleys and curves that couldn't make up their *verdammt* mind. More than a few times he lost sight of Katsuo's fender gleam—and whenever Luka checked his mirror there was a fifty-fifty chance that he wouldn't see Adele. That's how twisty the roads were. Too twisty, really, to be stealing rearview glances. The chance of straying off road was far too high.

But this was part of the reason he *had* to look. The mountain rocks echoed all sorts of noises. Pops, revs, shrieks... loud violent things that made Luka worry Adele had gone accidental lemming on him. (Later, he found out via the Reichssender's dramatic recap, a racer *had* lost his bike off a cliff. ~~Himura Kenji~~ of Tokyo managed to cling to the ledge as his Zündapp slipped, shattered into a dozen pieces below. Since the supply vans were taking their regular detour around the mountain range, the fourteen-year-old was doomed to wander the race path on foot for a day and a half until officials sent a search party.)

The mountains began petering off—raggeder to ragged. The road tossed this way and that. Luka's brakes began to reek of burning rubber from overuse and, though not normally one for prayer, he willed them to last through New Delhi.

On the fourth morning they reached the Seventieth Meridian. The line itself wasn't marked, but the space around it was decorated in as much patriotic flair as a wilderness outpost could muster. Standards not yet faded by the south Asian sun fluttered from buildings. Swastikas claimed the first half of the settlement, shifting abruptly into flags with rising suns. Border guards—Reich on one side, Imperial Army on the other—watched the racers cross into the Greater East Asia Co-Prosperity Sphere.

The day stretched on with the road, and the land started changing yet again. Colors other than the duochrome blue sky–dirt brown bled into the landscape. Green piled onto green: a tree here, a bush there, palms spiking every which way. Though the racing path had straightened out considerably, Luka's habit of checking his rearview mirror was unabated. Adele stayed just two meters behind him, hunched against winds created by her own speed. She commanded her stretch of pavement with ease, keeping cataclysmics and hopefuls at bay with quick swerves of her bike.

One racer in particular kept edging up. He wore a Japanese band around his arm and kept tailing Adele's tires with tireless persistence. Luka wouldn't have thought twice about the sight if not for the glint of metal in the racer's hand: a sharp fang of folded carbon steel that didn't belong to the bike. Takeo's Higonokami knife.

The sight of the blade catching sunlight cut Luka's breath. *Next, next, already?* But Takeo wasn't going for Luka this time; Adele was in the way, veering off to Luka's right, her arm in perfect swiping distance. A one-handed, drive-by stabbing took talent, but Watabe Takeo seemed well practiced in the maneuver. He pulled next to Adele, his knife slashed out, catching—

Adele didn't yell so much as bellow. The sound punched through Luka's back, came out of him chest-first, and seized him like a grappling hook. He slammed his brakes. Takeo drew up on Luka's right side, blade within easy reach. Luka lunged for the weapon, hoping to knock it out of Takeo's grasp, but the knife-fighter was too well trained. Punch, dodge, slice! Luka's riding glove bore the brunt of the Higonokami's edge, but Luka felt the color of pain across his palm. Red. Diagonal through his life line.

Luka's hand flew back to his handlebars, oozing blood on the throttle. Takeo, balance wavering, passed by, knife jutting out like an extra finger. Adele was still alive, still driving. She charged up Takeo's right side, and was now cutting him off with a sharp veer left. The move wasn't just daring, but completely insane—the kind of courage distorted by pain. Adele's rear wheel spun only centimeters from Takeo's front tire, forcing the boy to brake and drop back to a safer distance.

Luka gunned his Zündapp forward. The throttle was slick and hard to grip, especially with an injured hand, but Luka seized it anyway, shoving his conscious mind away from the electrical impulses that told him he was hurting. HURTING.

He stole a look at Adele's arm as he drew close. The knife had gone straight through her jacket, but Luka couldn't see much beyond the tear. Her jaw was set, white with pain. The colorlessness blended with the zinc oxide still streaked across her cheeks. Several times Adele caught his stare. Those eyes...they were starting to get addicting. Hooking him again and again. The asphalt ripped beneath them, the wind thrashed, and despite his right-hand fire, Luka was soaring.

Road high. *Her* high.

They drove side by side. Far enough away not to wreck each other, close enough to prevent Takeo from barreling through their center. Every time their attacker tried to move up one of their sides, they drifted apart, blocking him. After several attempts, Takeo eased off their rear, slipping his knife away just in time for the fuel stop and its accompanying press cameras.

Threat averted. For now.

Luka's high—adrenaline mixed with Adele—throbbed against his palm as he pulled into the refueling station. These stops were always short, five minutes or less, as the officials siphoned fuel from gasoline barrel to Zündapp tank. Racers had to choose which necessity was most pressing: a swig from the canteen, a hurriedly chewed protein bar, or nature's calling. Luka went straight for the first-aid kit, whirling through its contents: Iodine! Morphine syrettes! Gauze! Teeny-tiny bandages that looked more suited to patching up baby dolls than sixteen-year-old boys! The cut wasn't deep, but it was still oozing. He splashed the wound with iodine and wrapped it in gauze.

"Need anything?" he asked Adele, who stood by another gasoline drum, guzzling water and examining the tear in her jacket's black leather.

"It's just a nick." She screwed the cap back on her canteen. "I'll live."

Luka wasn't so sure, but before he could press, the official refueling his motorcycle began pulling the hose out. *Time to go!* He shut his med kit with such haste that several of the miniature bandages twirled out. Luka left them in the dirt.

CHAPTER 9

1st: Tsuda Katsuo, 9 days, 26 minutes, 8 seconds.
2nd: Luka Löwe, 9 days, 26 minutes, 23 seconds.
3rd: Felix Wolfe, 9 days, 26 minutes, 34 seconds.
4th: Watabe Takeo, 9 days, 29 minutes, 19 seconds.

The knifing incident cost Luka a few seconds and a tablespoon of blood. Nothing he couldn't reclaim over the next few days.

Katsuo dismounted at the courtyard of the New Delhi checkpoint with ease, standing just long enough to watch his name get chalked into first before heading inside. Takeo, on the other hand, looked skittish. Especially when Luka marched up to the boy's bike, bloody hand first. There were too many officials and camera lenses floating around for the Higonokami blade to make an appearance without Takeo's name getting struck off the list, but the boy's eyes darted to his sleeve, as if he was thinking about using it anyway.

Luka held his cut palm up, words cold: "You use that knife on me again, and I will use it to cut you to pieces."

He didn't have to ask if Takeo understood the German. Luka could see his threat being weighed and settled behind the boy's dark gaze.

"Same goes for Felix Wolfe," Luka added. Just on the other side of Takeo he could see Adele favoring her left arm as she pulled off her helmet.

Not just a nick, then.

Takeo followed his stare. "No more thinning the field?"

"Just stay away." Luka didn't quite snarl, but the animal signal was there, bristling between them long after he turned away.

Reichssender press crowded around, eager for updates, but Luka pushed them away as he followed Adele into the checkpoint. She walked fast—through the dining hall already fragrant with curry spices, down one of the building's many twisting corridors until she found the first non-communal toilet. *Thud, click* went the door before Luka could reach it.

"A—" He started to say her name, but caught himself. "Open up! It's me!"

Her voice came, faint through the wood. "I'm fine."

Luka didn't believe her. "I want to see it."

A pause. Faucet water started flowing. And flowing...and flowing... She wasn't going to let him in.

"Let me see your arm, Felix."

Finally, the door opened. Adele's jacket was off, slung over the sink. In her plain white undershirt she looked small, though not small enough in certain anatomical places. It suddenly made sense why she wore the jacket at all times, even when she slept.

"Stop ogling." Adele didn't sound angry when she said it, just pained. Her left arm was smeared in blood, as if her swastika arm-band had seared through her sleeve, branded into her skin.

Once Luka looked past the blood, he realized the cut wasn't as deep as he'd feared. There was no visible muscle mass or fat, only a red that made Adele hiss. It needed a thorough cleaning, certainly. Maybe even stitches. "You need to go see Nurse Wilhelmina."

Adele jerked away. "I can't go to the nurse, dummkopf! It will take her twenty seconds to realize I have breasts, and another twenty seconds after that to tell a racing official. I'd be out of the Axis Tour before you can say, '*Heil Hitler!*'"

"You want that to go gangrene central on you?" Luka asked. "Trust me, getting an arm amputated is *not* worth seeing this rat race through to the end."

"Rat race?" Adele's incisors flashed against the vanity light. Her question—as sharp as those teeth—caught Luka off guard. "Is that all this is to you?"

Words often had a habit of spilling out where Luka was concerned. Ones he didn't always mean, but usually did. *Rat race*: running in circles—around, around—just for show. What use was being the prize rat if you were still just a rat?

Would two Crosses really make his father see that Luka had bled, was bleeding? Just not in the way Kurt Löwe wanted...

"No," Luka said. His hurt hand throbbed against an uncertain pulse. "But I've seen what losing an arm can do—"

"Quite the one for melodrama, aren't you? The wound won't get infected. I'll clean out the cut myself." Adele went on, "You already have a future, Luka Löwe. One that matters. Not all of us have that luxury. This is my chance to live my life the way I want it to be lived. I'm not going to toss that away because of some playground scratch."

"What kind of playgrounds do they *have* in Frankfurt?" he asked as she moved to the sink. Her blood flowed down the drain—bold to pink and away. "Let me get some proper disinfectant. I need to go see Nurse Wilhelmina anyway."

Nurse Wilhelmina—a pretty woman in her early twenties with sun-colored curls—made quick work of bandaging Luka's wound.

"You boys and your knives," she tutted. "If all of you just followed the rules, there would be a lot less blood."

"But a lot fewer visits to the infirmary. I wouldn't want to cheat you of that!" Luka winked.

It took only a bit more flirting to wheedle an extra bottle of disinfectant, some gauze, and a handful of teeny-tiny bandages from the nurse. By the time Luka returned to the washroom, Adele had mopped up most of the extra blood. She sat on the covered toilet; wads of pinkish toilet paper littered the floor by her biking boots. Luka kicked these aside and knelt close to the wound. The sight of it—six centimeters of parted flesh—made him wince.

Adele didn't, even when the disinfectant cut into her exposed nerves. Her tolerance for pain was higher than most boys'. Including his own.

"Another few centimeters and that knife..." Luka thought aloud as he applied the bandages. "Adele, what if Takeo had hit an artery?"

"You sound like my brother." Adele gave an irritated grunt. "If Takeo had hit an artery, then I would've bled out on the road, and you would've gone on to avenge my death by winning the race."

She was right. But now all Luka could imagine was Adele sprawled on the road she loved so much, anchored in a pool of her own blood. The image made him shudder.

"I can't lose you," he said.

Adele's arm stiffened beneath his fingers. It was an instantaneous reflex: there and gone. Luka's touch responded in kind, pulling away to fumble with another tiny wrapper. Wrong. He'd said something wrong. It was too soft, too *feeling*. If she were any other fräulein, he might've been able to wink it off, but all the suave coolness Luka had channeled in the infirmary was gone.

"I can't lose you," he backpedalled. "Our plan to sabotage Katsuo on the ferry takes two."

Adele leaned down. Her eyes flowed straight through him.

"We'll get Katsuo." These words were formed by lips so close that Luka could count the lines etched in them—a delicate pattern traditionally hidden by lipstick.

Adele lingered. Had she been some Germania sweetheart, Luka wouldn't have thought twice about kissing her. But this fräulein was something else entirely....

He wrestled the urge back.

Nothing happened.

Adele pulled away.

The wound didn't look so bad once it was bandaged up. It might not even scar. When Luka told Adele this, she just shrugged and pulled her jacket back on, heading out the door without another word. Her blood was still everywhere—littering the floor in paper form and streaking the edges of the porcelain sink. Luka stayed behind to clean up, wondering if...indeed...nothing had happened.

It felt, in a way, as if everything had.

CHAPTER 10

Just as Nurse Wilhelmina had predicted, Luka's wounded hand grew stiff, griping against all efforts to STOP or GO as he handled the throttle and handbrake. The road to Dhaka was an easier leg than many of the ones before it. The desert's omnipresent dust had settled, tamed by tree roots and grassy plains. The roads were well tended, allowing for the fastest speeds and longest days since Europe.

Katsuo pushed on well past sundown. No dust meant excellent night visibility, so they were in for another test of endurance. By the time their drive hit the fifteen-hour mark, Luka's hand was in agony. His fingers felt frozen in place by fire—hot, hotter, hottest—until it took everything in Luka not to pull to the side of the road and let it rest.

Instead he followed Katsuo's taillight, with nothing but his thoughts to distract him. In any other race, these would be fantasies of the finish line: rolling through the gates of Tokyo's Imperial Palace, with flashbulbs bursting, the first double victor in the history of the Axis Tour. Best of the best.

But tonight Luka's thoughts were trapped in the New Delhi

bathroom, living and reliving his exchange with Adele. All that blood and their almost-kiss, the words flung at each other in between.

I can't lose you. But he would, after the Li River. Once Katsuo was out of the picture, the race would be down to him and her. First and second, neck and neck. No more laughter and cigarettes stubbed out by their pup tents. Luka thought of all the soft lines that made up Adele's lips. The kiss that wasn't.

Could Luka miss something he never had?

(It sure felt like it.)

For now Adele was still behind him, blocking any riders who tried to advance from the rear. Most didn't. Takeo had taken Luka's warning to heart, and Katsuo's pace was too grueling for most of the cataclysmic racers to keep up. The herd of headlamps that made it to Dhaka together was a small one, rolling into the city well past midnight, where a bleary-eyed timekeeper recorded their places.

1st: Tsuda Katsuo, 9 days, 19 hours, 41 minutes,
18 seconds.
2nd: Luka Löwe, 9 days, 19 hours, 41 minutes,
37 seconds.
3rd: Felix Wolfe, 9 days, 19 hours, 41 minutes,
50 seconds.

CHAPTER 11

There was another day of rest in Dhaka, used for napping, a second visit to Nurse Wilhelmina, and more Reichssender interviews while the last of the pack reached the checkpoint, filling the board from fourth place (WATABE TAKEO, 9 DAYS, 19 HOURS, 44 MINUTES, 6 SECONDS) all the way to August Greiser's sixteenth, followed by four crossed-off names. The road had been whittling away stragglers through accidents, illness, and sheer despair. The next few days were about to claim more.

If the desert was boring, the jungle was anything but. The journey to Hanoi was littered with perils. The luxury of pavement did not extend far beyond Dhaka. Neither did bridges. In several places the road's dirt vanished into riverbeds thinned out by the region's dry season. Shallow, but still dangerous. There were always one or two boys who submerged their air intakes or got mired in mud so deep it took an entire team of men to free the wheels.

Heat exhaustion was also common. Gone were the chilled temperatures of a European spring, replaced with humidity thick enough to swim through. The very same jackets that protected riders from road rash now clung to them with miserable sweat—black leather baking beneath the sun. Brown wasn't much better, but Luka didn't dare take his jacket off. He'd seen too many cases of mangled-meat skin to risk it.

Then there was the wildlife. Snakes, monkeys, tigers, creepy-crawlies. The jungle had them all. Luka had personally never seen a tiger, but several years ago a Reichssender cameraman had managed to catch the magnificent beast on film. Monkeys were much less rare and much more likely to rip apart the motorcycles' panniers in search of food. But by far, the worst creature of the jungle was the mosquito. There were millions upon millions of them, all starved for juicy racer flesh.

Smoke helped keep them away, which was one more reason to keep the cigarettes coming. Luka had no problem whatsoever ripping the final pack open, if it would get the *gottverdammt* bugs off his neck. He could only imagine how many of them were trying to poison his blood with tropical diseases—yet *another* hazard of the jungle stretch.

"Don't forget to take this." He tossed a chloroquine tablet to Adele along with her cigarette. "Tastes like tinfoil, but it keeps the disease away. You don't want to end up like Adolf Schäfer. Poor *Saukerl* won the race in 1952, but then he up and died of malaria just a few weeks later because he forgot his tablets."

"That's...anticlimactic." Adele opened the tablet, swallowing it in a swift silver-wrapper movement.

"He was a decent guy, Schäfer." Luka settled back down. They sat outside of their standard-issue mosquito nets, close enough to make Luka think of the almost kiss. "It was my first race, and I had no idea what I was doing. He took the time to give me some pointers in Prague."

They lit their cigarettes in silence. The evening's conversation had been sparse, mostly due to sheer exhaustion, but Luka couldn't help but wonder if the wordlessness between them held more. Was that tension in the air between them? Or just mugginess?

The sweat on Adele's face glowed bronze bright whenever she

brought her cigarette to her lips. She had to be sweltering, but she didn't take off her jacket.

"Aren't you warm, Adele?" Luka asked, desperate to keep talking.

"Aren't you?" She eyed his own jacket—still half zipped, despite the sweat stains on his torso.

"I'd rather roast than become a bug buffet."

"No." Adele shook her head. "That's not why you wear the jacket. It's not because of mosquitoes, and it's not because you look better in brown. You swagger around in your unofficial jacket and smoke for the same reason I try to pass as a boy."

The logic was bendy. Luka couldn't follow it. "To enter the Axis Tour?"

"To show you're untouchable. Nothing can get to you. Not even the official rulebook. Cigarettes and leather are just pieces of the armor." Adele's cigarette wasn't even half finished, but she stubbed it out in the dirt anyway. "If you take them off, if you seem vulnerable, then people will try their best to own you. Devour what's not theirs."

She wasn't far off. There were no crowds in the middle of the jungle, but Luka could still hear the chant of a thousand *Sieg heil*s drumming his ears. He could still feel his father's rough palm on his arm, pressing too hard, trying to mold Luka into his own image.

"But sometimes the armor just gets too *verdammt* heavy," Adele went on, unzipping her own jacket. The white undershirt beneath was just as dirty as his, but it wasn't the sweat stains that drew Luka's eyes. He tried his best not to stare, faking sudden interest at the embered end of his cigarette.

"The thing is"—Adele shifted closer, until they weren't just elbow to elbow, but arm to arm—"no one's untouchable."

Luka was still staring at the dying fire when she kissed him. The whole of it—motion, speed, flavor—caught him completely unawares. Her lips tasted of salt. They stung against his: warmth and movement, edged with teeth. She kissed him with fervor, a hunger Luka *knew*.

For a moment he was frozen, but the more her lips moved, the more he broke, until, finally he kissed her back.

542

Adele did not smell very much like a garden. Her scent was wild: sweat and sun and road-worn leather. No one would be rushing to make a perfume out of it any time soon, but Luka hardly cared. There wasn't much time for smelling when Adele's lips were pressing into his as if she were a drowning girl and Luka was oxygen. Hungry, hungry. They'd both been so hungry for something....

Turns out it was each other.

When Adele pulled away, she shoved her short hair from her eyes and smiled. "Not bad."

"Not *bad*?" Luka's eyebrows flew up. "I'll admit, it wasn't a peak performance. You caught me off guard."

"Kissing's not a sport," she told him. "It's an art. It's all in the spontaneity, going where the inspiration takes you."

"I'll have you know that art is very technical. Good art anyway. Not that there's much of that left in the Reich to judge by—" Luka cut himself off, watching Adele's face with care. It was well and good to talk about lemmings, but directly critiquing the Reich was a dangerous pastime. Though Adele had spilled her own doubts, he wasn't sure if he should say something so shadowed in her presence.

The tilt of her head was more curious than condemning. "I wouldn't have taken you for a connoisseur."

"Not me. My mother used to haunt museums when she was younger. It was her dream to go to art school."

"What happened?"

"She met my father. He didn't approve of the notion. They got married. Enter, stage right, baby Luka. She never really gave up drawing. We used to do it together, when my father was off at the war. We'd practice in the margins of newspapers when good paper became scarce." Nina Löwe's touch was so different from her husband's: gentle fingers guiding Luka's over the pen, coaxing something out instead of beating it in. "It was like racing to her—something to strive for. Something to make living bearable."

"Did it help?"

Not when his father came home and found the sketches. Kurt

Löwe hadn't yelled; he rarely yelled, which only made his words more frightening. Any of them could be hiding his anger. Instead, Luka's father had gathered up the drawings and shoved them, silently, into the fire. There were too many papers for his lone fist to hold. Five times he did this as Nina Löwe held a hand to her mouth, trying her hardest not to let a sob out. Luka did the same, biting his lip until blood seeped through. The papers were dry and their end was quick. They burned like so many of Europe's great masterpieces had at the stake of Goebbels's whim. Beauty into orange into ash.

The art lessons stopped after that. Nina Löwe kept drawing—in the shadows, in the dawn, in the edges of her life that Kurt would never see. As soon as her pen left the paper, she crumpled it up, tossed it into the flames herself.

These things were scorched into Luka Löwe's soul. Always remembered, never spoken of. He found himself telling Adele the story anyway. She flinched at the part about the fire, as if she, too, could feel it, eating away at so many futures, too many pasts....

Did it help? Luka did not know; he did not want to know. Thinking about the cinders his mother swept from the hearth every morning just reminded him of his own hollowness. The feeling he hadn't felt when their lips were pressed together.

He leaned forward. She leaned in.

This time when they kissed he was ready. Luka tossed his cigarette aside, brought his good hand to her face, explored all its angles with tender-brush fingertips. Their lips melted into a single motion: no clash of teeth, no too-hurried tongue. This kiss was about tasting; this kiss was about technique. This kiss was about being filled.

Warmth rushed down his throat, down his stomach, down...

Luka's hand fell, too, grazing the swan-slope of Adele's neck all the way to her shoulder, pushing aside the leather there. The skin beneath was so soft. His fingers couldn't touch enough of it.

It hurt this time when Adele leaned back, her lips parting from his, flesh drawing out of reach. Luka's whole body ached in a way that had nothing to do with the kilometers he'd driven.

"Much better," she murmured. "*Too* much better."

The jungle sweltered around them, yet Luka felt cold. Were his fingers *shaking*? Was Adele *that* strong of a drug, that he was already experiencing withdrawal? "Wasn't that the goal?"

"I don't need any...female lemming complications. If you know what I mean." Adele tugged her jacket back over her shoulder. White flesh vanished under the leather. "It's—it's not like I prepared for this."

Luka hadn't either. Fräuleins had been the last thing on his mind when he was packing his panniers. Now his brain was scrambling, a hormonal stew à la sixteen-year-old boy. "We could...we could just keep kissing!"

Those lips—the ones he needed so badly—twisted. Adele looked up to the sky instead of him, where the dark was crowded with leaves, stars dusting their edges. "It's late. Tomorrow. Maybe tomorrow."

Luka paid no attention to the constellations. She was all he saw. Adele, painting of a girl, mythic as she stood, her black jacket ascending, blending with the midnight sky. It was as if she pulled pieces of Luka up with her. A heartstring here, an extra breath there.

"Tomorrow, then," Luka managed. He wished he had a better argument.

Adele ducked down to her pup tent, pushing aside the mosquito net. She looked back over her shoulder at Luka. For a moment hers looked like any other pair of jungle eyes: luminescent against the electric lantern light, harboring some primal eeriness.

"I'm looking forward to it," she said.

CHAPTER 12

Lips.

Skin.

Warmth on warmth.

These thoughts feasted on Luka with mosquito-needle eagerness, gorging on his concentration. It didn't matter that the engine whirred beneath him or that Katsuo was fording every river in record time or that the actual bug bites on his neck itched until his nails made them bleed. Whenever he shut his eyes, he saw Adele, a movement away, ready to kiss him, to be kissed. Whenever he opened his eyes, he saw her, too, wheels in time with his own, driving through water with gritted teeth and steeled eyes.

Both of these things—thoughts and sights—made Luka's insides soar. Adele was distracting, yes, but she also drove Luka forward: much faster, much further than any Zündapp had ever carried him. He doubted his father had ever felt anything like it.

Zoom, zoom.

The second day out of Dhaka was as grueling as the first. Tsuda Katsuo's pace stretched everyone thin. Ten hours into eleven, mud splashing/gashing over everything, thirteen hours and still going, a darkening jungle blurring by, fourteen hours cramped by muscle agony, wavering wheels, exhaustion thickening the night, making the darkness impossible to pierce, even with the brightest of headlamps. Fifteen hours and they could go no farther. Hanoi was still over thirteen hours away, which was much too far to push without sleep, especially with the Hanoi → Shanghai stretch on the horizon.

Both Luka and Adele were covered in mud as they set up camp, checking the overhanging branches for creepy-crawlies and driving stakes into the soil. The electric lantern lit their movements. Adele looked more beautiful than ever as she worked. Luka's smile would not stay tamped down. He wondered, vaguely, if he was being the soft *dummkopf* his father had always feared he was. The one Luka had spent his whole life trying to prove he *wasn't*. He was strong. A *verdammt* victor.

But it wasn't enough; it was never enough.

And here was ... something.

Adele felt it, too. He could see it: in the subtle shift of her hips, in the glances she threw Luka's way when she thought he wasn't looking. He heard it, as well: in the perfect silence between her sentences, in the way she said his name.

"Luka ..." Adele let the pause stretch, until they were both taut. "This is our last night alone together."

Already? He realized, with a start, that Adele was right. Tomorrow night, Hanoi. After that, the Li River ferry crossing. Once they knocked Katsuo out of the race, their alliance would end. The thought gutted Luka more than it should have.

He didn't trust himself to speak on the subject. He chewed on his dinner instead, nodding to her sliced jacket. "How's your arm?"

"No gangrene. Yet," she added. "Your hand?"

"Getting better."

They fell back into a muggy, not-quite silence. Ration packets crinkled. Somewhere in the distance a tiger called out—burning growl against the dark. There was something profoundly lonely about the noise.

547

Is this all there is?

Adele cleared her throat of the last of her meal. "I never thanked you for distracting Takeo."

Luka looked down at his bandaged palm. He couldn't see the blood, but he knew it was there, in crusts, entombing its way back inside of him. The wound would be completely healed by the time he returned to Hamburg.

"It's what allies do," he said.

"Is it?" Adele tilted her head. "You shaved seconds off your time for me. You risked the blade. I've never heard of a racer doing that before. Even for an ally."

"I'm not most racers."

"You're not most men," she countered. "If any other racer had come across me in that washroom, they would've turned me in to the officials. But *you* chose to form an alliance with me. You see me as your equal."

Adele reached out, placed her hand on his. Her fingers looked as they had the first time he'd noticed them: delicate, built of bones slender enough to reach into Luka, rearrange the laws of his existence. "I don't want this to end. I know it has to, after the river. But..."

She didn't finish her thought. Perhaps because they both knew there was no *but*. The Iron Cross called to them both, and it was a strong siren.

"We can be together after Tokyo," Luka heard himself saying. "I'll come visit you in Frankfurt, or you can come to Hamburg. I'll try my best to hide all the fish."

Adele's laugh trembled all the way through her fingertips. "I'd like that. But..."

Another *but*. The word felt as sharp as fear in Luka's gut.

"If you win, I'll want to race in next year's Axis Tour. Everyone knows who you are, Luka. If the Reichssender sees us together, that will put me in the spotlight. I wouldn't be able to compete as Felix without somebody noticing."

She wouldn't, would she?

"Let's…." There was sadness in Adele's smile. "Let's enjoy this night while we have it."

Luka's exhaustion—the same one that had leadened limbs and lids alike while they set up camp—melted away. Kissing was an art, but with Adele it also felt like a bit of a battle. He didn't mind letting her win. They kissed and kissed and kissed, until the bulb of the electric lantern began to dim and darkness crept out of the jungle leaves, stretching across them both. They fell asleep in each other's arms, jackets still half-zipped, breaths tangling into each other's hair as they gathered strength for the dawn.

━━━━━

The jungle had taken its toll on the Axis Tour roster. Once all the times had been entered on the chalkboard at the Hanoi checkpoint nine names were struck through. There were only eleven racers left in the lineup. Only three times that mattered:

1st: Tsuda Katsuo, 12 days, 8 hours, 47 minutes,
39 seconds.
2nd: Luka Löwe, 12 days, 8 hours, 47 minutes,
59 seconds.
3rd: Felix Wolfe, 12 days, 8 hours, 48 minutes,
15 seconds.

Darkness bunched outside the checkpoint's open windows, pulsing with cricket song. Luka sat by his empty dinner bowl—eyes on first place, Katsuo and company lingering in the corner of his vision. Luka kept his back to Adele because he wasn't sure he could bear to look at her without…aching.

She pushed into his sights anyway, seating herself only two chairs away, hands wrapped around a bowl of pho. White blazes of hair stabbed into Luka's periphery. He kept staring at the chalked 1st until the board around it bloomed: cones and rods gone stale. A blue as vibrant as her eyes...

Don't!

Adele blew at the steam curling from her bowl. "Tomorrow?"

"The plan hasn't changed." Luka kept his voice low. "I'll push ahead, get on the ferry first. Try to let Katsuo stay in second while you pull in third. When we're crossing the river, I'll distract him; you cut his fuel lines."

"And then our interests diverge," she murmured back.

Interests change. Luka's lips buzzed with the memory of hers. All of him wanted to turn, push aside the empty chairs between them, taste the movement, the warmth, the whole of her.

You and I aren't so different.

The Iron Cross called to them both. Iron calls to iron, and Adele called to him.

There was only one way Luka could answer....

You already have a future. Why do you need the Double Cross so badly?

There was always something more, but what if a second Cross wasn't it? What if the answer was just a glance away, slurping spoonfuls of lime-tinged broth? What if... Luka let her win?

The thought alone was close to heresy. How many worlds' worth of kilometers had Luka ridden to get to this point? How many lungfuls of dust had he inhaled? How many ounces of blood had he spilled for a chance to make history?

Was a fräulein worth all these things?

She shouldn't be.

But that didn't mean she wasn't.

Adele cleared her throat. It was a sound that begged Luka to look at her, just look at her. He stared even harder at the 1st, his vision decaying into neon around it. When Luka blinked, the staleness cleared. He could see Katsuo across the room, watching him. Why the hell was the victor smiling?

It was *verdammt* unnerving. *All* of this was so *verdammt* unnerving. Kisses and long games and kilometers still undriven. Luka almost wanted to go back to the starting line: where things were—well, not exactly simple, but at least they were straightforward.

Now it was more than just road jitters fraying his insides.

Luka patted his pocket for a cigarette. There was only one left in the pack he carried on his person. He took it out and lit it. Flames' warmth prickled his insides at the first inhale, washed out with his exhale—*Scheisse* taste coated his mouth.

"Don't expect me to go easy on you," Adele spoke into her bowl, words mixing with meat bits.

Katsuo kept smiling.

Stay the course, Löwe.

"Likewise," Luka muttered.

CHAPTER 13

They were an exhausted lineup, eleven racers at the end of their proverbial rope, strung out on fumes of sleep and the promise of the end. Not quite in sight, but close. At 2,394 kilometers, Hanoi to Shanghai was the final exam of endurance. To be a victor, you had to complete this stretch without camping. It was a dangerous race against sleep deprivation.

The sun was all shine. Their motorcycles rumbled, weariless machines. Luka's wrist shuddered over the Zündapp's throttle, but the engine revolutions weren't enough to rattle the weariness from his veins. They did not banish the shadows from the edge of his goggles, the ones that threatened to shove him into sleep there and then.

Speed helped. Thick, humid ribbons of air smacked Luka's cheekbones, spurring him out of Hanoi, past rice fields of mirrored sky. Katsuo's fender flashed only meters ahead—something to chase, something to beat.

They were well into the day—zooming through a land of mountains without ranges—when Luka made his move. He was awake now. All awake. Wrist, hand, fingers, made of pure adrenaline as he twisted the throttle. Katsuo was so close Luka could see the vertebrae sloping along his neck. Their wheels were a turn away from touching, lunging along with a maniac hum. Katsuo lashed his engine forward. Luka's acceleration matched it, until he realized that bikes *did* get weary. Hot oil and rattling bolts. You could only push an engine so fast, so far before it broke.

The land blurred green around them: rice seedlings into hillside foliage into bamboo stalks. Luka's Zündapp—stretched with speeds faster than his speedometer needle could measure—made noises he'd never heard before. Katsuo's motorcycle joined the duet, refusing to slow.

The road curved, sloped downward to its first glimpse of the Li River. Its waters were as green as the rest of the landscape, threading around the hillsides like a jade necklace. Cormorants sat, widewinged, on docks made entirely of stone. A lone ferry operator stood at the end of the nearest one, waiting to transport the racers across.

The race path was ending, but Katsuo kept pushing. The dock's rocks flew forward—too narrow to drive on—and Luka knew it was down to nerves. Who would buckle first?

The cormorants—unsettled by the dueling engines—slipped into the water. The ferry operator gripped the edge of his hat, knuckles knotted. Luka was close enough to see the whites of the old man's eyes. Fear gleamed in them.

Luka had to fight the *put on your brakes, you death-flirting dummkopf* flex of his fingers. There were only a few meters left before not even a state-of-the-art brake system or years of mastered technique would save him.

Six meters. The ferry operator waved his pole in warning. He was probably shouting, too, but the engines clashed too loud to hear. Four meters. *Scheisse, scheisse, scheisse!* Two meters...

His bike made a terrible screech when he slammed to a stop. Luka's heart flung forward with the sound, disappearing into the emerald tangles of shoreline bamboo. He had no time to calm down, breathe, find it. The dock was at hand, and to Luka's surprise, he'd managed to outnerve Tsuda Katsuo by an entire meter.

The plan was working.

He shifted the bike into neutral, dismounted, and shoved it along the dock. The beast was heavy. Its overworked engine blistered against Luka's leg as he pushed, but he had no time to whine about it. Behind him Katsuo was doing the same.

The ferry sat at the dock's end, looking as shambly as ever. The craft felt that way, too, leaking water through the gaps in its bamboo stalks when Luka boarded with his bike. Every year he feared the raft would just keep sinking: ankle, knee, engine deep. Every year it didn't. River water licked the edges of Luka's boots, but that was as high as it would ever go, even when Katsuo rolled *his* bike onto the raft.

Luka kept his Zündapp at his back, well out of Katsuo's reach. An uneasy expression shadowed the other victor's face.

"Relax!" Luka grinned at him. "Enjoy the river cruise."

Other riders jostled their way down the dock—a frantic blur of armbands. Swastika, rising sun, rising sun, swastika, swastika. All shoved their bikes forward, hoping to claim the third space on the raft.

Come on, Adele.

He could see her at the front, jaw set. This time Adele's girlness was working against her. She simply didn't have the strength to push her 224-kilogram Zündapp as quickly as the others. A rising sun was closing in from behind—

Luka felt his smile going stale as he watched the Japanese racer—Takeo, he thought it was—push forward, draw even with Adele, go faster. The dock was barely wide enough for both bikes, too narrow for a fight.

This didn't stop Adele from trying. She shoved into the boy, ramming both his body and his motorcycle to the edge. But Takeo was firm on his feet. His Zündapp stayed grounded. He lashed back—Higonokami-less—knuckles hitting the sliced spot on Adele's jacket, the wound beneath.

Her scream was loud, stripped of fake-Felix huskiness. Luka's grin vanished. The raft's water level rose as the ferry operator took his place at the stern and removed the ramp.

554

No! Luka wanted to shout, but the word didn't quite make it out. *This isn't right.... What about the third passenger?*

The operator didn't look like he gave a *Scheisse* about his raft's capacity. In fact, he seemed eager to leave, turning his back on the skirmish as he shoved off from the rocks.

Adele and Takeo ceased fighting. Both racers stood, watching first place float away. The river swirled—green and gray—between themselves and the dock. More green, more gray, wider, wider. Luka's insides sank into the shivering waters.

No! No! No! Still the cry did not come. *Adele...their plan...*

Luka wasn't sure which loss hurt more—girl or a chance at first. Neither was a pain he could allow to show, so he twisted his lips into default: sneer mode.

Katsuo sneered back. The other victor had positioned himself in front of his tires, body rigid. Not that Luka would try anything now. Without Adele to provide a distraction, sabotaging Katsuo's bike would only lead to mutually assured destruction. It was useless.

Without Adele...

The raft pushed into deeper waters. Katsuo folded his arms against his chest, eyes heavy with dare. *What are you going to do now, Löwe?*

Excellent question, Katsuo.

Luka crossed his own arms. Stared back. It took everything in him not to look over Katsuo's shoulder, to the girl standing by the river's edge, drawing farther and farther away. She was just a dark speck on his periphery, blending in with all the other black-clad racers. Without a spot on the first ferry, Adele's time was hampered by ten whole minutes. As talented a rider as she was, there was no coming back from a loss like that this late in the race. Her Axis Tour was over.

It was just Luka and Katsuo now.

Victor and victor.

The race was on.

CHAPTER 14

1st: Tsuda Katsuo, 13 days, 5 hours, 53 minutes,
49 seconds.
2nd: Luka Löwe, 13 days, 5 hours, 54 minutes,
5 seconds.
3rd: Felix Wolfe, 13 days, 6 hours, 5 minutes,
19 seconds.

The victors' furies were well matched. No matter how fast Luka pushed his engines, Katsuo kept the same kilometer count. They raced head to head—snatching seconds, stealing them back—all the way to a predawn Shanghai. By the time Luka reached the boat that would take them across the East China Sea, he was too exhausted to wait up for Adele. Even the most basic tasks—taking a piss, eating some grub, collapsing into the oh-so-sweet embrace of a private cabin bunk—had become epic feats of strength after a twenty-one-hour ride.

He slept well into the next day, snoozing away the hours while the last of the cataclysmic racers reached the *Kaiten*. When Luka finally woke, the world was swaying. There was no wrinkled pup tent above him, just steel or iron or whatever metal Imperial Japanese warships were made with, painted the somberest of grays. The color overwhelmed the cabin, making Luka feel more imprisoned than private.

He needed to get up. Find Adele. Make a plan. Though Luka's front tire had been the first to hit the *Kaiten*'s ramp, Katsuo still had a sixteen-second lead. The Double Cross was so close: 1,229 kilometers from Nagasaki to Tokyo. Easy roads, straight shot.

Sixteen seconds seemed so short by the *tick* of a watch, but Luka knew the odds of gaining this time against Katsuo with nothing but an honest Zündapp were...dismal.

Which was exactly why he'd come prepared. Luka stood, assembling his uniform: boots, Luger, jacket, the illicit drugs sewn into its linings. One glance in the mirror told him he looked like *Scheisse*. He paused, just long enough to pat his hair back into place, splash two handfuls of water against his complexion.

It took a bit of nosing about to find Felix Wolfe's cabin. There were no names on the doors, but directions weren't hard to bribe out of the Reichssender staff. All they needed were a handful of Reichsmarks and the promise of an extralong interview. ("After you shower." Fritz Naumann wrinkled his nose. "The Reich could probably smell you through that camera.")

He was directed to a bleakly lit corridor. Second door on the left.

"Herr Wolfe?" Luka knocked. "We need to talk!"

The door opened and an eye peered out through the crack—blazing blue. The shadow beneath it matched the ship's walls.

"May I?" He nodded.

Adele blinked. (Or winked. How could Luka tell?) The door didn't budge.

"Ad—" Luka caught himself, midname. Thankfully, the corridor was empty. Fritz Naumann had fled from the road stench, and every other door was latched tight. "Felix. Just...let me in. Please."

"I don't—" She stopped. Her eye flashed. "I don't think that's a good idea."

557

Was she...angry? Something in Adele's words made him think so. If only he could see the rest of her face...

"What's wrong?"

"Nothing," Adele said, too quickly.

"Which means everything," Luka replied. "I know how fräulein-speak works."

"Don't *say* that word!" Adele hissed. The door twitched open a few more centimeters. She glanced into the corridor. Still ill-lit and empty.

"Which one?" he asked, casually. "Fräulein?"

Adele's hiss turned into a scowl. Her hand shot out, curled over Luka's lapel, dragged him over the threshold so quickly that his head clipped the edge of the door frame. Pain roosted on his skull, enough to make him wince.

Adele kicked the door shut without an apology. Her gaze was so many things: art and speed and sharp. Piercing far deeper than Luka ever suspected another person might be able to see.

"Are you pleased with yourself?" she asked.

"Not at all, actually." Luka rubbed his head. "Second doesn't suit me."

"Then why didn't you stop the ferry operator?" Adele stepped close—kissing distance, but not. She faced Luka sideways—her chin tilted away from his, creped with anger. "Why didn't you make him hold the raft until I got there?"

"I couldn't tell the operator to stop without giving Katsuo a window to sabotage *my* bike. Not to mention making him suspicious about our alliance. You should have pushed faster."

Judging from the expression on Adele's face, Luka realized it was the worst thing he could possibly have said.

"So it's my fault now, is it? You think I wanted Takeo to catch up to me? You think I wanted to lose ten whole minutes?" There was a sob in her voice—exhausted and fierce. "I came all this way. Nineteen thousand kilometers and nothing to show for it..."

Nothing? She doesn't mean that, does she?

"The race isn't over yet," he reminded her.

"It is for me." Adele's smile was quarter-hearted. Dead before it grew. "You said it yourself: 'Ten minutes is impossible to reclaim' now."

"We can still help each other. Help me oust Katsuo, help me win the Double Cross, and next year I'm all yours. I'll get you to Tokyo and first place."

"Why would you do that?" Adele asked.

"I like you, Adele Wolfe." He swallowed. "You're not just my equal. You're my match."

For all his motorcycle racing, for all the years he'd lived in the same house as Kurt Löwe, Luka had never felt a fear like this: heart pinned and pulsing on his leather sleeve. The girl who could crush it— less than a step away, blinking at his words, saying nothing in return.

"I know we can't be together after Tokyo, but I'll wait." His tongue felt so stumbly, tying itself into *verdammt* knots. "I'll wait, and next year I'll race alongside you. Help you win. Then we can both be victors."

Adele stared at him with a silence that made Luka want to run up to the *Kaiten*'s deck and jump into the East China Sea. *Heartbreak.* It was a term he'd always shrugged off, something he'd never needed to worry about. Until now.

Now it was terrifyingly real. Now he could feel his ventricles stretching, starting to tear, slippery blood raw everywhere—

"I like you, too, Luka Löwe." This time Adele's smile survived, climbed all the way to the corners of her eyes. "I didn't think—I didn't know—I didn't . . . expect you."

Luka felt his own eyes smiling. The bleeding in his chest had ceased, replaced by a soar that would not stop. Adele *liked* him. Maybe even *more than liked*!! She was leaning in to kiss him again, and it was by far the closest to heaven he'd ever been—wing tips brushing stars and all that poetic sort of stuff.

Both of Adele's hands were on his chest, her mouth just a breath from his when she paused. "Will you really wait a whole year for me? Make me the 1956 victor?"

"One year. One win." Luka's heart thudded against her palms, a closeness he could barely stand. "I promise."

"All right, then." Adele's grin widened. Her teeth flashed white as she moved in for the kiss. It was battle. It was bliss. It ended too soon. As much as Luka wanted the moment to go on, they had more important business to tend to.

"How are we getting Katsuo out of the picture? Shoving him overboard?" Adele guessed.

"Aren't you a violent one? No. Subtlety is the way to go. We don't want to do anything that could get us disqualified." Luka reached into his jacket. The glass he pulled out was unmarked, but he knew exactly what it was: vomiting-in-a-vial. "One sip of this and Katsuo will be planted by a toilet for days."

Adele's eyes narrowed on the vial. "Where'd you get that?"

"There's a lot of interesting things floating around Germania's black market," he told her. "American jazz records. Art that's not *Scheisse*. I hear there's even a guy who does tattoos if you fancy a bit of ink. And cigarettes, of course."

"Of course," she murmured. "Speaking of. Do you have any more on you?"

Luka shook his head. The truth: His pockets were empty, though he still had half a pack left at the bottom of his pannier. He was saving it for a celebratory finish-line smoke.

"So how are you going to get this"—Adele hesitated—"special ingredient into Katsuo's grub without him noticing? Am I supposed to play the decoy? Distract Katsuo with my not-feminine wiles?"

Luka shook his head, handed her the vial. "Won't work. Katsuo's been suspicious ever since I pushed ahead to get on the raft. If I'm in the messdeck, you can bet he'll be watching me."

She squinted at her palm. "And what if he isn't?"

"He will be," Luka promised. "But take care. If he spots you...run. There's a reason these doors have locks. Katsuo won't try anything too violent on a ship full of officials, but if he does, I've got your back."

Not to mention a second vial. You could never have too much insurance in a race like this. He trusted Adele—obviously—but the possibility of her getting caught was higher than Luka let on. The messdeck was a well-lit, open space, and Katsuo never sat alone.

"Be careful."

"You said that already." Adele's fist closed over the vial. She shoved it into her pocket. "Don't hurt your pretty little head fretting over me. I can manage on my own."

What a *verdammt* amazing fräulein. What a full, full heart he had, beating just where Adele's palms had pressed, just where the Double Cross would soon rest. In this moment, Luka felt more than strong.

Now he was invincible.

———

It took several hours—and many cups of green tea—before Katsuo graced the messdeck with his presence. As soon as he walked into the dining area, his eyes migrated to Luka: alone with a cold bowl of rice and his eighth serving of tea.

Caffeine sparkled through Luka's veins as he lifted his cup, "*Sieg heil*, Katsuo!"

It was the cold shoulder today. Katsuo refused to respond, giving Luka's table a wide berth as he settled down for his midday meal. Takeo and Iwao trailed him, both boys looking road worn, *almost home* reflected in their tired eyes. The group sat on Adele's side of the room, not even bothering to glance at the German racer hunched over the pages of a dated *Das Reich*.

Luka picked at some stray rice grains on the edge of his bowl, watching Iwao play waiter. The boy brought Katsuo some tea and a bowl of *kake udon* in turn. Both liquids. Easy to spike.

Luka popped a final grain in his mouth and stood. The messdeck was full of movement—cooks stacking plates, cataclysmic racers finishing their meals with smacks and slurps, Adele Wolfe folding her newspaper over her hands, presumably uncapping the vial beneath it—but Victor Tsuda only had eyes for Victor Löwe.

That's right. Eyes on me. Luka kept one hand on the vial in his pocket while he sauntered, as swaggeringly as possible, toward Katsuo's table. The other victor went rigid in his bolted chair. Takeo stood—hand in his own jacket—and because Luka really had no desire to go back to the infirmary with another Higonokami wound, he halted. Iwao remained seated, bruised eyes flitting over Luka, returning always to the hidden hand.

Luka had their attention.

Now he just had to keep it.

All three had their backs to Adele. None of them saw her glide in their direction, close as a shadow and just as quiet. The trouble? Katsuo's meal sat just under his nose. Not even Adele's hands were slight enough to manage that proximity.

If Katsuo turned…

"I just wanted to offer my congratulations on your imminent victory!" Luka's bow was sweeping, theatrical enough to disguise the vial slipping from pocket to palm. "Even I know when I've been bested."

Adele hovered by Katsuo's shoulder. Poison in hand. Waiting for her opening.

"We might not be friends, and we most certainly aren't gentlemen, but does that mean we shouldn't be civil?" Luka was babbling now. More concentrated on shifting the black-market vial in his palm than any words he might be saying.

Iwao was still staring at Luka's palm—a fact the victor counted on. He didn't show much, just a flash of glass, but it was enough to make Katsuo's ally point and yell.

562

Everyone moved at once. Iwao stood, eyes excited white inside their battered sockets. Takeo lurched forward, and Luka leaned back—out of knife's reach. Katsuo placed both hands on the table-top, his chest arched over his bowl of *kake udon*. The Japanese victor's attention was all forward, too centered on Luka to notice the fingers beneath his armpit, the dash of something new into his soup.

"No need to get stabby!" Luka tossed his hands up and let his own vial fall to the floor. Takeo moved forward, crushing the glass with his boot. "As I said, I know when I've been bested."

Adele had already returned to her table. *Das Reich* unfurled as if nothing had happened. It was time for Luka to get the hell away from this messdeck.

"Call off your cavalry, Katsuo!" He shifted away from Takeo's advancing knifepoint. "You win, okay?"

Katsuo couldn't help but smile. (So the *Saukerl* did speak German!) He allowed Takeo to advance a few more steps before throwing up a hand, motioning him back.

"Scheisse!" Luka swept past his old table in a huff, dashing both his teacup and his rice bowl to the floor and smashing through the remnants. Perhaps the exit was bit too dramatic, but Katsuo didn't seem to notice. The victor was smiling like a cat at a fish market: happy, happy as he brought the first few udon noodles to his lips.

Slurp away, my foe. Luka struggled to hold back his own smile as he ducked into the corridor, stood with his back to the wall in breathless anticipation.

He'd done it.

They'd done it.

"Katsuo wolfed down the whole thing," Adele whispered when she emerged into the hall a few minutes later. "Congratulations, Double Victor Löwe."

"Don't jinx me," Luka teased.

But her eyes just flinted, blazed. "Soon."

CHAPTER 15

Stomach flu. That's how the official reports labeled Victor Tsuda Katsuo's sudden onset of vomiting. To his credit, the Japanese victor tried to get back on his bike as the *Kaiten* drew into port, but dry heaves kept wracking his body with a violence that almost made Luka feel guilty.

Almost.

Today—April 2, 1955—it was hard to feel anything but triumphant. Luka's name was first on the scoreboard, his lifelong dream just a day's drive away. His tire pressure was full, and his engine ran flawlessly. The spring sun had nowhere to hide. Cherry blossoms covered trees and roads alike—strewn across the pavement in the fashion of confetti, as if nature itself were cheering him on.

This was, for all intents and purposes, a victory lap. Takeo, Iwao, Hans Muller, and the other middlemen didn't even try to maneuver for first. Their fight was with each other now, determining third, fourth, fifth. (As if it mattered!) The few cataclysmic racers left were just happy to reach the finish line. Most of them weren't really *racing* anymore, stopping for snacks and nature's call and any other minor discomfort.

Luka kept driving forward—hour after hour—until all the others fell away. Well, not *all* the others. Adele—his equal, his match—rode by his side. Once they got to the outskirts of Tokyo, he'd have to pull out all the stops, lose her to the horizon like the others. Crossing the finish line at the Imperial Palace was something Luka had to do alone.

As much as Luka was racing to this end, he also dreaded it. Adele had only been in his life for...what? Three weeks? Now the thought of spending an entire year apart loomed. Twelve months of waiting, fifty-two weeks without her wit, 365 days without her touch. Luka didn't even want to count the hours.

But the hours were counting down regardless. He and Adele had spent five and a half on the road already—driving out of the morning, past lunch, through Osaka's fervent crowds, back into a blossoming countryside. It was a long, wonderful stretch of nothing. No Reichssender cameras, no *Sieg heil*s, no other racers. Just Luka and Adele and the road.

Adele spurred her Zündapp forward. The gestures of her free hand told Luka she meant to pull over, take a break. *Would he join her for one last moment together?* Would he park his motorcycle next to hers, under the whisper and wave of the cherry trees?

As if these were even questions...

Luka's healing hand twinged as he pumped the brakes, guided his bike off the road into drifts of cherry blossoms at the end of their short life cycle. Both engines cut off. Luka dismounted his bike and removed his helmet, savoring the scene. Falling flowers and a sky scrubbed the purest blue—sights he'd never slowed enough to see before.

Even in this landscape, Adele Valerie Wolfe stood out. Luka's eyes went straight to her: the stretch of her calves, the shine of her hair as she removed her helmet, the faintest hint of curves beneath her riding gear.

How had he ever seen Felix there? It seemed impossible now that Adele was anything other than herself: inimitable fräulein. A girl worth waiting for.

Adele's eyes met his. A smile burst from her lips.

Luka grinned back. "You wanted to stop and smell the sakura?"

"They are pretty." She reached to an overhanging bough, snapped off the nearest blossom, and sniffed it. "Not much of a smell, though."

The petals brushed her lips, and Luka couldn't care less what it did or didn't smell like. Would he ever stop wanting to kiss her?

Adele blew at the petals, letting them join the blossoms at her feet. "You got any of that jerky left? All I have are protein bars."

He did. Luka turned and unbuckled the closest pannier. Inside was a hasty mess of food and camping equipment. It'd take a bit of rummaging to find the jerky....

"I could use a little extra fuel before Tokyo," Adele was saying.

Tokyo. The end he both desired and feared was close. In less than four hours Luka would be rolling through the Imperial Palace gate, camera lenses catching his triumphant image, sending it half a world over, so Kurt Löwe could see his son as he was: double victor. Hero of the Third Reich. Tough as leather, hard as steel. Worthy.

The crowd in Luka's imagination roared in time to the footsteps behind him: *Sieg heil! Sieg heil! Sieg—*

CRACK!

Everything went sharp. Pain bright. Luka's world turned sideways. Reality and dream alike, falling, falling. Pink sky, blue blossoms, black leather, black...

BLACK.

When Luka's eyes fluttered open, all black was gone. The pink was still there, smearing into blue. Nothing was sharp anymore. His thoughts scattered and blurred and the sun was so *verdammt* bright! Beaming through his retinas, into his head, exploding out the back of his skull, leaving an exit wound that felt roughly the size of an apple.

His hand migrated to the pain, not stopping soon enough. The back of his skull was wet, screaming against his touch. Luka screamed back, obscenities even *he* was usually loathe to say.

A new color: red. Blood covered his fingertips.

He'd been attacked.

They'd been attacked.

Luka tried to stand, but his entire body revolted, stomach first. He found himself on his hands and knees: acid scraping his throat, breakfast splattering his knuckles.

Adele! Where is Adele? He swung his throbbing head to the side, expecting to see her splayed out in the blossoms, sticky with blood of her own.

She wasn't there.

Luka looked to the other side, his vision barely keeping up.

No Adele.

He was about to call out when he realized what he was looking at: scores upon scores of crushed cherry blossoms formed a path back to the road. A path the exact width of a Zündapp's tire. Adele's motorcycle had disappeared, too....

"Adele," Luka croaked, but there was no one to hear him. He crouched over sticky petals, trying not to vomit again. Adele's absence—what it meant—was all around. Luka's skull flinched and cracked, trying not to believe the undeniable truth.

No one's untouchable.

He'd been played.

Kisses, cigarettes, brown jacket confessions...Adele had found Luka's every string, plucked him like a fiddle. She'd known parts of him he'd never shared with anyone, and now she was gone.

To make matters worse, the sun was lower than he'd last seen it. Low enough to tell Luka that his ten-minute lead was as busted as the back of his head. Luka's 1955 Axis Tour was over, and he was not the victor of victors. He was not tough or hard or worthy.

Just bleeding.

A breeze rattled the branches. It sounded like his father's sneer: *See? Weak.*

For a long time Luka sat, listening to creaking bark, waiting for the world to stop spinning. There were plenty of expletives he wanted to voice, but couldn't. This was a hurt beyond words. Beyond pain, even. His head throbbed, but all he could feel was the crater in his chest. Luka's heart wasn't broken. No—it had been carved out, stolen. His whole being gaped with its absence.

He needed a cigarette.

The last pack with the last few smokes—the ones he'd been saving for the finish line—was still squirreled away in his pannier. Luka dug it out and tapped it against his wrist. Only one cigarette tumbled out. Strange...

It wasn't a cigarette, Luka realized, but a piece of paper that had been scrolled tight. His fingers trembled when he unrolled it, discovered the words written within:

THERE'S ALWAYS SOMETHING MORE.

Luka stared at the script. His hands shook, harder and harder, until the letters blurred together and the paper tumbled into bloodstained blossoms.

He didn't bother picking it up.

CHAPTER 16

There was only one thing on Luka's mind as he limped into Tokyo: revenge. He'd fallen nearly two hours behind his projected time, and the Axis Tour crowds were already starting to disperse into the neon-lit night. The finish line—at least—was still waiting for him. It was a quiet crossing, no wild cheers or cameras flashing. Luka almost preferred it that way. He kept his helmet on as he parked his bike. No need to go displaying his head wound for the Reichssender.... If they found out what happened beneath those cherry trees, his reputation would never recover.

Tricked by a fräulein, you soft-hearted dummkopf.

It wouldn't happen again. It couldn't.

He was heartless now.

"Victor Löwe!" It was a reporter, shouting. "Victor Löwe! We have some questions!"

But Luka had no answers for them. He kept his lips sealed until the Reichssender staff took his silence for what it was: sore loser syndrome. Luka's name wasn't *quite* last on the final scoreboard, but rankings meant nothing now. The only spot that mattered was claimed. Felix's name had already been erased, replaced by the Wolfe's true colors.

1st: Adele Wolfe, 13 days, 15 hours, 7 minutes, 33 seconds.

Luka stared at the numbers. At the name he refused to let himself say.

I didn't enter the race to lose. Wasn't this what the fräulein had told him at the beginning of their journey? Before she lulled Luka into a false security, striking when he least expected it. The fräulein hadn't just used Luka's sabotage tactics, she'd mastered them.

She'd mastered them and won.

——————

The Imperial Palace was an ideal place to lick one's wounds, full of baths, beds, winding paths through manicured gardens.... Emperor Hirohito's staff went out of their way to make sure the Axis Tour racers were well cared for, even if they weren't invited to the postrace festivities. Luka knew from years past that only the *worthy* were welcome at the awards ceremony; only the victor was honored at the Victor's Ball.

It stung, the closeness and distance of everything. If Luka stood by the window of his guest quarters and looked out, he could see the party's lights, brimming gold against the night. Shadows of guests—high-ranking National Socialist officials and Tokyo's elite—flitted across the panes, with *her* somewhere among them. Eyes twinkling, laughing the laugh that once made Luka feel so full.

Is this all there is?

Is... Is...

He could hear it. The sound throbbed at the back of his gauze-bound head—freed from both imagination and memory. Some masochistic impulse had driven Luka to switch on the television, where the ball was being aired live. Most of the announcers were Japanese, but he'd managed to find a German-language station, its announcers all aflutter with Herr Wolfe actually being Fräulein Wolfe.

570

"Remarkable," one of them said. "It's simply remarkable, isn't it? That Adele managed to beat out both Victor Tsuda and Victor Löwe? By more than *two* hours, I might add. It's little wonder the Führer decided to pardon her rule-bending. She's fast on her way to becoming the Reich's sweetheart."

When Luka looked back to the screen, he saw that the cameras had panned to the new victor. She looked a completely different person—draped in a *homongi* kimono, lips made full with color. Her curtained bangs had been twisted, pinned back into a softer style. The ballroom lights lit her wintry features, making them glow.

"Breathtaking!!" an announcer gushed. "Don't you think?"

Luka certainly couldn't breathe. His chest was frozen and on fire, gaping and closed. He wanted to tear it open, get all of this hollowness *out*.

That laugh again . . . technically it was coming from the television, but the sound reverberated, through the window, around Luka's head. The fräulein stood by the Führer's side, surrounded by SS security—laughing at something he'd said.

Adolf Hitler seemed just as taken with *her* as the Reichssender announcers. His eyes had stayed on her the entire evening—through cocktails and toasts and a lavish dinner. Now the pair hovered at the edge of the dance floor.

As vivacious as he was during his *Chancellery Chats*, the Führer was the very definition of antiparty. Luka supposed that playing hermit for nearly three years would turn anyone into a wallflower.

The fräulein's magic seemed to be working on Adolf Hitler, too. He laughed along with her, was still laughing when he extended his hand and asked, "May I have this dance, Fräulein Wolfe?"

The ballroom and the announcers gave a collective gasp as the victor accepted the Führer's arm and stepped onto the dance floor. They swept along under bright lights: kimono shimmering, Adolf Hitler's hand pressing her waist. It was a magnificent dance, full of twirls and twists and notes that surged against Luka's skull. When it came to a close, the fräulein curtsied, smiling as she did. Painted lips parted to show white-point canines beneath.

Sweetheart, indeed.

Bile scraped up Luka's throat again, tickling the edges of his molars. He didn't swallow it back. *This* was the taste he had to remember, not some sultry minx kisses. *This* was the feeling he had to cling to in the weeks and months to come.

Hate made perfect training fuel, and he had a lot of training ahead. Iron called to iron, and there was always something more. Fräulein would enter next year's Axis Tour, go for a Double Cross of her own. When she did, Luka would be ready.

He'd be *more* than ready.

Nineteen fifty-six was going to be Luka Löwe's year.

Time flies when you're plundering history.

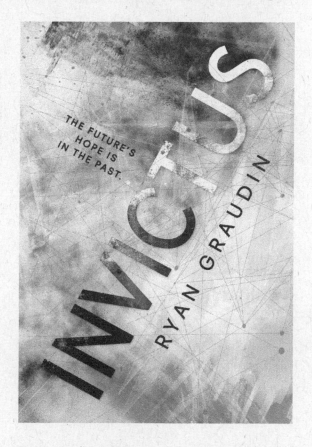

Keep reading for a sneak peek at *Invictus*, a
heart-stopping adventure that defies
the laws of time and space.
Available now.

1.

THE BOY WHO SHOULD
NOT HAVE BEEN

MAY 5, 2371

"STATE YOUR NAME." THE MED-DROID'S AUTOMATED voice was cut clean, every syllable filed down to replicate a Central accent. Why machines needed accents, Far didn't know. Maybe the programmers added this touch of humanity to put the med-droid's patients at ease. The tactic had failed, though the robot couldn't be faulted for Far's discomfort. Sitting tail-naked on an examination tabletop wasn't exactly Relaxation 101. The stainless steel surface was a few degrees shy of frosty, nipping places on his body where cold had no business going.

"Farway Gaius McCarthy," he answered.

The med-droid recorded the reply, shifted into the next query. "State your date of birth."

Far sighed. They asked this question. Every. Single. Time. And every single time he answered, the med-droid's computers would whir through the census databases, find nothing, and state in its elegant accent: "Answer invalid. Restate your date of birth."

This routine was old hat. He'd done it scores, if not hundreds, of times, for all the scores, if not hundreds, of Simulator exams he'd taken at the Academy. The anticheating measures—a full stripping and thorough identity scan before every Sim session—seemed extreme, but as Far's instructors had taught him, time travel demanded flawless precision. Cheating now could lead to world-ending catastrophes later. Maybe. Time's immutability was something much debated by the Corps, who were too afraid to test their theories in case they ended up changing the future they lived in—butterfly wingbeats and whatnot. Thus, perfection was their MO.

Traveling the Grid—exploring the past in real time—was all Far dreamed of. He'd been raised on a steady diet of serialized datastreams and Burg's expedition stories: outrunning velociraptors, witnessing Vesuvius's rage against the night sky, surveying the great Dust Bowl of the 1930s. But watching pixels flicker through screens and listening to an old man's recounted adventures wasn't enough to sate Far's hunger. Even the Sims' state-of-the-art sensory replications, with their sounds and smells and hologram people imbued with enough artificial intelligence to mimic an interactive scene from history, weren't enough.

He wanted to meet history face-to-face. He wanted to be

the blood in its veins, as it was in his. Far was a McCarthy—son of one of the most beloved Recorders of her generation. Everywhere he went, Empra's name followed. Older Academy instructors always did a double take when they came across Far in their class rosters. *You're Empra's boy,* they'd say, along with some version of: *She was a bright girl, one of my best students. It's such a shame about what happened to the* Ab Aeterno....

His mother's legacy and loss were always there, pushing Far to be the best, always the best. And he was. Today he'd pass his final exam with flying colors, like he always did, and receive his license. Today his Sim score would earn him a coveted space on the crew of a Central Time Machine. Tomorrow he'd be exploring many yesterdays ago, documenting momentous events for scholars, scientists, and entertainment moguls alike.

But first—first!—he had to get past this pragmatic med-droid. "State your date of birth."

"Can we just skip this part?" Far shifted on the table, a vain attempt to keep his unmentionables from going numb.

"Answer invalid. Restate your date of birth."

"April eighteenth, 2354 AD." Far tried the date that made him seventeen and a smidge. It wasn't his true birthday, but that didn't stop his cousin Imogen from buying him gelato and sticking sparklers in it every year. He'd tried to make 4/18/54 official, but no clerical worker could be persuaded to fill the blank gap on his birth certificate. Far's birth outside of time had to stay on the public record, for historical purposes. Med-droid malfunctions be hashed.

Speaking of: "Answer invalid. Restate your date of birth."

Far attempted the date he used whenever he was trying to impress a girl. The date that made him 2,276, minus a smidge. "December thirty-first, 95 AD."

"Answer in—"

"I know, for Crux sake! I don't have a hashing birthday!" Far knew it was useless to get mad—*he* was the glitch, not the med-droid's programming—but sometimes it just felt good to yell. "I was born on the *Ab Aeterno*!"

The examination room door slid open. A living Medic stuck her head around the corner. Her features were as edged and elegant as the Hindi on her ID card. A stethoscope dangled from her neck, competing for space with gold-tinted headphones. "Is something wrong—oh!" Her face brightened. "Hello, Far!"

"Hey, Priya." He grinned at the Medic and tried oh-so-subtly to tense his abdominal muscles. "Like the headphones. Where'd you find them?"

"Some hawker in Zone Four was trying to pass them off as genuine BeatBix, asking three thousand credits for them. Can you believe it? With the BB logo facing the wrong way and everything."

"I'd expect nothing less from a Zone Four hawker," Far told her. "One of them tried to convince my cousin that a kitten with an awful dye job was a red panda cub."

"Aren't red pandas extinct?"

"Exactly. So what'd you haggle him down to?"

"Two hundred and fifty credits." Priya's rip-off headphones gleamed as she shrugged. "Could've gone lower, but some prices aren't worth the fight. Hawker gets to pay his bills and I get to listen to Acidic Sisters through something other than my comm."

"Answer invalid," the med-droid informed them in its tireless cadence. "Restate your date of birth."

"Ah. Birth date question again?"

"Never not," Far said.

Being a Medic in an age where droids made up fifteen percent of the population required training beyond human biology, so like most of her peers, Priya doubled as a mechanic. She pried open the med-droid's chest plate and rearranged some wires—a routine Far had seen her perform scores of time—to bypass the question manually. "You'd think they'd have this bug fixed by now."

Far laughed as he offered his arm for the inevitable blood sample. Of all the Medics who came to intervene with his examination hitches, Priya was his favorite. She always pretended the problem lay on the med-droid's end and not his. And where her coworkers were quick to scurry off—their silence like fear—she lingered, often close enough for him to hear the notes beating through her headphones. Today it was a punk-tech ballad. Catchy to the max.

"So…your final exam Sim. I'd ask if you were nervous, but who am I kidding?"

He laughed again. Nerves were for people who didn't know what the future held, and his was pretty clear: valedictorian of his Academy class, acer of Sims. Sure, final exam Sims were the toughest of the bunch. You could get anything from Neolithic bonfires to a twentieth-century high school keg party to watching King John sign the Magna Carta. The goal was simple—record the event and study the people without being noticed. One misstep and you could be thrown out of the Academy tail-first, banned from time travel forever.

Far didn't make mistakes, however, just calculated risks. "Got any song suggestions for my impending victory dance?"

"Classic or current?"

"Classic. I'll need to get used to some historic beats once I'm licensed."

"Let's see." Priya tapped her chin. "There's Queen's 'We Are the Champions' and DJ Khaled's 'All I Do Is Win.' Oh—and you can't go wrong with Punched Up Panda's 'Top of the Rise.' M.I.A. has some good ones, too."

Far made a note of the band names on his interface so he could look them up later. "Queen, Khaled, Panda, M.I.A. Got it."

"You should breathe." The Medic's smoky eyes flickered from Far's exaggerated, oxygen-starved abs to the vitals graph on the med-droid's chest. "You're skewing the readings."

Ah! She'd noticed! Perhaps not in the way he'd intended, but still…

"When will you go once you pass?" Priya asked.

That was the question, wasn't it? Far had spent his entire life watching other times. A whole quilt of cultures and humanity… prehistory, ancient Greece, ancient Rome, medieval Europe, the Renaissance, the Age of Enlightenment, the Industrial Revolution, the Age of Progress, all the way to Central time. And that was just the Western Civilization track. So much was still unexplored—for while there were hundreds of licensed time travelers, there were only so many CTMs to go around. The finite life spans of the explorers they carried covered just a fraction of history.

The possibilities were endless. Almost.

"I could go back and kill Hitler," Far joked. "Isn't that every time traveler's dream?"

Priya shot him a *you shouldn't kid about that* look from under her bangs.

"Whenever the Corps wants to send me, I guess," he recanted.

"You don't have any preferences? You aren't scared you're going to get stuck trying to collect bubonic plague cultures from corpses in the name of science?"

When Far was fourteen, he watched a datastream of the Black Death. Even at that age he could tell it was highly edited: choppy shots, faded audio. The Recorder taking the footage had gagged at a blurred-out cart piled high with bodies. "Not my first choice."

When the med-droid finished its ritual pricking and prodding, it rolled toward the door, calling Far along. "Proceed to the next chamber to acquire your final exam Sim wardrobe."

"I want to see it all," he told the Medic.

"Speaking of seeing it all..." Priya bit her lip, but her smile was too strong to hide. Every other corner of her face lit with it as she nodded to the door where the med-droid had vanished. "You should go get dressed."

Far found his final exam Sim suit in the next room, pressed to perfection and composed of too many pieces. Wool stockings went on first, followed by knee-length breeches and a dress shirt with rabid lace frothing from its ends. These ruffles peeked out of a blue waistcoat embroidered with vines and some long-extinct flower Far couldn't remember the name of. A green-and-gold-striped coat weighted all this into place. The outfit was bookended with leather shoes and a powdered wig.

"Not the plague, then," Far muttered as he reached for the stockings.

He'd experienced a few Sims from the eighteenth century—witnessing the signing of the United States' Declaration of Independence, sailing the Pacific as part of James Cook's crew, watching the streets of revolution-era Paris crumble into parades and chaos—but it wasn't a time he'd studied thoroughly.

It made sense. The point of the exam was to demonstrate how well you could improvise. Time travelers had to use costumes, knowledge, and technology to blend into their surrounding environments. On board a traditional CTM, the responsibility for providing flawless covers fell to the Historian. They assembled the Recorder's wardrobe: clothes, hairstyle, and translation technology…the works. They were responsible for briefing the Recorder on the time period they were walking into. They ID'd key historical figures and sent instructions about how to behave over the comms.

During examination Sims, the Historian's role was played by a computer linked directly to Far's comm. It greeted him with the same accent as the med-droid: "Welcome to your final examination Sim, Farway Gaius McCarthy. Your mission is to observe and record an hour-long datastream. You will be graded on the quality and content of your datastream as well as your recording methods."

The usual, then. Far snapped his breeches into place. For Crux sake, they were tight. It was a miracle the human race managed to keep procreating after years in pants like these.... "When exactly will we be going?"

"May fifteenth, 1776 AD. Seven o'clock in the evening."

The shirt was snug, too, and the waistcoat pushed the ruffles up so they feathered Far's neck, making him feel ostrichlike. "Who wears this many layers in May?"

"The residents at the Palace of Versailles," the computer informed him.

Versailles. A glamorous den of royals, where the air was prickly with wig powder and the golden halls swished with gowns so voluminous they could second for circus tents. There were girls in Far's Academy class who would kill—or at least significantly maim—to be placed in such a Sim.

Far shouldered the overcoat, secured his wig, and ran through his pre-Sim mantra: *I am Farway Gaius McCarthy, son of Empra McCarthy. Birth date unavailable. With timelessness in my blood and nowhere calling to my heart. Born on the* Ab Aeterno, *for Ab Aeterno. I am a single Sim away from all of time.*

The Palace of Versailles, France, 1776 AD would be a cinch.

He switched on his recording devices and stepped into the Sim.

David Strauss

Ryan Graudin

was born in Charleston, South Carolina, with a severe case of wanderlust. When she's not traveling, she's busy photographing weddings, writing, and spending time with her husband and wolf-dog. She is the author of *The Walled City*, *Wolf by Wolf*, *Blood for Blood*, and *Invictus*. You can visit her online at ryangraudin.com.

CPSIA information can be obtained
at www.ICGtesting.com
Printed in the USA
LVHW092136070223
738959LV00028B/1138

9 780316 405164